THE ONE WHO EATS MONSTERS
Wind and Shadow, Book I

By Casey Matthews

For Emily.
The blood of the covenant is thicker than the water of the
womb.
But we have both.

"In the Long Ago, in the time before the gods wore human flesh, I lived apart from the warmth of a beating heart. In those times I was made from wind and shadow, and I danced beneath the lesser lights across a dark earth. The moon and the stars were my roof and the depths of the seas were my cellar. I traveled the world from horizon to horizon and loved everything that I touched.

"But then Man came. Man changed everything."

The Great Spirit

Not So Long Ago,
Far From Civilization

Aina bled to death in the dark and could think only of her younger brother.

When she opened her lips to say his name, no words came—just warm blood, which spilled from her cut throat, swallowed by desert sand pressed firm to her back. She stared straight up—stared into the bottom of the glittering sky—with the sense she might fall off the world and disappear into the space between stars. The shadows of the men who had killed her shrank away, tethered to their crunching boots. She pitied them all.

A dark cover slipped over her eyes. A year might have passed—or a minute. There was no time left to contain her. All she knew was her body lay somewhere beneath her, her life somewhere behind; she saw her life in picture-flashes, saw her village, her family, dragged backward on tides of memory all the way to her mother's labor pains. Released from the over-powering current, she burst forward and swam through the good years of walking, talking, and touching everything in her world. Then came the hard, sad years after Father died from fever.

A burst of white filled her vision and it was yesterday again—the day her brother's skin burned just as Father's had. Aina flew above it all, her mother and brother, above the missionaries who drove toward the city, intent on medicine that couldn't arrive in time. Above her very last yesterday. Her brother's fever worsened and he cried all day.

After dark when she was supposed to sleep, his ragged cries woke her and she couldn't wait for the missionaries one more minute. Aina's body sprinted from the village and across the far reaches with Father's machete in hand, her spirit flying high above in pursuit of the dream. She chased her body as it ran from cities and medicine and concrete, and instead toward the Fortress of Needles where the Great Spirit lived.

She had not anticipated the foreigners and their trucks, and her body couldn't hear her spirit's shouts of warning. They ran her down.

Another flash of white and she no longer flew. She was living her last memories from inside her own skin. They bound her wrists and placed her atop one of their crates in a stretch of featureless, flat ground at the doorstep of the Great Spirit's house of stones. The man with the scar through his eye questioned her, every word relayed through an interpreter.

"Tell me, Little Morsel, why are you out here in the dark with the monsters?"

"I seek the Great Spirit."

"Your prayers will be heard by nothing but hollow wind."

It was her second time talking to the scarred man and she felt less fear, since he had already murdered her. She answered more easily in the dream. "You do not understand. Just like the missionaries, you do not know the Great Spirit. It is not a god for worship. It is not a god swayed by words or burnt offerings. It is power, thirst, and it rules men as the wind does, without care for what they are. To plead for its mercy is to ask the lion to bow down."

It lived out there, in a forest of tall stone, alone and hungry, always hungry, but the scarred man didn't believe her. "Tell me more about your idols." His men wore bandoleers; they had sharp edges and thirsty smiles, and they chuckled while he ran a knife across Aina's cheek.

"Sometimes when the moon is high, it comes to our village and takes the men away. It likes soldiers, the ones with hard eyes and hearts, so they don't come to our village anymore. When I was small, it took my uncle. My cousin never spoke until the next night, and she told me it had dark eyes lit with blue fire, and that the Great Spirit promised that her father would never, ever touch her again."

Some of the bandits shifted uncomfortably, but the scarred man leaned close. "Do you mean to frighten us?"

"No. You do not understand well enough to be afraid. The missionaries didn't either, not with their God who forgives, and not you with your bullets and bombs. The Great Spirit cannot forgive, and it cannot die. You do not understand darkness or how it moves and breathes. You have forgotten magic and the shapes that lurk at the fringes of the well-lit places. My people do not forget. We live here, beneath the playground of gods, far from the thrum of electric wires."

He laughed and called out into the night, "Oh Great Spirit! Forgive my love of air conditioning! Of motor oil and gunpowder and the smell of money! Forgive my men the fun we intend to have with your fool of a worshipper."

"I do not worship. I fear." Aina shivered and wanted the dream to end, because she remembered what came next and didn't want to live it twice.

"Why did you come out tonight, Little Morsel?" the scarred man asked.

"To offer my life for my brother's."

"Offer your life to me instead."

"No."

"I am the only power in this desert. I am your Great Spirit. Offer it."

"You are not. And it will come for you." She lied, then, afraid because of where he slid the knife along her slight body: "There is more than one. They number dozens. They will all come for you. They are born from Hell and will burn you forever and ever." The only light about them was in their knives, and the void inside their eyes yawned so wide that their depths froze her skin. Her teeth chattered.

"There is no Hell but the one I make for you," the neatly dressed translator said. The man with the scar through his eye leaned close and she could smell his breath. "And I am your only god now."

Then they hurt her. And through the pain and the degradation she could not help the swell of pity, because each of them—as he took his turn—condemned himself to a fate ten thousand times worse, and she wondered for the first time if some people could feel Hell coming for them. Pulling them into its orbit. And whether the pain they wrought was because of the great evils that bore down upon them. She would not let the same evil that ate through their hearts take hers, and so she would not hate them, even as they worked their terrible will on her body.

They finished and they slit her throat and left her for animals to devour.

It was no longer before. The dream had ended.

Aina drifted into a snug and warm place like the heat under her wool blanket on a chilly morning, and she felt a stranger's heartbeat nearby. It drummed big, hollow notes, like a horse's. Was she in a womb? Had she died, and passed through gates, and become a person again, only not yet fully formed? Or was she being born an angel in some newer, stranger place?

She never found out even though she wished to. Something seized her center like a small, bright thread and tugged. At first, gently. Then, it pulled upon her like a swift river and dragged her from the cozy nest. Death was a threshold made of fire, she discovered, and though great comforts lived on either side, Aina now understood that it hurt to move through it, whether going forward or back.

She was cold. Blood was smeared on her face and an incredible ache in her throat pinched off a scream; she touched her neck by reflex, and felt the tight weave of fine stitches. The same night sky spun above her, the moon dark, but the stars shifted. From the temperature of the blood—her own blood—and the movement of the sky, she had been dead for at least an hour. She lay on her back on something so frigid it burned, a sheet of white, and specks of the stuff floated down through the desert air. Snow. Aina had only seen it in books brought by the missionaries, and yet here it was so beautiful that it hurt to look at.

The Great Spirit knelt over her, its body a hooded veil outlined by the drifting snow, and somehow she knew that the Spirit had made the snow, and it seemed very alone in their small patch of white frost in the middle of a vast desert.

"Did you save me?" Her voice came out a raspy whisper because of the threads through her neck.

It nodded. Its chin was pale like the missionaries, but its

eyes held no white; the scleras were black as deep skies with irises of blue fire. Blood wreathed the snow beneath its hands.

She had never hated the foreigners, but their bodies stained the patch of snow and she knew the Great Spirit had hated them for her. And it hated better than she ever could, cleaner and hotter, and for the first time in her life Aina felt no fear, because the most dangerous thing in the world had already decided in her favor.

"I came for you," she rasped. "My brother. So ill. Trade me for him, please. I will go with you to Hell if you save him."

It reached down and took white snow into its hands, which were bandaged in shadow like the rest of it, and exhaled until the water melted. Its breath hung, a cloudy mist in the air, and the snow became a gleaming pool that reflected more starlight than it should have. It drained the water into a canteen, which it passed to her, and Aina understood. The water carried the Spirit's breath, a rare gift that would save him.

But the expulsion of power caused the Spirit to collapse into the snow. Its fingers splayed there. She could see how it stooped, bent-backed, weakened, and wondered just how much of a god's power was required to drag her back through death's gates. So, too, was the moon gone, and she knew the Spirit was always strongest when the moon rode high. "What's wrong?" she asked.

The first shot rang from the dark. The bullet struck the Spirit's shoulder and Aina was shocked at the solid thud. Though it didn't appear to wound the Spirit, it loosed a beastly growl and pointed out into the desert. "Flee," it said, in a voice like rough sandstone. Rough, yet spoken from what appeared to be a feminine jaw.

"They will hurt you! They're monsters!"

It climbed to its feet. "I am the one who eats monsters." It turned toward the men—more of them than before. Undaunted, it charged its prey, loosing an otherworldly howl that rattled Aina's courage.

And so Aina ran and carried the water back to her sick brother, unsure if the Great Spirit could hear prayers, but saying one instead to any god who would listen: put wings to her feet and aid the Great Spirit in working its terrible will.

CHAPTER ONE
Clockwork Men

Hours Later

Helicopter rotors spun in the darkness and nothing that lived here knew that sound. Scrub mice scattered to their burrows and snakes tasting the frigid air from their holes slithered back into the deep places.

The headset crackled and Sergeant Kessler heard the communication from his position behind the cockpit: "Artemis One, this is Artemis Two. Package spotted. Converge at two klicks north by northwest."

The helo flew adjacent to limestone forests. The Fortress of Needles was a stony region of brackish rivers and mangroves protected by natural hazards that had stymied human settlement since humans first lived. Spires of rock jutted into naturally dagger-sharp points. Every ridge, crest, and handhold had been wind- and water-scoured to broken-glass edges. Razorlike stones chewed both climbing gear and flesh with ease. The deadly ridges rose above the helicopter's trajectory, and in the distance they looked to Kessler like the uneven, serrated contours of a medieval implement of torture.

A long desert scrubland flanked the east side of the fortress. Far to the west, though, stone spires protected a dense rainforest known mainly for its variety of poisonous reptiles. The rainforest swallowed the region's waters, cradled its rivers, flooding for entire seasons of the year. On one side of the vast stretch of limestone walls, a man would drown and be eaten by crocodiles. On the other, he'd die of thirst and have his softer parts swallowed by buzzards.

It lay not far from pirate-harried coastlines and warlord-controlled villages, a region once called by the British "a sort of natural anarchy" where man lived in suspicion of his neighbors.

The temperatures, venomous animals, wild carnivores, serrated rock, blinding sandstorms, seasonal floods, and bottomless sinkholes had chased off naturalists and explorers alike. It was the last untamed place. Kessler and the other members of his squad banked and flew along its feet, scanning the cold earth for traces of warmth and life.

Not every beastly thing in the Fortress of Needles was an animal. Their quarry used the desolate alcoves at the edge of the Fortress as a pit stop on their journey north, a sort of reverse underground railroad of human, weapons, and drug trafficking.

The helo cruised over flat lands until it found its twin, and they hovered like moths. Long cords spilled from their bellies and dropped to the sandy earth, and soft as snake hisses the soldiers boiled out and alighted among the desert scrub.

The soldiers were clockwork people who moved as they were taught to move—low and fast and outward-facing with their weapons, the first to land being the first to find positions until both helicopters had released their full, deadly payloads.

Kessler paid attention to the simple gesture-and-flick of his unit commander, cocked his carbine assault rifle, and moved stealthily into position. The air tasted thin and cold, the sky above him black as a bottomless pond, the stars especially bright and the darkness behind them especially empty. Out here in the primordial sand, all distance between the heavens and earth shortened so that he could have scraped his nails across the sky—and the emptiness stretched down from behind the stars and into Kessler. It swallowed him, so that he felt suspended between cold ground and the abyss.

Their approach was measured, slow. Their snipers took up position in the flat of the sands, on the peak of subtle crests that only rose after a hundred yards of effort, and even then, only a few scant feet higher than the rest of the terrain. They hid like insects camouflaged as their surroundings, beneath neatly folded wings of tarp, armed with rifles that could cut through a tank.

Kessler and the other soldiers crunched through the sand and hardened earth, with the same unnoticed forward advance as the moon across the sky.

The enemy had built a bonfire at the foot of tall limestone walls and nested in a dark alcove behind it. Three trucks with canvas backs were parked in a row, aligned so one's headlights was on the encampment and two others faced out, creating a perimeter of light that the soldiers studiously avoided. It also interfered with Kessler's night vision, so that he couldn't count them.

The outward-facing lights didn't fit and Kessler's mind buzzed in quiet alarm. The smugglers used this region because it was desolate. What were they so afraid of that they'd set up a perimeter?

No—it didn't fit. Something had happened. Something had frightened them.

"Eight contacts," said the radio. Kessler counted four, but the trucks blocked his view to the alcove.

He knew it wasn't his place to speak up, that radio frequencies could be monitored. He did it anyway. "Be advised, they're set up for us. Something's wrong."

"Number four, shut up," said the commander. "Team, proceed."

Kessler's lizard brain vibrated the fine hairs on his neck. He wanted to scream into his radio and order the team back. He couldn't. Just by speaking out, he put the whole squad at risk. He swallowed his intuition, forced it deep into his gut, and with jittery limbs he stepped forward.

The first explosion erupted twenty yards to his right, washing out his night vision as hot force swept over him. It filled up the desert with a soldier's rattled scream.

"Minefield!" said the radio in his ear.

High in the rocks a muzzle flashed, and the shot reached his ears the next moment. A near miss. He disobeyed his instincts again and didn't move, because there was no cover to be sought. The explosion from the mine had backlit him for a moment, but the shooter didn't have a good bead on him. If he moved—if he disturbed the darkness—that would change. Instead, he used his radio. "Contact, twenty meters above the campsite, sniper in the rocks."

A gunshot rang from their own side. His night vision registered the falling corpse that hit the dirt.

He remembered the scream and pivoted. Smoke drifted up from Jenson, who lay still. The other soldiers dropped to the ground and fired into the enemy camp.

Kessler sprinted for Jenson. Shots rang out all around. He slid to a stop in the dirt. Jenson's breath came in short gasps, his mask pried loose, so that Kessler could see the spark of his clenched white teeth, face contorted in pain. His chest rose and fell quick, like the sharp breaths of a woman in labor, trying desperately not to scream and give away their position.

The legs were gone below his knees and Kessler's stomach wrenched. He wasn't the primary medic but he had training and knew enough to save Jenson's life. He went through the procedures, hissing to Jenson's face so he could read his lips: "You're good, hang in there. Going to do a tourniquet and get you out of here. You with me?"

"Yeah," he said between sharp breaths. "I'm here. Sure as fuck not—anywhere else."

Horror froze Kessler's hands at first. Revulsion washed through him. The sight of the bloodied stumps struck a gong in his skull that wouldn't stop ringing. His training muted the noise, dulled the reverberation until it became a persistent buzz. He ignored the human being and focused on the stumps and the tourniquet and the bandages. Instead of operating on a person, he sought only to stop the bleeding. It changed him from a panicked surgeon to a competent plumber.

Shots like firecrackers erupted all around him, the echoing *pop pop pop* filling up the sky. Strobe flashes from the cliff sides and the scattered positions of his team ignited the darkness. The radio burst with frenzied messages: "... need helo support *now*, pinned down..." "Paint the target, Seven, unsure if there are non-hostiles on the ground." "Enemy behind the trucks, repeat, taking cover behind—" "Then push them back!" "Anyone get a look at the mine that clipped Three?"

Kessler glanced at the crater in the ground, then at Jenson. "You get a look at the mine?"

"Don't fuckin' know, might have been... might have been under some brush."

Made sense. The ground here was short scrub brush

sprouting from clay. A freshly buried mine would look like a discolored zit on the open terrain, so they would be hidden under brush. But there was too much dry vegetation to avoid it on their approach. And there had to be a lot of mines, since Jenson had triggered one only a hundred yards out from the trucks. One step could kill or maim Kessler or any of his squad mates.

No, he thought. *Don't think like prey.* He slammed the door on that. *Focus on the enemy, focus on what they're trying to do.* The outward-facing trucks and mines were a defensive perimeter. Something had spooked them enough to unload a cache of munitions and mines they must have been trafficking and create an impromptu minefield in the middle of nowhere. He looked at the trucks and their headlights, then the places in shadow where his squad had taken root.

That was it. The light and the shadow. Not a lot of mines, he realized. Well-positioned ones. The truck lights were meant to corral the enemy into the darkness, into the mines. He tapped his radio. "Four to squad, advise, the mines are in the shadows underneath the scrub."

First a pause. Then pops. The truck headlights shattered. "One to squad. Avoid the scrub. Approach in front of the trucks where there was light before. Suppression fire. Chase them back into the alcove and then drop the goddamn hammer."

A scrape of boot heels signaled the appearance of Hendrickson from the shadow, hopping and jumping over the scrub like some perverted battlefield game of "the floor is lava." He knelt by Jenson. "I'll finish here."

Hendrickson was the more experienced medic. Kessler stood and danced over the brush, blending light-footedness with the low, swift movement of a soldier. Alvarez had made it to a forward position and fired his light machine gun from prone. Seo had dug into a flank and together they'd chased back the traffickers hiding behind the trucks. Concussive booms in the distance signaled fire from their snipers. Three traffickers fled to the alcove and then dropped like puppets whose strings had been cut.

Kessler sprinted past; Alvarez stood and tagged along behind him. They ran parallel to a truck and took cover behind one of the tall spikes of rock just forward of the Fortress's cliff side, where the cavernous holes hid their enemy. The alcove was partly lit and partly obscured in their night vision by the fire burning in front of it.

Return fire hit the rocks above Alvarez's head. Kessler had an angle into the cavern and a glimpse of the shooter. He'd never killed a man before. It was a shot across sixty yards at a partly uncovered torso through the fog of shadow and glare of fire.

Kessler drew the bead. Gunfire cut through the night air to his right. A stutter of bullets from Alvarez's machine gun struck the shooter an instant before Kessler could fire. In the grainy night vision it looked to Kessler as if the man's head folded in, like a smashed pumpkin.

The ghost of an emotion filled him, irritation or relief, but no time to process it, and like a shadow it was gone. He poured on suppression fire and the squad caught up, then shifted forward under alternating fire.

"Paint the overhang," their commander radioed. "Aim high, don't damage the package."

The helicopter rotors grew in volume, desert sand flew past Kessler's ankles, and then its big guns opened up. Thunder cracked the sky in half and roared palpably into Kessler's shoulders. The cliff wall above the overhang transformed into powdered stone. Between bursts they could hear the rattle and collapse of rock formations crumbling under the onslaught.

"No rockets and keep it over their heads," the commander said between explosions from the heavy cannons. "Don't want to breach the package."

Blind spots for the overhang rested along the cliff wall. They could position there and sweep the inside. Kessler pointed at the wall to Alvarez, who nodded. Over the fire and noise from the helicopter, they sprinted for the cliff. He sensed Seo and Ike hustling to the right-side cliff wall as he and Alvarez went left. Return fire from the enemy position came in sporadic bursts. Not even aiming. Not chancing a glance around their stony cover from inside the overhang, lest the helicopter's fire rip them to pieces.

Kessler hit the cliff wall and spun. The motion ground one shoulder strap along a serrated rock, slicing the fabric halfway through. He and Alvarez looked ahead. Up close he could see a tall wooden post, like a short telephone pole, that they had planted in front of the fire. They'd tied a shapeless black mass of supplies to the top of the pole with baling wire to keep it from predators. A round from the helicopter snapped through the middle of the pole and obliterated half the thick beam. The big guns quieted and the wood groaned in the night air, threatening to snap.

"Go, go, go," said Ike. Kessler rounded the overhang's wall and stepped into the alcove.

Bang, bang, bang, each rifle shot a percussive beat in the tight confines. Seo's shots lanced through a trafficker who crumpled forward without a sound, like a wind-up toy whose spring had run down. Another trafficker popped up and aimed at Seo. Kessler's rifle snapped to attention. His finger teased the trigger.

Ike fired first and the trafficker's head snapped back. He collapsed.

Kessler finished rounding the corner while Alvarez strafed for a rock, wanting a spot to set up his machine gun. For a split second, it was only Kessler. A figure ran from around a stone pillar, away from Ike and Seo as they cleared the opposite side of the cavern. Running away rather than toward the fight, he had his rifle down. Maybe fleeing, maybe repositioning. He ran straight into Kessler's path.

For one split second Kessler saw him. Saw through the bandana on his face and to the surprised, black-eyed face beneath, eyes un-creased by age or experience. He had the lank body of a teenager. His weapon tensed.

It was going to swing up or drop to the ground. Kessler's gut told him it was swinging up.

He fired.

The trafficker hit the ground. His rifle skated away from his fingertips. Kessler pushed back the desire to second-guess himself and swept the rest of the corner just in time to see one more enemy step out from a rock formation and fire into the space Kessler had occupied a breath ago. Alvarez's machine gun kicked the camo-dressed man off his feet into the back wall of the alcove.

The team cleared the rest of the small opening in the cliff

wall. The helicopter's gunfire had killed three men and the rest had died in the brief firefight.

"Possible ID on the package," Seo said.

Kessler knelt and waved a handheld black box over the surface of a metal crate about the size of a garbage disposal. The black box clicked rapidly and he nodded. "Positive ID," he radioed. "Package is intact."

"This thing going to give us cancer?" Seo asked.

"I wouldn't lick it if that's what you mean," Kessler said. "But the seal's tight enough for short-term handling."

"Area secure," radioed Davis. "Bring in the evac bird. Sending the package and Jenson back in Artemis One, per Extraction Plan Bravo. Hendrickson, stay with Jenson."

Kessler and Seo went carefully over the rest of the bodies. "Got a live one," Seo said.

They both knelt around a young trafficker, his hood pulled back to reveal heavy black hair and nut-brown features. Kessler came in close to the man and lifted the night-vision goggles on his own face. Seo brought his penlight out. "Tell us where you were taking the package. Who was your contact?" Kessler checked the man's wounds, putting pressure on them. Two to the center mass. He didn't have long.

"Take me," he said in English. "Take me away. Before it gets me."

Seo and Kessler shared a glance. "Sure," Kessler said. "Just tell us who your drop contact was. We'll get you out of here, get you patched up." It was a lie. Without a new liver, he would die. "I need a name."

"No. I'm dead," he said, glancing down at the black blood on his vest. "Take my body away. Before it drags me to Hell."

"No one's dragging you to Hell," Kessler said. He was confused. There were old military tales of Westerners wrapping dead Muslims in pig flesh or filling their mouths with pork before burying them, ostensibly to threaten Hell on their enemies, but the mission brief said these traffickers didn't worship anything except money. So why the superstition?

"Took them. Took them to Hell. I heard them screaming. Only found pieces of my friend, *small* pieces. It was not from this world. Men cannot move like that. And the sounds it drew out of the other men... men do not sound like that."

"He's hysterical," Kessler said.

Seo shook the trafficker. "What screaming?"

The dying youth lurched up and grabbed Kessler, his fist tight around the front of his jacket. With the strength wakened at the precipice of death, he pulled Kessler face to face. Seo drew his sidearm, but didn't fire.

"We followed their howls. Followed the trail of... remains. It ripped apart seven more of us before we brought it to the ground. *Just one* did that, and the girl said there are dozens more out there. We cut it for hours to draw them out, but it made no sound. I— I do not think it can die. Please kill it. If you can. Then take me from here. Don't let it have me! Fly my corpse away and throw it into the sea. Hell lives in its eyes."

He collapsed, eyes wide open and staring straight up into the air, the motion and life in his body evaporated, so that only the husk remained and not the animating force of the man.

Seo scratched the back of his head beneath his helmet. "How many drugs you think that guy was on?"

"All of them," Kessler said.

They both walked out of the alcove and toward the fire, built with the remains of wooden crates. The post groaned in the breeze, threatening to snap in half from where the round had blasted through it. Kessler looked again at the bundle of supplies strapped to the top. It didn't look like much, just a lump wrapped in black trash bags, strapped to the stake with baling wire. A big, metal tent spike had been driven into the post up high to nail it in place. Seo gave it a firm push with his shoulder and the post cracked, falling to the side and away from the fire. "Timber."

The post hit the hard desert ground and the bundle of supplies growled at them.

"Holy shit," Kessler said. Had they tied a wild animal up? He leveled his rifle, clicked on the front-mounted light, and shone it over the misshapen heap of bags. He traced his light up the pole. Rust-brown bloodstains coated the wood below the bags.

Then he passed his light to the tent spike. "Oh holy God." It wasn't a strap they'd nailed to the post. It was a human wrist. "It's a person."

He and Seo dropped to their knees. He flicked his combat

knife out and sawed the baling wire. Seo worked from the bottom up and snapped a wire off, then forced the mass of garbage bags aside, baring small feet. *Please let them be attached.*

Seo clipped another wire. They were. Kessler ripped the plastic bag open where there was a lump like a head, above where the wire tightened around the shape of a neck.

"It's a girl," Kessler said, his throat and stomach contracting all at once. "I think." It was hard to tell. Her face had amassed brown and purple bruises, eyes swollen to slits, her mouth a bloody mess.

"Look at her wrist," Seo said.

He did. She'd been tied to the post by baling wire and covered in plastic, but her wrist was stretched straight over her head. They'd pounded a railroad tie–sized spike through her wrist just below where the bones in the forearm met. "Jesus. The wire on her throat's tight," Seo said. "Can't get my knife in. Think she's conscious?"

"Has to be," Kessler said. He swallowed. "Only way she could keep from choking to death..."

"...was by hoisting herself up on the spike in her wrist," Seo finished.

They glanced at one another, and then Kessler radioed. "We have a hostage in bad shape. Need an evac with Jenson. Badly injured left arm, low on blood, unknown number of other injuries," he said as they pulled the plastic bags off. Her skin was chalk-white wherever it wasn't bruised.

"How bad?" Davis radioed.

"Bad. Counting multiple wounds to her torso. Combination gunshots and knives."

Seo checked her scalp. "Someone shot her close range. You can see where the bullet glanced off her skull."

They'd half freed her from the wire when her eyes slitted open beneath the swelling. They were black.

She spat a wad of blood. White teeth flashed and for a split second Kessler thought he saw fangs. He leaned in to get a better look. Then she seized his throat. He gripped her skinny arm at elbow and wrist, pried, but he couldn't shake her. He wheezed, eyes watering.

Seo grabbed her and pulled from the other direction, but she gripped like a demon. Ike and Alvarez saw them and both jumped on. Finally they wrenched her loose. She fought them, a flurry of animal sounds, elbows, wild punches. One knocked Alvarez's helmet sharply down and to the side and he fell onto his ass blinded by his own gear. Kessler leapt onto her and pinned her midsection, forcing a forearm across her throat. "Settle! We won't hurt y—*fuck!*" She'd sunk her teeth into his forearm. Felt like a bear trap. Bled like one too. Seo went to rip her head back and Kessler yelled, "No, fuck, get back."

They stared.

"Just get back!"

The three of them did. He stared into the slits she had for eyes, blood seeping out of his forearm. He could see where her unnaturally pointed canines had penetrated the flesh. She had teeth like a wolf's, a bit too long on top and bottom.

He swallowed through the pain and looked down at her. "I'm a doctor. I won't hurt you."

She growled but didn't rip his skin off like he was sure she could.

His hand snaked around and he put the syringe into her neck. He pushed the plunger down. She spat out his arm, clubbed him with a tight-balled fist, and rocked him off her.

Seo dragged him back. "What'd you give her?"

"Enough. I hope."

It wasn't. She wriggled, arched, and a crack of wood sounded. She squirmed free. Then she grabbed the tent spike.

With one, two wrenches, she tried to rip it free. At last, she collapsed flat on her face, making a soft thump as she hit the dusty ground, where she lay motionless on her stomach.

They all stood and approached with weapons leveled on the slight, raven-haired girl. Ike toed her with his boot like she was a Fourth of July firework that had failed to detonate. "You think she's with the traffickers or being trafficked?"

"Neither," Kessler said. "They wouldn't ship just one person at a time. And she's white. Foreigner."

"Think she's American? English?" Seo asked.

"No idea," Kessler said. He knelt and checked her pulse. "Going to live, though."

"Jesus, look at her back," Alvarez said.

Kessler got on the radio again. "Subject's sedated. Highly combative. Looks like multiple lacerations on her back. On her everywhere, I think."

"Lacerations?" Davis asked.

"Torture," Kessler said. "A lot of it."

"Keep her sedated. She rides out in Artemis Two. Keep her away from Jenson."

"Copy."

CHAPTER TWO
Feral

Ryn woke bound and powerless. Her brain felt sticky from the drugs. She smelled lifeless plastic, tasted the iron tinge of human artifice on her tongue. A prickle of urgency tensed the muscles in her legs. They had her in a machine. In a whirling, thundering abomination, bound to a gurney, and two of them prodded her with fingers covered in man-schemed rubber. The stench of their gloves caught in her throat and alien hands probed her wounds.

Wounds.

It was a type of sacrilege, to be harmed by such temporary creatures, but dragging the village girl called Aina back from death had been no small feat; and she had given the mortal a second gift of breath to carry home to her dying sibling. Giving life back was the hardest thing she could do and she'd never dared it twice in a row before. That was why Ryn had fought with no more strength than a mortal, why her power had yet to return.

At least she knew Aina had succeeded. She had sensed the expulsion of her power across a vast distance, felt in that moment how her life force had punched into the heart of Aina's brother. Ryn was glad. Though she disliked mortals as a rule, Aina had the clean scent of rain on her skin—free of the stink that oozed out the pores of the species. Whatever the price, paying it had freed the little village girl who Ryn had watched from the time she'd swelled her mother's womb. Now Aina, too, would have time to grow old.

The two soldiers rolled her on her side. They both hailed from that new country that had been re-colonized in the last few centuries, a place where the blood of a thousand origins ran together. They were imperial in self-regard, and they spoke a faddish language that had swept the world. It was a great civilization in wealth and prowess, and arrogant, but she hadn't bothered to learn its name. She had stopped learning the new ones' names.

"What is this stuff?" asked the one called Seo. He tugged the strands of her kanaf, all that remained of the mystic fibers that normally cloaked her. Another thing lost in the battle.

"Can't tell," said the one called Kessler. "Fiber's stiff, like Kevlar." He tugged and it popped out of the slit in her back. "These six lacerations on her back are different from the others. Too symmetrical, not bloody enough, and this black stuff looks like it got... worked into it somehow. Almost like she's attached to it."

"They don't match the other wounds. Maybe two different guys worked her over."

"You'd need a scalpel to do this. Probably not even that. These remind me less of cuts and more of... gills."

The butchers cut away the last of her kanaf. How long before it would regrow?

Kessler took her wrist. Ryn feigned unconsciousness. She remembered Kessler, the one who had injected her with the drug. Normally the only thing she liked about soldiers was the sound they made when she broke them. But these ones didn't stink quite so badly, Kessler especially, and so she hadn't yet mutilated him. She'd lost consciousness around him and he hadn't harmed her. That didn't seem typical of humans.

He attached a sensor to her undamaged wrist and she felt a prick to the inside of her elbow. Fluid tried to drain into her through the needle but her body stopped it. A "beep-beep" sounded from one of their loud machines.

"This bag isn't flowing. No stoppage. What the hell?" Seo asked.

Ryn slitted one eye open.

"Don't know, but there had to be four pints of blood in the camp back there between the post and where they tortured her. Should be tachycardic, but her pulse is strong, slow." Kessler was a brown-skinned man with symmetrical features, eyes like black slate, and charcoal hair.

"You sound worried."

"It's too strong," Kessler said. "She's lost half her blood, ought to be in stage-four hypovolemia. She's not in shock, not at all. She's... stable."

"Strong kid."

Kessler absently massaged his throat and nodded. "Maybe too strong. She's what—five feet tall? Sixteen years old? She weighed a hundred pounds, give or take, when I lifted her."

"What're you getting at?"

"Ever seen a girl this size throw a punch like that? She's just a kid."

"Fear and adrenaline?"

"Could be. My friend back home sometimes works with troubled kids. Juvenile offenders from all kinds of crazy backgrounds. She said you'd be surprised what these kids can do. One of them—barely twelve—once put a three-hundred-pound caseworker on crutches."

"Good thing she's zip-tied down."

"Guess so." He pressed fingertips to her hair and smoothed it away from the gunshot wound on her scalp. "I'm not a surgeon, and she's scabbed over, so we'll let the ER docs on the ship take a crack at most of this. Maybe stitch up this mess, though. Pass me those scissors."

Seo passed scissors over her and she realized they meant to cut her hair.

No.

"Shit, she's awake," Seo said.

"Not with all the dope I put in her." Kessler met her eyes and she peeled her lips back, showed him her canines. He didn't shout, or curse, or sign himself with the cross, or throw salt over one shoulder—all mortals reacted differently to her eyes, to their cold depths and the spark of divinity that burned in her irises. She guessed her weakness had dimmed the spark, because he only shivered.

Ryn jerked at her plastic bonds. She twisted her spine in every way a spine could bend and a few more. Both men jerked away from her. "Fuck!" Seo shouted.

"Everything okay back there?" called someone from the cockpit.

"It's a scene from *The Exorcist*!"

Her gaze narrowed on the scissors and she sensed some

give in the plastic tie binding her right wrist, where he'd tied it looser because of the metal shard embedded there. They had sawed the spike off the post rather than pulling it from her flesh. She rotated her wrist faster and faster, using her blood as lubricant, never mind the bolt of pain that fired up her arm so sharply that she felt it in her jaw.

"Hey, easy, sh sh shh, it's okay. I'm putting them down," Kessler said over the flying machine's engine. He lowered the scissors.

She followed the motion of his hand. The monitor's annoying bleeps had sped with the rate of her heart.

"Do you speak English?" He touched his chest with both hands. "I'm Sergeant Kessler. This is my friend, Corporal Seo, and we're not going to hurt you. We're flying you to a hospital. Can you tell me what language you speak?"

Ryn didn't understand. Soldiers were men with weapons, hard men sent to the serene fringes of the civilized world, who bent it and subdued it and filled it with loud noise for the sake of colored pieces of cloth waved around on a pole. The idea that a soldier did not want to *hurt*—especially a female—only confused her. What else were they *for*? Yet this one spoke of hospitals. "Soldier," she said. "Soldier means no harm? No. *No*." She hadn't tried their language before and it sounded foreign to her own ears.

"Yeah, soldier," Kessler said, patting the metal tags dangling from his neck. "Not a bad soldier. We don't want to hurt any innocent people, or you, we were only hunting the bad guys."

Ryn shook her head. "Always hurt. 'Want' not matter. Always women, small ones, old ones—caught by bullets, swords, spears. If not on purpose, then accident. *Clumsy*." She spoke the last word like a curse because too few humans understood how *wrong* their clumsiness really was.

"I'm not clumsy. Let me fix your wound. I just need to cut your hair."

She snarled.

"I don't think she wants you to cut it," Seo said.

"Really? You think?" Kessler glanced down at her again. "Okay, okay. What if I put the stitches in and leave your hair alone?"

Normally she stitched her wounds with her kanaf, but that was gone. "I do it."

"I can't let you. But I can tell you don't trust me. That's all right. Here," he said, and rummaged for a tray bottom. It was reflective like a mirror and he gave it to Seo. "Hold this up for her." She could see everything his hands did to her scalp now. "You can watch, all right? That way you know I'm not being clumsy."

She glared, but until they untied her, she could do little. That irked her. Even worse, the cottony hold of the drugs had returned and she felt it lulling her toward the brink of unconsciousness.

He cleaned the wound and put sixteen stitches into her scalp.

"Done," he said. "See?"

"Not good."

"Was it clumsy?"

"No. Just *not good.*"

He chuckled. "Thankless brat." She didn't know what "brat" meant but it sounded good and bad at once, the way he said it.

"Let go. Let me go," she whispered.

"Don't worry. You're not in clumsy hands. You're all right."

"No. Not in hands. No one's hands. No one holds me." Her voice sounded far away and her heavy eyelids lowered. She felt only the rattle and vibration of the flying machine, and then nothing at all.

~*~

Kessler stepped into the cramped briefing room on board the USS *Tsongas*, one of the military's "floating cities" that deployed around the globe. It had the medical facilities—and then detainment facilities—to deal with the girl, and he'd been shuttled alongside her while the limitless wisdom of the military bureaucracy tried to decide whether she was a detainee, a refugee, or something else that fit into their check sheets. He was glad it was Major Blackmun who sat behind the desk, since he'd served under him before. Beside him was a bespectacled doctor with a receding hairline and his nose buried in a thick medical chart.

"Have a seat," Blackmun said. He had a square, boxy head, with the hardened frown of a bulldog, and he put his glasses on with the noticeable disdain of a middle-aged man who hated the small betrayals of his body.

"Yes sir."

"At ease. What's this I hear about your transfer?"

"Garfield thinks I'm too slow on the trigger, sir. Fraction of a second. Wants to move me for the rest of my term, put me in an investigative role. Said it suits my personality better."

"Can't say he's wrong. You've got great instincts, but you're the kind of soldier who has to be sure before he pulls the trigger. That kind of caution will suit you where you're going. Now. You're here because we still have a puzzle to solve. You went and found yourself a stray, Sergeant. And nothing about her quite adds up."

"No, sir."

He motioned to a monitor on the wall and judging by the time stamp it showed footage twelve hours old. The girl sat in an interrogation room at a metal table, cuffed, in an orange jumpsuit. She didn't move. She stared straight up into the camera, and from a distance her eyes were dark with bright sparks where the irises should have been. Kessler had never looked at her eyes and not shivered, this time included.

Blackmun never looked up. He kept his gaze steady on Kessler. "You don't think she should be a detainee, do you. Why not?"

"Because they tore her up bad, sir. Never seen it that bad before, and I didn't grow up in the best neighborhood. Broken bones, lacerations, bullet and stab wounds, two mashed-up eyes, burns, and those weird incisions on her back. I don't even want to know what else they did to her."

The doctor cleared his throat and said, "The report yielded little. They tried to get her to sign the consent form and she stabbed the nurse through the hand with a pen. However, we *do* think she was—"

"That's enough, Dr. Mellon," Blackmun said. "Yes, I read the report. They tortured her and she lost more than half her blood, although what concerns me is that a good deal of the blood on her hands and body belonged to other people. Her predilection for violence is a problem. She woke from her surgery and choked a surgeon. But beyond the violence, there are other questions."

"Yes," Mellon said. "Like how she's back on her feet so quickly. She's already got a red-cell count that's off the charts." The more he went on, the faster he talked. "Most of her wounds have mended. Her *bones* have mended. Her metabolism is unreal—I don't mean high, I mean *impossible*—because she hasn't eaten *or* lost any weight. My colleagues want to test her DNA, because we're not even certain she's genetically—"

"Doctor Mellon." Blackmun silenced him with a glance, then looked back at Kessler and hit a button on his desk. "Then there's this." On the screen, which Blackmun still refused to look at, the time stamp went from a slow crawl to extreme fast forward. Minutes ticked by faster than seconds, but the girl didn't budge. There was no jerkiness to her. She sat like a statue, a fixture as motionless as the table, unflinching, for eight hours. She stared through the camera, peeled back the circuitry and wires, and looked straight into the briefing room. Interrogators blurred into the room and tried to talk to her, and even when they put water in front of her it remained untouched. Kessler's skin crawled.

Blackmun hit stop. The only indication was the frozen time stamp.

"What are you getting at, sir?" Kessler asked.

"I believe three things," he said. "First, that she isn't allied with the nuclear traffickers, and we lack any other evidence to suggest she's either an asset or an enemy of this country. Second, that she's a foreigner to the country where we picked her up, origins unknown, and clearly a minor at that, which, let's just say, complicates things for an old man like me." For as long as Kessler had known Blackmun, he'd had pictures of his daughters on his desk. "And thirdly, that she's unusual in ways that make her... dangerous."

"You think she's a child soldier, don't you?"

"You tell me. She won't talk to us. You're the only one to successfully communicate with her so far."

"Wrong part of the continent," Kessler said. "Also, she's white and speaks some English, so she's from somewhere else.

Her verbal and interpersonal skills are stunted. Then there's the violent behavior, physical toughness, and neither of you even mentioned the eyes or the filed canines."

"Oh, *not* filed," Mellon said. "There's no evidence of dental—"

"Mellon, you can leave us," Blackmun said. The doctor frowned, sighed, and left through the ship's heavy steel door. When it shut, Blackmun said, "He's one of five doctors who want to write on her for medical journals. I'm not having any of that. This operation is still classified. The girl is a problem. I need her to go away, quietly. Help me understand her, Sergeant."

"What about feral children?"

"Like *The Jungle Book*?"

"Sort of. I researched it a little, and most feral children miss a developmental period. They don't pick up language, or learn how to eat with a fork and knife or use the toilet, and they never develop an interest in other human beings. Not my impression of this one. She's only half-feral. She recognized gestures, spoke some broken English. Sort of like a child who ran away very young, when she was halfway socialized."

"Ran from what?"

"Usually a rural home. An abusive one. The wilderness is sometimes more attractive."

"You think she survived where? The Fortress of Needles? I've read the briefing. Experienced survivalists have died there. One slip, one tumble, and you end up vivisected. The mission work-up explicitly forbade your team from engaging in that environment for fear we'd lose most of you. Then there's the question of *who* she ran away from, since there aren't that many white English-speakers in the vicinity."

"Missionaries, maybe?"

"Then you think she could be American?"

"It's possible. Have you asked her?"

"No. I want you to."

"I understand, sir. What do you plan to do with her? She'll want to know."

"If we can't figure out where she belongs? We'll treat her like a refugee. But I don't want her stateside unless we can find an institution for her."

Kessler recalled the other research he'd collected on feral children. "I have an old friend back home. A caseworker out of New Petersburg. She has a lot of connections, and she deals with children—some very violent. I think it's likely we could place her. There's private money there for it, some kind of trust fund, and a lot of professionals are interested in feral children."

"No research," Blackmun said. "She's connected to a black op. No research, no publicity."

"Like I said, I know someone. I can take care of that. What about citizenship?"

"I'll pull some strings at State. Grant her asylum for now. But make sure she's not Russian, or British, or God knows what else first. And find out if she has parents, if you can."

"Yes, sir."

~*~

The girl slipped her cuffs twice and they finally stowed her in a small cell with a thick locking door, then stationed two guards. It felt to Kessler almost like a joke to wrap so much security around a hundred-pound teenage girl, but he reminded himself of the vicious left hook she'd used to damn near knock him unconscious.

He and the guards exchanged salutes and he glanced through the eye-level viewport into the cramped bunk. Her sheet had been draped over the side of the metal cot and she was likely beneath in a makeshift tent.

"Blackmun told us not to fuck with how she sets up the room," said the guard. "Long as she stays put, anyway. Probably wouldn't even understand us if we ordered her to fix it."

"She understands us." Kessler reached into his pocket and took out an orange. "Open the door."

He stepped in and the guard shut the door behind him. The echo reverberated in the narrow confines. Kessler settled on the floor, back to the wall and his side facing her tent. He listened, hard, for the telltale sound of breathing or the small scrapes of motion. None came. He only heard the distant hum of ship engines through bulkhead. She made less noise than settled dust.

He set the orange down next to his knee. Then he rolled it, so that it lay between his leg and the curtain.

He waited.

It must have been an hour. His mind wandered. The guard poked his face up to the window now and then, but Kessler ignored him. He never once looked entirely away from the orange because some part of him felt certain that if he did—for even a second—it would disappear.

At last, a small hand darted from the curtain, snatched the orange, and shrank back in the bat of an eye. He could hear her peeling. She took her time even though she must have been starving. After a spell, orange peels slid from beneath the curtain.

"You're welcome," he said.

Nothing.

"There are citrus groves in the Fortress. I figured you'd like oranges. My name is Kessler. Do you remember me?"

"Yes," she whispered.

"Do you have a name?"

"No."

"What should I call you, then?"

"Whatever you like."

"You should at least pick something. Otherwise, I'll call you Butt-Face."

"Then call me Ryn."

"Are you afraid of me, Ryn?"

"No."

"Then why are you hiding?"

"The eyes. They itch."

"Your eyes itch?"

"Their eyes. They make me itch."

Her English had improved. A lot. "I'm supposed to figure out whether or not you're dangerous. Are you dangerous?"

"Are you?"

"Not to you."

"But you are. You are dangerous."

Kessler gazed off into nothing. "I suppose I could be. I suppose it's the same way with you, then? You could be dangerous. But I'll bet what you really want is to be left alone. Is that right?"

Nothing again.

"Where are you from?" he asked.

"Outside."

"You mean the wilderness?"

"I am from outside," she repeated.

"We need to find out who your parents are. Where you come from. So we can figure out where to put you."

"Put me back."

"We can't do that. You have to have a home. A place to be, with others like you."

"There are none like me."

"No parents?"

"No."

"No family at all?"

"Do you have family?"

He laughed. "This conversation is about you, not me. Tell me about *your* family."

"There is only me. Tell me about family. Tell me about yours."

"All right, fine," he said. "I grew up in New Petersburg. My father was a soldier and he died when I was very young. My mother passed away three years ago. Lung cancer. I have a much older half-sister who lives in Boston, from my mom's first marriage, but we never talk. Your turn. Where did you learn to speak English?"

"People. I hear them. I listen."

"What sort of people?"

"Every sort. They come to the places they should not be and fill them with their words."

"You say they shouldn't be there. Should you?"

"Yes."

"Why?"

She was quiet for a while. Then: "I am not allowed in the city. Or civilized lands. Ever."

"Why? Who told you that?"

"Does not matter who. Not allowed. Not welcome among kings or gods."

"We could send you back with us. To the United States. We don't have any kings there."

"Are you sure?"

"Of course I'm sure. We have a president."

"There are always kings. Always gods. Always."

"Not here. Not with us."

"Not that you can see."

"Is that what you're afraid of? Kings? Rules? Dictators? Is that what you mean by gods, powerful people who'll hurt you? Did someone hurt you? Is that why you ran away?"

"I am not afraid of them," she said. Then, quieter: "They fear me."

"I'm not afraid of you."

The drapery slid up, and Kessler scooted down so that he lay on his side. He could see just one of the girl's eyes, with blackness instead of whites and the unsettling irises that seized the brain, drained it of thought, and covered his skin with a slow prickling sensation that radiated from the back of his neck. "There isn't anywhere left, is there?" she asked.

"What do you mean?"

"Nowhere to go anymore. Nowhere people aren't. They are everywhere. In every small and large place in the world. Nowhere to run. Nowhere to be unseen, untouched, unthought-of. It is all close together now. Too close together. Like this room. Walls, ceiling, floor, all so close you can touch the two sides with both hands."

"I guess there's not much in the way of frontier left, no," he said.

"Then put me where you will."

"Tell me where you're from and we'll try to put you back there," he said.

"You don't understand," she said. "The place I am from doesn't exist. Not anymore."

She dropped the veil back down.

CHAPTER THREE
Through the Gates

Eighteen Months Later
New Petersburg, USA

The elevated train rolled along at window and rooftop level, channeled through corridors of brick and graffiti. The rhythmic clickety-clack of the wheels over the track joints accelerated and they jostled each time the aluminum car swayed outward on a turn. The press of bodies in cramped space had concentrated the salty odor of anxiety that clung to the city and now it suffused Ryn's clothes as well. She rode beside Victoria Cross, a dark-skinned woman dressed in a crisp suit and slender-framed glasses. Ms. Cross managed the chaos of her unruly hair by pinning it into a clutch, but stray locks danced over her right cheek.

Ms. Cross talked on her cell phone. It went about as well as all her phone calls.

"Level with me, George: are you thinking of hurting yourself? Or someone else? No? Good. All right, slow down. The first thing you're going to do is sit down and breathe. Ten breaths. Tell me when you're done." She paused for a spell. "Now, why did she leave? Did you hit her?" Another pause. "Did she deserve it? Oh, she did? Did she burn your winning lottery ticket? Then no, she didn't deserve it, George. Well, that's what happens when you hit a woman. No, I won't tell her that. Because she *shouldn't* come back. Yes, I am a bitch. You don't get to be a program manager without being a bitch. It's on my résumé. I underlined it twice."

Ryn liked riding beside Ms. Cross. She could focus on the faint aroma of rose-water perfume that Ms. Cross wore so often and lightly that it might have become her natural scent, and it drew Ryn's attention from the oily layers of stink that plastered the inside of the cramped train car. It was the smell of city people, of gnawing worry, the kind that applied constant pressure. It pushed a person into a perpetually frayed state, where they proceeded fugue-like and unaware that their credit cards, overdue bills, and inboxes had settled into their shoulders and bent their gait. They lived like a man forced to walk, never stopping, until he died.

The train's vibration nudged down Ryn's dark sunglasses. She pushed them back up before anyone could see her eyes. Best not to cause a panic on her first day in the city.

The train doors opened at a South Dock Street platform and she followed Ms. Cross into the frigid January air with her bag over one shoulder. Ms. Cross speared through the crowd and continued her conversation.

"Yes, I think it's very possible she's talking to the police. I'm sure they do hate you, George. If I had to come down to your place and arrest you twice a month, I'd hate you too. As it stands, I'm sitting at severely disappointed." She changed ears. "Uh-huh. And how am I supposed to do that if you're not at group? Yes, you'd better be there. I know 'sick' means hung over, and your meds don't mix with alcohol. I'm not as naïve as my various degrees would suggest." She led Ryn down the platform stairs and through the brown-slushed avenues. "Glad we had this talk. Remember: meds, group, no alcohol. Hanging up now." Ms. Cross snapped shut her phone and glanced at Ryn. "How about you? Ready for big changes?"

"Yes." So ready she could feel every slack tendon in her legs tingle, too long unexercised inside the tall, beige walls of Sacred Oaks. Ryn juked between the shouldering masses and tried to stay in the bubble of space Ms. Cross projected by force of will.

"Out of the institutional pan and into the group-home fire. You won't be as closely monitored there."

No. And every inch of freedom returned a portion of her strength. The ancient banishment that had cast her from civilized lands left her power strangely susceptible to mortal laws.

Somehow, though, she had avoided the pain of a curse that normally afflicted her whenever she set foot inside their borders.

"You're ready for this," Ms. Cross said. "No more regimented schedule, no more group therapy, no more orderlies."

No more watching the days, weeks, and months zoom by through her window, patiently awaiting release, no more trying and failing to figure out what parroted words the men with clipboards and pens wanted to hear.

"You can meet people your own age. You can get a part-time job. You can go to a real school."

She could break out into the night and hunt down one of the ten thousand horrific smells ground into the asphalt. Find the most hateful monsters and spirits that fled to the cities to escape the ones like her—to escape the bigger monsters. Find, stalk, kill. *Yes.* She could nearly taste it.

"Tell me: what are you going to do once you settle in?"

"Behave." In front of the mortals, at least.

"And see me the first Tuesday of the month. *And*, no hospitalizations."

That had happened only once and Ms. Cross refused to forget it. "I understand." But she didn't give her word.

"You're an awful liar."

It was true. Mortals were practiced at lying and seeing liars. Ryn barely understood what their faces meant most of the time, and they could divine her every mood based on the tics of her mouth or tone of voice. She'd never realized until now how strangely good people were at interacting with one another—maybe twice across her countless centuries of life had she socialized with a human. "I will try."

"You say that now. Sixteen months ago, you knocked a tooth out of an orderly. I liked that orderly."

"He smelled wrong."

"And from now on when people smell bad, you will use your words."

Except Ryn could not. She could do many things without effort—anything at all with her hands or body, or with the acuity of her senses. But after observing the human species from the fringes of its campfires for as long as it had built campfires, Ryn had concluded they were not meant to be understood by something like her.

Which suited her. What was there to like, besides how the wicked ones tasted?

Salt caked the cars and the slush pushed into her thin-soled shoes. The brick buildings were many stories tall, windows dark or dingy, and graffiti decorated building sides, mailboxes, and street lamps. Shop fronts were squashed together and steam rose from sewer vents. Wintry gusts swept in from the bay and people screwed down into their coats. Ryn hardly felt the cold, and kept her face up to greet it, savoring its salty sting and lonesome moan.

"What is the name of the couple who run your group home?" Ms. Cross asked.

It was a test. "Judy and Albert Birch."

"Yes. And how do they feel about girls who growl at them?"

"They don't like it."

"Good. And how are you to treat them?"

"With respect."

"And?"

"Check in every night. Check out every morning when there's school. No exceptions."

"And?"

Ryn scrunched her face up. "...no hospitalizations?"

"Good."

She hated Ms. Cross's quizzes, and her finger point that indicated where Ryn ought to go or stand, like a trained dog. But Ryn couldn't read humans, or decipher lies, or sense their true motives, and she discovered considerable diversity in their trustworthiness. Her instincts insisted Ms. Cross was *safe*, a non-predator, no matter how grating. All she could do was cling to the woman, otherwise adrift in a complex web of social interactions and cues that meant nothing to her.

They stopped in front of a seven-story, brick apartment complex that was squat and perhaps a little sad, labeled with a cornerstone: "Roosevelt Place, est. 1922." Its crumbling stoop led to incongruously modern glass doors. Ms. Cross buzzed in and they rode a rickety elevator. Ryn hated elevators. They reminded her that humans didn't enjoy the feeling of their hearts beating inside their chests. Sometimes she wondered if they enjoyed being alive at all.

On the fifth floor, they knocked and an apartment door swung wide. Ms. Cross smiled, chatted amicably with Judy and Albert Birch, and introduced Ryn, who remained silent and non-aggressive and stifled the reflexive growl when Albert Birch came too close. Instead of being pleased, Ms. Cross chastised her for darting back.

"How many?" Ryn demanded.

They all stared and Ms. Cross scolded her for interrupting. Ryn hadn't been paying attention to their words, so they probably hadn't been important.

"What do you mean?" Albert asked, stooping to her height with his hands on his knees. Ryn liked him even less at eye level.

"How many?" she repeated, counting chairs at the table. "How many stay here?"

"Oh, well, my wife and I, you now, and six other young people, ages nine to seventeen."

"Where am I?" People liked to assign rooms. Organized like that.

"Right this way; I'll show you," Judy Birch said.

Ryn was guarded with Judy and Albert Birch. They didn't feel safe like Ms. Cross or Sergeant Kessler, and Albert Birch had something in his eyes she couldn't place. Too beady. He smelled like salami left out in the sun, and she was happy to get away. Judy led her through a living room cluttered with knickknacks and toys, but no filth.

There was a cuckoo clock in the kitchen and Ryn smelled an asura living inside of it, but of course the humans didn't notice the little spirit.

Her room was a converted dining nook with two doorways into it, one from the living room and one from the kitchen, curtained off by thin sheets. It had nothing akin to privacy. It was barely large enough for the bunk beds and a dresser, which sported two drawers labeled "Rin." She had no idea what to do with two entire drawers.

It had one good feature: the bay window. It stuck out from the side of the building and Ryn immediately perched on the cushioned seat beneath the frosted panes. She gazed through the bars and into the ice-glazed courtyard between Roosevelt Place and the surrounding buildings. It was littered with rusty bikes, a bent basketball hoop, and jacketed people working charcoal grills.

Ms. Cross came in. "That's no good. Those bars are a fire hazard. They come off."

Albert Birch scratched the back of his head. "I'll see what I can do," he said, and after Ms. Cross looked at him in a way Ryn didn't understand, he added, "The bars are on the outside of the window and five stories up. Can't get to them until spring, when they wash the outside of the building. I'll talk to the super."

"You have rules for people coming in and out of this room, right? I don't like the curtains at all, not for girls; they should have a door," Ms. Cross said. While they talked, Ryn noticed the other bunk's occupant, an eleven- or twelve-year-old girl, silently swept away in a thick book. She was reedy and large-eyed, with dust-colored hair and a tendency to blend in. Ryn liked her.

Ms. Cross stayed long enough to levy a dozen more criticisms of their accommodations until Judy and Albert Birch made a series of attempted farewells, following every new requirement with something to the effect of "Fine, fine, it's been a long day, we'll see you to the exit." Perhaps a half-hour after the first time they said that, Ms. Cross let them push her out the door.

Ryn leapt onto the top bunk in a clean motion and lay back, staring at the pattern of plastic stars on the ceiling. Judy and Albert came in and said some things, none of which seemed terribly important to Ryn, other than that dinner would be soon. Judy in particular asked a lot of questions and Ryn found the best way to deal with too many questions was to not answer any of them.

Judy left muttering things about attitudes.

"I don't think she likes you," the girl beneath Ryn's bunk whispered.

Ryn slid off the bed halfway, gripped the edge, and dangled to have a closer look at the other girl. "Does she ask fewer questions when you read?"

"Yes."

"Is that why you read?"

"I suppose so, at first. The house gets loud. The boys are all out at the Y and they'll be home for dinner. That's when it's loudest. I'm Susan. What's your name?"

"Ryn."

"Why do you have those glasses on?"

"I have an eye condition," which Ms. Cross had coached her to say. Ms. Cross had had a friend write the prescription for dark glasses after a bad group-therapy session—of all the people to react to her eyes, schizophrenics liked them the least. Ms. Cross said keeping her eyes covered let them save on haloperidol costs.

"You mumble some," Susan said.

"I do." It hid her teeth.

"You don't like to talk, do you?"

"I don't know why people fill the air with so many words."

"The conversations in my books are better. So are the people." Susan held up her book for inspection. "I guess I don't like small talk either." That was the name for it, then. No, Ryn did not like small talk.

Susan found a thinner book and gave it to Ryn. She lay back on her bed and leafed through yellowed pages, which gave off a mildly vanilla odor. Most of the book in her hands had been alive once—paper, ink, glue. It was dead now, but inside, the words lived in front of her eyes. She had learned the mechanics of reading English, of long division and algebra and other pointless tasks, at Sacred Oaks as part of a plan to "mainstream" her into a place called high school. Her book featured a very useless female who kept getting into trouble, except that she attracted the interests of a man who was a pirate and whom Ryn would have preferred the book to be about.

Soon, the apartment filled with tromping feet and the brash voices of "the boys." They met at the dinner table and Ryn regarded them, with some unease, as a rabble of disparate youths, two of them twins, who operated in mob-like togetherness. They pounded their silverware on the tabletop and chanted, "Feed us, feed us, feed us!" and Albert turned up the volume of a television set on the kitchen counter.

Judy served rice, two microwave family dinners, and the contents of three cans of vegetables mixed together. This was treated as a big affair. Albert poured about a fistful of salt onto his food and the Rabble battled over the leftover Salisbury steaks: "...give, it's mine you *ass*..." "*Ow*, he bit me!" "Did not!" "I'm bigger, give it." The patty smelled to Ryn like the train and she avoided the vegetables for the same reason. She scooped her patty to the quietest of the Rabble and ate rice, wishing there had been fresh fruit on the table.

"You a vegetarian?" Albert Birch asked with his nose at an upward tilt.

"No." She'd eaten her share of animals and people, but she wouldn't call what they ate "meat," and she preferred to only eat flesh when she'd killed it with her hands. Animals that lived wrong or that ended wrong carried wrong flavor. Nothing here tasted right.

"Picky eater, then?" he asked, muting the television. Was it a challenge of some sort? Did he want to fight Ryn for dominance? Probably not. It had never turned out that way with the orderlies. Humans never wanted to fight for anything.

"Not hungry," she said.

"We don't take special orders here," he said. "Eh, boys?"

The Rabble laughed and Judy murmured her agreement.

"No orders," Ryn said. When she had first arrived at Sacred Oaks and refused food, they had tried to jab her with needles attached to bags of fluid. That was when she'd realized the horror of that place—to the authorities there, she was not competent to fend for herself. She had to be taken care of. Like cattle. Every time they'd said "for your own good" she'd had to bite off the desire to demonstrate her core competencies. At least now she could forage.

"So what's her malfunction?" asked one of the twins, nodding toward Ryn.

"Not my business to say," Albert Birch said. Then he leaned forward. "But she's from Sacred Oaks."

"I hear they put crazy people there," another one said. "People who write on the walls with their own poop."

"Robby!" Judy said. "Not at the table."

"It's true," he insisted under his breath.

"Well, they've downsized," Albert Birch said. "That Ostermeier Trust Fund's run about dry is what the television says; some kind of bad investment deal. So they're kicking out some of the parasites."

"Suppose she's dangerous," the twin said.

"She's not dangerous, look at her," Albert Birch said. "Little stick like that? Figure you boys can keep her in line, am I right?"

They laughed and shared pet theories about why Ryn had been in Sacred Oaks, and Ryn absorbed it all in silence. She hated this place and everyone in it except maybe Susan.

She cut a quick path back to her room after dinner because the Rabble pushed and shoved a lot and she didn't trust herself not to play rough. As enjoyable as that might be, she didn't want trouble with Ms. Cross. The Rabble skirted only briefly into her bedroom before Susan shooed them out, and Ryn sat at the barred windows looking out at the darkened world. She shut her eyes until Susan asked to turn out the lights.

Near midnight, the last boy nodded off and the entire house breathed in the easy rhythm of sleeping humans. Ryn alighted soundless to the floor.

Freedom had strengthened her—she could feel it in the needled anticipation of unsprung calves as she crept from the bedroom, past a snoring boy wadded up on the sofa, and to the kitchen and the cuckoo clock that slept unmoving beneath layers of dust. "Wake," she whispered.

Nothing. Not a tick. Not a twitch of its ornate clock hands.

"I smell you," she growled. "Come out."

The clock doors whined open and a streamer of dust motes sprang out, curling through the air like a serpent, igniting gold against shafts of street light. It curled twice around Ryn, took her measure, and flitted back to the clock. The thick sheet of motes all over the aged clock shimmered as they caught the light. It spoke in the raspy voice of an old man: "What right've you got ordering me around, deva?"

"I am Ryn. What are you called?"

"Dust," and when he said it, flecks sneezed from within the clock. The asura did not give true names, as it was dangerous for their kind. "What's a goddess doing, bothering an old soul's rest?"

"I am no goddess."

"Eh? Tell me. If you ain't a goddess, why're you lurkin' around here?"

A good question—one she had not yet answered to her own

satisfaction. "I am here, and I am no goddess. I am a monster."

"Monsters don't get to do that, dearie. Their lot was banished from cities—but here you are, spry twerp without your bones set on fire, which tells me you're dead wrong on at least one count. You're a deva? You can caper about with mortals? Only one thing you could be: a goddess."

"I will never stop being a monster. That is the first and the last of what I am."

"Some kinda loophole?" he asked, intrigued.

Ryn didn't know what that was and she waited. He seemed like the sort who enjoyed prattle.

"Way I recall," he said, proving her right, "the deva who couldn't pass for anything but monsters were banished. But that curse never actually made 'em susceptible to the laws of the gods—made them weak to mortal man's. If man's rulers invited you in, well, there you have it."

Ryn snorted. "Man does not rule man. Every king belongs to a god."

"Funny place, this one. Ruled by pencil pushers, bureaucrats, by screaming moms on the news and scared old men in ball caps and angry young ones with no fucking clue; ruled by everyone and no one. A thing happens, and half the time you're lucky just to know who did it, forget why. And here you are, wriggling through a crack in the door like a shit-covered cat."

His explanation satisfied. "They invited me."

"Poor, dumb fucks."

"Why do you live in that clock?"

"I live in a lotta places, darling. Places like this one, for the quiet. For the taste of old wood and paint, rusted springs and gears. There's life in 'em. More life than the average person. Never trusted flesh riders anyhow. They get one taste of human insides and go batshit. Gimme a musty attic any day. Only proper house for an asura's the one that's dry, none of that wet biology for me, thanks."

"Are there many flesh riders here?"

"Damn straight. Flesh riders love a good loon, and New Petersburg's got a few thousand on the streets after shuttin' down the rubber rooms. There's a couple nasty asura out there, the kind who don't take well to deva and their rules, so watch your ass."

"You should pass the word around. I am not like other deva. I have few rules. But I do not tolerate the stink of torture, rape, and murder, the screams of the innocent weak, or the arrogance of the evil strong. I am the monster who eats monsters, and this city is mine now. My territory, my hunting grounds."

"Warn them? Ha! You think I like the devils who shred souls and eat babies? I'd rather sit back and watch."

"Then we have no quarrel."

"Music to my ears, baby monster."

He didn't understand her—not fully—but she preferred it that way. Ryn pried open the unbarred kitchen window and crawled into the rising moans of nighttime wind. She clung to the mortar in the wall by her fingernails. The wind snapped at her T-shirt, licked her torso, and her jeans rasped against rough bricks. She shut the window, faced the half-full moon that clouds skated across oh-so-swiftly, and scaled to the roof. Every motion warmed the tight cords of her muscles, until they were hot with anticipation.

She crested the roof and perched on its lip. The black sea of staggered rooftops stretched around her, with deep valleys lit yellow by headlights and street lamps.

The air teased her black hair. She pulled her shirt up and angled one arm behind her back. Her finger traced the faint groove of a scar that covered the six slits holding back her kanaf. They tingled beneath the moonlight and she plucked a single, loose strand and examined its knife-edge gleam. By the full moon, she would have her cloak again.

She pulled down the uncomfortable, unnatural fabric of her T-shirt. Without the kanaf against her skin, she felt naked.

She leapt off the rooftop and glided soundlessly to another. Then she sprinted, vaulted, climbed the brick and the black-iron fire escapes, savored the whip-kiss of cold wind on her chest, and with every step her heart pushed hot blood into her fingertips and toes.

She lived again beneath the limitless sky, and though her jungle was brick, concrete, asphalt, and metal, it still had a pulse and life of its own beneath her soles. She loved the city even more after dark, when people emptied the streets and she was free to roam unseen. She explored the rooftops in her block, learned the best routes, the easiest jumps—though she performed the hard ones, too, pleased that her season of near-mortal weakness had passed with something so simple as a stroke of Ms. Cross's pen.

Only mortal laws bound her here. If she could stay free, she would only grow stronger and stronger.

When the dark gave way to deep-blue twilight, she slid down the outer wall to her bedroom window. Clutching a brick protruding a scant fraction of an inch, she took hold of black metal bars with her other hand. She braced both feet and pulled with the whole of her body.

The bars groaned, bent, then tore from the brick wall. Powdered stone puffed into the air. She dropped the bars into the alley, where they rang loud and distant. Then she rapped on the window several times until Susan woke, approached, rubbed tired eyes, and opened the window for her.

"Am I asleep?" she asked.

Ryn swung into the bedroom and shut the windows. "Go back to bed," she whispered.

Once Ryn settled into her bed, Susan sleepily returned to her own. "You aren't going to jump, are you?" she asked through a yawn.

"Why wouldn't I?" Ryn asked.

"Please don't jump. My last roommate jumped. Albert put the bars in after she died. Promise you won't do that."

"I will not die." Ryn lay back on her bed and Susan's comments nagged at her. How foolish and clumsy Susan's last roommate must have been, to try to jump from the window to the rooftop. It was impossible for their species.

She really didn't understand them.

~*~

Naomi didn't often think about suicide, but today was different.

It was a Saturday afternoon and she rode the train back from the Docks, changed stations in Commonwealth Plaza and headed to her home in Garden Heights. The transitions between the three districts always bothered her, from brick and graffiti, to mirrored buildings that sparked in afternoon light, to the wide lawns and proud, old homes where she lived. Guilt gnawed on her, but not solely because of her neighborhood's affluence. She mentally reviewed the last six months and thought about all the ways she was to blame. She still wore the shroud of feeling that always followed her after funerals. Iosef had a sister who was almost the same age Naomi had been at her last graveside service.

Her phone buzzed on the short walk from the train station to her street. She checked it. Denise. Could she handle Denise after a funeral? Naomi had been brushing her off too much, sensing today was coming and unsure how Denise would treat her feelings. She loved her friend, but on suicide, Denise could be weirdly judgmental.

Naomi answered the call anyway. "Hey," she said, projecting a happier tone than she felt.

"You went, didn't you?" Denise asked.

"I don't know what you're talking about."

"To his funeral. That kid, the one who shot himself. The one you tutored. That was today. You went, didn't you?"

"Uh." Naomi shut her eyes. *Of course she knows. She knows everything.* "Yeah, I went."

"You told me you were 'fine.' "

"I am. I was just paying my respects. I knew him pretty well."

"No, you knew him a little. You tutored him after school one day a week for a semester and a half. He drew you a picture once and—unless it was a different kid—awkwardly hit on you last year. But now you're inflating your role in his life so that you can beat yourself up. You're doing that *thing*."

"I have a thing?"

"Oh yes. The whole messiah-complex thing. It was sweet in third grade when your Barbies always saved my Barbies with their superpowers, but it's not fun anymore. It's angsty. You're not responsible for everything other people do."

This was why she had avoided Denise today: the aggressive insistence that Naomi should let things go before she was ready. Before she figured out for herself exactly what Iosef meant, and what to do with the fact that a kid she had tutored—and mentored—could do *that* to himself. To his family.

And before she had counted and tallied all the signs she had missed.

"Now you're thinking about all the ways you could have stopped him, aren't you?"

I hate you, Denise. "No."

"Lies. Disgusting lies. Let me come over, though, and cheer you up with ice cream. Even liars deserve ice cream. I won't say another word about it. You can pick the movie and tell me about all the horrifying things you did and I promise I'll just nod and agree that you're a terrible human being."

Naomi had a distinct Charlie-Brown-going-to-kick-the-football feeling but she sighed and said, "All right. But after six. I've got homework."

"You didn't do it on Friday night, Miss Perfect? Slipping."

"I couldn't. Dad picked me up right after basketball practice. He was back from the Hill. He wanted to have dinner. Trying to convince me to volunteer at his office this summer. Had to tell him no, and that always takes *hours*. We're doing Habitat again this summer and between that, Scouts, staying in shape for cross country, and wanting to have an actual job, I don't have the free hours to give."

"Harsh," Denise said. "But working for a senator—even if he is your dad—has got to look good on college applications."

"Yeah, then everyone expects me to be a College Republican or something, and that's just not my thing. My dad kept all the political genes."

"I can hear you doing the blech-face from here."

It was true. She had.

"Your dad has you ridiculously over-scheduled. Too many things. You should come out with Elli and me next week."

"I can't. Dad's fighting that big security bill and he's only back for one day a week."

"Tell him to take an extra day hammering at Big Brother and you can come shopping with us. Elli's dying to get out and see non-Madison boys, and she's been talking my ear off about clothes for this trip all week. If you don't come, I'll have to deal with her going full-blown man hunter without your backup. Besides, we can do something bad."

"Something bad?"

"Yeah. I don't know. I'll smoke a cigarette near you."

"You don't smoke cigarettes."

"Maybe I'll smoke something else near you."

Naomi rolled her eyes. "You're awful."

"And you need to do *one* bad thing before college or—I swear to God—you will go former-child-star levels of crazy once you're there. You'll drop acid and shave your head."

"You're wrong. I'm the daughter of a U.S. senator and I never do bad things, especially when they're so photogenically bad."

"Do something bad with me next week. Your pick."

"We will buy dissident literature, watch an R-rated movie, and try on sexy clothes. How's that?"

"It's a Republican's idea of bad," Denise hummed.

"Someday you're going to get me arrested."

"I'll be sitting right there next to you."

"But only one of us will be featured in negative campaign ads."

"I'll talk to you later tonight. Mint chocolate chip okay?"

"Yeah." Naomi disconnected and, despite herself, felt somewhat better. Maybe she had cleared the pall from Iosef's funeral.

~*~

Splat picked at the stitches he had put into the meat's face. His excitement spiked when the auburn-haired girl crossed the sidewalk on her usual path. He leaned forward, snapping rapidly with the digital camera.

It wanted her now. But no, not just yet. It was still gathering supplies, waiting for the right moment. But it was close.

It had to be perfect. It *would* be perfect.

CHAPTER FOUR
Hunting Grounds

Ryn explored her new territory by night. She learned the skyline's ridges on each block, mastered the rhythm of the elevated train and let its steel roof whisk her to and fro from riverfront to Dock Street. She stalked Oakland Avenue's neon-lit holes and boarded-up properties. She never rode the train westbound underneath the bay, to the heart of the city with its glassed skyscrapers and electronic eyes. Until she had her bearings, she didn't want to stumble upon a god.

She swept across rooftops in the Docks, ghosted between the bowed, wooden struts of water reservoirs, breezed between coils of razor wire, and blew up the iron fire escapes. She dropped through the crisscrossed maze of wash lines full of flapping laundry. The firelight of burn barrels underneath the Goldwater Bridge gave her pause. They called the place "the Draintrap." It was inhabited by bearded old men and wild-haired women who were so skittish they glanced Ryn's way and—not quite spotting her—shuddered. She savored the spicy smells in Bourbon Alley, a packed-full bazaar that swam with the pungent aroma of narcotic herbs and a thousand other things from across the world. She touched the gray rasp of the city's walls, tasted the brick and exhaust, and it was filthy from top to bottom in a way that settled into her skin and hair and made her feel like she was a piece of it.

Ryn loved the night. The days confused her.

She didn't understand the group home. Judy Birch never stopped asking questions and Albert Birch was often confused. He would wander around the house, often into Ryn and Susan's room, especially if Susan was changing clothes. Susan

would yelp and Albert Birch would apologize, backing gradually through the curtain. Ryn suspected someone had damaged Albert Birch's brain. She knew better than to damage a
human's brain, not unless she meant to kill one.

But then two days later he burst into the bathroom as she
stepped out of the shower. She felt his eyes on her. She knew
then it wasn't confusion, knew what it *really* was. Somehow
the sin was harder to spot when she was trapped in the center
of this whorl of human activity, as though the ocean of lying
eyes and deceptive words dulled her knack for spotting predators.

She stood her ground, dripping cold water as Birch
gawped. At first she could only think about cracking his head
through the porcelain sink and how little she cared about his
brain.

No hospitalizations.

Ryn stood her ground until he backed out of the room—far
too slowly and not without making her skin feel grimy from
what his eyes and his tiny imagination were doing. Fire flared
in her chest, and she wanted to eat his heart. She couldn't in-
jure or maim, though—she couldn't even threaten, couldn't
even look up to bare her eyes at him without betraying her
savage divinity and endangering her new freedoms.

And so she bowed her head. Like a supplicant. Something
in her almost broke from the rage.

The Rabble was its own kind of trouble, a chattering tide
of energetic bodies that filled the cramped apartment with unwelcome noise and smell. Between them and the itching presence of Albert Birch, the apartment frayed her patience, and
Ryn was always grateful to leave.

She savored the walk to her first day at Parker-Freemont
High School, a boring, tall stack of cinder blocks with shadowed windows, a few smashed and covered with plywood.

The apartment Rabble was nothing set next to the high
school. Between classes the halls flooded with students
packed tighter than cattle, and the noise—it staggered Ryn.
The scents of a thousand oily bodies choked her and she
stowed herself in a narrow space at the base of a stairwell with
hands clamped over ears.

The students filtered into classrooms and the bells rang

again and all fell silent. Ryn crept through empty hallways full of long echoes. She liked the school much more without the people; it felt like a locker-lined cave.

Ryn turned a corner and came across a stocky woman in a uniform. The grooves of middle age scored her face. Humans invested authority in uniforms, and this one even had an electrical weapon jutting from her hip. Ryn was supposed to respect the weapon and the uniform both. They got angry if she didn't. Ryn tilted her head inquisitively and let the human make the first move.

"Hey. You." She stuck her thumbs into her belt and strolled closer. "You lost?"

"No." Ryn folded her hands into the deep pockets of her hoodie. She wore baggy cargo pants and kept the gray hood up. Sinking into it soothed the itching from their eyes just a bit.

"Let me see your hands." She tapped the electric weapon.

Ryn didn't understand the woman's face, but saw tension in her shoulders. She showed her hands. The woman ordered Ryn to her class and followed to ensure she arrived. The force of thirty sets of human eyes centered on her at once and made her spine itch. She flitted to a seat.

"If you're all settled in, we can continue," said the teacher. Her face blended together with all the other faces Ryn had seen today. "Also, I have a very well-lit classroom, and you are not Tom Cruise. Remove your sunglasses, please."

"I have an eye condition," Ryn said, precisely as she had been taught.

"And *I* have a condition. That condition is: if students don't do as I say, I embarrass them in front of their peers." She squared her palms to the front corners of Ryn's desk and leaned over it, and Ryn wondered once again if she had to fight for dominance. If Ryn won, did she have to teach the class? She hoped not.

"The one with the weapon said I should be here," Ryn said.

The instructor's face changed color and Ryn could track the small explosion of tics and tremors through the right side of her upper lip and the corner of her eye. "Fine. If the glasses stay on, you'll be punished. Detention."

"What is 'detention'?"

"It means you sit in your chair, shut up, and suffer through the afternoon until I'm satisfied!"

Ryn couldn't figure out how that differed from where she was now.

The classrooms brimmed with students. After the bell rang, their chatter filled the air and they reminded her of the Rabble: loud, pack-minded, yet each one a mystery to her. She couldn't fight or flee, couldn't intimidate or growl. They had clipped her claws and locked her in a building and mandated by law that she spend her days with a thousand unknowable animals, and only one survival strategy remained.

Stealth.

She kept her hood drawn up and pressed through the hallways, their odor and noise putting the screws to her braincase. Then there were the classes. She struggled through English. She understood words and could follow the rules of punctuation, and spell or recite definitions. But they saw things in words that weren't there, like shamans who smoked herb and stared into the sky, imagining shapes in clouds.

In history, they missed important details. Their instructor discussed the Soviet Empire, a collectivist state encompassing much of the world that had collapsed only after the turn of the millennium. They only talked about its human rulers. There had been deva, too, pulling strings, propping it up and allowing it to live longer than it should have. The instructor seemed to hate them, since decades ago they had assassinated two people called President Paul Tsongas and Vice President Bill Clinton.

Mathematics interested her, but she doubted its application. Biology seemed strictly limited to the modern era, ignorant of the Long Ago, of magic, gods, the things hidden from humans behind the Veil, and they only knew about the material parts of the cells—and they taught a very crude version of even that.

Gym was the most difficult. It challenged her every conception of humans as her sister species. They ran as if wading; they used their hands and fingers with all the nuance of flippers. They played elementary games of coordination with ball and bat, only interesting because they couldn't perform them consistently. They couldn't even repeat a single basic motion, let alone a complicated sequence, like a toddler who beat—poorly—upon a piano key over and over. She felt embarrassed for them, even more so because they didn't know to be embarrassed for themselves. Ryn tried to blend in and mimic their ungainly motions, and it made her conscious of her own body in a way that she hated. She hoped they didn't all live that way.

At night, away from the school, she forgot the ungainly stumbling and exploded across rooftops. She savored the gorgeous sensation of matching her movement to the contours of the city. Like two pieces fit perfectly together, like hand in pocket, her sprint pushed her into a groove, the only thing in her life that worked right. Every night she ran, from black midnight until pre-dawn blue, and every night the moon filled and filled, grew brighter, and poured its jittery energy into her limbs.

Most people left her alone. One girl who hid behind her bangs tried to talk to her, but Ryn's stony silence chased her away. Then on Friday, the waxing moon became unbearable. She stared across the cafeteria, inhaled the stale scent of bland food, and wished for clear, frigid streams, and for the feel of wriggling fish in her hands. The moon teased her from the other side of the Earth. It tugged subtly on her slight shoulders. She wanted to drop to the floor, press her cheek to cool linoleum, and listen for its approach.

A boy sat at her table, directly across. He wore neatly pressed slacks and a buttoned shirt, his hair crisply in place so that he reminded Ryn of a well-clipped porcupine, and stank of spicy body-wash odor that burned her sinuses so that she couldn't even tell if he smelled wrong.

"You're in my gym class, aren't you? I'm Harper." His face did a lot of different things and he had very straight teeth.

Ryn fixed him with a steady look, one that chased most humans off after only a few minutes.

"So what's the story with the shades? I know you're not—ah, you know—visually impaired. You get around pretty well in gym."

Ryn stared.

"I mean, it's the only class I see you in. I'm taking all advanced-placement stuff this year. Trying to really get everything I can out of this school—it's not a great school, but my parents are kind of snobby about supporting public ed. I'm a senior. Doing college next year. How about you? Plan on getting out of here anytime soon?"

She stared.

"You look like you belong at a college. You've got the whole alternative look down. I'm into alternative stuff. Very, you know, open-minded."

"Leave now."

"Look, I know I've got the preppy look a little too cornered, but I swear it's just to keep my parents off my back. What do you like? Horror movies? Politics?" He leaned in. "Handcuffs?"

"Solitude."

"I even know where you can find a lot of quiet. A place no one would bother you."

Ryn wondered if someone had damaged his brain.

"I'll show you. It's a great place to get away from crowds. Promise I'll be a gentleman." He sneaked out of the cafeteria, and Ryn followed him, even though she didn't like him. A hiding place might prove useful. He led her up a flight of stairs and pushed open the door to a janitor's closet with the heavy odor of chemicals.

Ryn stepped in and frowned. "Small."

"Cozy," he said, shutting the door. "Hey, want to listen to my playlist?" He offered her an earbud.

"You promised solitude," she said, glaring at him.

"Right. Just you and me."

"I don't think you know what that word means."

"Oh c'mon, don't be like that. No one goes into a closet with a boy unless she's a tiny bit curious. Aren't you curious?"

"Only about what you taste like."

"Oh, holy *shit*, it's like that, huh? The guys were so right about you." He slid a thin plastic-wrapped wafer from his back pocket, its surface worn and crumpled. "Safety first, right?" He reached for her.

Ryn flicked back a pace. It took him a moment to reorient, to find her again with his eyes. She had been wrong to dismiss this one as an annoyance—he reasoned like a child, but he was full grown, and while he wasn't a threat to her, what if she had been a mortal girl?

"Relax, I don't bite." He reached again.

"I do." She braced him with her palm flush to his chest and his hand went to her shoulder, trying to urge her to her knees. His intentions offended her so deeply that her pulse spiked. "No." Anger flashed through her with the word and her free hand curled, finger by finger, into a rocky ball.

"Oh. I get it. You punk girls like it a little hardcore." He grabbed her shoulders and tried to drag her close.

Every fiber of muscle in her arm groaned for use. The full moon had left her in a fog of hunger. She salivated at the thought of pulling an organ out and showing it to him. Instead, she wrapped her hand into his buttoned-up shirt and cracked her skull into his.

He flew back into the door. It burst open. He flopped out of the closet and onto his back. Ryn strode after him and knelt atop his chest. She seized him by the spikes of his hair, and glared into his eyes. "I will forgive the confusion because we are not the same species. But this word. 'No.' You understand it?"

"Uhnn."

"Remember it."

It took his eyes a moment to focus on her and Ryn realized she was being observed by the uniformed woman from earlier, now standing over them both. The woman drew her weapon. "Back off!"

"He will be fine." Ryn stood and slunk back a step. "No hospitalizations."

Harper sat up, wobbled, and swayed back to the floor.

"...I think."

~*~

Ryn sat in a neatly arrayed office made to feel smaller by having too many people in it. There was a desk and a man in a crisp suit behind it in a high-backed, black chair. The desktop marker labeled him "superintendent." Ryn was separated from Harper Pruett by Harper's mother, who emphasized several times how upset she was at being summoned from the art gallery she managed.

Mrs. Pruett pushed up the tiny glasses on her nose and

said, "I think it's clear this isn't a parental matter anymore. It's a police matter. My son was assaulted. It's not a question of whether I'll press charges, it's a question of whether or not I'll sue. My husband works for the law department at Graystone University and we know a lot of excellent lawyers."

"It's still unclear who started the fight," the superintendent said.

"Look at my son!"

Blue and black bruises had amassed around the bridge of Harper's nose and a cotton ball was stuffed up either nostril. Ryn only felt thankful she had restrained herself. The full moon made her blood sing. It clouded her brain, and whatever she did always seemed foolish in retrospect.

"Well?" Mrs. Pruett asked, looking at Ryn as she examined Harper's face. "Are you satisfied?"

"No."

Mrs. Pruett's mouth snapped shut. Her eyes got very large until Ryn could see the whites and tension filled her small, bird-like shoulders. "You *filthy* little—"

"That's enough, Mrs. Pruett!" The superintendent leaned forward. "Ms. Miller." That was the last name they had assigned Ryn. "Harper claims that you lured him into the closet—'seduced' him—and then tried to mug him. What about your side?"

"What is 'mug?' "

"Pardon?" the superintendent asked.

"Do you think playing stupid will get you out of this?" Mrs. Pruett snapped.

"Mugging is when you rob someone by force," the superintendent said. "Did you try to rob Mr. Pruett?"

"He has nothing I want."

"Then why were you in the closet?"

"My head hurt from noise. The closet was quiet. He wasn't supposed to stay."

"All right, so he took you to the closet and stayed. Then what?" He had to cut off Mrs. Pruett's objection with a pinch of his fingers.

"He reached for me. I warned him once. He touched me. I struck him."

"How many times?" the superintendent asked.

"Once."

"Once?" His eyebrow did something.

"Yes."

"He never hit you?"

"He cannot hit me," Ryn said.

"What, because you're a *girl*?" Harper asked. "Like that'd stop me, you crazy bitch."

She leaned out to peer around his mother at him. "Because he is slow."

"She's crazy!" Harper said. "She said she wanted to fuck and when we started, she flipped out!"

"Harper!" Mrs. Pruett said.

"What!"

"Did she tell you to stop?" the superintendent asked.

"No! I mean, not at *first*, not until we already started. I mean, it's not like—I mean, what is this, Red Light Green Light? I didn't hear her. And then she just whales on me! She's a liar."

The superintendent cleared his throat. "You can press charges if you like, Mrs. Pruett, but this sounds to me like a big miscommunication."

"It was *assault!*" Mrs. Pruett said.

"Yes," the superintendent said. "And sexual assault is a very serious matter. So I understand if Ms. Miller would also like to press charges."

For a while, no one said a word. Finally the superintendent glanced at Ryn. "Are you all right? You're shaking the entire floor."

Her knee bounced steadily. "I'm fine," she said. The moon still teased her.

"You're making us all nervous," the superintendent said.

"I'm fine," Ryn repeated, gaze zeroing in on the window behind the superintendent's head. A fly batted against the pane. Its *tap, tap, tap* made her toes curl and her stomach turn over twice and she wanted to stalk it.

"Might you stop?"

Her knee still bounced. She willed it to stop. The buzz was not in the fly, then—it tremored up her calf instead. Her knee bounced again. "No. I can't."

"She belongs in an institution!" Mrs. Pruett said. "Not

around my boy."

"I'm sure a woman of your means can afford all sorts of alternatives if you're unhappy with where Harper is," the superintendent said. "In the meantime, if Harper is saying he was physically assaulted and Ryn is saying Harper attempted to sexually assault her, I have to turn this over to the school resource officer. There will be a formal investigation. Possible criminal charges. If, however, you both admit to a big misunderstanding, it can go away."

The superintendent and Harper's mother both seemed very interested in making things "go away," and Ryn doubted it was to her benefit.

He motioned them out, and while Ryn couldn't read Harper's face, she assumed the look he shot her meant this wasn't over.

She went to the roof. She lay on her back, shut her eyes, and waited. Lunar gravity took hold of her like a second, alien world, pulling from another direction. When it crested the night sky, the pull was from above and below and the moon's power made her weightless. She rose, stood on her toes, pocketed her sunglasses and let the moon touch her face.

Then she tore through her territory, her senses so sharp that she could hear screams from decades past, smell blood spilled into the paving stones a century ago. The six scars holding back her kanaf glowed red hot. Every noise and smell and sight pushed into her brain at once, too fast, like Ms. Cross's driving on the highways.

Pressure built behind her scars. She stripped on a dark rooftop, tearing off mortal cotton, until all that remained were faded, red tennis shoes. Her scars peeled open, split by black strands of razor wire beneath her skin. Countless thin fibers exploded from the slits and filled the air like a black cloud. They flexed and Ryn arched her back at the exquisite sensation of an eighteen-month cramp finally stretched and soothed. With a thought, she wove her kanaf into sheets and smoothed them over her bare skin. She willed them soft and airy as a breeze and reveled in the sleek feel of them covering her—adjusting them to the same shape, color, and apparent texture of her hoodie and dark cargo pants.

She no longer felt naked. The kanaf was as much a part of

her as a bird's feathers.

Unfurling her wings had not released the deeper tension that coiled in her center. It was a spring prepared to release, crushed tighter and tighter by the institution, the school, the humans she couldn't hurt but who desperately deserved it. There was still one thing she could hunt, though, that mortals wouldn't miss. She filtered through the overlapping trails of old blood, the layers of killers and rapists and all manner of beasts on two legs until she found a fresh one. One that stalked right now, under the same full moon she did.

Perfect.

Ryn slid down a drainage pipe and vaulted across an alley, angling between two close boards on an upper-floor window. She dropped into the dingy room, which was cold from the gaps that exposed it to January's elements and delicious in its lonesomeness. Street sounds crept in unfiltered, the walls laced with mildew and the smell of aged wood. There was a taped body outline on the bare floor and an incongruous, wooden rocking chair that creaked in the draft.

She knelt before the rocking chair. "Dust. I thought you hated flesh riders."

He didn't answer at first. Then the chair groaned, its wooden struts protesting as if put under an invisible weight. "Mind your own business, deva."

"I am."

"On the prowl, eh? You're wound tighter than a three-day clock. Splat's got it too. Full moon gets him riled up."

"Splat." She rolled the name around in her head. It gave her ideas—delightful ones—for how to deal with him. "He was here. I can smell him. Why?"

"Just a little, ahem, territorial dispute. Splat keeps a hollow in Whitechurch and I got an attic in the same apartment. Like to visit. Has old photos on the wall. Black-and-whites, full of flavor. Tastes like old-fashioned romance, a dash of tragedy, just the way I like it. Don't find it on anything newer than Great Depression."

"A hollow?"

"Spare body. Call it that 'cause he and his cabal pulled the soul outta her. Did it with one of them plastic porn boxes, those buzzing, noisy what-do-ya-call-'em... laptops. So he and his asura buddies, they infest the laptop and convince this girl they're real flesh-and-blood people on the other end, isolate her, cave in her world. Grind her soul down to just about nothin'. Keeping her on tap, see, in case he needs spare skin. A good hollow's already half dead, soul partway out the door. Gotta get 'em so low they don't feel the asura slipping in to fill the fat, gaping void they carved out. Lotta ways to do it. Torture. Rape. This one was subtle. I kinda ruined it for him, I guess."

"How?"

"The photos. One of 'em was the hollow's grandmother. She kept a diary in a locked trunk, one with sweet, old pages dusted in perfume and tears. I knocked it onto her floor one night. Those old pages filled the hole they put in her. So Splat stopped by to tell me—covenants be damned—he'd eat me if I did it again."

"Who is he in?"

"Some nutcase he's been grooming. Dunno much. He's got a place on Oakland above the Big Shots Tavern. If you scent his hollow, you'll find it there. This isn't gonna come back to me, is it?"

"He won't bother you."

"You say that, but somehow I doubt you got a mirror box. How you gonna trap him?"

"I won't. He won't eat you because I'll eat him first."

"Hate to be the bearer of bad news, but you must be too young to know. Deva can't kill asura. Unlike you, we got no bodies to kill."

"I am from the black places and the Long Ago. I can kill anything that can die, and a few things that cannot."

Oakland was only a few blocks away. Ryn found the apartment and cut a circular hole in the window with one fingernail. She popped the lock and seeped into the room's shadows. The urine-and-mold stink saturated a bare mattress. The hum of a refrigerator and computer fan didn't quite drown out the skitter-clicking deluge of bed bugs in the shadowy parts of the walls. They moved at once, poured from the ceiling like grains of sand, but left a neat ring of clear space around Ryn. They sensed death on her.

Her eyes peeled back the dark and she examined papers

heaped onto the computer desk and pinned to the walls. There were maps with tacks clustered in different locations, short-hand notes with times of day, surveillance-photo printouts, and a reminder note taped to the computer monitor, scribed in disjointed letters. "To get: duct tape, needle-nose pliers, 45-cal, rivets (various)," with a final line in different marker, an afterthought scrawled at bottom: "car battery?" It was under-lined.

A rotten smell came from the bathroom and she peered in long enough to be sure there were no corpses. Just blood in the sink and two clipped-off, human toes in the bathtub, shriv-eled and black with weeks-old gangrene. The asura hadn't taken care of its hollow, perhaps because it was nearly done using it. Whatever its plans, they happened soon. Probably to-night.

The photographs depicted groups of teenage girls who ap-peared outwardly near Ryn's age. One recurred—a very pretty, pale girl with auburn hair. She was the target. But for what? It involved bullets, pliers, and a car battery.

Ryn had to settle her imagination before it could offer a suggestion.

She took the scent of Splat's hollow from a ball cap near the door and returned to the rooftops. With the moon full, she could have found him from three cities distant. She trailed the street he'd driven and rode the steel spine of a tractor trailer across the Goldwater Bridge. Terrain mattered, and she didn't know the rooftops of Commonwealth Plaza, so she darted from the truck, spidered up the exterior wall of a train station, and scented the air. Northeast.

Another train line whisked her that way. At each stop, she bounded to the station roof and sprinted over top, avoiding the prying eyes of humans and their cameras. She recalled Splat's maps. Most pins were in Garden Heights, where the new line terminated.

She picked the scent up again just before Garden Heights, in unfamiliar terrain between the suburbs and Common-wealth, called Center Square. The buildings were shorter than in Commonwealth, but crowded with bus stops and neon lights advertising department stores, coffee shops, and the bright arches of fast food. She rode the train into the station this time, dropped to the platform among startled passengers, and slid beneath the turnstile. She tracked the scent across an elevated walkway that crossed six lanes of traffic and connected the station to a massive parking deck that fed into a sprawling, four-story shopping complex called Center Square Mall.

Ryn paused. The predator's scent had filtered down to her mouth where she could taste it; she savored the moon's bright light and opened her senses. The dark was wide with possibilities. Deciding on her next move, she hooded herself from prying security cameras and tracked Splat's scent to a white van on the top deck.

She darted between camera rotations and found a blind spot by the van's windowless rear doors. Locked. She stiffened her fingers into a knife-hand punch and drove it through the smooth metal. Though her nails appeared mundane, they parted the aluminum hide like oily liquid. She wrapped her fist around the locking mechanism and tore it out with a firm twist. It banged against the asphalt and she cracked the door open.

A duffel bag reeked of Splat. She opened it. It contained a car battery, phallic-shaped plastic objects, handcuffs, duct tape, and a roll of cloth that, when unfurled, revealed a shiny collection of corkscrews. Sitting at the bottom of the bag was an acetylene torch.

Ryn lit the torch and examined the inside of the van by blue-hot glow. She set the shag carpet aflame and tossed the torch into the center of the crackling fire. Slamming the back doors, she ducked behind a row of cars and evaded the cameras until she arrived at the walking bridge into the mall.

She walked into a wall of noise and stink. Bodies and wares pressed and puréed together—fried foods, sweets, paperback books, detergent-stiff clothing, hard plastic, and human oils mashed into one thick soup. Then the perfumes hit her: a meteoric explosion of a thousand compounds that each combined a hundred other scents detonated inside the front of her brain and slumped her into the wall. She lost Splat's trail. The noise and color, too, the riot of signs and the music intermingling with three or four hundred chattering voices collided together like ten trains in her skull. She stumbled forward into a fourth-story railing over the food court.

Too much. No time to adjust. She'd gone from the bright full moon sharpening her senses in the empty city to the crushing mall interior in just two steps.

Clapping her hands to her ears, she shuddered a breath in, then out, and shut the door on the world and everything in it except the measured thud of her inhuman heart, hard and sure. It dimmed the universe outside her skin.

The first sound to cut through the deep well she'd dropped herself into was the voice of a young woman. "Are you all right?" It ran through Ryn smoothly, except for a faint rasp that brushed at her senses. The girl's scent hit next. Her soul smelled different, like a rain shower that washed out the salty taste the entire city bled from its pores. And her skin had the faint tinge of a citrus shampoo that made Ryn think of sunlight.

Ryn slitted an eye open behind the dark sunglasses that shielded the world from her, and every fine detail of the pretty girl's gleaming, auburn hair burned through. She stood a head taller than Ryn, with a slender and long-limbed build that brought to mind the strength and flexibility of willow branches. She dressed in a calf-length skirt, trim blouse, and a red, hooded jacket. She had poise, the sort of grace other humans forgot, her hands clasped. Her large eyes were soft and deep brown, fixed on her, and when Ryn looked at them she couldn't move.

"I asked if you were all right," the girl repeated.

It was the girl from Splat's photographs.

CHAPTER FIVE
Dinner with a Demon

Naomi realized she was talking to a girl. It had been hard to tell from a distance because of the formless outfit and dark sunglasses that—truth told—kind of made her look like the Unabomber. The tips of Naomi's ears burned as she asked her question a third time: "Are you okay? Sorry, clearly you are. And I'm being weird now." She withered under the girl's stare.

Up close, the other teenager looked more her gender. She had pretty enough features, with a straight, expressionless mouth and a stray wisp of darkest-black hair dangling loose from her hood. She might have been goth with a bit more effort, but seemed more than anything like a tomboy dressed in the slapdash apparel of secondhand stores. "I'm fine," the dark-clad stranger bit off.

"Good." Instinct had demanded Naomi approach her. Instinct, and maybe Iosef's ghost still walking around in her shadow. Something in the girl's stance at the railing, in the way she clutched her head as if under attack, had drawn her closer. It could have been a migraine. But it could have been something worse, too, and she'd forced herself to make sure. "I'm Naomi."

The strange girl examined her with a cant to her head, like a dog trying to figure out whether or not someone was speaking to it. "Ryn." Her nostrils flared and she snapped her gaze to a spot behind Naomi, where Denise and Elli stood.

"Those are my friends," Naomi said. "Denise is the long-haired one with the affected expression of boredom and Elli is the one in black-frame glasses." Denise made a show of checking her phone impatiently and Elli held the bags while examining her toes. Naomi turned back to Ryn. "We were just buying some books. Do you have friends here?"

"No." She didn't elaborate. It came out as a dismissal, an invitation for Naomi to leave.

Naomi took a deep breath and ignored the critical gazes that no doubt bored into the back of her head. Sometimes she wished she could ask the obvious: *Are you okay?* But that never worked, so instead: "Want to hang out?"

"No." Ryn glanced back at the railing.

Okay, the direct approach it is. "It's the crowds."

She caught a hint of Ryn's eyes narrowing behind those dark glasses. "How did you know?" An accusation.

Naomi lowered her voice, too quiet for her friends to hear. "The skittish way you looked at Denise and Elli, at the people around us."

Ryn's eyes sparked beneath the shades and a current of alarm shot up Naomi's spine. "I am not afraid," Ryn growled. Naomi had never heard anything like it, never heard someone wrap the English language so perfectly into a snarl, and it switched down some kind of primordial breaker in her brain.

"Sorry, no, of course not," she hurried, the words matching her quickened pulse. Forcing a steadying breath, she ordered herself against every instinct not to scurry off with tail between legs—*What is it Dad says? Timid doesn't look good on us.* "Okay. Full confession, you're the kind of girl more likely to elicit terror than to feel it. I get that."

A solemn nod, as though Ryn were satisfied.

Clasping her hands in front of her, Naomi added, "Promise you won't murder me, and I might even feel bad enough to make it up to you."

"I won't harm you." Ryn's tone softened. "You smell right."

Naomi blinked. The fear, though, had fled her, the invisible fist that squeezed her heart unclenching so that she could breathe again. "Glad to hear." A jolt of exhilaration followed, her body's reward for surviving an encounter with this strange, almost-goth creature. "So you'll let me make it up to you."

"I'm fine."

"I know you are, but I'm not over it. You want to grab food with me?"

Ryn bit her lip in a way that hid it in her mouth, no teeth on display, and it was a strangely sweet gesture that made Naomi think: *cute like a cat; like someone who thinks she's apex predator, but also doesn't mind when you bring her tuna.* The self-serious girl shifted and looked in the other direction. "Not hungry."

Naomi had never met a worse liar. "Not at all?"

"I can feed myself."

"And I can buy the food that you feed yourself with. Teamwork."

"There is... food at home." Oddly, another lie.

"There's food here too. Come on. My treat." Naomi used her brightest smile—a dirty, low-down move that usually worked. "Just this once and I'll never bother you again. Scout's honor." Three fingers held up, somewhat guiltily since that was probably also a lie if they spent any time at all together.

Ryn opened her mouth, shut it, gazed back into the crowds, and finally back at Naomi. "What do you want from me?" She wore a look of such desperate frustration.

"Naomi!" Denise called. "Getting hungry. Let's go. Let emo kid be emo."

Naomi shot her a warning glare. "Stop." Facing Ryn, she offered her hand.

Ryn danced back, hands clenched to the rail, tension filling her body like a spring compressed tight. When Naomi backed off, palms out in placation, Ryn relaxed.

Not just the crowds, Naomi realized. *Like an idiot, I cornered her.* She really was a stray, in more ways than first surmised. "Sorry," Naomi whispered, lowering her arms to her sides and relaxing her posture. This seemed to relax Ryn slightly as well, and the girl eased back to her full height. "I'm not trying to trick you into going to my church or voting for my candidate, and I won't let Denise make fun of you. Just wanted you to grab a bite with us—if you want. Do whatever you like. If it happens to be eating with us, I'm buying. That's all. Sorry again."

Naomi expected that to be the end of it. This was a girl who had seen violence. She could sense it, could tell Ryn needed a basic charity without a covert quid-pro-quo. But she couldn't force it. For certain wary souls, the harder one tried, the faster they sprinted the other direction. Yet something happened between the two of them in that moment, a calculation in Ryn's mind that Naomi couldn't intuit. The other girl examined the floor between them and murmured, "I will go with you."

"Awesome." She smiled over her shoulder at her friends. "Guess what? This is Ryn, and she's joining us for dinner."

Elli and Denise both forced smiles and Ryn did nothing to acknowledge them, keeping to the other side of Naomi as they all walked. Naomi struck up a conversation and found out Ryn went to Parker-Freemont. It was a high school in the neighborhood next to Thatcher High, where Iosef had attended. Ryn's school competed with Madison Academy in a few sports, and since Elli had been a cheerleader and particularly hated their teams, her face scrunched up in scorn.

"Parker-Freemont is on the other side of the city," said Denise. "Did you really come all this way to shop?"

"No." Ryn's stare was on the crowds.

"Then why commute over here?" Denise asked. "Planning to rob someone?"

"It's a nice mall," Naomi said. "Maybe she likes it here."

"I'm looking for someone," Ryn said.

"I thought you said you didn't have friends here," Denise said.

"I'm not looking for a friend."

"Family?" Naomi tried to verbally separate Ryn from Denise, who tended to get catty when her blood sugar dropped.

"No," Ryn said.

"Who, then?" Denise asked.

"A man."

A boyfriend. That made sense. Naomi grinned. "Is he handsome?"

"I doubt it," Ryn said.

"Wait, you don't know?" Denise scoffed. "Is this some digital hookup? That's a little trashy."

Ryn's attention was fixed elsewhere. "I am not hooking with anyone." Naomi wondered for the first time if English was her first language.

Elli sighed. "The animal-vegetable-mineral game is kind of annoying. Just tell us what it's all about. Are you dating this guy or are you planning to murder him?"

"I have to find him first."

"So it *is* murder," Denise teased. They all laughed except for Ryn.

"She doesn't have to say what she's doing here." Naomi motioned with her jaw to a café. "Come on. Let's eat here, before Denise dies of starvation."

"I won't starve." Denise grinned. "I'd eat one of you two before I'd let that happen."

Ryn glanced at Denise for the first time. Naomi saw suspicion in it.

They sat at one of the café's outlying tables, separated from the mall proper by a divider covered with advertisements. Ryn fumbled with the menu and paid a lot of attention to the three of them, mimicking their movements and reading the sections they read from. Naomi made sure Denise and Elli ordered first. She figured Ryn was a foreigner and picking up the customs. Ryn ordered some kind of salad with oranges in it. "That looks good, I'll have that too," Naomi said. She glanced at the strange girl. "What do your parents do?" It was one of her surreptitious tricks for gauging how a person was doing. The more willing someone her age was to talk about their parents, the more likely they were okay.

Denise lifted one eyebrow a fraction of an inch, which meant, *Could you be any more obvious?*

Naomi shot back with a slight narrowing of her eyes: *Shush!*

Ryn didn't follow the best-friends telepathy at all and just shrugged. She appeared highly interested in the grooves on the lip of the table.

Naomi could have kicked herself. Maybe she had no parents. This wasn't a Madison girl; she was from the Bad Part of Town.

"My parents are both Dr. Kwon," Elli said, trying to fill the vacuum of Ryn's silence. "Just one of them works exclusively on bones and the other on... gunshot wounds, mostly, I think."

"My mom's a lawyer," Denise said. "Dad is a house husband."

Elli laughed and Naomi was happy for the change of subject. They discussed Denise's father's nontraditional family role a while, cracking the same series of jokes they had since grade school. Ryn sat quietly in her chair, observant but not saying anything, shifting and bouncing her knee at a steady frequency. She fidgeted and scanned the crowd.

"He's a good cook," Denise insisted. "He could open up a little bakery if he wanted."

Ryn spoke up for the first time. "What about you?" she asked Naomi.

"Oh. Well, my dad's a politician. Senator Bradford?" She prepared herself for the usual litany of reactions to that. There were only a few: stunned silence if they were impressed by senators, or an awkward joke about either voting or not voting for her father if they knew him from politics. Naomi had a few established responses, such as her crack that she wouldn't have voted for her father some days either, or that it sucked to have a parent who debated professionally.

Ryn didn't follow the script. She skipped over Naomi's father and asked, "What about your mother?"

Naomi hated that question—no matter how anticipated, it always made her breathing go shallow. "She passed away. A few years ago."

Ryn tilted her head. The typical responses were *I'm sorry* or *That's terrible*, and Naomi had her autopilot ways of making people feel less mortified. However, Ryn threw her for a second loop. "Tell me about her."

The table quieted. Denise picked through a packet of crackers meant for soup, sucking the crumbs off her fingertip. Elli played with her necklace. Ryn eyed Naomi with laser-like focus. Her knee still bounced. The quiet stranger had killed their small talk, shattering through niceties like a bullet through an Emily Post book.

"She died in a car accident," Naomi said at last. "Drunk driver." The words tightened her throat. If anyone asked her, she'd tell them it was a long time ago. It gave people the impression she was over it, because whenever she said she was over it, it didn't sound like she was, not even to her own ears.

"But tell me about her," Ryn said.

"Oh." Now the stray had cornered her.

Elli and Denise pretended they hadn't heard the inquiry, and Naomi didn't trust her voice at first. "Mom was a very brave woman. She was from Russia, back in its Empire days, and she won a visa to study economics in the U.S. She stayed, illegally for a while, and lived in the ex-Soviet diaspora in the Docks. She met Dad at Graystone University in the city and kept turning down his marriage proposals. Dad says she only gave in because the feds were getting close, but I never saw anyone look at him the way she did. *She* said she married him because he had a dryer and she was sick of clotheslines."

The words had broken loose and came faster. "She was brilliant, and tenacious. She eventually earned her Ph.D., but they wouldn't award it for years because she was illegal while she worked on her credits and there was some bad blood in the faculty. Then her work earned a Nobel Prize and they sort of had to. Dad put it on the shelf next to his high-school track trophy and always asked her, 'But how high can you *jump*?'

"Later, she taught at Graystone University here in the city. She taught economics but she knew basically everything. She and Dad used to argue all the time, too, but in a good way. She was the only person I ever knew who could make the phrase 'anarcho-capitalist hardliner' sound like a term of endearment. Dad used to call her his little ex-commie renegade. She loved that."

Their food came. Naomi was glad; talking even that much had left her emotionally winded. Denise and Elli went back to chatting. Naomi didn't feel like talking, but she watched Ryn, who had seemed so much less important five minutes ago. Now Naomi wondered how she'd pulled exactly the right thread to make Naomi's heart unspool in front of everyone. *Are you especially clever? Or especially clueless?*

Ryn ate briskly between scans of the food court, sniffing the air periodically. Naomi hardly touched her food, inventing stories that explained this girl: the form-obscuring tomboy outfit, the too-large sunglasses indoors that weren't even cool, the soft-spoken words that were entirely too bold.

She'd seem awkward if she were not objectively adorable, made so by her apparent conviction that she was five feet taller than she was.

"So. Ryn," Naomi said at last. "What do you do for fun?"

"I run."

"Are you on a track team? I run the four hundred and I pole

vault."

"No," Ryn said. "No team. Just outside. When I need to move."

"A lot of energy, then," Naomi said. "Your leg's been bouncing this whole time."

Ryn examined her leg. "Yes." It didn't stop bouncing. "What do you do for fun?" She asked the question in the same tone Naomi had used.

"Plenty of things. Basketball, Girl Scouts, camping, swimming, running. I like to dance."

"What is Girl Scouts?"

"Really? It's an organization. Our troop does some volunteer work and wilderness trips in the summer. Do you ever hike or camp out?"

Ryn laughed just once. It seemed to escape from her throat, and she clapped both hands over her mouth. The displeasure with which Ryn treated her own laugh warmed Naomi's heart, made her kind of love the little weirdo. Ryn seemed to have even more trouble looking her in the eye, though. "I've been in the forest," she said after a moment. "I didn't know people went there for fun. I didn't know about Girl Scouts."

"Is English your second language?"

"Not my first."

"You speak it well. Where are you from originally?"

Ryn shrugged. "The wilderness. Some other places."

"Maybe someday you can show me around your home," Naomi said. Ryn didn't like to share details and Naomi's mind swam briefly with suspicions. She thought of her mom and wondered if Ryn was also in the country illegally. Then she cut off that thinking—it didn't matter. Her dad had always taught her that immigration laws were too evil to be respected by decent people. "In the meantime, you must be new here. Let me take you out. Next weekend. There's this great dance club—it's under-twenty-one on Friday night. Do you have a piece of paper?"

"No."

"I mean, she doesn't *have* to come with us if she doesn't want to," Denise said.

"Don't be silly," Naomi said. "Here." She reached across

the table and took Ryn by the wrist, clicking out her ballpoint pen. The click shot Ryn backward. For a moment, Naomi thought she'd fall off her chair. Instead, the chair slanted onto two legs and Ryn somehow alighted onto it, balancing it with a foot on the seat and another on the chair back. She crouched, focused on the pen in Naomi's hand.

Denise and Elli stared. Naomi raised the pen and presented it to Ryn. She clicked it a few times for Ryn's unwavering gaze. After a few clicks, Ryn glanced back at Naomi. Only then did she tilt forward. The front chair legs banged onto the floor and she dropped into her seat in the same motion.

Naomi had taken eight years of ballet, swing dance, and gymnastics, but had never seen anyone move like that in her life. The speed. The fluidity. "Sorry," she whispered. The low current of alarm had returned, and she licked her dry lips. "I should have asked." She set her hands at the table's midway point. "Do you trust me?" *Do I trust you?*

Ryn averted her gaze, and without looking up she slid her cool hand into Naomi's. Expecting calluses, Naomi was surprised by the smoothness of the palm, softness of the fingertips, and perfectly tended fingernails. Each nail's edge had a strange gleam. Rolling the sleeve up two inches to write there, Naomi startled at the glimpse of a scar. She flicked the sleeve back down to conceal the mark from Denise.

But the memory of it burned. *Enormous, and not from a razor.*

She wrote the information on Ryn's palm. "Now you won't forget."

Ryn looked at the address and time. "I won't." She stood, staring at the words on her skin. "I must go."

She pushed away from the table, hopped the divider into the mall proper, and disappeared into the crowd before Naomi could react.

~*~

The mall had too many eyes. The prickle of human gazes skittered across Ryn's flesh like a swarm of ants. Naomi's gaze had been a different kind of itch, one that made her feel small, uncertain, but kind of good. She couldn't tell if it was the too-gentle press of Naomi's fingers or the ballpoint on her palm that had made her so ticklish.

Ryn wove through the crowd. She could still feel Naomi's heart pounding against her through the fleeting contact of fingertips. The magnetism of her words still tugged on Ryn, confusing her and almost propelling her back to the café. Those words convinced her to do things she otherwise wouldn't.

No, not just the words: the smiles, the motions of her body. Ryn had never seen a smile before Naomi's, or at least, none had ever made sense before hers. It was like a codex, unpacking for the first time not just what smiles signified, but what they *did*. The surveillance photographs hadn't been enough, since they were too frozen, like capturing the ocean in still-frame when it could only be understood in motion. Naomi was animated. Her soul pushed to the surface of her face. Her movements added a dimension that drew together her whole meaning. And that clean rainwater scent... it was like Aina's, and alien to the city—a scent Ryn might catch once in a century, a scent with no evil in it. But most of all, Ryn could not figure out why she hadn't stopped *thinking* about Naomi. Why her mind and her feet kept trying to lead her back to the female.

Then it struck her: the full depravity of what Splat intended. The fugue of the full moon had almost blotted the hunt from the forefront of her mind, but now she sharpened her intent. No one would hurt Naomi. She fell now into Ryn's sphere of influence, and therefore, Ryn's territory.

Ryn ascended the stairs and paced a circle around the food court. She inhaled. Splat was out there. His presence tickled her brain in its darkest corners and her fingers clenched and unclenched with delight. The stalking had begun. By far her favorite part.

CHAPTER SIX
The Devil You Know

"**M**ost awkward dinner of *my* life," Denise said on their way out of the food court, bags in their hands.

"It wasn't that bad," Naomi said.

"A close second to my eighth birthday party when Bragan Coates went to kiss me on the cheek and threw up down the back of my dress," Elli said.

"Bragan was just in love," Denise said. "Still can't figure out what that girl's problem with chairs was."

"Don't be mean," Naomi scolded.

"I'm not being mean; she just needs to be careful. Like maybe someone should start a nonprofit to educate people. On how to sit on chairs. Or maybe put the instructions *on* the chairs."

"You're being mean and it's because you're livid about my inviting her out next week," Naomi said.

"Was that for the best, though?" Elli asked. "I think she might be uncomfortable hanging out with us. You have to admit, she's not our usual thing."

Denise snorted. "Not our usual? You mean like how you can't tell she's a girl until you're right on top of her? Or do you mean like she might have some kind of chair-related dysfunction?" Her eyes lit up and she leaned in conspiratorially. "Or maybe the chairs offend her, because all chairs are imperfect shadows of the Platonic ideal of a chair. And so she's disinclined to sit. Philosophically."

"You're not going to manipulate me into uninviting her," Naomi said.

"Whatever do you mean?" Denise asked, her saintliest expression on display.

"You're trying to convince me you'll pick on her endlessly so that I'll uninvite her. Maybe instead you should humor me for one night."

"Fine—if you promise it'll help you get over the Iosef thing," Denise said as they boarded the escalator. "Because that's what it's about, isn't it?" she pressed.

"Maybe. I mean, I saw her at that railing, and she looked..."

"Aloof?" Elli nodded and let out a small sigh. "Aloof and mysterious."

Denise chuckled. "You thought she was a boy at a distance too, didn't you?"

Elli shrugged. "So I have a type; sue me. I thought Naomi was going to hit on her. Was about to go all green-eyed monster, too, until I saw she was tiny, and then a girl, and I realized the tragic failing of baggy cargo pants." She shook her head sadly. "Such unfortunate choices."

"Too bad she wasn't a boy," Denise said. "Then Naomi would have a date next week."

Naomi was rubbing the corners of her eyes. "I didn't see or care who she was, just that she was alone."

"There's a reason some people are alone." Denise turned her back to Naomi and stared ahead. "Some like it, and some are that way for good reasons; reasons you would have no clue about." They rode to the top of the escalator, and she added over her shoulder, "Drugs, by the way."

"What?" Naomi asked.

"She was here to sell drugs, Miss Perfect. Hence the internet stranger and the way she kept looking around. That's why she didn't want to come eat with you. She thought you were trying to buy from her, and she figured you might narc."

"I don't think that's it." Denise had a point, though—that explanation fit better than anything she could come up with. "I hope not. And if she was here to sell pot, I hope she doesn't think I was trying to buy any. Do you think that's what she thinks?"

"No idea," Elli said. "But she was jumpy."

"I'd be jumpy too if I were a waif who sold drugs in the Docks," Denise said.

"You don't know it was drugs," Naomi snapped.

"It's only ever two things, and she's wound too tight for the other thing. Drugs. She's buying or selling, and my money says she shows up next week either high or trying to sell you shrooms. Anyway, my point is: bring cash to pay her off, because you'll look like an idiot if you try to use plastic."

"Stop trying to talk me out of next week."

"Are you kidding? I've changed my mind. I want to watch this train wreck. Don't worry. You can pay her, but you don't have to take the shrooms."

They stopped because they had arrived at a crossroads, with Elli and Denise needing to exit toward a different parking deck. Naomi faced them. "Look. I don't think she was a dealer, and she looked like she could use a few friends. If you can't be that, then don't come out next week."

"I will be there next week and I'll be myself," Denise said. "Just because you tuck it all in for Daddy doesn't mean I will. However, I do promise I'll be gentle with your new charity project's feelings. Because I love you. Also, I don't want this girl to knife you in the ribs."

Naomi took a breath and expelled her irritation. "Good night, guys. Drive safe."

"Night. We'll see you Monday. Oh, and bring at least fifty bucks for your dealer. Because if *I* have to pay her off, I'm getting my money's worth."

Naomi pushed through the heavy glass doors and crossed a walking bridge to the parking deck. Frigid wind struck her from the right. She hunkered into her big coat and her hair did a wild dance. She entered a cavernous middle deck and passed through a deserted maze of shiny cars, the echo of her footsteps pinging off distant walls.

The deck lights flickered once and it went dark.

She stopped.

The shape of the once-familiar concrete space was transformed by shadows; everything lay still, gleaming car windshields visible only because of distant illumination through the deck openings. A single warning shiver rattled up her spine, and out of nowhere her brain recalled the percentage of assaults and rapes that happened in parking garages. *I hate you, brain.*

She rummaged through her purse and flicked on a penlight. She took a deep breath. Likely a circuit breaker. She walked again.

The deck was silent but for the wind, which caught a plastic bag, crinkled it, and scraped it across the concrete. The sound raised her fine hairs and she gripped her bags tighter in her left hand, speeding her steps.

A singsong voice echoed off the cold pillars: "Here pussy, pussy."

She wasn't sure she heard the words right, but hurried along as cold fear prickled her skin. She'd borrowed Dad's car. It was still a dozen down and two aisles deeper.

"Don't run, pussy." She'd heard it right. *Oh God.* "Going to do such nice things with you; promise."

Behind her. Panic dulled her senses until she heard only ringing and she spun, dropped her bags, and snapped up her can of pepper spray. She jogged backward toward the car and flashed her penlight left and right across an empty floor. *Where is he?* Nothing back there except cars and the dark front of an unlit Coke machine.

"Step out, you coward," she said, projecting confidence she didn't have. All the while, she wove between cars, spun to check each corner, and worked toward her vehicle. *Keys, keys, keys. Left pocket?* "I'm armed!"

"Bad kitty. No scratches or I'll pull out those pretty claws." The voice came from everywhere and nowhere.

Where are you!

"You want to see me, don't you? Bet you scream." His voice was melodic and made her queasy. She spun toward her car, now in sight, and sprinted. She hit the key fob for the doors to unlock about eighteen times and heard them pop. She hit the panic button too so that its lights blinked and the horn blared. The side windows were shattered but she kept going. It wasn't until she grabbed the door handle that she saw it.

Someone had torn off the steering wheel.

And scratched "BEHIND YOU" into the side panel.

"Are you ready?" he whispered, his voice in her left ear and his breath far too warm on the back of her neck. "To scream?"

Naomi twisted around. Fingers vised around her throat, choking off her cry. He lifted her into the air with just one hand. *How can he be so strong?* She tried to say "Please" and only heard a weak gurgle. Her eyes watered and her vision filled with sparks. She gripped his wrist and kicked, but it felt like hitting a frozen slab of meat.

She thrust the pepper spray into the dark space near his face and squeezed.

It was a ski mask, but she unloaded into it. He choked, dropped her back onto her feet and slammed her flush to her car, gripping her neck without entirely cutting off her air. Her lungs worked fast to suck in oxygen.

He coughed and laughed at the same time, free hand wiping at his eyes. "Bad kitty really wants to get declawed. Don't worry, I can do that. Oh, but first: am I handsome?" He peeled off the mask.

That's not a face. Not really. It was a skull with skin stretched across it, yellow-toothed grin so wide she could see all the way to the back molars. He'd slit his cheeks from ear to ear. The gashes were stitched with thick, black wire, and messily, as if by the hand of a drunken boxer. His bugging eyes seared through her, the veins in one having burst, turning it red. "So, pet? Would you like to scream now? Or do you find me handsome?"

Naomi swallowed her revulsion. She shuddered out a deep breath and dropped her pepper spray. It rolled noisily away. Reaching up, she touched his mutilated cheek with her fingertips. "Maybe once. Before this." She covered the gashed part with her hand, until she looked only into his eyes.

He blinked, confused, and Naomi tried her best to hold him there in her gaze. It was a low-down, dirty trick, but she even managed half a smile.

That caught him off guard. For a moment, he was only trying to figure out the kindness in her eyes.

A moment was just enough. She sought with her right hand a loose black wire on his gashes and ripped it out with all her might. It made a *p-p-p-pop*, like the important stitch from a jacket sleeve.

He howled. She looped the wire around two fingers and kept pulling. His shriek pitched up an octave.

He threw her. The psychopath and the ground shrank. She sailed too high and too far, spun partway, and saw the hood and windshield of a car rise up at her. Rolling her body, she threw her arms down in a breakfall drilled into her by gymnastics, and the windshield cracked on impact. Pain jolted through both her forearms and her back, but evenly, and nothing snapped.

No sooner had she hit than she rolled off the hood and dropped to her feet, sprinting away.

Footfalls echoed behind her. She realized in her panic she'd sprinted to the wrong end of the parking deck. There was no ramp or stairs ahead, so she tucked around a corner and ducked between cars, working her way to another row. She stopped by an SUV and pressed her back into it, breathing heavily, and listened. *Find him. Then sneak around him.* It was hard to hear over her car horn.

A corner of the garage strobed in her car's headlights. She heard the psychopath snarl. The sound told her where he was, so she scampered down the aisle a few more car-lengths before something stopped her in her tracks.

Something moved out in the shadow, a patch that was blacker than normal black.

"Here kitty, kitty," the psycho called. He sounded far away, his voice from another direction than the twist she'd spotted in the darkness. "Here pussy. Such a bad girl. Wish you thought we were handsome. Maybe you'll grow to like our face once we carve you to match."

Naomi settled into a crouch. *Trying to scare me,* she realized. *Wants to flush me out, and he's getting frustrated. Just keep your head.* His voice made that hard, but when she glanced back at the weird knot of shadows, something else stole her breath.

Something else—that was all she could make of it, because it looked like nothing more than a distortion in the darkness that blew like smoke from behind a column, flitted across the floor, and merged into another column. Her heart thumped against the inside of her ribcage at what she'd seen: at something more fluid than form. Dread squeezed the air from her lungs and erased every rational explanation from her mind— for that instant, there was something wicked staring at her from the blackness; something had crawled from Hell and watched her with an ancient patience.

It terrified her in ways the psychopath could not. She sensed they weren't together, because the Hellish thing crept toward the madman's singsong voice—liquid shadows peeled from the column and appeared for an instant as the silhouette of a person, bounding to the rear of a truck and joining the shapeless ceiling. So quick it might have flown. So purposefully toward the stitch-faced man, she realized it wasn't hunting her. She was merely in its way.

No. She'd lost track of it, and with it gone from her sight, she closed her eyes and likewise emptied her mind. *It's not real. Just the fear playing tricks. Focus on getting out of here.*

Her feverish mind pushed through the haze of terror, grasping for an escape. There was a stairwell and a ramp, and the psychopath would only have a general idea of where she was. He'd split the distance between the two, in case she ran for one of them. But Naomi was closer to the stairs now. Maybe close enough.

She sprinted for them.

She heard a commotion. A wet, animal snarl. The collision of bodies.

Every step up the stairs, she envisioned hands ghosting from behind to grab her ankles and drag her backward. Each stride across the bridge to the lit mall, she swore that furnace breath gusted against the back of her neck.

She hit the heavy glass doors. They resisted her and opened so slowly. She burst through one set, and the second was heavier than concrete. She stumbled through and ran until she reached a shocked, frozen gaggle of shoppers.

Everyone stared. Naomi collapsed, inhaled sharply, and gesticulated toward the exterior doors. Through hot, thankful tears she managed to focus on a round security guard—a badge had never seemed so lovely before—and struggled to say, "Parking deck! Someone. Some... man. Psychopath."

"What's he look like? Miss, are you hurt? Your hand."

She looked down at the black wire looped around her fingers, sticky with blood. It was all over her.

"Not my blood. He— had this. In his face. Oh God." She clapped her other hand over her mouth and shuddered, realizing how much of her own horror she'd swallowed in her effort to escape—but that sticky blood and black string sent the nail straight into the deepest part of her. *He almost had me. That thing with half a face almost had me.*

~*~

Fear was delicious. It was sour and pooled in the sweat of wicked men. It dribbled into their sinful blood, and like discordant sounds arranged suddenly into the loveliest kind of music, turned bittersweet. And it made stalking delightful. Fear caused paralysis, fogged the mind, and lent her prey the impetus to run. And when they ran, it twisted all the right places inside Ryn's stomach.

Naomi's fear was different. She fled the asura and trailed the musk of terror chemicals on car hoods and concrete. It wasn't a right smell. It was ripe-things-turned-rotten, like a rain shower filled with heavy oil. It was profane.

She flowed along the ceiling like wet ink, her hoodie and cargo pants dissolved into the formless black wings of her kanaf, bleeding her shape and color into the negative spaces around her. Every nerve buzzed, a sensitive conductor. The asura passed beneath her and Ryn's pulse quickened with voyeuristic pleasure. She could have reached out to flick open his carotid, yet she remained unseen. The waiting almost felt better than the bloodletting, savoring the moment before full, kinetic contact, her visceral urges piqued but teasingly denied for just a few heartbeats longer.

Naomi cut short Ryn's stalking when she sprinted for the corner staircase. Splat whirled to follow her.

I could let him catch her. I won't let him hurt her, but then I could stalk him more. No, she decided. Naomi was her territory now, and she didn't share.

Splat passed beneath her again. Ryn tore from her shrouded place on the ceiling and snarled her hunger at the asura. "*Mine.*" The word came in the midst of her growl and she didn't know why she said it. He spun in time to see teeth and shadow, no more.

She hit him. They tumbled. Her force punched him into the concrete. She cracked him across his face, and because he was slow, she did it nine more times.

Then he fought back, throwing a wild punch. She rolled

backward. His fist whiffed the air and her fingertips settled
onto the concrete floor as she eased into a low crouch at his
feet. She had to wait for him to stand. It took forever. He
wasn't much faster than a person, not at all.

But she could smell some person in him. The asura wasn't
in a hollow, strictly speaking; there was something of the human being left. She didn't want to kill the person if he wasn't
either evil or completely gone, but getting Splat out of the human would be tricky. There were tales of holy men who could
draw out an asura with words from their Almighty, but monsters had a messier alternative.

Pain.

He cocked his fists and she shot in low, wove a dance
around his two blows, and vaulted onto his chest. Her deft fingers gripped one of his incisors and she leapt over him.

"*Fuck! Fucking fuck!*" He clutched his face and Ryn tossed
the incisor aside.

"One," she said. Asura hated pain. They were not accustomed to it. Even the ones who mutilated their flesh preferred
to do so with only one toe dipped into the host. As heady and
intoxicating as the flesh could be for the pleasures it brought,
they didn't have tolerance for agony. Life granted that tolerance only to creatures who wore their skin each day.

"Are you my new plaything?" he asked, practically singing
the last word. But when Ryn advanced, he retreated.

She flew at him again. He tried a punch and missed, his fist
crumpling in a car hood.

Ryn's hand whipped through the air and he shrieked. She
twirled around him, then ducked an elbow strike. She tossed
away a molar. "Two."

"Tell me, plaything, what do you— *fuck!*"

"Three."

The singing was gone from his voice. "You're going to run
out of teeth eventually, you bitch."

"You have more than teeth." The dark was full of things
that glittered, but none so bright as Ryn's eyes.

"I'll teach you respect." He wrapped his fingers into the
soft metal of a car hood and spun the vehicle out of its spot.
Its tires scraped on the floor and he swung it like a bat. Ryn
rolled over top. The car crunched into the front grille of a Jeep.

"What are you? Not asura. You're a damned goddess, aren't you? Think you can come down here and piss all over *me* on a full moon?"

He swung into a concrete pillar and powdered it. The choking dust flew into Ryn's face, an attempt to blind her. He followed it up by snagging a coupe and rolling it through the air at her.

Ryn dove through the car's passenger window, passed mid-roll through the cab, and burst through the driver-side door just before it crunched onto the floor. She alighted on the ceiling, gripping a metal rafter. "I will hear you scream," she promised.

Her cloak shrank at the fringes, tightening so it wouldn't get in her way. She was prepared now for battle.

He pounced from the floor; she descended from on high. They tangled in the air, where she allowed him to grapple her because it would limit her advantage in speed and agility. Ryn had been lit and left burning for too long; she needed to stretch, to taste blood, and to destroy him in all arenas—even those where he had an edge.

Together they whirled and sank to the concrete in a flurry of shattering blows. They traded fists and knees; Ryn deflected Splat's, and as they tore at one another, his blows pocked a trail of tiny craters in the concrete. He brute-forced Ryn into a steel girder. She snaked a leg around his knee, flexed him into the ground, and loosed a hurting volley into his ribs. He tore one arm loose, backhanded her, and she spat the blood into his eyes. Then she cracked her forehead down into his temple. He went limp.

But not for long. He lurched with new vigor. He grabbed a fistful of her kanaf and slammed her back into the pillar over and over until it dented. On the fifth slam, Ryn clung fast to the pillar. She pincered his throat with her legs and jerked him to the side, into a car hood so soundly that his face left an impression in the soft metal.

Splat took her knees in both hands, spun, and tossed her across the parking deck. Ryn let him. She reoriented in the air like a cat, landed gently on the face of a parked bus, and slid to the floor.

"Next time I get a hold of you I'm going to rape every part

of you," he snarled.

She laughed at him.

"What's so funny? You think I'm going to tickle you? You think I'm playing games, you bitch? I'll make you feel every inch."

"You talk too much. Is that why you're so bad at this?"

He lunged and she melted away. He let loose an onslaught of blows, each one slow. He hadn't overpowered her in a grapple where Ryn's mobility was limited, and on open ground he simply couldn't touch her. She angled her body around one blow, rolled her shoulder to avoid a second. Each step he took, she countered, and each blow met vacant air. He backed her into a pillar, but she knew it was there. She ducked.

His fist powdered a chunk of concrete and Ryn stepped behind him. Four strands from her kanaf unfurled and tightened like a noose around Splat and the pillar. She cinched it with one pull, fastening him there.

"The hell—"

"I promised pain." Lashes from her cloak whirled around his forehead and lower jaw, and anchored below his armpits, so that she could place one foot between his shoulders, tug, and his head snapped back with his mouth forced wide. He struggled. But Ryn took her time and gripped two more teeth. She twisted the molars in their sockets very, very slowly, until his wails echoed. "Five." She scattered the teeth across the floor like dice.

He coughed blood, unable to fully close his lips. "Enough."

Ryn released him and absorbed the strands of her kanaf into the cloak.

But he hadn't ceded, not really. "What are you? You're no goddess. They don't fight that..." He coughed out more blood. "...that dirty." He was trying to distract her; the tension hadn't left his shoulders and his fists were still clenched.

Ryn didn't answer. She intended to demonstrate what she was. With her hands.

He lunged and Ryn caught him. She tossed him over her shoulder and folded him in the front of a sedan. He pushed out from the metal cavity and Ryn met him with her fists, because her claws would have killed host and asura alike. She painted him with concussive blows. Side of the neck. Ribs,

ribs, thigh. He tried a kick. She broke the femur. No more kicks, she decided.

He produced a gun. She punched the weapon with a knife-hand strike of her claws. It cut the weapon into two neat halves.

Splat's other hand produced a knife. She deflected it with her hardened palm and threw her shoulder into him. He stumbled onto the broken leg, screamed, and fell to his knee. She flattened him facedown and drove a hundred razor wires from her kanaf into the space below the bump on the back of his neck. He tried to push up, but the syringe-thin wires coiled along his spinal column. She threaded gossamer into his nervous system. His arms twitched and went limp.

"It's mine," Splat whined. "It's my body. I earned it."

"Now it's mine." And with the slightest vibration of her kanaf, she fired pain through every nerve. He screamed. She vibrated the wires lower, longer, and the scream changed volume and tenor. Ryn tilted her head to the side, intrigued by the new instrument she had made. Then she scraped the wires, hard, and he cut loose with obscenities that evolved into a sound no longer human.

He jerked. His flesh went limp. The words came from a slack, unmoving mouth, his voice different when it was just the asura and not the human vocal cords: "Fine. You want me out? Fine. But, monster—"

Ryn felt pleased he'd figured it out. Demonstration successful.

"—whoever you are, wherever you're from, I will punish you. You wait. You won't see us coming." A thin vapor dissipated from the host's lips into the air.

Ryn retracted her cloak and her skin buzzed. She could sense the asura in the room. She could not see an asura without consuming psilocybin mushrooms, but she detected his presence. Car lights flicked on and off, signs of his power.

"You've earned enemies tonight, demon whore. Powerful enemies. I had plans for that mortal and... Oh. I see your face now! I saw you in the food court. You dined with my kitty. Oh, yes. I know how to hurt you now."

"And I, you." Ryn swept her claws through space. She slashed marks across a concrete pillar, then a second blow that left similar grooves in the front grille of someone's truck. Splat shrieked. She'd struck off a piece of him.

"*Get away from me!* What are you! You can't—"

"I did." She slashed the air twice more. She had only wounded him.

Splat's howl faded. He had fled.

Ryn stood alone in the parking deck. She crouched over the bloody, shallowly breathing human she had spared from death. His soul without Splat didn't smell especially clean, but he was just a man with a broken mind, and she no longer cared about him one way or the other so long as he stayed out of her way.

Distantly, she heard shouting voices from the walking bridge. Mortal security. Then, without Splat to keep them turned off, the deck lights flashed once, twice. Before the cameras could turn back on, she pulled up her hood, leapt through the open side of the parking deck and tumbled out into the moonlit sky.

CHAPTER SEVEN
Black Binder

Kessler crossed yellow police tape into a world full of twisted metal and broken glass. The parking deck was littered with crumpled cars and shattered pillars. A Chevy Cavalier lay on its side dripping oil from its broken engine block. He jogged to the ambulance and flashed his badge at a paramedic who shut the wagon's back door. "Where you taking the suspect?"

"Mercy General. Guy's a wreck. Can't hold this train up, sorry."

"Define wreck." Kessler followed the medic to his door, since he didn't break stride.

"Compound fracture to the femur, missing teeth, and his ribs are like a bag of broken sticks. Somehow the femur break didn't nick an artery, or *he'd* be in a bag. Face looks like he made out with a sausage grinder, but that's old. Didn't happen here." The medic got into the cab.

"Got an ID on him?"

"No ID, but said his name's Walter Banich."

"He say who did this?"

The medic gave a short, cynical laugh. "Yeah. The Grim Reaper." He slammed the door and drove off.

Kessler absorbed the scene and tried to sort out what could cause this much damage. There were no burn marks on the broken pillars or the cars, no evidence of explosives. No shell casings, either. It looked like collision damage, but somehow they had limped away in whatever car had done it.

"It's a black-binder case," said a gruff voice from behind him.

Kessler swiveled and came face to face with an obese detective with thinning red hair and a bushy mustache. His clip-on tie was half tucked in and had a food stain. Kessler had never met a more out-of-shape or ugly detective in his life. "Black binder?" he asked.

"Oh yeah. A weird one. I put 'em in a binder, the weird ones. Going to write a novel someday. You the one from the Four-Three?" He clapped a firm hand into Kessler's. "I'm Detective O'Rourke. Central."

"Detective Kessler. Central called me out. Word came down the pipe that a van belonging to one of the freshly released mental-health patients had caught fire. Wanted me to check it out, since the van's registered in the Docks and I have some rapport with the mental-health people. By the time I got here, all this happened."

"Military, huh?"

"Former. Making the transition. How'd you guess?"

"You've got the look. All neat, straight lines. What brings you here?"

"Home sweet home."

"What's your experience like?"

Kessler sensed scrutiny in the fat detective's deep-set eyes, so he said, "Only a year as an investigator. Before that, my main job was putting bullets through bad people."

O'Rourke rubbed the bristle on his double chin. "Why the transfer?"

"Slow on the trigger. Fraction of a second."

"Hn." O'Rourke turned from Kessler and he had the distinct impression that O'Rourke didn't like him.

"You going to fill me in?" Kessler asked. "What the hell happened to these cars?"

"No idea. Not going to bother."

So he was one of *those* cops. "Ah."

O'Rourke turned partway around and gave him the fish eye. "The cars are black binder. Trust me, when it's black binder, you need to simplify. Ignore the pieces that are incidental. So let's forget the cars. They either help us solve our puzzle or they obfuscate it. Core to the heart of the puzzle: who did this? Banich and a stranger. Our job is to find the stranger."

Okay. Maybe *not* one of those cops.

"Blood trail tells half the story and our vic fills in a little more," O'Rourke said. "Banich jumped her over there. She ripped stitches out of his face, then fled. Tough girl. Made it behind that SUV over yonder, then sprinted for the stairs. That's when it got interesting. That's when Player Number Three entered."

"A second assailant?"

"Girl says she saw something else."

"Something?"

"There you have it," O'Rourke said. "I ask her, she says 'something.' Not someone, something. I ask her to clarify, and she says she didn't get a good look. I ask her: animal or person? She says probably a person."

"Probably."

"There you have it again. Careful, if you turn out to have a brain, I might end up liking you. Now, I figure the vic is scared and seeing things, but damned if we don't have cars tossed around, and then *that* fucking thing." He motioned to a handgun on the concrete.

Kessler knelt. The gun was sliced in half. It was bisected straight down its barrel, a cut so clean it looked like it had been manufactured that way. Even the bullet that had been chambered was sliced length-wise, the powder from the cartridge dusting the floor. "What could do this? It's like someone took a diamond saw to it."

"No. There'd be shavings, irregularities at the edges—nothing portable cuts that way. So. What do we do with the gun?"

"Black binder?"

"You're spoiling all my preconceptions about you, detective."

"Wait. Preconceptions?"

O'Rourke kept going. "Way I see it, Banich had his rental van over yonder loaded with a rape-and-torture kit. It was torched. Third Player is the likely culprit. He burnt up the van, then beat Banich into half a lifetime of rehab. Now, I'm not going to lose much sleep over Banich, but if there's someone out there who can do damage like that, I want to know."

"Isn't the damage in your black binder?" Kessler asked.

O'Rourke waved a hand. "The binder's a method for cutting through the bullshit. It's not for assessing threats. This person? He's a threat. We should find him. Because it's possible he was working with Banich."

"How do you figure?"

"Accomplice who got cold feet," O'Rourke said. "Maybe a fellow wacko. The girl was a senator's daughter. Think about it: two creeps meet and share an obsession with this girl. One proposes the kidnap-and-rape scenario, and the other goes along with it and figures, 'I kill the other guy, I get into her good graces.' "

"All right," Kessler said. "Maybe I can get something from the security cameras."

"Good luck. Report said the power went out on this deck. One of the maniacs probably cut it. But find what you can."

"How's the vic, by the way?"

O'Rourke shrugged. "Scared. Get ready to put in some OT on this one. Like I said, her daddy's Senator Bradford. He'll be leaning on the captain, and the captain leans on us. I need everything you've got."

"Mind if I ask you a straight question, O'Rourke?"

"Best kind."

"You under the impression that I'm bad at my job? That I'm slow on the uptake or that I need a senator breathing down my neck to solve crimes?"

"Let me ask you something. Can you run a mile in under five minutes?"

"Yes."

"Bet you can bench, what, two hundred? Two-fifty? And you probably spent enough time on the range to put a consistent two rounds into a man's skull at a fair distance."

"So?"

"So you trained a long, long time to do all that shit for God and country. You ought to be proud. But a man's only got so many hours in his life to get good at things, especially if he's only been trying for a year. And I've seen a hundred tough guys come up from street patrol and make detective. Good cops. Diplomatic and streetwise. Excellent lung capacity. But shitty puzzle solvers. Try to understand, Detective Kessler, I love puzzles, and I know way too many guys doing this job who don't. That said, I'm pleased to have you here."

It didn't seem like it to Kessler.

"You're probably thinking, 'Sure doesn't seem like it,' but you strike me as earnest. Dedicated. It's not worth as much as you'd like it to be, but I can work with it."

"So what now?"

"Do the security footage and work your contacts in the mental-health system. We compare notes tomorrow. You need any resources, drop my name at Central. If that doesn't work, drop the senator's name. This is a high-priority case."

"Why?"

"Because it's mine."

~*~

Kessler hunched over a bespectacled guard at the wall of monitors in the mall security station. "I swear, I'm really good at this," the guard said. "But I haven't found anything—and I mean *anything*—on the van fire. It was set by a ghost."

"That can't be right. There's got to be twelve cameras on that deck."

"Eighteen. Here's the van door pre-blaze and here it is post-blaze, but no one approaching or walking away. If he came in or out of the mall around the time of the fire, though, he'll definitely be on the camera that overlooks the walking bridge. No rotation, no way around it. But there had to be forty, fifty people passing in that time frame."

"Copy me the footage. What about the fight on the parking deck?"

"Almost nothing."

"Almost?"

"Cameras came back on after the fight. Got a glimpse of... something. Here, it's easier to just show you."

The monitor blinked on. It was static at first and then showed the parking deck. Banich lay on the concrete. "What am I looking at?" Kessler asked.

"Took me a few times too. Let me put it on loop."

The video looped. Kessler strained his eyes. Shadows seemed to shift. *No, not shadows.* He leaned in close. On one of the loops, something inky-black slid from the corner of the frame and leapt out of the parking deck's open side. Kessler shot back three steps. "The *hell* is that?"

"I know, right? I think it's a person going over the edge. And the drop is five stories. We've had a suicide off that parking deck."

"Those light fixtures above the opening," Kessler said. "How high up would you say they are?"

"I don't know. Eight feet?"

"If that shadow's a person, even crouched like that, he can't be over five feet tall. Small guy. Banich had to weigh two-fifty at least. How's someone that size do that to a person?"

"With a baseball bat? Or a car."

"Copy that footage too," Kessler said.

A thought crept over him. He knew a person in New Petersburg who was about that size, who could scale a sheer wall, fight like a demon, and send the shivers straight up his spine. She'd just got out of Sacred Oaks less than a month ago.

On his way out of the office, he dialed Victoria Cross. "Victoria. It's your ex. Uh, David. We need to meet." More quietly, he added, "It's about Ryn."

~*~

They met at a sandwich shop in Whitechurch. When Kessler had left New Petersburg more than a decade ago, the crime rate in Whitechurch had been dropping. The graffiti had since been replaced by spray-painted murals, the fire escapes dotted with spice-garden planters that would bloom come spring, and the streets flooded with educated people who wanted to live in the city between Graystone University and where they worked in Commonwealth Plaza. Its revitalization had driven up property values and chased out the poor. Now it was full of trendy restaurants, the sandwich shop flanked by a sushi bar and a vinyl record store.

Kessler found Victoria at a booth, surrounded by a fortress of case files. She'd been nothing but bones and wit in high school, and she'd kept her lean physique, except now her hair had a done-up, professional quality that projected competence. Nevertheless, the clasp could not quite contain her energy, and a few curls busted loose. She worked her case files at the pace of a mad scribble.

He sat. "Victoria. You look good."

"You should order the house club," she said.

"Not hungry."

"Order the house club and you will be."

"I'm here about Ryn."

"I know. And I don't talk about my cases, so you're wasting your time. Unless you order the club—then it won't be wasted at all. It's that good."

"You need to trust me. Especially when it comes to her. She wouldn't be under your care if it weren't for me. This isn't business, Victoria. This is personal."

"Personal?" Her voice had an edge.

"Yeah."

"Personal like, say, what we had in high school?"

Shit. "This isn't really the time—"

"It's relevant. Do you remember the Tuesday after graduation, David? Because I do. That was the day my boyfriend of four years broke up with me, by phone, while on his way to *boot camp*. Which surprised me, since I had thought we'd decided to move in together."

He ran his hands through his close-cropped hair, trying to contain the same surge of frustration she'd always incited. "Moving in was your plan, goddamnit. I didn't want to go to school, and I didn't want to meet all my girlfriend's college friends and explain that I worked in the Docks. I didn't want to stand still. That life would have killed me."

"What—living with me? I grew up two floors beneath you, you dolt. We were practically living together already by the end of high school. I used that fire escape next to your bedroom more than the alley cats."

Kessler deflated. "It wasn't you."

She made a face.

"I swear. I know everyone says that, but it's true. It was... well, my dad."

"I loved your dad, too. He was important to me. He used to walk me home when I was a little girl, down both flights, to my door. A gentleman, your father. Don't use his memory to excuse your meltdown. When you told me you were going into the military, you didn't say 'because my father died in a war,' you said 'because I have to.' It was duty. Honor. You chose that, and you chose it over me. So when you say Ryn is personal, I say I don't believe you. I know your priorities."

Kessler had avoided this conversation for ten years.

She removed her glasses and folded them. "It's not a bad thing. Duty, honor, service. Great things. Just... not for eighteen-year-old me. Maybe not for her, either."

"I tried to talk to you about my plans." Folded over his spot at the table, he lifted his jaw and squared her in his gaze. "A hundred times. But you weren't the sort of person who took 'no' for an answer. I'd say the words, but you'd never hear them. I'd say, 'I'm not sure about moving in,' I'd say, 'I can't find the kind of work I need.' You'd try to argue me out of it, like if you could present enough points in a logical enough way, I'd feel differently."

"So," she said, grinning. "It *was* my fault."

He sighed. "Fuck. Yes. All right? Yes, it was."

Victoria paused over her case files and actually smiled. "I know."

Kessler threw his hands up. "Then why the fuck are we talking about it?"

"I needed you to say it." She shook her head. "You're too damn noble. We broke up because I was a selfish girl who thought she could drag you along anywhere I went. You don't get to take the bullet for me, years later, after I figured all that out through the awesome power of a graduate degree in psychology." Pausing, she added, "You're exactly like your father."

"Not in a good way."

"What do you mean *not in a good way*? Your father was the best."

"Yeah. Big, dead hero who wasn't around for my first fight in elementary school. Had to learn to shave from my mom. Had to learn to drive from *you*, and that's done me no favors. So there I was, doing big-hero things an ocean away and ignoring all the pain in the city where I grew up. Don't think I left for the nobility of it, or whatever else you think. I was just running. Same as him."

"Bullshit." Victoria leaned in. "They were murdering children."

Kessler had read the report a hundred times—the real one, not the press release when they'd awarded the posthumous medal. It had been an ugly border incursion from the Soviet side—"freedom fighters" who had holed up in a school with enough firepower to push back the small NATO contingent stationed there. They'd started the executions as some insane bid to erase the line drawn through their country by the Soviets and NATO. "It was a goddamn trap, Victoria. They'd done it before—wreak some havoc, kill some kids or some soldiers, then fade back across the border."

"And your dad walked into a trap," Victoria said. "Outnumbered. While everyone else tore for cover. He lived long enough to fire every bullet they gave him. Sixteen monsters walked into that school; only two walked back out. And the kids? All those little hearts kept pumping because just like you, he couldn't follow an order, even if it might have saved his life. That's not what a runner does."

"He was *my* dad. I was eight. I didn't care about gradeschoolers half a world away. It was my birthdays he missed." Sitting up straight, Kessler said no more until he had his voice under control. "Selfish, I know. But I was eight."

"You can't be a father and see children—anywhere—without seeing some of your own kids in them."

"Maybe not."

"You never told me any of that when we were kids."

"You wouldn't have let me get away with bitching." He cracked a smile.

"I'd have definitely told you to suck it up." She closed her last file. "I trust you more when you act like a human. Explain this thing with Ryn."

"I think she's in deep shit. Last night someone beat a two-hundred-fifty-pound, would-be rapist named Walter Banich into the concrete. They dodged two dozen cameras and disappeared off a seven-story parking structure. Torched a van, too."

"Sounds like ninjas. Have you put an APB out on ninjas?"

"We both know who it sounds like. And the lead detective on the case thinks Banich had an accomplice. He had a history in the mental-health system, same as Ryn. Then there's this." He slid a folder from his coat and showed her a surveillance still. The blurry image showed Ryn crossing the mall's walking bridge.

"That might not be her."

"It might not be. But it is."

"Ryn is not this man's accomplice. That I can tell you with absolute certainty."

"Why?"

"You know why. Ryn's not like that."

"Treat me like I'm a hostile prosecutor. Convince me so I can convince the other detective."

"Fine. Ryn has an aggressive form of reactive attachment disorder. She doesn't socialize with anyone unless she trusts them, and she trusts so few people it's less a circle than a straight line connecting her and me. To conspire, you have to talk to people. Ryn doesn't do that. If she beat your man up, it wasn't because she turned on her buddy. It was probably because he tried to rape someone. That, actually, does sound like Ryn."

"Then how did she follow Banich? Do you think a maladjusted teenager could stalk him?"

"Yes. And you do, too." Victoria leaned forward. "You know things about her. Don't you? Things you haven't told me."

He sighed. "Fine. Here's how I met her." He told her the story, start to finish, and he even showed her the scar on his forearm. When he'd first sent Ryn her way, he had left out the details, but now that he filled in the blanks, she didn't seem at all surprised.

"Just how classified is that story?"

"Enough to put me in a cell," he said. "I'm a little bothered that you're not more... incredulous."

"I have a three-inch-thick file documenting the impossible things I've seen her do. Nothing surprises me as long as it's something she can do by herself and without smiling."

"Like what?"

"Promise me that Ryn is not just a case for you."

"Pulling her out of that hellhole is probably the best thing I've ever done," Kessler said. "I've visited her a dozen times since I moved back home. She matters to me, okay?"

"Okay. CliffsNotes version: Ryn's the strangest case I've

ever seen. Her brain isn't human. I'd bet good money that if you put her into an MRI, the neuroscientist would reach for the whisky in his drawer five seconds later. He wouldn't even have words to define what he saw.

"A concert pianist came to Sacred Oaks a month into Ryn's stay. She was rapt because she'd never seen a piano before. Three days later, I caught her playing Beethoven in the rec room. Flawlessly. She's never done it since. She came in with broken English and no reading, writing, or math, and now she nearly has her GED. It wasn't until she was under 24-hour observation that we realized she only sleeps one day a month—and always on the new moon. All day and night, like she's hibernating.

"Then on the full moon, she's half crazy. Tried to have a session with her once on the day of the full moon and she couldn't focus on anything. Kept telling me it was the moon distracting her. Ended up taking three coins on my table and spinning them. Never seen anything like it."

"Never seen someone spin a few coins on a table?"

"Not one on top of the other, no."

"And she still doesn't... understand people?"

"Not at all," Victoria groused. "She learns quickly—even the mechanics of language—but she only understands facial expressions in the most clinical sense. Can't lie, doesn't grok money or manners or the basics of friendship, love, or even family. She's atomized, and on some level... I question whether she wants to learn. I know the way she processes expressions and the tendency toward sensory overload probably put her somewhere on the autism spectrum, but it's not her only barrier. There's a lot she won't learn just because she resents it."

Kessler sat back. "What about the physical differences? The teeth. I thought she'd filed the teeth at first but the canines are actually too long. And her eyes? That's not normal."

"I'm not an expert, but maybe she's a genetic offshoot. Imagine a group of humans with those traits: sleeplessness, antisocial intelligence, sharpened teeth, bright eyes, and nocturnal habits. Getting close to a lot of Dracula-style fairy tales there. A small band of humans with those traits might end up isolated. Living on the periphery. Maybe they'd be nomads, probably secretive enough to go unnoticed. But that's all speculation. What I know for certain is that Ryn could have probably tracked Banich down. And beat him. But she'd never work with him."

"All right. I want to talk to Ryn."

"I'll tell her."

~*~

Kessler was used to the Four-Three Precinct by now—a rundown station with exposed pipes showing through patches of broken wall—so walking into Central, he had to adjust to thrumming, black computers and new-carpet smell. It seemed like the sort of place where solving crimes did more than hold back the tide. It possessed smooth, clean architectural lines, and natural light poured in through tall windows, which provided an unobstructed view of busy streets in Commonwealth Plaza. Those windows made him feel exposed, but then, building sides were rarely shot up in Commonwealth Plaza.

O'Rourke had a small, windowless office, its walls lined with photos and commendations. Two monitors displayed browsers with forty tabs open, case files were heaped on every available surface, and one stack balanced an open pizza box. O'Rourke ate and scrolled a mouse wheel. His reading glasses comically enlarged his small eyes. "What'd you find?" he asked between bites, without looking up.

"Rough image on a possible accomplice." Kessler paused. "Still working on the ID." *More like working out what to do about it.* He passed the stills to O'Rourke, who rubbed his oily fingers off on his tie and leafed through them. They included the shadowy image from the parking deck and the blurry one from the walking bridge.

"Can't see a damn thing. Based on the light fixtures in the parking deck, our perp's five-foot, give or take. Slender. Matches the one you found from the walking bridge. Good job. Except if he's this big, can't figure how he wrecked Banich."

Kessler removed some folders from a chair and sat. "How about you?"

"Talked to the senator and found something damn disturbing. Let me bring it up."

Kessler glanced around the office. There were action figures on the desk: R2-D2 and Han Solo. The bookcase's lower shelves held textbooks on statistics, something called "Stata," and forensics, but higher up it turned into paperback science-fiction and mystery novels. "You read a lot?"

"You don't?" O'Rourke clicked a few more times with his mouse.

"When I have time."

"Find more time. Keep your brain sharp. Hungry. That's your most important tool now, and you need to learn obsession and curiosity. Otherwise your work regresses to the mean." He focused a moment on Kessler and said, "The mean in New Petersburg is pretty bad. Now. Look at this." He swung his monitor around.

It was a wall of text on an internet message board. Kessler scanned a few lines:

> ...best way to dump her corpse? Use lime, like the mob.

> Noob. That's lye, ur killing a whore, not makin cocktails lol.

> Why dump it? Put her on display at the end. Or during. Make it public.

> When I think of all the people Bradford murdered to get where he is it just makes me want to cave his skull in with my fist. Wonder if he'll cry when we do to his daughter what he's been doing to DEMOCRACY...

Kessler stopped reading. "There's got to be a hundred sites like this on the internet. Just people blowing off steam, right?"

"That's what I figured at first. The premise for the board is sick—point-scoring system for who can hurt Bradford the most. Last two weeks, it's been a nonstop circle jerk about kidnapping and raping his daughter. They doxed him—" O'Rourke paused, peering up to see if Kessler knew what that was.

"Posted his address and phone number." Kessler waved his partner on.

"—and a few weeks ago, one of them called the cops pretending to be Bradford, saying he had a gun and was gonna kill his daughter. Tried to get a SWAT team to break into his house. Luckily, the operator was on her game and figured it out before the wagon arrived. Bradford said they changed their number, but he was apparently keeping his daughter out of the loop until now."

"This is crazy, though. Do you really think this website inspired Banich?"

"He's one of their top five posters."

"And you think his accomplice was someone on the site?"

"Someone helped him. He had professional surveillance on his wall, and Banich wasn't the sort who blends in well. I don't think it's everyone on the site—"

"—but we need to figure out who helped him, and the site's a good start." Kessler considered what was on the screen. "The web stuff is out of my depth. Can we track them somehow?"

"We'd need a warrant for the IP addresses, and that still might not do it. Banich was a dumb shit by all accounts, but whoever took the surveillance and pieced it together for him... he's different. Has that slippery feel, sort who might be hard to find. Meantime, we split up the board posts and try to find anyone who chatted up Banich's account or looks especially suspicious. Banich's computer didn't have much, so whoever it was probably had another way of talking to him outside the boards, too."

"Even if we find this accomplice on the website, how do we get to him if he's as slippery as you say?"

"I can root around. Even if he covered his tracks, a lot of these assholes are vain and like to talk about themselves. We can still try to connect anything he gives away about his background, try to figure him out based on his habits or interests—or maybe he's got other accounts somewhere else with a similar ID. Burns my ass, though. You know how much easier this'd be if Bradford wasn't blocking that Senate security bill?"

Kessler didn't follow domestic politics much. "Hadn't heard about it."

"Some big plan to import static IDs to internet users. They'd still be anonymous to one another if they wanted, but everyone's name would connect back to their real-world identity in a federal database. Trying to crack down on cyberterrorism, but Bradford's opposed for some blah-blah-blah rehearsed civil-liberties reason. Since the bill's dead in the water—and 'unconstitutional as hell,' says Bradford—guess we do it the old-fashioned way."

Kessler looked at his partner a moment. "Isn't it a little strange the Bradford kid gets attacked by an anonymous internet maniac the same week her father's fighting a bill that would make the guy's accomplices easier to track down?"

A twinkle appeared in the fat detective's eye. "Another good reason to follow this rabbit hole all the way down, don't you think?"

"So you're saying conspiracy?" *That's crazy, but at least it doesn't point toward Ryn.*

"Saying I'm going to find out. If there's one thing I hate, it's a puzzle with missing pieces."

~*~

Roosevelt Place was a decrepit building in the Czech part of the Docks, based on the language of the graffiti. The elevator lights flicked out twice on Kessler's ascent. It was a medium-bad group home, but Victoria didn't have room to be picky in the crowded New Petersburg system. He suspected she'd placed Ryn knowing her to be a tougher-than-average girl.

Judy Birch answered the door. Her smile was plastic. "Are you the detective?"

"I am." Kessler showed her his badge. "I'm here to talk to Ryn Miller."

"She isn't in any kind of trouble, is she?" Mrs. Birch leaned close. "Because between you and me, that one is always up to something. Don't trust anything she says, especially about my husband."

Shit, that's not suspicious. "If I could just speak with Ms. Miller, that would be fine."

She let him through and he stepped carefully into the living room. The frayed sofa only had a body's width of clearance from the wall, all of the furniture too large for the size of their apartment. It was cluttered but clean. The absence of roaches or animal droppings alone put it above the cutline at which group homes might get written up.

He felt the air move and glanced over. Ryn stood in front of a curtained doorway and he wasn't sure when she'd arrived. *Always with the little cat's feet.* He noted the cargo pants and hoodie, same as the photo.

"Ryn." He didn't bother with a pleasant smile, since he knew she wouldn't care. "That look suits you."

"Sergeant Kessler. I prefer when you aren't covered in the stink of war."

"Such a charmer."

They stared from ten feet apart, Kessler in his jacket and tie, Ryn barefoot on the carpet with a paperback in hand. Judy Birch stood in the kitchen doorway, hands clasped and forcing a smile that, as the seconds ticked down, dissolved more and more into a frown.

"You two are friends." Her fingers tapped hastily together. "What fun!"

It clearly was not.

"Good book?" Kessler asked.

"About a cowboy and a woman. I don't understand why she hasn't shot him yet."

"You taking care of yourself?" She was still too thin—but she'd always been that way.

"You know I have."

"Keeping busy?"

"I read. I run."

"How about chasing? You do any chasing?"

She said nothing.

"You chase someone in the vicinity of Center Square Mall? Enjoy a little arson? Beat a guy named Walter Banich into a full body cast?"

Still nothing.

"Body cast?" Mrs. Birch tapped her fingers together again.

"I'll just... go put together a cookie tray." She fled to the kitchen.

"The roof." Ryn disappeared into her curtain.

Mrs. Birch tried to pry information from him about the arson and beating; he just stepped close. "Your husband had better not touch any of these kids. If he does, what I'll do is the least of your concerns. But it should still be a very big fucking concern. You feel me?"

She blanched and nodded.

Kessler took a cookie from her plate and chewed on it going out the door. *Raisins.* Scowling, he tossed it into a garbage can in the hall and climbed to the roof, where Ryn stood on dark tarpaper, still barefoot, collecting snow in her raven-feather hair.

"Albert Birch ever touch you?"

"His eyes bother me."

"See that his hands don't. If he ever does anything to you or the other kids, call me." He knew she wouldn't. "And you should have called me about Banich, too."

"Will you arrest me?" she asked.

"Depends. Did you help Banich?"

She snarled and flashed her teeth.

He took a step back. "Point taken."

She turned. Her gaze lengthened over the rooftops. The wind tugged her hair, which was loose and long. Her features seemed somehow girlish and hard at once—soft cheeks, firmed mouth. He knew what her dark sunglasses hid and the thought made him shudder.

"I didn't know him," she said. "I didn't help him."

"But you were at the mall that night."

"I was."

"What were you doing there?"

"I walked. Met a... what is the word?"

"Friend?"

"Friend." It sounded alien on her lips. "Perhaps."

"You assaulted Banich at the mall and lit his van on fire?"

Again, the silent treatment.

"Someone your size, with your skills, assaulted him. You were there. There's probably footage of you in the mall. Ryn. You could go to prison."

She stood like a statue, her gaze on rooftops far away.

"Jesus. Look. Do you use the internet?"

"No."

"Ever?"

"People use it around me at school. I don't like the way the light moves in the screens. It bothers my eyes."

"So you don't have your own computer?"

"No."

"You don't know anything about an anti-Bradford hate site? And you never took any surveillance of Naomi Bradford?"

"No. That was another."

"Wait. You know the guys who helped Banich?"

"I know of them."

Kessler stepped closer. "How?"

She seemed lost in something happening in the alleyway. "He told me, in between screams. Naomi is still in danger. Isn't she?"

"You know her?"

No answer.

"Oh, naturally, of course you know her. Is that who you met at the mall?" Her silence indicated "yes," and Kessler let out an elaborate, pent-up curse. He stretched it into eight extra syllables. "If you're spotted around Naomi Bradford and someone links you to the Banich assault, it's going to get ugly. Keep your distance."

Ryn didn't speak. Kessler wanted to shake her. Then she said, "Be careful, Sergeant Kessler. There is more danger than you realize."

"What's that supposed to mean?"

"They move in packs."

Kessler realized she was talking about Banich. "How do you know?"

"Whispers. Places you cannot go. The stories worm their way out of deep crevices."

"Then how many are there?"

"Hard to say. At least three. Never more than six, because seven is holy. But Banich is... unimportant. He isn't really one of them. The one who controlled Banich escaped."

"The ones who took the surveillance? And you know

them?"

"Only as prey."

"No. *No*, Ryn. You cannot be involved. This is not the Fortress, we have laws here. And we're very good at this. We'll get DNA, prints, we'll track them down."

"You will find shadows and rumors. No more. These ones are ghosts."

"Stay *out* of this."

Her gaze met his, so hard it caught his breath. "Tell me again what to do. I dare you."

His mouth went dry. "Telling you what to do is my job."

"I have no job, only purpose. Unlike you, I must obey it, because my purpose is all that I am. And my purpose is to stay close to Naomi Bradford. She is safer with me. You don't understand this threat, because it doesn't come from civilized places."

"Then where?"

"They are born from great sins and powerful emotions, and they are more and less than human."

I'm talking to someone who grew up in a place where they take gods and monsters literal-fucking-serious, he reminded himself. "If someone pins the Banich assault on you, you will go to jail, because they will assume you met Banich in the mental-health system and that you helped him plan it. Do you understand? Spend time with Naomi Bradford and you go to jail. You will be exactly where you were a year ago, only worse."

"Then arrest me. Or don't. Until then, I'll do as I like." She hopped onto the ledge, turned her back to him, and stepped off. He ran to the ledge in time to see her spider into her bedroom window.

A feeling, a shiver, like a dark premonition, wriggled all the way up his spine. "Stay away from that girl, Ryn. Stay away, or this isn't going to end well."

CHAPTER EIGHT
Invited

The wane of a full moon peeled back layers of noise and sensation until Ryn was left with slack limbs and a steady heart. What she lost in power she gained in control, and in her clearer state of mind she had regrets.

She had declared Naomi Bradford her territory. True, she'd announced it only to herself after a moment of unusual feeling that she chalked up to the excesses of a lunar hunt. But no deva—not even a monster—took such words lightly. It was not a vow, but close to one, and Ryn had never regarded a human that way before. Worse still, she found herself thinking about Naomi, and not in the usual ways. Sometimes when she closed her eyes, the teenager's smile greeted her, and she would remember Splat's cruel promise.

Splat was a rank terror. He would suck the humanity from Naomi like the yolk from an egg, hollow her into a pale and decorative shell. To Splat, human skin was an instrument, their spirits a troublesome noise to be cleared out of his engine. That must have been why she thought so much about Naomi—it reminded her of the importance of killing Splat and his cabal.

Naturally, the thing to do would be to get as close as possible to Naomi.

Kessler was right. She risked prison in doing so, and mortal laws could contain her. But a deva her age was a constant, and like the orbits in the sky she would do the same bloody things always and forever.

Splat would rather attack Naomi while she was alone to

avoid another touch from Ryn's claws and to keep himself hidden from mortal authorities; he had to, if he wished to avoid punishment by the secretive gods who despised mortal entanglements in their world. However, from Kessler she also learned he had mortal resources—and they could strike during the day and in public. There was little she could do about that, as Ryn was usually trapped in school on the other side of the city when the sun was out.

At night, though, she expanded her influence, commuting across the city and exploring Naomi's neighborhood, her school, the nearby rooftops of two- and three-story houses. It was called Garden Heights and featured grand, old trees and large backyards. The space between people eased a tension in Ryn's mind she'd forgotten was there.

She mastered the rooftops and hunted for fresh signs of asura, but all the scent trails were days or weeks old. She also prowled the city for the mushrooms that granted vision of the asura and poached a handful from a distracted vendor in Bourbon Alley. Humans enjoyed them for the hallucinations, but not everything they revealed was a lie.

School busied her during the day and Ryn eluded the notice of her teachers. She was introduced to the concept of grades and realized they marked her efforts. To avert attention, she strove for mediocre marks. It meant pouring effort into her English literature class, because the arcane interpretation of texts was impossible for her. In math and science, she varied her answers strategically to earn lower marks. In history, she simply answered truthfully. If an essay asked what the medieval era was like for women, her answers included a lot of detail about the main kinds of edible roots and the quality and range of military weapons.

Harper Pruett and his pack mates ignored Ryn, their attention having shifted to a girl with dyed blue hair two grades lower, who they mocked because of something she might have done with boys more times than they wanted her to. It bothered Ryn even more when they focused on the dye-haired girl, and Ryn wished she could get Harper into that closet again. She wondered how Naomi would handle the situation. *Probably with less head-butting.*

At the apartment, Albert Birch avoided her, often sweating

his anxiety in fat beads. He also stopped bursting into their room, and Susan said that when Ryn was around, the Birches rarely bothered her.

"Does Albert Birch bother you when I'm gone?" Ryn asked, sensing prey-fear on Susan. It was something she scented on many girls and boys at school.

"No," Susan said. "Not me, at least."

"Who?"

"The girl before you. Before she went out the window, Albert bought her expensive things. Clothes mostly. I wondered what it was about."

"I don't understand."

"Well." Susan closed her book. "I figure—and I guess I don't know, but I figure—maybe he tried to keep her quiet about something they might have been doing, something they weren't supposed to. Anyway, he's creepy, but he never does more than gawk. How about you?"

"He sweats fear when I'm close."

"Hope it lasts."

On Friday, she rode the train to meet Naomi because daylight made the rooftops impassable—too many human gazes to avoid. It shrank her routes through the city almost to nothing. New Petersburg was uglier in the sunlight and there were too many bodies filling it with prattle and odors.

The city rolled past her window. She rode beneath the bay, changed trains, and then wandered Porter Avenue, a downtown spot near Whitechurch that blended the graffiti and panhandlers of the Docks with the noisy bars and nightclubs of younger neighborhoods. Salty brine and mud-slush caked the streets and cars so that everything had a grimy coating, but a sharp winter breeze lit Ryn's spirit on fire. She wasn't certain why she felt so buoyant, but the evening felt wide and unexplored.

She waited outside a club called the Nine Lives for Naomi and her friends. Near sundown, Elli and Denise arrived together.

Naomi isn't with them. Ryn's heart fell. "Where is she?"

"Couldn't come." Elli's smile was large—the shape of it meant something other than happiness, because why would she be happy her friend had stayed home? Ryn would have had better luck deciphering patterns in frosted car windshields than in Elli's face.

Confused, Ryn looked to Denise. *This one doesn't smile at all.* "Tell me more."

"Her dad freaked out." Denise got in line beside Elli and refused to look at Ryn. "Not sure if you heard. She was attacked last week at the mall. It was serious. She's okay, but it was close. Been on the news all week; made national. You don't own a TV?"

Ryn felt strange then. If her only task was to stand watch, find Splat, and exterminate him, this should have been fortuitous—Naomi was a lure, and watching the auburn-haired teenager from her rooftop narrowed his paths of attack, forcing him to fight Ryn straight-on. So why had the fire in Ryn winked suddenly out? There was nothing desirable in a club stuffed with oily, aggressive, aroused teenagers. *Disgusting.* Naomi would have had to drag her in.

It made no sense, what Ryn was feeling, and she scowled at her own sour mood.

Elli shuffled, seemingly unable to make eye contact. "You know, if you want to bail since Naomi's not here, we'd understand."

The question escaped Ryn's mouth ahead of conscious thought: "Did she want to come out?"

Denise's smile was thin—did that make her only a little happy? Why were her eyes narrowed to slits? "Doesn't matter. Her dad said no, and the princess always listens to dear, sweet father. The way is blocked. Verboten. Her social life shall commence sometime after, hm, I predict graduation."

Ryn bristled and had to suppress a flash of her canines. "She is human. She has will."

Denise snorted. "Not in that house she doesn't."

Outrage blossomed fresh and invigorating in Ryn's chest. "I shall see." She strode away from the girls.

"Hey. You leaving?" Elli did that smile again. "That's fine! Nice seeing you."

"I am going to have a conversation with Naomi." Ryn didn't break stride. "I may return."

"Did you hear what I said?" Denise called. "Are you dense or are you actually going on the warpath against a senator?"

"I would rather go around than through him." *But either works.*

Already half a block behind her, she heard Elli whisper, "At least that's over—she gives me the creeps."

Denise scoffed. "Just now? I started to like her."

~*~

With sunset at her back, Ryn clung to the train's filthy spine and rode it across the city. In Garden Heights, she danced among satellite dishes and outpaced cars on the suburban street.

The Bradford home was guarded by a tall rock wall that might have kept out a particularly stupid human or one who couldn't operate a ladder. The trees were the right height to cross from wall to branches to rooftop. The house possessed the sort of recesses and nooks that, along with the trees, hid her from the street. It was an ideal perch.

The security wasn't terrible: one bored cop in a squad car passed sometimes on the street and a soldier in a dark suit walked the perimeter at intervals. The soldier looked competent for a human. With enough bullets and luck, and on a new moon, he might have slowed down Splat.

Naomi's rain-clean scent rose from the back of the house and Ryn dropped from the roof to her window. Her toes caught the sill and she perched on the three-inch sliver, fingertips flush to a window with drawn curtains on the inside. Ryn felt a flutter of anticipation and knocked.

Would Naomi or the soldier answer?

The curtain whipped open. Naomi stood on the other side of the glass in a halo of warm light, dressed in pajama pants and a too-large, faded T-shirt whose wide neckline sloped almost off one of her shoulders. Ryn filled her window, and Naomi yelped. She shot back a step, tripped over a book, and flailed for balance, hitting the bed.

Ryn tilted her head to one side. She nudged the window open. "May I enter?"

Naomi propped herself on her elbows and gaped. "How did you get up there? Why are you here?"

"May I enter?" Ryn asked again.

"Yes! Hurry. If Mark catches you out there he'll shoot you."

Ryn eased in and shut the window. Naomi's room was filled with her scent and it immediately wrapped around the deva, overwhelming her with a sudden swell of feelings—a curious blend of longing and comfort, as though happy to be in the warmth of Naomi's presence, but made acutely aware she was an outsider; that she lived in the dark, and was only meant to watch from beyond the light's reach. *That is why I declared her my territory,* she realized. *Not the full moon. This. I wanted this.* That thought froze her with sudden alarm, because she was standing in the place she least belonged.

Naomi heightened that fear as she paced a circle, inspecting Ryn from every angle—inspecting a body meant for the shadows and hands suited for violent deeds. Her skin prickled in ways she... didn't hate, though her heart galloped.

While Naomi examined her, she in turn examined the teenager's room: clutter, clothing draped on chairs, and a bookcase with English and Russian titles. A high shelf contained famous monuments built from interlocking, plastic blocks. One—the Eiffel Tower, recognized from her school books—was only partway finished, as if some invisible hand had obliterated half of it.

Naomi breathed out. "Weirdo." She stood in front of Ryn again, fists to hips, and even though she'd called Ryn a word she knew to be insulting, the girl smiled after saying it.

Ryn didn't have any trouble whatsoever interpreting this smile—it sent warmth radiating from her stone heart.

"How did you do it?" Naomi begged. "How did you slip past Mark?"

"I climbed."

"*How?*"

"I don't understand." Ryn felt a hopeless tug because she'd explained and Naomi still stared.

"My dad's got police protection, motion sensors in the yard, and an armed guard. It's crazy you would even try. Seriously, how? And *why?*"

"You don't believe me," she realized.

"Of course I don't!"

"These things are easy for me. I don't move like anyone you know."

"You're agile, I get that. But you're not on Delta Force, and I'm pretty sure Mark could sneak up on his own shadow." Naomi peered out the window again, sliding her curtains closed, and Ryn moved into her blind spot—then bounded to the wall, skirting higher. When Naomi turned back, Ryn was perched in the corner of her ceiling, braced by fingertips and feet.

Naomi's back thumped into the far wall and she pressed her shoulders flat against it. Her breath quickened and a strange urge to touch her cheek floated briefly through Ryn's mind. "This is how I move." She dropped to the floor.

"You could have just said so," Naomi blurted, heart hammering in her chest like a cornered rabbit's.

Ryn softened her bunched-up stance, and tried to approach with one hand raised as she might an animal she didn't want to spook. "You didn't believe me."

Naomi folded both arms protectively around her middle. "You're right. Sorry. Still jumpy I guess." Fear had indeed darkened her rain-clean scent, less profane than a week ago, but something in the shape of her eyes made her fragile—made Ryn want to fold her in protective wings. "You heard about what happened to me?"

"I know about it."

Naomi opened her mouth as though to speak. Blanching, she folded back into the room's corner with her arms tight around her body, and she seemed, in the very midst of her home, to be somehow lost.

"Nothing will harm you here." Ryn approached carefully as the girl's heart slowed, but fear still overwhelmed her scent. As though she were that cornered rabbit, Ryn set a hand on her shoulder and stroked it with her thumb. Not knowing any other comforting gestures, she tried some human words: "I have no interest in eating you."

A snort of laughter, and Naomi stared with glassy eyes that seemed distracted from their troubles only long enough to notice her. "Thank you. I won't eat you, either."

Ryn nodded solemnly.

"I'm going crazy," Naomi whispered, her full attention locked on Ryn in a way that charged her with excitement. "Can't sleep from all the nightmares. No more than a couple hours at a time all week." She swallowed. "I don't want to be a mess in front of you, but I'm exhausted and my filter's burned out. For an instant, when I saw you up there, I thought you were... *it*."

"Banich."

"Kind of." She turned sharply, pacing, as if it would toss off the memory, and Ryn's hand fell away. "I don't like to think about it." She stopped and pressed her palms against her eye sockets. "I see things in every shadow of this stupid, creaky house."

Ryn wondered what, exactly, Splat revealed to her—how much Naomi knew.

"I realize it was just the fear, but I remember the whole thing clearly when I sleep, except now I know more about what Banich was planning than I ever wanted to. The news had all the details. The things in his van..." She covered her mouth suddenly, eyes going still. "A blow torch," she murmured. Blinking, she lost control of her tears. "Corkscrews." Her scent bloomed into a more acidic flavor, typical of horror-fear—familiar to Ryn from all the ways she'd taken men apart. It didn't belong on Naomi. "I try not to think about it, but I can't stop dreaming... Want to know something morbid?"

Ryn didn't know how to answer, as most of what she knew already was morbid.

"I Googled pictures of the corkscrews. Hoped that if I stared long enough the horror might somehow pass through me, like I needed to get to the other side of it. Stared until my skin turned to ice, but I think I just invited all of it in. I wonder if it ever goes away." She strode to her bed and collapsed there, thumping face first into a pillow.

"It will," Ryn whispered.

She shook her head, around which her wavy auburn mane had settled in a bright pool. "It won't," she groaned through the pillow. "And I'm an idiot."

"It will." Ryn took two small steps forward.

The girl rolled into a sitting position, clutching pillow to lap. "Dad wants me to take a semester off at Madison and attend cyber-schools. Maybe he's right."

"You fear leaving your cell." Ryn's lip curled, not at Naomi, but at what Splat had poisoned her with.

"It's not a cell." Her voice faltered at the look on Ryn's face, and she squeezed the pillow to her chest. "And I'm not afraid."

"It is. And you are." Ryn could taste it in the air, bilious and foul. "It turns strong legs wobbly and fills you with the need to vomit—yet you cannot, because the thing wriggling within you isn't bad meat. It's horror-fear."

Naomi stared, lips somewhat parted. "Horror-fear?"

"Why do you lie about it? I smell it." Ryn tapped her nose.

The smile was small—on any other mortal, a mystery, but on Naomi it made such wonderful sense: small because it was the mark of light weakly penetrating whatever pall afflicted her. "Smell. Right." She tapped her own nose, teasing. "That obvious, huh? I guess I don't *want* this to be a cell, and I don't want to be afraid." Her eyes glistened, and she brushed at them with both hands. In spite of it, tears still streaked down her face after.

Ryn's chest tightened. Before she thought better, she reached out and brushed one of those tears aside—a gesture she'd only seen humans do; why did it feel so right?

Startling at the contact, Naomi watched her a few moments while sucking on her lower lip. "Thanks. You're sweet."

"I'm not."

"I mean you're nice, not that you taste sweet."

Ryn thought on it. "I still am not."

Her giggle almost broke Ryn open. "You must think I'm a flake. Afraid to sleep, afraid of a dark hallway in my very-well-protected house." She pushed her tears away with the heel of her hand. "Banich is hospitalized. I know that up here." She tapped her temple. "Just can't shake the sense it isn't over."

Fingers wet from catching a tear, Ryn smudged them together, the tactile evidence of Naomi's terror filling her with sadness. She spoke the ugly, true words. "It isn't over."

Naomi's eyes were large, and made Ryn realize why not all lies were spoken with malice. "Why not?"

Staring at her fingers, Ryn refused to look back up. "There will always be more. There is no end to monsters. Even if there were, it wouldn't be over for you. Because it..." She didn't know the right words; she tried the best ones she could find. "It echoes. Even in safe, well-lit places, it echoes."

"The fear?"

"Yes." But Ryn couldn't let that be the end of it, so she

looked at Naomi again and showed her a tight fist. "But there is me."

One of Naomi's eyebrows went higher than the other as she examined that fist. "Counting the change in your pockets, you might weigh a hundred pounds. Thanks, though."

Ryn wished she knew the magic of words—Naomi and Kessler and Ms. Cross all did, and had the power to make people see with nothing but strung-together sounds, yet that distinctly human magic could never be hers. If only she could hunt a bull elk and drop it dead at Naomi's feet; if only she could show her with deft hands what her idiot words couldn't: *Look now at me. The dark is terrible, surrounds you, and is never empty as it seems. Though monsters lurk, know this: none is hungrier than me.*

Instead, Ryn had only: "I am one hundred and three pounds."

"Oh, all right then." Her smile was radiant. "So long as you keep an eye on me, I think everything will be all right."

Ryn's hand did something it ought never do—and the oath came too quickly to stop. With a sureness she shouldn't have felt, she crossed one finger over her heart, an action no deva could do without binding her immortal will. "I vow to protect you."

And like that, Ryn's course would never alter. She could no more break a vow than she could die.

Yet Naomi laughed through her tears, hiding her smile behind that pillow and peeping over. "How are you like this? You're putting on an act, aren't you?"

Ryn scowled. "My vows are absolute."

"You're the most adorably intense creature I've ever met."

Adorable! The outrage stiffened her every fiber.

"Easy! Whoa, sorry." This time her giggle ended in a snort, which made her hide her whole face in the pillow. "It's a—a tough adorable. Relax." Lowering the barrier again, she gave Ryn another one of those searching looks. "Bet you're a hellcat in the ring."

The levity in her voice—that tone was mockery, Ryn realized, and she pressed her fingertips to her own face, because it had warmed in response. It had never done anything of the sort before, and the realization fired her cheeks hotter.

Naomi stood, eyes soft. "You're amazing at cheering me up; but I'm sorry, now you're going to get hugged. I'm an unstoppable force so don't even try to avoid it."

Before Ryn could figure out whether to hide, Naomi wrapped both arms around her unyielding frame.

"Thanks, Ryn." Those words came on soft breath against her ear and neck, plucking away her anxieties; relaxing into the embrace, Ryn let the scent overwhelm her, inhaling as quietly as she could for fear it wasn't a normal thing to do—and the heat in her cheeks made her worry for once what a mortal thought normal.

When Naomi backed up, Ryn could feel the vacancy left behind.

They both stood, the silence that Ryn normally loved turned awkward. She hoped Naomi would fill it with more soothing words, but Naomi seemed at a loss for them too.

Ryn said the only thing she could. "Come out to dance."

"I'd freak out."

"I vowed to protect you."

"I remember." Naomi smiled with not just her mouth, but her eyes. "Going to beat up all the bad guys?"

"To the last," Ryn swore.

"One problem. My dad would have an aneurysm, and I'm not old enough or crazy enough to fill his Senate seat."

"Don't tell him."

"And the armed guard? The one with the gun?"

"A small gun."

"But full of bullets."

"*Small* bullets."

She shook her head. "You're insane."

"I can show you how. If you follow." She pointed to the window. "I will lead the way—if you desire to leave your cell."

"It's not a cell!"

Ryn disagreed, but also couldn't figure out a way to convince her otherwise.

Naomi folded her arms and narrowed her eyes, seeming to mull Ryn's offer. "Fine. You win." She picked her pillow up, wiping the last moisture from her cheeks with the pillowcase. "Just let me get ready." She made a whirling motion with one finger. "Turn around."

Ryn stiffened again. "Present my back?"

"It's your paranoia or my modesty." She crossed her arms again, waiting.

Squelching her anxiety, the deva faced the window curtains. Naomi flitted through the room, rolling drawers in and out. Ryn heard pen scratching paper. "A note for Dad—he won't be back until morning, but don't want him worried I was kidnapped if he changes his plans," Naomi murmured. "Now. Breaking-out-to-go-dancing clothes. Bingo."

If modesty meant hiding herself from view, it would fail— a sliver of window through the curtains reflected the room, easing Ryn's feral distaste for turning her back—right up until Naomi shed her nightshirt. It flicked over her head into the corner. Ryn caught a flash of her long back, the groove tracking the path of her spine, and the delicate contours of her shoulder blades.

The urge to stare and absorb every smooth line competed with the urge to snap her gaze to the floor. Ryn tucked her chin to chest, studying her toes as heat blazed from her ears to the back of her neck. Twice, she nearly glanced up; twice, she shook off the desire.

And it all electrified her body in unfamiliar ways, currents of air making her too aware of her exposed skin.

Naomi tapped her shoulder and Ryn whirled, hissing.

~*~

That cool, dry hiss was like a snake's, scraping at Naomi's dulled survival instincts and rousing them to full, heart-pounding alertness. Her mouth dried and she stared at Ryn, who bowed her head to hide her teeth as she made that sound, as though she had venomous fangs she was embarrassed to show.

But it passed, and Ryn's body relaxed.

Only after it did could Naomi catch her breath. She swallowed, remembered herself, and spread her arms to show off the dark blue jeans, gray hoodie, and a slim white top. She liked it for subtly highlighting her shape, for how easy it was to move around in. "How do I look?"

Ryn—who wore the same hoodie, cargo pants, and dark

sunglasses as last time they had met—clinically scanned Naomi's attire. "Not warm enough."

"You're bad at girl-ing. Look, my winter coat is downstairs. The hoodie's all I have up here. If we hurry to the train, I'll be fine. You got here in yours, after all."

"I am unlike you."

Naomi couldn't figure out if Ryn was arrogant or delusional, but it had a way of comforting her. It was precisely the bravado she'd needed all week. Maybe some of it would rub off. "Fine. How exactly do we get out? You bring a ladder or, I don't know, a grappling hook or something?"

"Follow." Ryn opened the window and hopped onto the sill, disappearing around the side in a flicker of motion.

Startled, Naomi toed to the window and peered out, seeing that Ryn had leapt onto a lip of roof four feet to the right and slightly higher up. She took one purposeful step back into her room. "Nope! No. I'll fall."

"Do as I did," whispered Ryn from her perch.

"Wasn't paying attention. Bring me a harness and carabiners and we'll talk."

"Step out." Irritation in her voice now.

She's crazy. I should not be listening to a crazy person. Yet Naomi wanted to follow. The idea of Ryn skirting into the night, leaving her to rot in her room one more evening... Sucking in a breath, she stepped onto the windowsill and refused to look down even as vertigo seized her. A tremor shook her calf. She mouthed "crap crap crap" like each iteration kept her steady.

"Now jump to me," said Ryn with too straight a face.

"It's too high." She peeked. *Mistake.* Her stomach turned over and the driveway spun, seeming more like fifty feet down than twenty.

"If you fall, I will catch you."

"Your arms are short."

"I will catch you."

Why did she believe her? It wasn't even physically possible. *That arrogance.* She loved it. "Okay, it's not much higher than a pole vault," Naomi reasoned. "Just pavement instead of a pad. What do I care, they're only legs." A breeze caught her hair. She sucked in a sharp breath, readied herself, looked at Ryn—that seemed to help the most—and jumped.

The ball of her right foot struck shingle. Flailing forward, Naomi slapped both hands flat to the roof's slope. "Did it!"

"Good."

Her pride glowed at the compliment, until Ryn spidered up the roof's slope with preternatural ease. "How is she so good at that?" she whispered to herself, following in a halting crawl that never peeled more than one hand or foot from the incline at once.

At the apex, Ryn guided Naomi with a finger point to walk the length of the roof to the crown of a tree on the other side of the house. "You first."

Sensing Ryn's penetrating stare as she took her first cautious steps, Naomi found herself wondering what the strange girl thought of her agility. No one had ever made her feel uncoordinated before; she focused on not messing up—and wouldn't have, if her heel hadn't planted on a rotted shingle.

It skidded down the roof and carried her with it. Naomi pitched toward the roof's edge. She toppled shoulders first, sensing the ground more than twenty feet below. Her mouth went slack, a scream leaping from her center.

Before she'd fallen two feet—before she could belt out a scream—she landed lightly in Ryn's arms, cradled at roof's edge like a dancer swept back. Her hood flopped down, auburn hair spilling out, and Ryn's other hand clapped to her mouth.

Panting, staring wide-eyed into the raven-haired girl's emotionless sunglasses, she could feel the riot of her pulse in her own throat. Her hands clutched Ryn's forearm. It was corded, lean, and though entirely too small, Naomi sensed power beneath her fingertips—a lot of it. And she was confused. *She was behind me a second ago. How did she move like that? No one can move like that...*

The smile that crept onto Ryn's mouth was slight and satisfied, yet it thoroughly intimidated. Before now, Naomi had been in her element, but out here in the winter air and on the rooftop, this wildling seemed more in hers—and that was the reason for the smile, she realized. Ryn had gotten to show her a piece of who she was, and the brat was proud.

Glancing behind her at the concrete far below, she focused

back on her savior. "Going to help me up or hold me here all night?"

Ryn waited a beat too long before easing her upright, and Naomi felt her racing pulse skip a beat.

She found herself regretting for the first time that Ryn hadn't turned out to be a boy when she'd approached her in the mall last week. *Would have made things much more interesting,* she decided. "Thanks for the save."

"I told you I would protect you."

"How did you even get down here in time? That's incredible."

Ryn skittered to the roof's apex, offering a hand, which Naomi took, and the girl with curiously soft fingers didn't bother answering the question.

As Ryn led her, Naomi took notice of how fluid her steps were—how sure. "You remind me of these monkeys I saw at the zoo as a kid. Didn't even look like they were climbing, just scampering straight up a tree or upside down on a branch. Like gravity didn't matter."

"Gravity matters." She glanced back. "For you."

"Cocky much?" Naomi realized she was using her flirty voice and wiped the egg-her-on expression from her face. *She kind of looks like a boy. If I squint.* Except no, not really. She was actually pretty beneath the overly large shades and hood, her curves subtle, mostly erased by baggy clothes. *A pretty boy, maybe.*

"Between gravity and me, I am the superior force."

"So that's a 'yes' to the cocky question?"

"Yes." Ryn hopped almost six feet from the roof to the farthest branch of her father's oak. Naomi stood fascinated by the balance of weight as she landed, straightened, and spun, all the work in the balls of her feet. It was beautiful. A ballerina at the Met couldn't have done it better, yet Ryn just waited, expectantly, for Naomi to follow suit as though it were the easiest thing in the world.

Naomi shook her head. *No.*

Sighing, Ryn gripped an upper branch, leaned out, and closed the distance partway with her hand.

Swallowing her doubts—and her stomach, which had risen into her throat—Naomi threw herself off the roof. Her fingers scraped Ryn's in the air, the other girl's grip firmed, and when her feet thudded onto the branch, the girl's opposite hand clapped hold of her hip.

It steadied her. Somehow, just that hand on her hip was all it took to sap the wobble from Naomi's stance even as the branch they shared bobbed up and down. Once more, she sensed power there entirely out of proportion to Ryn's lithe build and short stature.

"You're strong for your size." Naomi glanced down at the hand on her hip, feeling her cheeks warm.

"I am." Ryn twirled her on the branch, somehow changing their positions without looking away.

And Naomi had done it with her, on instinct, their bodies able to communicate without words. "You're the most bizarre person I've ever met," she whispered.

Ryn broke the tension by pointing her toward the wall. It was only as she climbed across branches toward it that Naomi realized why her spirit felt so light.

She wasn't scared anymore. It was the first time in a week, and the very air tasted sweeter for it.

Ryn dropped to the sidewalk on the other side of her dad's stone wall, lifting hands to signal she'd catch Naomi. Sitting on the wall, glancing down at the raven-haired girl's come-down-here gesture, a swell of joy rose in her center. *She makes me feel safe.*

Pushing off the wall, she let Ryn clap hands to her hips again, absorbing the shock of her descent more thoroughly than anticipated. It wasn't until she was lowered gently to her heels that she remembered to breathe.

"This way." Ryn led her down the sidewalk toward the train station. "You're shivering."

It was from the cold, which was worse than expected. But Naomi was also bursting with excitement to go dancing. In addition to washing the horror from her mind, Ryn had reminded her how fun it could be to move in time with someone's body—and if she knew Elli and Denise, they'd have boys lining up.

~*~

Their train accelerated, whisking them from the station. Ryn stood guard over Naomi, who huddled in her seat, teeth chattering. Her nose had turned bright pink, but she wasn't huddling entirely from the cold. Ryn could tell she wilted at the presence of a nearby passenger who wore a scarf that covered most of his face.

From Ryn's place in the aisle by Naomi's seat, she could kill that man if he approached. She could kill or maim virtually anyone, no matter their approach. That was why she stood there.

Naomi didn't know these things, though, and so when the man in the scarf shifted abruptly, she shrank one size smaller.

At their changeover station in Commonwealth Plaza, Naomi hurried from the train and Ryn kept to her shadow, scenting for asura and worrying faintly about the way Naomi rubbed her shoulders for warmth.

Naomi blew warmth into her hands. "You stand and look around like Mark—the bodyguard my dad hired."

"Then Mark knows how to stand and look."

She felt Naomi inspecting her; it should have bothered her, but it didn't. "Are you some kind of professional criminal?"

"No."

"Recreational crime only, then?"

Ryn thought on it a moment and nodded.

"Explain it to me. Why you're guarded, and stealthy, and creepily acrobatic. Were you bitten by a radioactive goth? Should I be worried you'll bite me and turn me vampire?"

"I don't bite people I like."

Naomi snorted. "Even if they ask nice?"

Ryn frowned, knowing she had missed something.

"Where does someone like you even come from?"

"An older kind of place."

Another silence. "The place you're from was violent."

"Very."

"That's how you knew about my fear. Horror-fear, you called it."

"You also have prey-fear."

"Explain that to me too." Naomi leaned into her and stuffed all her frigid fingers at once into one of Ryn's pockets.

Going rigid at the unexpected contact, Ryn was at a loss.

"You're warm. Mind if I borrow some body heat?" Even her voice felt good, humming into Ryn's ear, and it took her senses time to adjust, to become aware of anything in the world besides Naomi.

When she had, she remembered the question. "Prey-fear." It was hard to think. "It comes from being ambushed and realizing predators exist. It sharpens your vigilance at first."

"So it's good?"

"Awareness is. But prey-fear fosters paranoia. Overreaction."

"So when Dad wants to pass a law so that seventeen-year-old assault victims can carry concealed firearms, he might have a teensy bit of prey-fear?"

It sounded like a good law to Ryn.

"Are you afraid of anything?"

"No," she snapped.

"Come on," Naomi sang, stretching the second word. "You know too much not to have felt it." She made a "hmm" sound, one that put her warm breath on Ryn's neck, eliciting a squirm that wasn't entirely from discomfort. "Crowds. Are you afraid of those?"

"I hate them," Ryn growled.

She laughed. "Yet you're going dancing?"

Ryn glanced away. "To guard you."

"If you hate crowds, why are you even hanging out with me? My dad's a senator, and during campaign season there are reporters in our house every other day. You might have picked a bad friend if the public eye bothers you."

A good point. There was danger in getting close to Naomi. She was no anonymous mortal; hers was the kind of life gods and nations alike might notice. Ryn had no more time to think on it, though, because their connecting train arrived and she stepped inside to the sight of Harper Pruett and his pack. *Did he follow me?* No, she realized. They were discussing the Nine Lives—they had the same destination.

Naomi sank into the first seat and turned to hide her face from the pack, and Ryn drew up her hood to hide her own, watching their reflections in the train window.

Their talk was loud, speckled with boisterous shouts, lewd comments, grating laughs; completely interchangeable with every conversation she'd overheard at Parker-Freemont.

Ryn knew the instant Pruett noticed Naomi. She felt a shiver of discontent ripple through her muscles as he strutted nearer, leaned off a pole, grinning down at her with that mass of purple bruising still decorating the bridge of his nose. "I know you. You're Naomi Bradford—Tom Bradford's kid. One who got jumped at the mall last week."

"Sorry," Naomi murmured, "but I don't know you." She shifted away from him.

"My mom can't stand your dad. Hey, why so jumpy?" He tried easing closer; Ryn stopped him by turning her back, swaying her shoulder into his path. "I'm not some stalker," he insisted. "I'm kind of surprised I never met you before. I'm on Parker-Freemont's Model UN, and you're what—a Madison girl? We visit your school all the time."

"I don't do Model UN. I don't do any of that." Naomi didn't look up at him.

"Bet if we hung out, our parents would both have strokes. C'mon, you and your friend can link up with my crew. We'll keep the sickos away."

"That is my job." Ryn turned, lifted her jaw, and drew down her hood.

Pruett flew backward, shouting, "Shit! It's her. It's the one I was talking about!" He stumbled and collapsed into one of his pack mates.

"*That's* the girl who broke your nose?" one asked. They all stared, but at the next stop, he and his friends got quickly off the train.

"Friends of yours?" Naomi smiled shyly from her seat.

It wasn't exactly a bull elk, but it sufficed.

CHAPTER NINE
The Body Electric

They walked four blocks from the station to the Nine Lives. Naomi hugged her jacket tighter against the nipping cold, nose and ears tinged with rose. Her delicacy made Ryn steal occasional, anxious glances, until at last the deva opened her hoodie—an extension of her kanaf—and draped the protective part of herself around Naomi's shoulders.

"You'll f-freeze." Naomi tried to shrug out of it.

"Unlikely." Ryn turned Naomi to face her and sealed the jacket.

"Wow. This thing is amazing." She snugged into it. "*Really* amazing."

Ryn's kanaf could take on a variety of material properties, but the heat radiated from her heart. Even on another being, the hoodie wasn't truly separate from Ryn. However, just as Naomi could feel the deva's warmth, Ryn could feel her friend's soft shape as though pressed against her. It sent an alien tingle through her stomach, and on their trek, she clutched at the new sensation in her middle.

"Turns out you really are sweet," Naomi grinned.

The tingle grew. "The cold doesn't bother me."

"Nice *and* tough."

The warmth was joined by a smile that twitched the corner of Ryn's mouth.

There was a line at the Nine Lives. The bouncer argued quietly with men a few positions ahead of them about their identification, and Ryn didn't care for their scent.

"Get outta here," the bouncer said. "It's under-twenty-one night, not 'skeevy, bearded perv' night."

"Bullshit. I'm seventeen, check the ID." The goateed man was lean with a knit cap, and his soul was almost entirely rot.

"It's not even laminated. Looks like you ran it off a printer."

"Our school's got budget issues. Look. I'm just here to dance the night away in this great, free country of ours."

They exchanged money through a handshake. The bouncer glanced down at the crumpled wad in his palm and then growled. He opened the door and whispered, "Your shit better not land these teenyboppers in Mercy General, or I'm coming for you, Ben Franklin."

"Relax. We're top shelf. All about the repeat business." Franklin and his two hulking friends went inside.

"What was that all about?" Naomi asked. "I think my ears are frostbitten."

Ryn had no idea. Humans could speak their language with exacting nuance, their faces, hands, and tone all playing a role. Apparently, they could also communicate by exchanging scraps of money. It was all so sophisticated, mysterious, and dumb. "Something about boppers."

The bouncer scanned their IDs and nodded. Naomi gave him money. When Ryn just stood there, Naomi quickly gave him another money and dragged Ryn through the door. "Don't be embarrassed, but are you broke?"

Ryn bristled. "I function. Flawlessly."

"No. Money. Do you have money?"

"I have a fare card." She produced it. Ms. Cross had said there was money and it was "on" the card.

"Right. Here's twenty dollars in case you need it—just where *are* you from? I thought the concept of money was pretty well saturated." There was something sophisticated to Naomi's smile, and Ryn realized she was being teased. It made her ears burn.

"I understand fine." Moneys were very important pieces of paper, and when the numbers on things got higher, people needed more of them. It was as perfectly stupid as anything humans did.

Stepping into the Nine Lives was like dipping into a pool of viscous sound. The scuffed walls, shadows, and ocean of bodies squeezed Ryn from every side, the music and voices gathered into a roar that vibrated through the floor. The bass pounded against her skin. The bottom floor had booths and tables, and there were only narrow avenues between all the people.

"The dancing is upstairs!" Naomi hollered.

Ryn choked on the odor of too many bodies, all too close. She tailed Naomi, but when someone brushed her bare arm, she jerked away. Another bumped into her from behind and she twirled, but collided with a third. Ryn spun around two times avoiding the flailing, awkward riot of humans. She realized the avenue from her entrance had closed and panic jolted through her. They were everywhere, pressing inward, crushing her, and she hated them all; she needed to claw her way out; she snapped her gaze to the ceiling in search of escape.

Then her hoodie slipped over her shoulders. She felt Naomi's hands on either side of her, steadying her. "You okay?" she whispered from behind. Ryn had backed straight into her.

Ryn closed her eyes and shook her head.

"Just breathe with me a second."

She nodded, hearing Naomi's breath and feeling the drum of her heart. It was steady and slow and soon Ryn's matched its rhythm.

"Stay close to me."

It was easier with the hoodie back on. Naomi had removed her own sweater, but the heat didn't bother Ryn.

They wound through the crowd, Ryn in her friend's wake. Males tried to talk to Naomi, but she just yelled, "Sorry, we're here with other people!" and pushed on.

The upstairs music flowed through Ryn's marrow with its tribal rhythm and synthetic flair. Smoke rolled across her ankles and sharp, unnatural colors bathed the swaying masses, shifting from green to blue to indigo. Even when the twisting dancers weren't pressed together, their movements knotted them anyway, so that the crowd moved as a single writhing body.

Ryn, too, felt the tidal pull of the music. It stuck to her hips, tingled up her spine and into her shoulders, and beat inside her brain with its loud demand that she lean into it.

And then she realized something else. She didn't itch. At all. No eyes were upon her. The crowd's attention was pulled deeply inward, and Ryn's core filled with the discreet thrill of anonymity, the same one she felt on the hunt.

There in the crowd, Ryn stood alone. She shivered.

Denise shouted from the bar and Elli bounced up and down to be seen. Naomi shouldered through the crowd, Ryn chasing her.

"You made it!" Elli shouted over the music. "Unbelievable!" Then she glanced at Ryn. "Oh. Both of you."

"This place is lame without you." Denise hugged Naomi. "No amount of bribe money will get a shot of rum in my Coke."

"That's why I like it," Naomi grinned. "The last thing my dad needs is to turn on the news and see photos of his daughter and her drunk friends getting felt up by boys."

"So 'no' to the booze, but can we still have the boys?" Denise kissed Naomi's cheek. "I love you, but take off the Good Little Girl mask for *one* night."

"For the thousandth time, it's not a mask. And I'm just here to dance—so yes to boys, and no to fondling. Deal?"

"Boring! Cut loose a little."

"I am cutting loose. This is me being loose." Naomi wiggled.

"Right. Hey, I see someone interesting. Be right back." Denise waded toward the other side of the bar and talked to Franklin and his tall pack mates. Ryn tensed, careful to watch their exchange, not trusting Franklin and his rotten smell.

Elli and Naomi shouted their conversation over the noise, watching the crowd. "We've been here a while," Elli said into Naomi's ear. "Place is full of high-school guys who get scared unless they outnumber you."

"Let's just dance." Naomi motioned to Ryn. "Come on."

Ryn shook her head. The floor was jammed with interlocking bodies and she wanted no part in that.

They both shrugged and pushed into the motion on the floor while Ryn hovered at the bar. Not everyone danced the same. Some rolled with the music, in a trance, their hearts fast and blood spiked with stimulant chemicals. Others danced with form, coordination. A few women added more flare, accents with their hips and touches from their hands, teasing their males. A lot of the dancing looked more like a mating ritual, and some of them seemed sufficiently fused to have been actually mating.

Then there was Naomi. She laughed at first, her eyes scrunched into joyful half-moons, and she and Elli danced playfully. Gradually, a tension in Naomi's joints dissolved. Her body loosened, her frame became sinuous, and she slipped into a groove—like the groove Ryn fell into while traversing rooftops. She became a ribbon, caught the music's pulse, and Ryn couldn't look away.

Naomi danced like an artist, a woman pressed skin-to-skin with the room's naked sound. She did it naturally, without mortal clumsiness, and across the raucous expanse and through two dozen bodies and bass vibrations, Ryn could feel her heartbeat locked onto the music.

"Like what you see?" Denise asked.

Ryn startled and glanced at the bar, where Denise curled around a fizzing glass of soda, her expression somehow feline. There were no words to speak—she sensed Denise had seen something that gave her insight into the workings of Ryn's mind; she didn't like that feeling one bit.

Denise sipped her drink and shifted her gaze to a mirror over the bar. Ryn could hear very well over the noise by now. "Don't know what to make of Naomi?"

"No." Ryn had to raise her voice.

"She's not hard to get. Imagine a person without an evil bone in her body. Then make her stubborn, unyielding, and persuasive. An angel's graces and the devil's charisma." Denise slipped a tiny, white pill between her lips and drank her soda. She swallowed. "I wish for once she'd let her hair down. How about you? Be bad with me. I could use a partner in crime."

"I am my own kind of bad. You wouldn't like it."

Denise considered her and chuckled. "Probably wouldn't. But I'll try anything once."

Now Ryn felt like they were talking about different things. She glanced across the dance floor at Franklin, who hadn't taken his eyes off Denise since they had spoken. "Stay away from him. He smells wrong."

"Oh, not you too. Christ. I don't need to get it from two friends at once."

"Friend?" That surprised Ryn.

Denise chuckled. "Can't tell whether I like you or not, can you?"

Ryn shook her head.

"Yeah, me neither." She exhaled and took a moment to study Ryn. "Can't figure you out. At first, I thought drug dealer. Now I'm not sure. I mean, obviously you're into girls—only surprise there is Naomi hasn't caught on."

Ryn frowned. "I—"

"Don't deny it. Way you stare at the princess breaks my heart, because she's saving herself for her future investment-banker husband. How do I know? She told me when she was ten what her life plan was, and she doesn't deviate. Naomi Bradford knows what she wants, goes after it with single-minded determination, and watching you pine is like watching Wile E. Coyote salivate—just makes me pity you."

"Pity?" Ryn snarled.

Denise slid off her chair to stare into Ryn's sunglasses, speaking softer now that they were close. "Let me lay it out for you. First boyfriend, hand-holding only, age twelve. That was Davie Raines, check." She made a check motion with her finger. "First dance at Homecoming, age fifteen, invited by a junior—that was Arjun, and he was a perfect gentleman. Check." Again with her finger. "First kiss? That's sometime this year. Bet she's looking for a candidate tonight. First fuck? I'd always thought after marriage, but no, it's going to be her college boyfriend. She'll wait three months to let him under her skirt, then at six months she'll give it up, sometime after he proposes and on a suitable anniversary."

"Why are you telling me this?" It felt wrong; it was an invasion of Naomi's life.

"Only thing that's gone off the rails is when she lost her mom. Klara's job was to take pictures before the first dance and grill her future husband in advance of their wedding. I took the dance pictures, for the record. Also: I'm her maid of honor at the wedding. What I'm saying is, that girl is the daughter of a genius and a senator; she's nobility. You understand that, right? She's not going to make a mistake with you, if that's what you're sniffing around for."

"I am no mistake." The words purred from Ryn's throat and for the first time Denise faltered. "I am no hanger-on, no sycophant. And I have no interest in Naomi Bradford." *I am her protector and she is my bait; that is where it ends.*

Yet her final statement made Denise shake off her fear and smirk. "The red on your cheeks tells a different story."

Ryn could have cut her down, but Franklin appeared and sidled into Denise's personal space, his hips close to hers, hands in pockets. "Want to dance?" he asked, grinning down at her. "My boys can run the sales floor for a few songs."

Denise's stare seemed hard, but softened so quickly that Ryn wondered whether anything in her was authentic. Turning her smile on Franklin, she said, "First you take my money and now you want to dance? Ballsy, old man."

"I could give your money back."

"Keep it," Denise said. "I don't dance for money. Only fun."

Ryn seized her elbow. "Don't go. He smells wrong."

Denise lifted an eyebrow. "Don't ever tell me what to do." She shook free and took Franklin's arm, heading to the floor with him. "Let's show my friends what a good time looks like."

Ryn stalked the edges and corners of the room, away from the gyrating humans and their unwelcome touches. She prowled in the places that fell between mortal gazes, scented the air now and then for asura, watching Franklin to ensure he never got too close to Naomi.

At first, the three females danced with one another, alongside Franklin and males whom Naomi and Elli had secured. Denise pressed into and grinded on Franklin, seeming to cast Naomi various looks throughout—but the senator's daughter kept some distance from her own partner, playful yet not intimate. Just her smile seemed to keep his interest.

After two songs, Franklin departed for a corner his pack mates had staked out. Denise and Naomi argued, the distance drowning out the details. Naomi inspected Denise's eyes and put the back of her hand on her friend's forehead. Denise batted the hand aside, yelled, and stormed off toward Franklin.

Elli's hand fell on Naomi's shoulder, stopping her from pursuing, and those two reluctantly folded back into their circle of males.

Ryn glided along the periphery of the room, now keeping track of two different parts of it. In one, Naomi's heart pounded a steady tempo, her skin glistened, and her auburn hair burnished into darker, messier tangles. Her scent changed into something spicy-strange.

Denise orbited Franklin, along with his two pack mates and a female they'd found. Denise danced with other men, but mostly Franklin whenever he wasn't exchanging money and white pills with strangers. The pills were stimulants—whoever took them ended up with a racing heart and a different chemical odor in their sweat. Oddly, Denise's heart slowed instead, her eyes glassed, and her movements seemed entranced. Franklin danced nearer and nearer. Though she slapped at his hand once or twice, she became more languid the longer they went. Finally, she stopped protesting altogether and he found a seat on a nearby dais, pulling her into his lap, and though his rot was so thick Ryn could taste it even now, Denise fused her mouth to his. The deva's stomach turned.

During a song transition, Naomi scanned the bar area, frowning in disappointment. She swiveled, as if to look for something, striding off the dance floor as her search turned frantic. Ryn glided through the room's dark places. Naomi, in a bout of panic, nearly backed into her.

"I'm here," Ryn whispered close to her ear.

Naomi's shoulders tensed and she spun. Her eyes had a slight sheen and the spicy-strange scent mixed with fear. She ran quaking fingers through tangles of her loosened hair. "God. *Ryn*. I thought you left. It freaked me out."

"I promised to protect you and I will."

Naomi managed a grin. "You really are a cocky little thing. And I don't know why I believe you. But I do."

This pleased Ryn.

"You don't want to dance?"

She shook her head. "Too many people."

"And finally, I know your dark secret."

How had she intuited that Ryn wanted to break the arms of everyone who bumped into her?

"You're shy!"

"I am not."

"Come on. Elli and I will dance with you. Hey. Have you seen Denise? I just want to check on her."

"She has her mouth on a man named Franklin."

Naomi furrowed her brow and glanced worriedly around.

She spotted Denise and Franklin and covered a giggle. "Oh! You mean kissing. Okay, come on, dance with Elli and me." She seized Ryn by the wrist and dragged her through the mass of people.

The monster should have snarled, and had any other being tried to physically move her, it would have uncoupled her wrath from her rationality. But it was Naomi, so she allowed it.

This once.

Elli was already dancing with three young men, and she didn't seem to mind having been left the center of attention. "Hey guys, this is Ryn," Naomi shouted.

They nodded, made brief introductions, and everyone danced again—Naomi beginning as before, conservative and almost hesitant until she shed her inhibitions; and then, weightless. In that moment, gravity didn't own her.

They weren't so much dancing with the males, Ryn realized, as in a tight circle—females to one side, males the other. Ryn stood, wary, bumped once by someone behind her.

"Move a little!" Elli coaxed, her smile different now—more obviously a smile.

"Find the rhythm." Naomi showed her how with her hips. "Just try a little two-step, like Wes. See? He's got it."

"Yeah," said the male named Wes. He was lanky and awkward in the way of a young giraffe. "Do whatever. You'll look good next to me, trust me. I call this move the Turtle." He swayed like he wore something ponderous on his shoulders.

Ryn let go, exhaling in a slow hiss, and closed her eyes. Another person bumped into her; they snapped back open.

It had been Naomi. Her friend slid nearer and intentionally tapped Ryn's hip with hers. "With me," she whispered, encouragement in her dark eyes.

So Ryn ignored the room. She fell deeper into herself, reached out to the music's tidal forces and surrendered to it. She buried the red-hot alarm caused by unwanted touches and focused on Naomi, because—she realized—Naomi made her feel something she had never felt among humans: welcome.

For a moment it was just Ryn's heartbeat next to Naomi's and the vibration of music pushed through floor, heels, spine.

She shucked off gravity, grasped the same thread of music that held Naomi aloft, and they moved together. Ryn had danced before to thunder, had played tag with lightning, but this was new. Their dance shrank the chaos in her mind to nothing, tossed out the heavy clutter in her head until all that remained in those great, vaulted spaces was the rhythm, the magnetic sound—and she came to realize her heart now drummed in time with Naomi's.

She opened her eyes. Naomi danced beside her. Elli and the others were there too, but most of all it was Naomi. Neither quite mimicked the other—but their bodies threaded close without quite brushing. Part of Ryn wanted it closer still; part worried she'd overstepped, that she was stealing too much pleasure from the roll and snap of her partner's shoulders.

Naomi caught her gaze for an electric instant, the worry erased. Those eyes were entranced and some thought was happening behind them, one Ryn couldn't fathom—but it wasn't fear or disgust. It seemed an invitation to stay.

"She's got it now," Elli said.

Naomi only smiled, and glanced away. She said nothing, all her fear gone, replaced with that spicy-strange fragrance; and Ryn liked it.

Although they danced in a circle, they each appeared to have a cross-wise partner, and Ryn's was Wes. She didn't like him. Nor did she dislike him, exactly, which wasn't typical for her—it was usually one or the other. He only came too close once, but stayed away when her lip curled. Sometimes he would dance in a jerky way that made everyone laugh at him, except he seemed to encourage it; he didn't gnash at being made a joke. She sensed no aggression in him whatsoever.

Elli and her male tired, slowed, and for two songs they leaned against one another for support, moving at last toward a wall where they sat.

"Can't believe she's still going." Wes nodded at Naomi. "Your friend's a machine."

Naomi had paused only to find Ryn. Even after the point of normal mortal exhaustion, she still lived in the thrall of the music.

"Horatio, you want to get some water for us and the girls?"

Wes asked, glancing at Naomi's partner. Horatio was tall, broad-shouldered, and had the trim look Ryn associated with soldiers, except with longer, more rakish black hair. Both his hair and brown skin shined from exertion. Ryn saw nothing in him to like.

"Yeah, sure." Horatio and Wes left for water.

For a moment it was just them, and Ryn's pulse spiked—but Naomi stopped dancing. "Can I ask you something? Did you keep an eye on Denise earlier?"

"She's near. Her male smelled wrong."

"Did she look... okay to you?"

"Lethargic." Ryn still sensed her faintly through the crowd.

"Come with me. I'm worried she might have taken too much."

They crossed the floor and, in fact, Denise no longer danced so much as slumped into Franklin while his hands held her aloft—held her at the curves, held her carefully, but with the ill intent of a spider. She was trapped in a fugue, the poison from his hand having done its work, and Ryn's stomach tightened as the reality settled: this was a web-spinner, a human who had played shell games with pills, and snared his prey so gradually she had let him. This one was a monster.

Which made him food.

Naomi skipped ahead, bolting over to Denise, the auburn-haired girl seeming somehow doe-like. She wound up inadvertently surrounded by Franklin, his two pack mates, and a female brunette affixed to one of their arms. The female's breath was ashy from cigarettes. At the sight of her rain-clean doe amidst them, Ryn's fine hairs bristled.

"There you are." Naomi set her hand on Denise's shoulder. "Guess you hit your limit." She glanced at Franklin. "I'll get her home safe. Sorry about this."

"No worries." Just the corner of Franklin's mouth tugged up. "She's cool where she is." He shifted Denise to his opposite hip, where she murmured unintelligibly, and he reached to brush Naomi's hair. "If you want to tag along, though, I got something that'll—"

Ryn seized his wrist, a growl rippling from her throat, one that spoke a simple truth: *Mine*.

Everyone stared, even Naomi—and Franklin jerked his

wrist free. Ryn let him keep it, as well the hand. "Where'd you come from?"

"From Hell."

"Fuck you, Ted Kaczynski."

"Easy!" Naomi glanced nervously between the tall men. "My friend's high, so she leaves with me—that's our rule." She focused on Franklin. "If you give me your number, I'll—"

"Won't be necessary."

"What do you mean—"

"Didn't you hear? You're dismissed." He waved his hand. "Your friend's a good tongue fuck; guessing she can do a lot more. So unless you're offering better, we're done here."

"Relax, sweetie." The brunette lit her cigarette, leaning off one of Franklin's pack mates. "She's been hot and ready all night; little girl needs a rough dicking." She blew smoke their way. "No shame in it. We're all animals."

Naomi stared, subtly shaking her head in disbelief. "She's drugged."

"And she paid good money for those drugs," said the ash-mouthed female.

"She's not conscious!" Quietly, ferociously, Naomi hissed: "That's rape."

"Or maybe she's not like you," whispered Franklin. His voice drew Naomi's baleful stare. "She told me a story. About this 'princess,' she calls her, who can't get high, can't dance too close, can't fuck." He showed her his teeth; even Ryn could tell it wasn't a real smile. "This princess makes her feel like shit."

Ryn peered through the crowd, counting witnesses. *Too many. Have to kill him later.*

Naomi swallowed. "Give me my friend."

"You don't get it, do you?" Franklin asked. "You're not the white knight riding in; you're the thing that chased her right into my arms." He tilted his head to the side, as though to examine the hurt spreading across Naomi's face, selecting each word like the perfect sharpened knife and sliding it in with relish. "She's high 'cause of you, with me 'cause of you—and I'm the thing that's gonna cure her. Of you."

Naomi shook, a leaf at the mercy of strong winds. "I'll call the police."

"And I'll be gone." He made a poofing motion with one hand, still clutching his prize with the other. "See, you don't understand how well I know trust-fund bitches. Sluts like this need to be stoned to get what they want, 'cause frigid princesses convince them they're filthy."

He knew words—powerful ones, because they made Naomi shrink, made her eyes tense with hurt. With no words of her own, Ryn rotated her jaw to one side, listening to the audible pop, and in the space of that pop, she decided to kill him here—and would have, if one hadn't come from behind.

So focused was her attention, she allowed the mortal's hands to touch her. They clapped to her hips, his disgusting pelvis mashing into her from behind. "This one wants it filthy too," he bellowed. "Got that wildcat look, doesn't she?"

Twisting around, her palm lashed out, tossing him into his surprised pack mate, showing only a flicker of her power and a hundredth of what she marked him for. The murder-itch tingled at the roots of her teeth and claws, in every tightening joint, and she'd have reached through his stomach to break his spine if the moon were any higher. She refrained because she was fairly sure humans couldn't do that. What saved his life was only the desire to kill subtly enough to remain unjailed. Weighing her options, she decided on a more believably human response—she'd rip off an arm.

No sooner were her claws flexed than both Horatio and Wes stepped in front of her, stymieing her again.

With Franklin joining his pack mates, the two boys formed a wall separating Ryn from her foes, and she nearly ripped the boys open for protecting them. When she realized their intent had been to guard *her*, it angered her more.

"Back off." Wes's voice seemed high, thin. "If you couldn't tell, the murder-look meant 'you're not my type.' "

She didn't need an interpreter. Ryn had an uncanny knack for communicating her displeasure across language barriers.

"You're not anyone's type, you little bitch," said the pack mate whom Ryn had marked for maiming. "But no one needs to get hate-fucked harder than tomboys. Can see it in her face—I lit her pussy on fire; she's just beggin' to look me in the eye while I tame it." He grabbed his groin.

"First of all," Wes said, "that metaphor was mixed. You

tame animals, you put out fires. I scold you, sir."

Horatio's fists tightened and he hissed, "Stop helping!"

Wes wasn't in a fighting stance—flat-footed, a sudden breeze could have knocked him down. With no clue how to brawl, he stood in front of three thick human warriors. *Is he brave or stupid?* "No one here wants trouble," Wes intoned.

Stupid, apparently.

Franklin slugged Wes, knocking him back into Ryn, who caught his shoulders. The drug seller had let go of Denise, who pooled on the floor.

A split second passed as mortals tensed for combat, but Horatio was faster than the rest. Before Franklin had reset from the blow, Horatio delivered one to the drug seller's gut that folded him in half.

Both the pack mates rushed Horatio, scuffling until they had their huge arms under both of his, holding him a moment before tossing him; Ryn didn't care for him enough to play catch again and let him drop to the floor.

Wes tried to rally, but couldn't make a proper fist, so Ryn squeezed his shoulder. "You will *stay*, or I will let one break you."

"Sorry, what?" Wes asked.

"You two fags need to leave," snarled Franklin, hefting Denise back into his grip. "This party just got dangerous. As for your slutty friend, you just sealed her goddamn fate. I'll fuck her stupid and send you the—"

Everyone went at once: Naomi screaming her outrage, Horatio scrambling, Wes summoning his courage. As for them? Aggression odors spilled from each, even the brunette, who seemed thirsty to see violence.

Ryn stepped between both tribes. "I claim her."

Franklin blinked. "Excuse me?"

"The girl." Ryn pointed at Denise. "I knew her first; she called me 'friend.' Give her to me, worm."

"Suck my dick. Possession is nine-tenths of the law."

"There is *one* law," Ryn snarled. "That is me." These lowly mortals decorated courtrooms in *her* image, as though they had the right—as though they knew justice, or what to do with monsters. "You cannot have her because I will it."

Hoots from the brunette and pack mates, who jeered: "Just

slap the bitch." "Knock her back into her women's-studies class."

Ryn slipped her glasses from her eyes, pocketing them, stepping forward almost into Franklin. *With apologies, Ms. Cross.*

Denise blinked slowly and froze at the sight of Ryn's bowed head and eyes, her blue-burning eyes that proved Hell was a cold place she carried inside her; Denise slipped mercifully back into unconsciousness.

"Make your move." He bared teeth again. "Show me, you puffed-up cunt."

Lifting her jaw, she showed him.

Franklin stared back into the absolute assurance of the supernatural and stopped baring his teeth, stopped speaking.

This was a magic older than words. The magic in her eyes marked Ryn for what she was; they set her apart, gave the gods cause to banish her from states and nations—they were solid black except for the searing light of her irises, and no mortal could look upon them and doubt her inhumanity.

A closing throat choked off his scream and he couldn't tear himself from Ryn's gaze; his color drained from pale to chalk, and he reclined his head as far as he could, fighting to look away, but unable until she released him. A thin whimper rose from his lungs.

Ryn snapped her canines at him and he released his prize. Denise landed softly in Ryn's embrace as Franklin windmilled his arms in a mad backward leap that sent him crashing to the floor. He crab-crawled away on all fours, screaming a string of "fuck"s until his back hit a wall.

Ryn eased her glasses back on, shifting Denise into Naomi's arms.

She pivoted toward Franklin's pack mates, who'd never seen her eyes—that display had been Franklin's alone. The one Ryn had marked bolted at her, reaching for her hoodie. "You're mine, you little—"

She snatched his wrist, twisting. The pop satisfied on nearly a spiritual level, as did his shriek. He buckled and Ryn backhanded him, snapping his head violently to one side. He crashed to elbows and knees at Ryn's feet.

Using his back as a springboard, she leapt and sailed onto

the pack mate behind him. Pincering her knees to his shoulders, she punched straight down into his face. Again and again and again, she hit him; he couldn't get his arms up to block, so she took her time. A dozen shots changed his face's shape and color, from pale to purple under her thorough ministration. Teeth and blood flew over her shoulder; she broke his nose, the orbit of one eye. When he collapsed, Ryn sprang free, alighting to the floor.

The marked man she'd floored attempted to stand, so she planted her knee into his jaw, flattening him again.

"My God, you psychopath, you broke his nose!" cried the brunette, rushing to tend the marked man.

"Nose once, jaw twice; wrist in six places." *I'm not done yet, either. Heal, you dog. I will be back for you all.* She steered her gaze to Franklin. *Especially you.*

Perhaps Franklin understood, because as Ryn held his gaze, even the memory of what lurked behind her sunglasses spread a dark stain at the crotch of his pants.

From her knees, Naomi held Denise in her arms while gaping at Ryn, as though seeing her for the first time.

Wes and Horatio, too, stood still as statues, unmoving since Ryn had first acted.

It was Wes who broke the spell by clapping his hands three times. "I feel like... I mean, take this however you want as long as it's not badly, because dear God I don't want to offend you, *ever*, but—for what you just did—I should offer myself to you sexually. And not like, 'wee, fun for me' sex. I mean I would let you penetrate me. Not that you'd want to. Or should. But... holy God, what was that? Kung fu?"

Ryn furrowed her brow, unsure if she should be offended at Wes for suggesting a sexual liaison, except it seemed curiously harmless.

"We— We should go," Naomi said.

"Agreed." Ryn hefted Denise into a fireman's carry. Naomi stood. For an instant they shared a kinetic moment of eye contact that made Ryn's nerves buzz, heightened further when Naomi mouthed "thank you."

"Uh. Okay, not kung fu then." Wes chased after them. "Krav maga? Ninjitsu? Do you do lessons? *Do you need a sidekick?*"

"Easy," Horatio whispered. "Nerd out after we get help for their friend."

"Oh. Yeah, sorry."

Downstairs, Naomi explained the situation to two bouncers who intercepted them. She had a way about her, making eye contact, explaining everything quickly and clearly. Whatever magnetism she possessed, the bouncers believed her immediately and told her to get Denise to a hospital.

It was cold outside the Nine Lives, sweetly empty of synthetic light and loud music. Elli met them and said she'd been in the restroom during the fight, and she'd seen the bouncers escorting Franklin and his badly injured friends out a rear entrance. Ryn sat Denise on a bench and Naomi checked her pulse with two fingers while tapping her phone. "I'll order a ride," Naomi said. "She needs a hospital."

"We'll come with you, make sure you get there okay," Horatio said.

"No chance. My dad's been on high alert for a week, and I've never seen him so stressed. This isn't the night to add boys to the mix."

"He doesn't know you're out?" Horatio asked.

Naomi clasped one hand on her opposite wrist, twisting anxiously. "Not... exactly."

"Take it easy on the old man." Horatio leaned too close for Ryn's liking. "Pretty sure he's got a good reason for all that stress."

"Oh my God—you knew who I was?"

"You've been on the news all week. And my dad's got your old man's campaign sticker on his bumper. Sorry I didn't say anything. Just figured you were here to dance, not talk about shitty current events."

Ryn definitely didn't like the way Naomi laughed and dipped her nose slightly while still looking up at him. "Such a gentleman," said the auburn-haired doe.

"After you get your friend settled, let us know how she is. Please." He took Naomi's phone—the way he just reached for it made Ryn's claws twitch. He typed digits into it, passing it back. "My number."

Wes nodded at Ryn. "Any way I can get in touch with you?"

"I don't have a phone."

"A themed signal I could flash into the sky, maybe?"

"My therapist gives me messages."

"That is perhaps the most creative way a girl has ever blown me off," Wes said. Horatio grabbed Wes's arm, dragging him away, and Wes walked backward while shouting, "I was serious! About lessons, not about the penetration."

"Come on, every second you talk it gets more painful." Then, as they passed from human earshot, Horatio whispered, "What part of our *thoroughly* drilled 'dial it down' hand signal did you miss back there?"

CHAPTER TEN
After Hours

Walking into an emergency room after midnight was like wandering past a plot twist in other people's lives. Everyone there was living that moment out of sync, interrupted. Naomi glanced from face to face. A nervous mother in a business suit with rolling luggage held an icepack to her listless six-year-old's forehead. A bearded man with a sleeve of tattoos on each forearm clutched a rag over his bloody hand. His blood plinked onto the floor and he fought with a nurse over the mess: "Maybe if I had a fuckin' doctor, I wouldn't still be bleeding."

Ten minutes before, they'd carted a gunshot victim through. He'd yelled at his brother in Russian to find his wallet and keys. He was belligerently drunk and asked the surgeon if she'd like to have dinner tomorrow night. They tried to pry the liquor bottle out of his hand, but he said, "*Nyet*, is not empty!" He still gripped it when they wheeled him into the operating room.

Ryn stood next to Naomi's seat. "I could take you home."

She shook her head. "I need to make sure Denise is all right."

Elli had left with her father. He'd blown through the ER like a tornado, apologizing profusely to the staff he knew, checking Denise's chart and talking to her doctor. He'd insisted to Naomi that her friend was in good hands and would be fine. Then Naomi had wilted as he'd grilled Elli about drugs. On the ninth iteration of the same questions, Elli had erupted into tears and confessed to taking a hit off a boy's joint in the restroom line. Overall, her father had seemed relieved.

Ryn perched on a chair and seemed intent on the room. A pinch of anxiety sharpened in Naomi's stomach the longer she watched Ryn. She'd felt silly putting her trust in the tiny girl's vows, but that was before. Now she had only questions. What she'd done to three grown men had been unreal—no one had ever moved so blindingly fast. But seeing her after the melee shifted everything Naomi thought she knew: no trembling, no relief or bragging, nor any sign of exertion. Like she'd simply... scratched an itch, the same as a hundred times before.

Ryn had fought a war. Naomi didn't know where, or how, but suspected she'd fought it nearly all her life. Almost certainly, this graceful predator had taken human life, and probably with her hands. *Who the hell is this person?*

A shiver worked through her, though not entirely from fear—also from the perverse sense of safety she felt, knowing now that she'd been protected all night. Ryn's formidable presence had replaced fear with a tangle of feelings she couldn't quite unravel: warmth, a jittery charge whenever Ryn looked at her, and the pleasure of watching the strange girl move, akin to the fascination in seeing a housecat prowl.

When emergency-room doors parted for her father, Naomi was filled with a more recognizable anxiety. He'd abandoned his charcoal suit jacket and had rolled his sleeves to his elbows, his red power tie loosened and his hair disarrayed from a long day on the Hill. Mark and his aide, Carol, flanked him and Carol worked twice as fast to keep up with his long strides.

Naomi jolted to her feet, with Ryn stuck to her like a shadow. The teenaged soldier positioned herself so that she met Mark face to face, forcing him to stop short, and the two took one another's measure. Naomi's father rushed past those two, dragging her into an embrace that drove the air from her lungs.

It felt good and sturdy and right, but she couldn't savor it, because he pulled back and wore his fatherly face—not Dad, but Senator Dad.

She smiled weakly. "Heyyy, Daddy." Clearing her throat, she shifted back and put an unconscious step between them. "So nice of you to swing back from the Hill to... pick me up."

"Are you hurt?" His voice was tight, which alarmed her.

Fear, she realized. She shook her head decisively. "No. I—"

"You're sure? No one harmed you? Physically, emotionally, verbally, tangentially, or existentially?"

"No. Dad, *I'm* fine, it's just—"

"I'll ask once. Did you take anything?"

"Of course not."

He ran his hand through his hair in frustration. "That's exactly what I said to your grandfather the first time I smoked pot."

"I'm not you." She tried a smile she couldn't feel. "I take after mom, remember?"

"Who the hell do you think rolled it for me? Do they do drug tests here?"

No one answered him.

He hated that. "Carol. Check with the nurse. See if I can have my daughter take a drug test. While she's at it, ask her what kinds of drugs they have. I'd like a few myself. Find the ones that make tonight go away and put them in my briefcase."

She split off to find a nurse, sorting through which of his requests to take seriously. Carol had worked with her dad a long time.

"Where's this den of drug dealers and ne'er-do-wells? Please God tell me you bought them at a public university or something I can defund."

Wincing, she whispered, "Private business. The Nine Lives."

His face darkened—that old rage of a principled libertarian looking for a loophole. Partway through, he seemed to give up. "Fuck it. Fuck private businesses, fuck drug legalization, fuck sentencing limits and due process and bans on capital punishment. I'm having them shot." Probably not, but he looked ready to do *something*, pressing one fist to his forehead, bouncing on the balls of his feet as though to exorcise the frenetic energy that possessed him. "Who took you out tonight?"

Naomi wasn't ready for this turn. He was hunting for somewhere to vent his fury.

"Well? Speak up."

She opened her mouth, but no answer came.

"Denise or Elli? Which one dragged you from your room? Put you in danger? Never mind, it was Denise. She's the one who OD'd, wasn't she? She going to be all right?"

"Yes, but—"

"Good. I want to talk to her. She awake?"

"*No*. It wasn't Denise. It was—"

"Elli? Swear to God, I don't believe Elli's assertive enough to convince a dog to eat red meat. Don't lie to me."

"No! Listen! *I* left. It was my decision."

"You're covering. You were terrified. You told me—"

"Let her speak," Ryn snapped.

Silence.

All eyes turned to Ryn. Naomi swallowed and inched a step away, fearing that lightning might peal from the heavens and zot the raven-haired girl into ash and vapor. When her father made no immediate answer, Naomi remembered to exhale.

When he did speak, it was pure senator. "Excuse me, you must be confused. You're new, so I'll be concise. Walk away." He narrowed his eyes. "Walk somewhere far away from my daughter and me, because whoever convinced her to risk her life tonight—and now I'm pretty sure it was you—"

"It was."

"That simplifies things."

"No, Dad," Naomi pleaded. "She's just—"

"It needs to be said." Though he stared, Ryn tilted her head in a display of curiosity rather than fear. Her father went on: "This friend is stricken from the book of my daughter's companions. You never show your face at our home again. Don't even speak to her."

Ryn stepped forward, earning a warning look from Mark which she ignored. "Tell me once more what I may not do."

Naomi's heart caught. No one had ever spoken to her father with such anger.

"I will find your parents and make you wish—"

"I have none." Ryn tilted her head to the other side.

Her father cupped a hand over his mouth, dragging it to his chin, a gesture he mainly used to conceal his anger in front of the press or opposition party.

"Dad," Naomi soothed, "she's not from around here. She—"

"You put my daughter's *life* in danger." The catch in his voice wasn't rage, Naomi realized. It was nothing less than the distilled helplessness of a father.

"Nothing can harm her when I am close."

"Do you have any idea who tried to hurt my girl? She was attacked, nearly murdered—nearly tortured—" His voice broke off and left volumes unsaid; cold panic passed from her father's words in waves through her every capillary. "*Last week.*" He could barely speak, holding his sleeve to his mouth. "And you took her from me? From my home. Dragged her across the goddamn city..." He turned away and punched the wall.

Mark and Naomi jumped, but Ryn stood unflinching. There was a crack in the plaster. The whole ER stared.

"Shit," her dad said to the wall, as if he and the wall were the only two in the room and he felt compelled to explain himself.

"She did protect me," Naomi insisted, knowing how crazy it seemed.

"Six. Damn. Days ago." Everything in him sagged and at bottom he seemed to be drowning. "There are more out there, God knows where, and all they want to do is hurt my girl. We can't find them, and they might be anywhere—might be anyone. And you took her."

Her father's attention on Ryn, Naomi reached out and touched his forearm. He startled, as though she'd scalded him. "Dad." She tried to swallow the tightness in her throat. "Listen. Just for a minute, please."

He nodded. "You have until Carol brings my drugs." Shutting his eyes, he sucked on his scraped knuckle.

"Ryn didn't drag me. She came to my room and made me realize those walls and guards and motion sensors weren't just keeping bad things out. They kept me in. I can't live that way, Dad." He tried to interject, but Naomi lifted a hand and raised her voice to cut him off—a trick she'd picked up from him. "I *know* it's only been a week, but it wasn't making me feel safer. Just isolated."

Again, he opened his mouth to talk.

"—*yes*, I should have taken Mark."

His mouth clapped shut.

"It was stupid not to. I could have called you, convinced you—and Mark would have been there when we needed him.

But in my defense, I left a note."

Her father wasn't trying to get a word in edgewise, so she had a moment to think. Her heart sank as she realized how grave her mistakes really were.

"I'm so sorry," she blurted. "I'm not sorry for going out, but I'm sorry I didn't call, and I'm *especially* sorry about Denise. I could have kept closer tabs on her; I shouldn't have freaked out when she took that pill. She ran straight into that bastard's arms." Her stomach twisted at the memory. "Oh God, Dad, it wasn't just the drugs. Those guys... they were trying to do things to her."

"What happened?" His expression was far too schooled.

"I couldn't stop it. There were three of them and they were so big." The words came in a torrent of feeling. "No matter what I tried, what I said or screamed, they were going to take what they wanted. They would have." She was trembling. "They didn't care, they were getting off on making me realize it—making us helpless."

She glanced sidelong at Ryn, whose hands squeezed into fists on hearing the story told. "Except she was there. Don't be mad at Ryn. I know you think she's full of it, but she's *not*. Tonight is my fault." Every last piece of it—ditching Mark, scolding Denise, letting her friend fall in with those scumbags. "I didn't mean to mess up this bad," she sobbed, tears starting to form, trying to force her apologies around the tightness that choked off her voice.

Her father crushed her against his chest in an embrace so firm her ribs compressed, the words no longer necessary. He didn't speak either. His vise grip and the single ragged sob told her everything. That sound alone broke her open.

She wept, eventually ushered into a waiting room where she cried herself nearly dry. Mark blocked off the space, and somewhere in the shuffle Ryn disappeared without a farewell.

That stung, but Naomi chalked it up to whatever strange, war-torn place the wildling had come from.

Her dad sat beside her, never asking again about drugs, but explaining, "I called Bill Holowaty." He was the only cop in the world who liked her dad. "Said they've got the same detective on those three punks as they put on your case. He's supposed to be good."

Naomi sniffed and smiled. "That was lucky."

"Not really. Guy insisted on taking the case—maybe he thinks it's related. Point is, Bill seemed confident, so I don't think they'll get away with it. It's likely the drug dealer switched her pills, so there's a raft of charges they could nail him with if Denise testifies."

"I don't think she'll want to," Naomi murmured. "How about you? Is this a problem for your job?"

He snorted. "I'm a second-term senator and I'm fucking adorable. Old ladies love me; they think I look like a smarter George Clooney. Look at me, Naomi."

She did.

"Not one of my constituents cares what you do. You know that, right? That's not how elections work anymore. You can shave your head and snort a line of coke off a clown's ass and all I have to do is give the 'I love my coke-snorting daughter, clowns and all' speech. Situation defused. They elect me because this state is packed full of Republican gun owners and ex-Soviets who get twitchy about big government. Scandals involving kids won't even move the needle."

"I know, Dad."

"The reason I want you out of the news is for your good, not mine. As I do not place a 'D' after my name, the press are not fond of us, and what few rules they have about kids and women won't apply to you. You shouldn't have to pay that price—it's my political career. But that's why I worry. My politics make you a target for some of the media's less savory gossips—not to mention the conspiracy nutters."

"Do you think someone has footage of tonight?" Naomi asked. "The room was crowded."

"Maybe it ends up on YouTube, maybe it doesn't. We'll figure it out if it does."

"Thanks, Dad."

He wrapped an arm around her shoulder, dragging her close, squeezing. "You're a good kid. Not sure what I did to deserve you."

She leaned into him a while, thoughts allowed to wander. They kept coming back and sticking to Ryn, who danced her ferocious ballet whenever Naomi shut her eyes.

"We do need to talk about last week," Dad finally said.

Naomi's gut pinched, but she nodded.

He fetched his briefcase from Carol and both sat on the other side of a coffee table, where he opened the case and removed a thick ream of paper. Taking the top sheet off, he tapped it twice and glanced at Carol. "You need to tell her what you found."

Carol pursed her lips briefly. "Are you sure?"

He passed the sheet to Naomi. "These are highlights. It's from the webpage, where Banich was posting about hurting you. Normally this stuff is bullshit—there's loads of it out there, nearly all of it pointless screaming and naked id. Ninety percent of the internet is just kids trolling or crazies howling at the moon."

"So why is it printed out in your briefcase?"

He frowned at the stack of paper, fingering its edges. "Because one of them tried to kidnap you, and he wasn't alone. For whatever reason, this group—they're different."

The sheet rattled in Naomi's hands, and at first she read without feeling the words, a curious delay between their meaning and impact. But like poison, there was no stopping them once they were inside her—she grew lightheaded, sweating from her palms so that the page stuck to her hands. She sucked in a gasp, only then remembering to breathe.

It was strange that the words that echoed weren't the sickest, but the most profoundly earnest: *I want to see her face and watch how it goes still when she dies. Then her dad's eyes when he sees it happen—how it changes him forever.* They clung to her, because a real person had written them. A real person craved *that*.

"Enough." Her father plucked the sheet away before she'd finished more than half the messages.

"They aren't serious," Naomi whispered, stomach churning.

"At least one more is." Carol sat straight and pale, her mouth a thin line. "Someone sent... something to the office today. In the mail."

"What?" Alarm tingled through Naomi.

"A body part. Police are testing it against who they have on record. Based on the letter, we think he's someone who helped Banich, and who posts in that group. He cut it off himself.

Mailed it as some sort of threat."

"He mailed a *piece of himself*?" The room felt crooked, her head spinning. "What— What kind of piece?"

"What's important is you know these people aren't joking," Carol said.

"What piece?" she whispered.

Carol glanced at her father, who nodded, so she looked across the coffee table and told her.

Naomi threw up.

~*~

Tom Bradford kept his bearing in the waiting room and on the short walk into the hallway, where he shut the door, leaving Carol and Naomi inside. Crumpling against the door, he sagged, the universe turning too fast as he tried like hell to catch his breath. *Feels like someone's been sitting on my chest for six days.* He squeezed his eyes shut, rubbing them through his eyelids, and desperately tried not to think—to avoid the white-hot anger or cold panic that washed through his blood whenever his thoughts strayed.

God damn it, I hate this hospital. He glanced at the ceiling, knowing his wife had left him one floor up. Was Klara's shadow staring at him now? She'd tap her jaw in that thoughtful way that meant she was dissecting him. *Keep frowning like that, Mishka, and people will think we are both economists. Where is that belligerent optimism I married you for?*

"Fresh out," he told the shadow.

His phone chirped. It was Detective O'Rourke, the one who'd interviewed him last week. O'Rourke hadn't seemed like much—irritable, immensely fat, hairy like a Tolkien dwarf, and a slob. That was why Tom had liked him. He'd met his share of people on the Hill who skated on charisma or looks, but this detective who'd garnered so much praise would have had to come by it honestly. "Hello?" he answered.

"Bill called. Told me you were at the hospital." O'Rourke slurped something, probably coffee. "There's a uniform driving down to visit those pushers who attacked your daughter's friend. A bouncer can testify he saw them slinging dope—club threw the bouncer under the bus after finding out he let them in. They're afraid you'll lean on the city to shut them down. He's trying to cooperate his way out of charges."

Tom grimaced. "I should shut them down." He *wanted* to. It had been advertised as under-twenty-one, and one of their employees had let foxes into the henhouse. He was within his rights to push it as a parent, but using senatorial clout was a gray area for him. "You think Denise will need to testify?"

"Maybe. Maybe they plead out. Not my department."

Tom should have been more concerned, but this wasn't the problem he needed solved. "Anything else?" He tried not to sound desperate.

"I could give you the canned 'pursuing all our leads' answer, but I bet you've given the senator version of that a hundred times."

"Hundred and one."

"Sit tight. I've got half a dozen little threads I'm pulling at, but it's a hell of a knot. I'll need some time."

Tom changed ears. "I'm just trying to keep my daughter safe. Can you tell me anything—anything at all—that'll help me do that?"

The pause on the other end lasted too long. "Who's your daughter's friend?"

"Denise?"

"The short one."

"I think her name's Ryn. Why?"

"Sending you some footage. Only video that came out of tonight, and it only exists in two places right now—my phone and yours. Keep it that way."

Tom frowned. "I don't understand."

"Look, this city is weird, and I can't—" He muttered under his breath, starting over. "It's evidence. I'm not supposed to share it. Breaking the rules some. Wouldn't do it if I didn't think you needed to see this."

"What are you—"

"Watch the video. You'll understand. Oh, and this 'Ryn' girl? She was at the mall last week with your daughter. Can't say anything more, but you're a smart guy. You'll connect the dots."

"Thanks. I owe you."

"You don't owe me a goddamn thing. This is my job and

I'm paid on the public dime. Just keep it in mind, next time you slash taxes."

"I only slash the federal ones. But sure."

The detective grunted and the line went dead.

There's a man who loves what he does. Tom had never felt comfortable around cops, but he liked O'Rourke. The detective seemed interested in the work and not the club-y camaraderie—cops tended to be cliquish, defensive, and they despised most of Tom's stances on criminal rights and unions. The only reason Bill was still his friend was because they'd spent a short term in the military together getting shot at in Haiti.

Mark padded silently up the hallway. "News?"

Tom nodded. His phone chirped again. "Just got video from the club. Guess there really was a fight."

He shared the screen with Mark, tapping the file open. It played bouncy footage and he wasn't surprised at all to see two boys barricading off Naomi and Ryn, though the size of their assailants was breathtaking. *Those are not teenagers.*

"See the tattoo on that guy's forearm?" Mark said. "That's a Ukrainian gang tattoo. Been in the Docks two generations, guns and drugs mostly. Surprised they made it all the way out to Whitechurch."

The teenagers filming whispered about it "going down," the camera giving one more annoying jounce, and then it happened. The skinny boy took a punch, the narrator singing "Daaa-amn!" and Ryn caught the boy. She slipped to the front and Tom suppressed the spectator urge to yell, "Get back, you idiot!"

Ryn removed her glasses and the rest came too fast. The skinniest gangster, who seemed their leader, panicked and flailed away like she was a rabid dog. The slight, raven-haired teenager caught Denise. *Kid's strong for her size.* She passed Denise to Naomi.

The biggest gangbanger came at her and Ryn did something to his arm. It bent wrong. He fell and she flew off his back like a demon, clobbering the last thug. That one dropped too and she turned to deliver the big one a parting knee to his jaw.

"What the hell," Mark said. "Play it again."

It had been terrifying in its speed and brutality, its unexpectedness, and something in Mark's voice prickled Tom's skin. "Why?"

"What she did there— Just play it again."

Again, he watched. He saw more this time—saw details concealed by speed. The girl had done too much in too short a time for him to understand before, but it looked like she'd caught the big one's wrist, broke it with a jerk, and knocked him down with a backhand before launching into the last punk. It wasn't just a clobbering, either. It was at least six blows, shots like cobra strikes that blurred together. The knee to the big guy's jaw looked like an afterthought. She didn't even look down at him.

"Shit," Mark breathed. "From the top."

"You going to tell me—"

"Just play it."

They watched a third time and now Tom just noted her expression: a twisted, animal look of hatred, and through pixelated footage her bared teeth seemed somehow wolfish.

"Jesus," Mark whispered. "Never even touched the first guy. Just *looked* at him. Whatever those sunglasses are covering, it's got to be disturbing. Scars maybe. Whatever it was, it must have told him the truth."

"What truth?"

"Everything was smoothly executed, right down to the way she caught Denise and transferred her to your daughter. There's economy in every step. She's a veteran."

"You mean a soldier?"

"She's fought. Who for, and why? Hard to say. But she knows how to hurt people in ways you don't learn in a studio. Her backhand nailed a nerve in the big one's jaw—broke it, too, I'd say. Maneuvered his body in the other guy's way, blocked his advance. And then her leap—it's fast. I wouldn't have seen it coming; it's an ambush maneuver. She pinned his shoulders, seized his hair in one fist, and delivered ten, twelve full-impact blows in less than a second. No one I've met can do that—not with that speed and force—and I've met guys I wouldn't take on without a SWAT team. That knee at the end? She's got either near-perfect peripheral vision or a spatial awareness most fighters would kill for."

"What was your first impression of Ryn?"

"Thought she was full of shit. Teenagers, right? Thinking back now, though, she was hands-free and moved to intercept me. She was protecting Naomi. Same deal on the video, until she attacks. Her stances are on the aggressive side, but she's always mindful of your daughter."

"Could she have put down Banich?" It seemed insane, given the extent of injuries dealt to the parking-garage attacker, but O'Rourke had hinted at it.

"If I hadn't seen this video, I'd say it was impossible."

Tom shook his head. "Still seems impossible to me."

"Because you're not a fighter." Mark tapped the phone. "She didn't do as much damage to those men, but the skills on display—it's all there."

"You think she's serious about being able to protect my daughter?"

"Let me see it again." Mark took the phone, replaying it four more times before passing it back. "That's not luck. It's uncanny. You can't do that unless you fight like a motherfucker on fire."

"And your gut?" Tom asked. "What's it say about her?"

"She's dangerous."

"To Naomi?"

Mark considered it. "To anyone who fucks with her, I'd say."

~*~

After staying long enough to see Denise, it was nearly morning when Naomi left the hospital with her dad, Mark tailing them in his car. Emotionally winded and raw, she was blindsided by her dad's question.

"Where'd your tiny bodyguard go?"

"The one stricken from the book of my companions?" Naomi smirked at her dad's faux-innocent expression. "She... disappeared."

"Going out on a limb: I don't think I scared her off."

"She's just not well-versed on finer points of etiquette." Naomi settled tiredly back into her seat. "Someone feels guilty for yelling, huh?"

"She's not stricken from any books yet. Consider it a suspended sentence, eventually lifted for good behavior. She's actually got no parents, though?"

"I didn't know that about her." *Suspected it, though.*

"Not a Madison girl?"

"Does she *look* like one?"

He laughed. "Sadly, no. Your school's got a stick up its butt."

She rolled her eyes. "I thought you loved all things private, Daddy."

"I love that my yelling at Madison feels more effective, what with all the money I give to the people I'm yelling at."

"She's Parker-Freemont."

"So she's from the Docks. Maybe from abroad, like your mother."

"Maybe. English isn't her first language—she speaks it fine, but she's got no idea how to use most idioms." *Or currency.* "She's not talkative. But the things she says—I don't know, they're blunt and insightful." Talking about her made Naomi smile. "She's just... interesting, I guess."

"Like how?"

She hadn't gotten farther than "interesting" and struggled with why. "Did you know she dances better than anyone I've ever seen? That includes all those ballets you and Mom took me to when I went through that phase. It's in every step she takes. And she knows things about the world—I don't know, like she really sees it. In ways I can't. But other times, she's got no clue, and whenever she's not teaching me something new, I'm teaching her." Naomi clicked her mouth shut when she realized she was rambling. Then: "Is that weird?"

"Reminds me of your mother." Dad smiled. "Smartest woman I ever met—but God, that dark sense of humor got her into trouble. We were at a faculty Christmas party at Graystone when we first dated, and she brought me along—just a lunkhead undergraduate she was scandalously dating. I'm ex-military and there on an Army scholarship, so she introduces me to her very-Marxist dean with, 'Here is Tom Bradford. He shoots Communists, but don't worry, only Soviet ones sent to Haiti and paid by the Kremlin to fight. You are not paid to support Communists, you do it for free, so Tom probably won't shoot you.' "

Naomi chortled, but her mom had told it slightly differently one New Year's after drinking too much wine. Instead of introducing her dad by name, she'd called him "a handsome student I am sleeping with." Glancing at Dad, she asked, "Was this the same dean whose kids she complimented?"

He laughed. "Yeah. First time she met him, she looked at the pictures on his desk and said, 'Your children are beautiful in America. Not like our children in the Soviet Empire, because they are starving.' "

Mom's droll cynicism was the source of many a family legend, particularly when her parents had first gotten to know each other. Naomi wondered if those bumpy misunderstandings were part of what she liked about Ryn.

"Will I see Ryn again?" Dad asked.

"I hope so." She felt a tug at her heart. "Oh no—I still don't know how to get a hold of her."

"Can't call her?"

"She's completely off the grid. No phone, no parents—I don't even know her last name!"

"Relax. The same thing happened the first time I met your mom. Remember, she wasn't entirely legal then, so she didn't exactly pass out her information."

"What did you do?"

"Just kept going back to the café where I saw her working on her dissertation. Told myself, 'If I run into her again, it's meant to be.' Have a feeling you'll meet Ryn again."

~*~

Kessler woke from a dead sleep and answered the ringing phone.

"It's me," O'Rourke said. "Got a break in the case."

"What time is it?"

"About five in the morning."

"God Almighty." *Can we go back to him being one of those kinds of cop? Those kind sleep.*

"Don't worry. There's a Denny's nearby. It'll be open."

"Because that's what I was worried about."

"Meet me at the one on Eighth and Lincoln."

O'Rourke had coffee waiting when he arrived, but the world's unhealthiest detective didn't appear the least bit run down. He had a tower of books, including one on child soldiers, and that pinched Kessler's stomach. O'Rourke's tablet was open to a martial-arts webpage and he was looking at video of various moves.

"That a library book?" Kessler asked.

"City librarian gave me keys. I come and go; leave them notes on what I took. Comes in handy if you need a textbook at midnight. Be surprised how much that happens to me."

"Less and less surprised every day." Kessler drained half his mug in one long pull.

"Take a look at this." O'Rourke slid the tablet over and Kessler watched Ryn beat down two gangbangers and scare the piss out of a third. She used the moves he'd always suspected she knew. The vise on his gut tightened.

"Those guys are Black Sea mafia?" he asked.

"The punks are. The girl, though—the one rolling them like they owed her lunch money. What do you make of her?"

Damn it. "What do you mean?"

"Her name's Ryn. Fits my theory of a crazed stalker who turned on Banich. She's latched onto the Bradford girl, and she broke those two guys—not as bad as Banich, but it proves she *could*. Right body type for the images you pulled, too."

"Except she's got no internet access and her only contact with Banich was of the hand-to-hand variety," Kessler said.

"Wait. You had this lead?" O'Rourke's shaggy eyebrows lowered in anger.

"I ran it down." Kessler sighed. "I know Ryn, her M.O., and her caseworker—professionally and, uh, personally. We suspect she was following Banich and happened on Naomi Bradford as a result—she's too antisocial to conspire, too easily set off by abusers to fraternize with one.

"I was on the fence about telling you. My concern is that the media's already on a witch hunt against the mentally ill, thanks to Banich. The same trust-fund implosion that put him on the street put Ryn there too. The narrative right now is, 'Crazy people are everywhere, lock them up.' We throw Ryn into that meat grinder, she'll get kicked back into the system. For good."

"Christ. Fine, whatever, but you keep me in the fucking loop."

"Yeah, I get it. You're the lead."

"Bullshit. I'm your partner."

Kessler narrowed his eyes. *Didn't you assume I was an incompetent meathead last week?*

"Look, you might not be as dumb as I thought." O'Rourke frowned. "Most guys who say, 'I'm not book smart, I'm street smart,' *might* be smart as the bricks they paved the street with. You? You're bright, you actually get people, you do good legwork, and you'll meet me at ungodly hours to go over casework. So, sure: partner."

"You don't have a lot of friends, do you?" Kessler asked, folding his arms.

"I got a bad track record with hero cops. I'm judgmental—but that's what cops do. We judge. The good ones, though, know when to eat crow."

"You going to give me hell for holding back the info on Ryn?"

"Not if you're sure this girl's safe. You vouching for her?"

"She's not safe. But she's not dangerous to the Bradford girl. I know her because my unit pulled her out of a wilderness people aren't supposed to survive in, and let's just say nothing on that video surprises me. I'm sure she's got blood on her hands, but when we found her she'd been beaten and tortured almost to the point of death. She hates abusers. Hunting down Banich is exactly like her."

"So, a vigilante?"

"Sure."

"Not exactly legal to hunt people down," O'Rourke grumped.

"But she pounced on him after he went for the girl. If Ryn were anyone else, we'd be giving her a medal. With her mental-health record, and the public scared, she'd get kicked back into the system and buried."

"Not necessarily."

"Look me in the eye and tell me what she did was wrong."

"Why's she with the Bradford girl if she's antisocial?"

"Seems to agree about Banich having accomplices. Wants to keep the girl safe; might be hunting the accomplices too."

O'Rourke nodded. "How's she know about them?"

He sighed. *There's no way to explain this that doesn't make me look crazy, or Ryn guilty.* "She knows things. Said it creeps up from dark corners, or whatever, and that there's between four and six of them. Thinks they're... ghosts. Somehow."

Surprisingly, O'Rourke just nodded.

Staring, Kessler asked, "You believe her?"

"You don't?"

Was it a trick question? A test? He said nothing.

"It's a weird city. Don't worry about it." O'Rourke leaned in. "Black binder for the ghosts, and how Ryn figured it out. The number of assailants is worthwhile data, though."

"And what do we do about Ryn?"

"She's not a conspirator. Now that I've got your read on her, that look on her face during the video tells me all I needed to know. She's not hurting those men to get closer to the Bradford girl. Hate that pure and clean isn't instrumental."

"You sound impressed."

"I tell people my idol's Sherlock Holmes, but not really. I didn't read Arthur Conan Doyle as a kid. I read Batman."

Kessler snorted. "You're jealous of her."

"Incredibly."

CHAPTER ELEVEN
Namaste

Every darkfall, Ryn shadowed Naomi by rooftop. She coasted on the metro and listened to the auburn-haired girl's heart through aluminum. She lay supine on Naomi's pebbled shingles, hearing the tosses and gasps brought on by nightmares. When the brassy sun rose, Ryn trailed on the street, learning to obscure herself in the city's flow of human bodies.

Weeks passed with no trace of asura. Ms. Cross complained that Ryn had not signed into her group home at night and about absences from school.

The moon waxed fuller each night and teased the blackest regions of Ryn's mind. Its light prickled her skin, her humming nerves attuned to the flutter of moth wings in the sky. On the night the moon burned its roundest, Naomi went ice skating in the city with Elli and Denise.

Ryn eased through the crowd, raw and moon-sick with bedlam pounding in her chest. Danger filled the air like fog, with Naomi at its epicenter, yet she scented no asura. All she smelled was aggression and sex from a slouching male who sat rinkside and stared too hard at little girls, always from the corners of his eyes.

He kept a cup of hot drink in his hands, another beside him as bait. A predator. He hunted, but not so well as Ryn. Though dull human eyes skipped over him, he stuck out to her, and in that instant they were the only two beings in the world. There was no asura in him, though. Was he the source of the danger Ryn sensed?

He distracted Ryn from hiding herself.

"Hey! *Hey!*"

The familiar voice snapped Ryn's gaze to attention: Naomi coasted across the rink to the wall where she stood. The doe-ish girl wore a too-thick, teal coat and a poofy hat and scarf that made her seem tiny even though she stood a head taller.

"You're here!" Her enthusiasm lit a fire in Ryn; her smile took away the air. "I was afraid I'd never see you again."

"You see me now." The moon amplified the pounding of Ryn's heart, and some enigmatic magnetism drew her in while at once making it impossible to look Naomi in the eye.

"Tell me where you live. Please?"

This female's power over her was such that she feared Naomi coming to find her; she could only barely stand to feel these things on her own terms and from the safety of the shadows. "Why do you want to know?"

"So I can get in touch. Where do you stay?"

"Roosevelt Place." *Why did I tell her? The moon is making me a fool.*

"Does Roosevelt Place have a phone?"

This must end. I am a monster and will not be hemmed in by the glances of a mortal girl. "Do you need something from me?" she growled.

Naomi's face fell and Ryn's heart dropped with it.

She'd said the words wrong, and moon sickness made her want to shrink. She examined her fingers, realizing with horror that somewhere along the way Naomi had been stitched into her—what the girl felt, Ryn did too. It took only a glance for the magic to happen, a power as surely as the basilisk's.

"You okay?" Naomi asked.

"Was that a frown?"

"I guess."

"I don't like them."

"I'm all done. See?" She pointed.

But Ryn's gaze was fastened to her hands.

So Naomi crouched and set her chin between Ryn's hands, peering up, startling the monster. "I've waited weeks to see you and I'm excited," said her friend. "I've wanted to talk to you like eighteen times a day, and then here you are—out of nowhere. Sorry if I come on strong, but in my defense, you totally knew that about me ever since the mall. Want to skate?"

Dozens of humans sailed effortlessly atop sleek ice, and at the sight Ryn quivered. She could think of nothing she'd rather do than fly on ice. Besides, her intuition wanted her close to Naomi. Checking, she ensured the child predator hadn't moved and nodded. "I would like that."

"I'll rent your skates for an address." She leaned in conspiratorially. "Though I'll tell you a secret." She spoke in a whisper that Ryn felt brush against her: "I like you enough that you could bargain me down, if you really don't want me to know where you live."

It was not in Ryn to deny her friend; not when she'd whispered so sweetly. "Your bargain is fair." She told her the address and Naomi went through one of those human gestures with a vendor, trading paper moneys for skates. It was done with exhausting precision, counting them out, being handed a few back because it was not the exact right amount. Their obsession depressed and amused Ryn at once.

Finally, Naomi passed her the skates. "These look your size."

The skates were inflexible and Ryn missed her worn-down tennis shoes or, better still, the sensation of rock and snow underfoot. But the moment blades touched ice, Ryn sensed the potential velocity within them.

"Have you skated before?" Naomi asked.

"No."

"It's easy. I'll show you."

Ryn remembered that humans were supposed to be clumsy animals, and she used her social camouflage honed in gym class. Holding on to the rail, examining one of the less adept skaters in the rink, she mimicked a tremor up her calf. But her camouflage felt dishonest here.

Naomi's hand clapped onto Ryn's elbow. "Easy. I've got you." With the moon so high and bright, she could feel the girl's fingertips, her pulse, almost as if it were skin-to-skin. It made Ryn want things, and she didn't know what. "Come on, with me." Naomi drew her off the wall, into the stream of people.

Ice flowed past her feet and the cool slice of blades over the frosty sheet slaked Ryn in a deep place. Her friend spun and skated backward, taking Ryn's hands in hers to guide, and with her face and its basilisk's magic right there, the monster became very interested in the ice at her feet.

"Don't look down," Naomi scolded. "Eyes forward."

Ryn couldn't resist; the magic was in her everything, even her voice.

"There, like that." And she was rewarded with a smile— such a smile, one that taught Ryn delight.

Yet in holding eye contact the feeling intensified, jolting from Naomi through Ryn until she felt her ears and cheeks flush with heat. A crinkle knit Naomi's brow and then she blushed too, turned away, and skated with just one hand in Ryn's. "I think you're getting it."

"Yes." Ryn allowed her feet to move more naturally, easing into clean strokes that propelled her side by side with the other girl. Through the static of cool air and the riot of full-moon sensation, she could feel the shape of her friend's body. It distracted her.

But then a cool dread pooled in her stomach.

Danger. It prickled the fine hairs on the back of her neck, but she didn't know from where it would come.

~*~

Casper Owens had slipped into the office and cleared off the desk, pushing it near the window so that he had something to lie prone across. It was not flush to the wall, but set back far enough that he could balance his Winchester away from the cracked-open window facing the skating rink.

He lit a cigarette to steady his nerves, smoking, ashing into someone's coffee mug.

Through the scope, he observed the rink. It sat in a gap between buildings a city block away. Fast-moving revelers zoomed across the lens and he struggled to pick out Naomi Bradford.

~*~

The moment stretched, Ryn scenting and listening, finding no obvious threat. Yet the danger was there, unsprung.

Denise broke between them and shattered the tension of

the moment. "I'd say I'm surprised to see Ryn here, but there's a full moon. Seems somehow appropriate you'd show up."

She bristled.

"Relax! So testy. I'll keep my claws to myself if you do."

"She's lying about that," Naomi said. "But I do think she had something to say." She shot Denise a look that communicated something without words.

Denise rolled her eyes, retrieving a velvet case from her jacket. "*Here.*" She thrust it at Ryn, who took it cautiously and sniffed it. "God, it's a gift, just open it, dumbass."

"Gift?"

"Sure. It's what people who suck at nice words do to make vaguely apologetic gestures. Don't read anything into it, it's just to make *me* feel better, okay?"

Denise was better at explaining human customs than anyone else Ryn had met.

"Did that burn so badly?" Naomi asked.

"Right down to my soul," Denise said.

The box contained sunglasses with blue-tinted lenses and elegant, wire frames. Though the lenses were smaller, the side shields would protect her eyes from view.

"They'll make you look less like you're casing government buildings." Denise tapped one lens. "If you're hanging out with us, I'd like it to be with a modicum of style." She hmmed softly and went to touch Ryn's hoodie. "How attached to this are you?"

Ryn recoiled. "As spirit and flesh."

"Unfortunate."

"Try them on," Naomi encouraged.

Ryn changed glasses by shifting her face down to hide her gaze. They tinged the world blue, the color not too different from her irises.

Denise examined them. "Just your color."

Does she remember my eyes?

"I can see more of your face." Naomi reached out to straighten the glasses, and the sheer liberty taken in the act somehow thrilled—no one before had dared. "You're pretty and now it shows."

Her smile was too spontaneous to stop.

"Holy shit, I made an emo girl smile." Denise shook her

head. "Guess my karma's balanced." She skated away, leaving Ryn to feel abandoned under Naomi's scrutiny.

"You should smile more," her friend said.

"It's odd."

Naomi laughed. "Looks odd on you, but not bad. You know, I think you might have won over Denise in just about record time. She normally takes months."

"Won?"

"That's what a fully 'won over' Denise is like. The wild Madison brat, you see, expresses her affections through complex social signaling. Once she's been reduced to playful snark and taken an interest in your wardrobe, it means you're invited to the tribe."

Now it made sense. Why couldn't humans always be so succinct?

"How about it?" Naomi leaned closer in a way that made a loose tangle of hair dance against her cheek. "Want to spend more time together?"

Though excitement leapt in Ryn's chest, she bit it down before she could too reflexively nod. *Of course, with days lasting longer, there's strategic sense to it...* She cleared her throat. "Very well."

~*~

Too far, Casper thought.

He hadn't been told the shot was five hundred yards—his benefactors had only texted him the vantage point an hour ago. If he'd known, he'd have asked for a larger rifle. His favorite .308 could bring down a bear at two hundred yards, but the cartridges were packed for efficiency, and outside of 250 yards there wasn't enough powder to give the round punch. It would go rainbow-arced and wide.

True, in the military he'd used the same gun to shoot at commies at seven hundred yards, but this wasn't a communist: it was a seventeen-year-old girl. He didn't want a kneecap or a gut wound, he didn't want her to die after a half-hour of bleeding out. He wanted it clean—it had to be humane. Casper had a girl about that age and, necessary though this was, he'd never sleep right again if she died screaming.

And it was necessary, because her father was the Antichrist. Casper had read the prophecies, seen the scripts with his own eyes at the anti-Bradford site. The benefactors had shared photos of the ancient scrolls found in a Jerusalem dig site, but the mainstream media never talked about them because they detailed the End of Days, and the MSM was full of atheists.

Tom Bradford couldn't be killed by normal means. His black heart beat in the ribcage of his own daughter, carried beside her own.

A stark choice: Kill Naomi Bradford or let the whole world burn.

Including his daughter.

~*~

They skated a wide circuit through the rink, the din of voices softened by an envelope of quiet that held them both, punctuated only by Naomi's intermittent talk of classes. She loved them all except government, since her teacher singled her out for being the daughter of a senator.

Listening, Ryn tracked the crowd; the air still held a dark energy, and while she smelled no asura, she sensed their meddling.

Naomi changed the subject to those boys from the Nine Lives, so Ryn focused on locating the source of danger—but it was still a fog, not yet sharpened into a threat she could dispense with.

"So do you want to?" Naomi asked.

Ryn's attention snapped back. "What?"

"Go on a date. Wes has been asking about you, and Horatio invited me out. So a double date, technically."

Her nose crinkled. "A mating ritual?"

Naomi laughed. "You don't have to mate, I promise. It's just to figure out if you two like each other."

"I know already who I like."

"Who?" She came closer then, as though it were a secret.

But it wasn't. "My psychiatrist."

"Holy *crap*, your therapist? Um, not judging, sorry. Is he... handsome?"

"She smells of rose water."

Naomi's cheeks turned slightly pink.

"I like you too."

The pink bloomed further across the bridge of her nose.

"As well a detective named David Kessler and my room-mate, Susan. Wes is acceptable. I don't want to kill him."

Now she was tittering, the fits shaking her shoulders. "*No*, God, I didn't mean who you *like*. I mean... well, you know."

I do not.

"Who you want to go *out* with."

Ryn opened her mouth to speak.

"Don't you dare tell me you go 'outside' with your thera-pist."

Now she didn't know what to say.

"I don't mean outside. I mean—geez, you're going to make me spell it out for you, aren't you? Dating is about romance. They have that where you're from, don't they?"

"So it *is* a mating ritual."

Exasperated, Naomi threw her head back. "*Fine*. But it's one that doesn't have to include mating at the end if you don't want."

Ryn had seen humans mate, but from the dark beyond their campfires their rituals always seemed hopelessly com-plex and demeaning for all parties. In principle, the silly dances served their purpose, but she'd never wanted to in-volve herself. Realizing Naomi *did* want that, she felt an ab-rupt surge of anxiety. "How do you want it to end?"

"I don't know," she said, pinking again and glancing away. "Maybe a kiss."

An image of Naomi's mouth joined with Horatio's heated Ryn's blood. "You can't," she sputtered.

"Okay, fine." Naomi beamed. "I will lay down the law with the boys and make sure they know it will be utterly chaste. No mating, no kisses. Will you go then?"

Again, it was hard to tell her no. "When?"

"I'll set it up, but probably not for a few weeks at least. Ho-ratio's out of town. Now that I've got you roped in, how about we celebrate with some hot chocolate? I'll be right back." Na-omi skated off and Ryn shivered in the void left behind.

She waited at the wall and kept an eye on the auburn-haired female, who waited in line. There was only a distance of forty-odd feet to cross, should the noose tighten.

Denise skated over again. "I heard you two."

Ryn ignored the comment, unwaveringly focused on her ward. Naomi briefly caught her gaze from the line and smiled, which made the corners of her own mouth twitch in sympathy.

"I guarantee you won't 'mate' with Wes."

Truth.

"Because you'd rather with Naomi."

"No." Her cheeks blazed at the lie, and she shook her head to cast off the fleeting impression of her mouth pressed into Naomi's. Yet the image was so searing it burnt Ryn in places deeper than she'd believed her nerves could root.

"God, you're hopeless." Denise leaned into the railing, silent as her hands twisted into knots. "Listen, about the other night." Yet for several moments she just stared at a featureless spot on the ground. "People don't like me, as a rule. I come on strong and bite too hard."

"So do tigers."

"I know, right? And everyone loves tigers, but they don't like it when *girls* are mean—that's somehow defective. At least you understand that much."

She did.

"I'm a tiger because Naomi is very much not. See, we grew up together and I admit I might sometimes be the tiniest bit protective. I scratch people I don't think are good for her, and because she doesn't know how vulnerable her big, dumb heart makes her."

"You guard her."

"Wouldn't you?"

Ryn nodded, again satisfied with Denise's explanations.

"Here's where it gets weird, though. I am not Naomi, and there's part of me that's wild and stupid and wants to be that way. Maybe I'm just naturally contrarian, or maybe Naomi drives me so crazy with her goddamn soul of pure white light that I need to introduce some bad into the picture. Like a kid bouncing on the ice, yelling, 'It's okay! Come out and play, it's really thick!' And the way she looks at me, like it's *not* okay to be out there—makes me want to be on the ice more than anything."

"Children shouldn't play on ice. They're stupid and fragile."

"Well put. And the other night at the Nine Lives? I was stupid. The ice was thin, I fell through, and you pulled me out. Maybe Naomi's right and I should just stick with her from now on."

"No. You're not her."

"Then what do you suggest?"

"Break the rules better." Ryn thought on it a moment. "Whether you break or obey a rule, if you don't understand the rule, you're not a person. You're a..." She had no word for it. "A thing. A thing that only does what it's allowed. Not free. A..."

"A cog. Like in a machine?"

"Yes. That. A working cog is better than a broken one, but still just a cog." Ryn glanced at Denise. "Break a rule because you understand it, though, and you are no longer a cog. You become a god."

"O-kay." She seemed to suck on the idea. "What do you call it when you're halfway between a cog and god?"

"Humanity."

Denise nodded. "Want to know something about Naomi?"

Always. She was greedy for more, for anything, and that terrified her.

"When she came to my hospital room, I expected the most elaborate 'I told you so' of all time. Never happened. There's hugging and crying, but no lecture. I even tried, masochist that I am, to bait her. 'Oh Naomi, If only I'd listened to you from the start.'

"She doesn't nibble. She says: '*No.* If only those men hadn't tried to rape you. If only the world weren't full of scumbags ready to pounce on the first sign of weakness.' I don't think there's anything evil in her. You need to understand that about her—that, and even after she said those things to *me*, the hypocrite blames herself for the whole night."

Ryn frowned.

"Yeah, and girls like that—who blame themselves first— they don't do well in relationships with selfish people. They don't know what they're owed. They get hurt and then blame themselves for standing in the way of his fist. She's a good kid, but goodness makes you vulnerable."

Now Ryn understood. "So you will protect her." *From me. The monster.*

"Oh yes." Denise leaned in. "But I'm not telling you to scram; I'm telling you not to hurt her. My best friend is precious fucking treasure. Remember that." Tilting back to her original posture, she added, "Not that you have a shot, because if she were gay she'd have obviously hit on *me* by now." Clearing her throat, she added, "But then again..."

Ryn paid close attention.

"Naomi's good with people and usually sees straight through them. Understands things she shouldn't, weird things, things a princess shouldn't understand. Told me she knew right away at the food court that you'd seen 'violence.' How does a senator's daughter from the Gardens possibly intuit that? But she did." Denise shrugged. "Except there's a blind spot when it comes to... a lot of you-related things. You confuse her, you drive her up the wall; she talks about you constantly. You *frustrate* her."

Ryn scowled, as none of that sounded remotely good.

"Oh, you don't think that's good news? It is. I told you once, Naomi has her little ten-year plan. Maybe she doesn't get you because you don't fit. You're not from her world. You're the thing she never expected." Denise stretched, positioning herself to skate away. "Someday she'll figure it out, though. It's going to be awkward and, I admit, I really want to see her face if you kiss her. It'll be a disaster—at best, a beautiful disaster."

"I don't kiss," Ryn growled.

"God, you're adorable." Denise pitched her voice into a low purr. "Imagine that soft mouth getting closer to yours—her breath all aflutter; her never-been-kissed eyes staring back at you."

The magic of Naomi's basilisk stare worked even from memory, a surge of prickles covering every inch of Ryn. Her whole body tightened in response. "Stop it," she snarled.

"Horatio's going to kiss her if you don't."

Ryn liked that even less, the way it emptied her of some hope that had been quietly mounting. She leveled a warning glare at Denise, who she knew was toying with her.

"Though he doesn't know Naomi's dirty little secret."

Ryn narrowed her eyes, resigned to wait.

"No one's ever gotten her flowers. The boys at Madison are too chicken. A girl will always remember the first boy who gets her flowers. Even if that boy's a girl."

Then Ryn felt it like a change in air pressure: *Something is wrong. Very wrong.* Her teeth ached and she wanted—no, needed—to find Naomi.

Cutting her way across the ice, she darted for the auburn-haired girl, who drifted back toward Ryn from the concession line, smiling and unaware of what was on its way.

Not even Ryn knew what—only that it was close.

~*~

When Casper's crosshairs first touched Naomi Bradford's chest, the tiny demon swerved into his scope and matched his target's pace exactly. His shaking hands faltered; it was the guardian. The benefactors had told him the Antichrist had a guardian. *I must avoid her. She is Death.*

Each time his crosshairs drifted close to Naomi Bradford, the demon's gaze would pivot and scan the crowd, sometimes the building sides too, her attention dancing closer and closer to him.

She senses me, he realized, an ice-water chill radiating from his heart. *The demon's proof of it—no one's that sharp, not without a piece of Hell on her side. It's true, then. Every word is true.*

The benefactors had put bait out for the demon, so he waited. His thumb clicked off the safety and he tried not to think of his daughter.

~*~

Naomi coasted along with two white styrofoam cups in hand. "Wow, did you miss me already?"

Ryn took her elbow and steered her through the crowd, toward a corner, where the hairs on her neck relaxed. "Here. Stand here."

"Okay, weirdo." There was amusement in Naomi's tone.

Ryn wheeled and sought her foe. She tasted him now. Mortal.

The asura were using mortals.

~*~

"Shit." Casper lowered the rifle's barrel. The guardian demon had taken Naomi Bradford to a part of the rink blocked by trees and a building corner. *I wasn't fast enough. I hesitated, and now the world's fucked.*

He took a finishing pull on his cigarette before grinding it out on the desk. *Stop freaking out—it's not over.* He wiped a sleeve across his sweaty face and scrounged for his phone, texting the benefactors.

A moment later, they replied: "Wait for the bait to do its job."

Casper settled behind his scope and pushed the butt of the cigarette into his ear to muffle the report of a shot he still intended to take. He imagined he was in one of those yoga poses the counselor had told him was "as good as a beer," which was bullshit—but he couldn't drink a beer, so he went through the poses in his mind's eye from first to last, until his heartbeat slowed enough to straighten the bullet's path.

~*~

"Looked like you and Denise had one very intense discussion." Naomi settled into the wall, passing a steaming cup of dark liquid to Ryn. "What about?"

"Nothing." With her intuition as guide, Ryn now guessed a sniper. She had him triangulated, and Naomi tucked safely away.

"So you talked about me." Naomi held her cup between both hands, steam rising to touch her pretty face.

The heat from Ryn's own cup calmed her riotous pulse and she inhaled the savory aroma of cocoa bean and sugar blended together. *She is safe for now.* "How do you do that?"

"Do what?"

"Know things—things I haven't told you."

"People talk in layers." Naomi sipped, her mouth a soft

pink contrast to her pale skin. Her lips were sensitive to the heat, fascinating in how gingerly she applied them to the rim. "What we say is only the top layer. Guess I'm more interested in the stuff underneath." She looked at Ryn then, in a curious way that made the monster realize she'd been staring too hard.

She snapped her gaze down and shielded herself by drinking from her own cup.

Something happened in Ryn's mouth that had never happened before and her body responded with a shudder. She drank again, more deeply, tipping the cup back as sweet, rich flavor coated her insides. "What is this?" *Witchcraft, surely.*

"You've never had chocolate? Hey! Careful, you'll burn yourself!"

Ryn finished it. "That..." She inhaled the inside of the empty cup, eyes shut. "That is the best thing I've ever had."

Naomi shook her head in amazement. "Welcome to civilization. You seriously don't have chocolate where you're from?"

"Seen it before. Smelled it." But it had been foreign and different. "I prefer the old things."

Naomi eyed the emptied cup. "Except for chocolate and ice skating, apparently."

And you.

"Want me to grab you another?"

Ryn shook her head hard. *No. Stay and do not move.* "The memory suffices." The heat was still in her center, the taste on her lips.

"What color are your eyes?" Naomi asked, leaning abruptly closer.

Ryn leaned away. "Why?"

"I'm trying to imagine you without your glasses."

"*Why?*"

"Humor me."

Ryn fidgeted, feeling somehow chased; more perversely, as though she wanted to be caught. "My irises are blue."

"And your glasses protect you, don't they?"

"How did you know?"

Naomi grinned. "Layers, remember?" Then she grew more serious. "I get the feeling you hide a lot—that you have to, to blend in. If you ever want to stop hiding from me, though... I'd like that."

Ryn had no answer to give. As powerful as Naomi's stare was, Ryn's eyes contained the dark secret of the universe—that storybook nightmares were real and made flesh and walked hungry through the world. If she tore off her person mask, everything would change.

"Did someone scar your eyes?"

My eyes would scar you.

Restless, Naomi finished her hot chocolate. "I guess it was really bad where you're from."

"It's bad here." Ryn didn't understand why no one saw that. "Men tried to rape your friend. Others torment a girl in my school for mating too many males; they sneer at me for mating none at all. Another mated a girl too small to stop him, until she killed herself. Where I am from, predators are not so cruel." Or if they were, they met her and didn't remain predators for long.

Naomi's face went lax, as though Ryn's words knocked all the feelings out of her. "What about you? Did someone—"

A snarl peeled the corner of Ryn's mouth, but she twisted her face from Naomi to disguise her fangs, and perhaps a corner of a dark memory buried now for eighteen months. "No."

Naomi made no answer and that weighed heavily on Ryn. She felt exposed, and Naomi didn't rush in with a new topic.

It reminded her of the child predator and she glanced at the bench.

It was vacant. Ryn jolted in that direction. "Stay here."

"What? Why?"

"*Do not move.*" Ryn skated into the crowd and scanned it. Bodies crisscrossed her field of vision, but she let the sound, scent, the heartbeats and the hormonal odors traffic through her brain. She skated for the bench and then past it, following a ribbon of chemical arousal.

She realized Naomi hadn't listened. The warm-hearted female pursued, straight into the path of danger. "No." Ryn pivoted in a spray of ice flakes, terror rolling through her as Naomi approached her, a confused smile on her face, as if to ask, *What? Why do you look so frightened?*

~*~

The demon took the bait. The benefactors' other man on the ground—the pervert Casper wished he could shoot instead—drew the guardian away and lured out the Bradford girl. He made the final adjustment to his scope for the crosswind.

Five hundred yards. Ten-mile-per-hour crosswind, partly blocked by buildings. To the right of her heart. Past her guardian demon. Not impossible, but...

He should have asked for a larger rifle.

What if I miss? The crowd...

Casper prayed to God that he didn't kill a child.

His crosshairs stroked Naomi Bradford's slender throat, then dipped to her heart.

"Namaste." He fired.

~*~

Ryn gripped Naomi's arm and tugged her close. She spun and let the bullet strike the cup of her hand. The only sound was a muffled crack five hundred yards away that the humans didn't hear, a zip, and the soft spank of jacketed lead against her unbreakable palm. She held the hot slug and steered Naomi through the crowd.

"Hey, easy," Naomi said, shrugging off Ryn's hand. "Your grip's like iron."

She kept between the distant window and Naomi, but the danger had abated—the danger to Naomi, at least. She still smelled the child predator.

~*~

Her hand. Casper lifted his face from the rifle. *She caught the bullet. In her hand. She didn't even know where I was until I fired.* How could anything move like that?

He slid off the desk and ripped his rifle's carrying pack open. One-handed, he texted, "It's over. Guardian spotted me. Bugging out. Will try again later."

And then: "DEFINITELY need bigger gun."

At least the demon will eat the pervert, he decided.

~*~

They wove through the crowd, Ryn only as far in the lead as she dared with a shooter still out there, albeit no longer at the open window.

Through the shifting skaters, she spotted the predator. His wide bottom and tapered shoulders made him an ungainly triangle, and he chatted with a dark-skinned child perched on the rink's wall, her hot chocolate held between two blue mittens. The child kicked her feet playfully. When the predator brushed her hair, Ryn tasted copper from her own bitten lip.

She scraped to a stop and dusted his ankles with ice, glaring up at him, carefully considering her options. *Do not break him in front of the child. Unless you must.*

Naomi hit the wall behind her, scooting nearer with one hand on the rail. "Hello," she said to the child before Ryn could challenge the predator to battle. "Is this your daddy?"

"No, I'm lost," the girl announced, more from excitement than fear. "This is Dylan. He had an extra hot chocolate."

"That's right." Dylan's smile was wrong. Ryn could only tell because, unlike Naomi's, it never touched the other parts of his face.

"Well, my name is Naomi. This is my friend Ryn. Ryn is *really* good at finding people. I'll bet she could help you find your mommy or daddy."

"But I get to help, right?" the girl asked. "I'm Amanda." She waved at Ryn.

Ryn didn't know what to say or do around children. They were stuck in between being monkeys and people. She glanced up at Dylan, whom she knew precisely what to do with.

Naomi skirted around him, though, and interposed herself between Dylan and Amanda, catching the predator's gaze with her own. "Nice to meet you too. Naomi Bradford."

"Dylan," he said, his voice too soft.

"Dylan what?" Naomi's face lit with cheer and Ryn instantly wanted to break one of Dylan's legs and drag Naomi out of his orbit.

"Um. Dylan Crane."

"Give me just one second, Dylan." Naomi tapped on her phone, glanced over at the child, and added, "That's a cute jacket, Amanda. Where'd you get it?"

"Santa," she said.

"He did a good job with that." Her finger flicked the screen.

"Santa is *way* better at picking out clothes than Daddy. I think Santa's a girl. She picks clothes like Mommy."

"Dylan Crane." Naomi skimmed her screen. "You live over on Akron Avenue?"

"Um." Dylan rubbed the back of his scalp and looked all around him.

"Because this website says you live there." She presented her phone to Dylan. Ryn could see his picture, address, and a block of bulleted text on the website.

"Hey. I'm allowed to be here," he said defensively.

"Sure. But maybe your parole officer doesn't want you buying hot chocolate for young girls?"

"I was just helping. I'm leaving anyway." He skated away, stumbling on his way toward the exit.

"Why's Dylan scared?" Amanda asked.

"You shouldn't talk to strangers." Naomi helped Amanda to the ice and took her hand. They skated into the circuit of people, scanning for her parents.

"You're strangers," Amanda said.

"True. Don't trust us. We're probably Russian spies." Then, in Russian, she said, "I'm really glad my friend spotted you. I don't think you understand the trouble you were in, little one."

"She does not," Ryn said, also in Russian. Something about what Ryn said startled Naomi and Ryn wondered if it was offensive.

"You don't *look* like spies," Amanda said.

"That's what makes us such good spies." Naomi winked.

"Da." Lying to children was actually kind of amusing, since they would believe anything, even from Ryn. Maybe that was why humans liked them.

"Was Dylan bad?" Amanda asked.

"Yes," Naomi said.

"He didn't seem bad. He was nice."

Naomi's tone became serious. "That's why he was so good at being a bad man."

They found a middle-aged man and woman in the midst of a frantic search through the crowd of children at the concession stand. Naomi guided Amanda over. The father drew his girl into a crushing embrace, the mother hugging Naomi. After they spoke a moment, Naomi showed them her phone and they went wide-eyed. The woman cried. The man mashed numbers into his phone. Ryn watched and thought it would have been simpler to break Dylan's limbs.

Naomi skated back. "That was terrifying. What were you going to do to that guy? How did you see that from across the rink? And Denise. And all of the stuff you told me. How?"

Ryn shrugged. *He was a distraction,* she realized. The asura had put both the sniper and predator in play. *Clever.*

"I don't get you. You can't figure out dating, but you can sniff out a pedophile or a rapist from eighty feet away. You beat up a guy who was like three times your size. You speak some kind of crazy old-fashioned Russian." Softer, she asked, "Who *are* you?"

"All those things and many others." But Ryn could tell it wasn't what Naomi wanted. She wanted a label, a category, but the monster was too old, too large for those things.

So she edged away from Naomi, coasting backward on the ice. With the danger passed, the moon high, and the power in the auburn-haired girl's eyes raging through her, she whispered, "I must go."

"Wait! I don't understand—Ryn! You're skating backward." She glided quickly after. "You've been skating twenty minutes and... you're already better at it than anyone I know. I don't understand. Who are you?"

"You know more than you should." *More than any other mortal has,* she realized, shivering—and turned to flee. She sped from Naomi, hopped over the rink's wall and kicked off her skates, exchanging them for shoes. In an instant she was fading into the crowd while sliding them on, casting a final glance back.

Behind her, Naomi stood still on the ice and only watched, mouthing words she couldn't expect Ryn to hear, but which electrified the blood: "I don't understand yet—but I will."

CHAPTER TWELVE
Just Friends

That night Ryn listened to the wild pump of Naomi's heart from the shadows of her rooftop. A nightmare dragged the teenager under black waves. Her panic sweated into the sheets and her thrashing transformed the covers into knots, pinning her arms. Each terrified moan cut Ryn—brutal cuts, a novel pain inflicted on the only pink and uncallused part of her heart.

No knife was sharper than her friend's soft plea of "no, stop." This new pain was felt in sympathy for another, allowing no defense. The faintest whimper upset the immortal's patience and set her to pacing.

And how much worse would the nightmares be if Naomi knew the truth? An asura cabal using humans could attack from almost anywhere: any mortal they could buy, blackmail, or deceive might become their instrument.

Ryn rolled the deformed rifle slug across her palm and didn't think too carefully about what it would have done to a wet, mortal body like Naomi's—how its speed and hardness would crack human bone like soft wood, shred skin and muscle, how so much of Naomi's soul depended upon the preservation of that fibrous mass behind her eyes. Ryn had seen brains cleaved in two, had seen them slip out large fissures in the skull and smear against stone. Those humans didn't have heads one iota less durable than Naomi's.

And so that became another thing she didn't think too carefully about.

Instead, she scouted widely and thoroughly, yet always keeping close enough to her ward to sense imminent danger. She no longer attended school or spent time in her group home, and left Ms. Cross's increasingly terse phone messages unanswered.

She stayed awake even on the new moon, all the way through a freezing rain that drove like needles and soaked through every part of her. Too tired to move, she perched like a gargoyle on Naomi's rooftop and waited for asura, for mortals, for any kind of malice to show itself. A cold river ran between her shoulder blades, a waterfall poured off the point of her jaw. The wet worked between fingers, toes, until no part of her was dry.

When the wind struck, the wet froze to ice. It encased her in glittering crystal and the rain turned to snow, which piled atop her, layer by heavy layer. Her cloak became a stiff burrow and Ryn tried her best not to drowse.

At the first touch of dawn on her forehead, the weariness of the moonless night lifted. Ryn moved and snow shed from her shoulders in great mounds. Her ice encasement cracked and slid off her in sheets as she stood. Her fingers flexed, released, and she listened to Naomi rouse with a start from another nightmare.

And throughout the day, still no sign of asura or their mortals.

Ryn could keep this up forever, but she worried if she didn't find the asura first, they would prod her defenses until a gap was laid bare.

~*~

"I understand," Casper Owens told his ex-wife over the phone. "I'm working on it. The check's literally in my hand." He polished the barrel of a custom rifle smuggled to his cookie-cutter motel room by benefactors he'd never met. Its mysterious black metal was too cold to the touch—too cold and too dark—and it was longer by half than anything he'd ever fired. He didn't recognize the design; there was no manufacturer's stamp, just stenciled silver scribbles in a bizarre language, and though he didn't understand the words, they made him queasy.

"I swear, I'm putting it in the envelope now." Casper lifted the weighty scope, disconcerted at the way a low-frequency hum emanating from the metal lifted the fine hairs on his arms when he touched it. "Take a picture? I don't have a smart phone anymore, I can't. Can I please just talk to our daughter?"

The line went dead. *Figures.* Frustrated, he set the scope on his desk and shut his eyes, trying to remember what Julia's voice sounded like. He'd give anything to hear it again; once he was finished, he never would. He'd be dead or incarcerated for life, and had no illusions that Julia would visit him in prison—she'd disown him, change her name, and pray her new friends never asked about her father. If they asked, she'd tell them he'd died in a war.

Hell. I basically did. Last time he'd felt alive had been that hot skirmish in Greece, shooting Soviets so Hillary Clinton could avenge her dead husband. Funny how he'd thought life would get better after the service, but his last job was on the road selling pharmaceuticals to doctors who were too busy or stupid to realize the latest "novel molecule" was a substandard repackaging of the last—different only for the fact it wasn't off patent and sometimes caused nausea.

He'd justified it at first: had to sell the drugs if his company was going to make new ones; he was only bilking the insurers, really; those doctors ought to know better; not like the drugs aren't doing their job. *That's how this world eats you. Doesn't make you do evil; makes you believe heroes aren't possible. Squeezes you under the weight of its mediocrity. The best you can hope for is a nice-paying job that's only a little selfish— and a daughter who calls.*

He missed war. He missed the way—when he'd first come home—a dropped dish in the other room would rip him from a dreamless sleep and drench every cell with adrenaline. He missed the smell of spent powder and brass, missed the feeling of purpose when he woke, the sense of mission. Sure, he'd laughed at the idea then. But if he'd known what was waiting for him, he'd have seen war with clearer eyes. Even the shitty things he'd done in the service—and there were a lot—had made a kind of sense. They were for a *reason*, something more than hawking a slightly worse cholesterol pill.

Casper booted his laptop's video chat. *Time to corral two dipshits.* The benefactors had warned never to meet Trevor

Wilkins and Paul Burns in person. The guardian demon had Casper's scent, and his associates could wind up contaminated by it, so they met digitally.

He wished either of them had spent even a day in the service, but Wilkins was some moonbat who hated Bradford's drilling policies and wanted to sterilize everyone with an IQ below his—he claimed it was 140. Casper had his doubts. Casper had once asked him, point blank, what he'd do if he could push a button that'd kill half the human population.

Wilkins had told him he'd hit it twice.

The Gaia-hugging hippy wanted to save the Earth from humankind, but Burns was just rancid in every way. He'd claimed way back in the day his great-great-grandfather had owned a hundred slaves and a plantation, and he'd talked about it like it was a good thing. Bitched and bitched about how Northern aggression had destroyed his inheritance, and now—apparently—the Mexicans were going to do it again. Bradford had spearheaded a couple immigration bills, which was all the excuse Burns needed to unload his bile.

Ludicrous, Casper thought, rankling. *I'm trying to save the world, and all I've got to work with are two guys who aren't even believers; not in anything that's real, anyway.*

The video chat picked up Wilkins and Burns. It took them a while to get Burns's computer unmuted since he wasn't very good with technology. After wasting ten minutes on that, Burns asked, "Did the admins get your BFG?" He had on a baseball cap and was bristle-necked, with the blocky face of someone who might have been a linebacker in high school, a contrast to the fancy hotel room behind him. He was in New Petersburg proper, somewhere, and Wilkins appeared to be inside a dark van, sucking on the paper of a joint. He wore those black-rimmed glasses that were popular among stupid people who wanted to look more like their favorite pundits.

"No idea where on Earth this monster came from, but yeah," Casper said, holding up the impossible rifle cartridge. It had a red tip and felt ice-cold and heavy. The bullet didn't look like any metal he'd ever fired.

"*Shee-it,*" Burns said, "could shoot through a fuckin' school with that thing."

"A tank, at least," Casper agreed.

"This country has a serious gun problem," Wilkins muttered.

Casper sighed, because that led to an eruption of shouts between his two cohorts. He couldn't figure out who he hated more between the two. "Stow it, both of you. We're here for our own reasons, but we're all here."

"Damn straight," Burns said, the crinkle in his eyes suggesting he only argued to see other people get angry. "Nothing wrong with a li'l tree hugging, we're all friends here." They weren't. "I'll personally fuck a redwood gentle-like if it'll get Wilkins here to help me wax that traitor Bradford and his uppity bitch of a girl."

Casper had yet to figure out why Burns also hated Naomi Bradford, except that she was pretty, rich, and talented: three things Burns had never been.

"Get fucked, Neanderthal." Wilkins pronounced Neanderthal with a hard "t" and it made him insufferable.

"Plan to," Burns said. "Got a couple buddies coming in this week and we're gonna hit the Red Light district. You wanna come, Wilkins? Do you stop being feminist if you pay for it? Or do you just have to tip real well?"

Casper could tell Wilkins was close to exploding, so he schooled his expression. "This is not spring break, Burns. We're here to do a job, and here are your orders. Wilkins, you follow the Bradford girl and monitor her routines. Be on the lookout for the girl in the hoodie, but don't approach her for any reason. Observe. Report. Figure out when she's not guarded, when she's vulnerable.

"Burns—do what you do best. Dig up everything on the dark-haired kid in the hoodie, but don't engage her. Figure out where she lives, who she knows, where she sleeps, and what her routines are. All our benefactors know is that she's centered somewhere in the city, but she's often close to the Bradford girl. You've got a description. Looks like she's a teenager, so start with the schools."

They both scowled. "What about you?" Wilkins asked.

Casper showed them the round again. "Target practice."

~*~

Friday was special, because Ryn was invited into Naomi's home and didn't have to hide on the roof. Instead, she watched the girl fan out notecards on the table. Naomi had dark shadows beneath her eyes, her posture bent from sleepless nights—but her smile was somehow still glorious.

"What are these?" Ryn leaned down, sniffing a notecard.

"I can't get over the never-tasting-chocolate thing," Naomi yawned. "But you must know some kind of food. If you can find it here, I'll cook it for you. As thanks for the Nine Lives."

Each card had a recipe. Ryn scanned them all. "I know none of it."

"None? There's fourteen nationalities of food here. What's closest?"

Ryn seized a rolodex full of notecards and spun it, the cards going *flickity-flick* past her vision until she snapped it to a stop. Plucking one out, she examined the ingredients and recalled the hearty beet aroma rolling from peasant homes at forest's edge. The script was Russian and by an unfamiliar hand, the cardstock bearing faint impressions of a woman's scent that was... half Naomi. "This."

"Borscht? You've had borscht?"

"No. But I could smell it in their homes."

Naomi gave her a worried look, nodded slowly, and examined the card. "I could make it." She sucked on her lower lip, uncertain.

"This was your mother's?"

"Uh. Yeah." She breathed differently—as though air was catching too high in her lungs. "I haven't had this since... well, not for a while."

Since her mother died. "Do as you wish." Then, more quietly: "I will try new things if they are your things."

"Let's make borscht." Naomi placed the notecard reverently on the countertop.

They ordered a ride to a nearby grocery store, one filled with too many smells, though the food was surprisingly fresh. It was there she realized not every human in New Petersburg fed from boxes and cans. While none of the meat had been properly hunted, the vegetables were only lightly poisoned and hailed from so many different places that Ryn had never seen some side by side. Naomi insisted on pork for the borscht, but picked meat that wasn't as thick with human-schemed hormones.

The Bradford kitchen featured hard marble surfaces, bright knives and wooden cutting boards, copper pans dangling from a ceiling rack, and a gas-burning stovetop. Naomi yawned again and her knife slipped on the onion. "Ah!" She clutched her finger, body seeming to fold around the wound. "Shit!"

"Let me see."

"Could you grab me a towel, it's bleeding."

"Let me see."

She was reluctant to turn over her hand, drops of bright crimson dripping from her closed fist.

Ignoring the blood, Ryn took the auburn-haired girl's hand and let trickles of it pool into her palm. The cut bled freely, so Ryn bent close and gently blew.

"That's so unhygienic," Naomi said.

"Better?"

Naomi rolled her eyes, but then furrowed her brow and muttered, "Yes, actually. It doesn't hurt at all." Glancing at her digit while running it under tap water, she frowned at a cut now noticeably shallower than before. "It's not as bad as I thought."

The blood on Ryn's hand excited her, filling her with an unnamable frisson. It didn't feel like hunger—but seeing part of Naomi imprinted red on her hand was right. *Part of her on me.* It was only with reluctance that she washed it off.

While Naomi rummaged for a bandage strip in a cabinet on the other side of the kitchen island, Ryn took the knife to onion, beets, carrots, and potatoes.

"I can hear you chopping like a maniac," Naomi laughed. "Trying to murder the onion for hurting me?" When she turned at the sound of Ryn planting the knife point down, she took an involuntary step back at the sight of minced vegetables. "How'd you do that?"

Ryn shrugged.

"They were— They're all done."

Ryn nodded at her bandaged finger. "You're too exhausted."

Suppressing a reflexive yawn at mention of exhaustion,

she narrowed her eyes. "Show me this time." Fetching the cabbage, she tossed it underhand across the island.

Ryn thrust her knife through the cabbage, spearing it between them. "If you wish." A thrill jittered through her whole body and she realized she'd decided something without ever thinking on it: to drop her social camouflage. It kicked her pulse, to know she was about to show her friend a secret—to expose it. Watching for a reaction, she was unsure if she'd see terror or shock or, perhaps, something better. As with their species' mating rituals, this was a disrobing. *Desire. That is what I want to see in your eyes.*

Releasing the cabbage from its seat on her knife with a graceful roll of the blade, she halved it with a *thunk* to the cutting board.

Whether at the fluid gleam of metal or the sound, Naomi straightened, and for a slow-moving second, Ryn savored the blossoming surprise in her eyes. *I like when your face does that.*

The knife flashed in her hand. *Let me make you do it again.* She showed with the singing knife what she couldn't with words, and she held back nothing: *This is what I do.* The lightning strokes made clean arcs at a speed no mortal could follow. Something the earth and sun took months to make whole, she had reduced to tiny, regular pieces in less than a heartbeat.

Naomi gripped the counter's edge tighter at the sight.

Now you see. I destroy, and I am good at it. Ryn again planted the knife point-down to punctuate the act, and her friend breathed, as if having forgotten how until that moment. Her gaze seemed to drink the deva, realizing only gradually what she'd witnessed—and how little she'd been able to see.

Ryn had never done this before. Never... shown off. Even she was breathing quicker in anticipation. "Is it as you like it?" she whispered. *Or did I show you too much?*

There was stillness to her friend at first, and then—her mouth somewhat open—a look of quiet awe that pleased Ryn so deeply, so thoroughly, that she now understood why some gods craved worship. "Where'd you learn to do that?" Naomi asked.

"There was never a day I couldn't do that."

She snorted in disbelief, the awe wiped clean. She was too sure of her world's boundaries and things taught in school to take Ryn at her word. "Fine, don't tell me. But since you already did the hard work, and I promised to cook for you, how about you let me finish? Unless you think I'm too sleepy to stir a pot."

"I don't mind watching."

Once the ingredients were set to simmer, Naomi led her upstairs and showed her books—showed her one called *The Brothers Karamazov* with her mother's notes in the margins. It seemed as though her mother's ghost lived in those notes, in the smell of the soup downstairs, and the auburn-haired girl's voice trailed off as her fingers danced over the spines on her bookshelf. She brushed one in particular, saying she could nearly hear her mom reading it to her. Ryn especially liked its title: *Where the Wild Things Are.*

The models of monuments made from plastic blocks also came from her mother, given to her "so you will not play with the slatternly dolls your friends play with," and they built them before visiting places. Ryn didn't ask why the Eiffel Tower wasn't finished. She sensed the answer.

Leaning back into her pillow with Ryn on her bedside, Naomi talked about needing to pull a new book from her mother's shelves over the summer. Then, yawning so wide it seemed to expel the last of her energy, the girl relaxed with eyes shut and she talked more quietly until at last the book she held slumped to her chest.

Listening to the rhythmic, slow breathing, Ryn tilted to face the girl, and Naomi rolled her way at the same time, curling almost around her, coming nearly to the point of touching. Half lost to sleep, she murmured, "Haven't slept much."

"Sleep now."

Something unintelligible—all Ryn could make out was "have company."

Leaning down, she whispered close to her friend's ear: "Nothing will hurt you when I am close. You are safe now."

A stale air left Naomi's lungs, as though releasing the last tension inside her, so that she pooled by Ryn's hip. Impulse seized the deva and she settled her hand into that auburn hair and tucked its glossy locks behind the girl's ear. Watching her breathe for two hours, watching her enjoy her first dreamless rest in weeks, Ryn felt strangely content. There was no other place she'd rather be, nothing else she'd rather do than stand guard so that Naomi could sleep in peace.

She heard Tom Bradford's car pull into the drive, so she gave him time to come inside. Sliding from the bed and prowling downstairs, Ryn found him on a stool at the kitchen counter eating borscht and watching the news on his tablet, a lone overhead bulb highlighting his haggard expression. The weeks had eroded him. She'd seen mortals crumble under far less. The hot, bloody-purple soup relaxed his shoulders and he slumped with arms circled around his bowl.

The Channel 5 news played on his screen and reported rumors of a "shadow" that street dwellers had seen in the Docks jumping from rooftop to rooftop. An elderly man with missing teeth told the anchorwoman, "Like some kinda animal. No sound. Made no sound." Bradford snorted and sipped the borscht off his spoon.

He jolted when Ryn paced around him; gawked a moment, then relaxed. "Jesus, be careful sneaking up like that. If I'd had my gun I might have shot you." He winced. "No need to tell any Democrats I said that."

"It isn't true anyway." She put the lid on the soup and turned off the burner. "Your daughter isn't sleeping enough."

"That makes two of us."

"Three," Ryn said. "But she is the worst off."

"I'd sleep better if Mark didn't take days off, though my daughter insists you're quite the badass. Where'd you learn that?"

"Many places."

"What was the last?"

She told him a country—if it could be called that. There were regions recognized on maps as states which weren't, where the rulers had power in name alone, and Ryn could still walk those lands uncursed.

He nodded, the two of them saying nothing. She sensed he inspected her almost as closely as she did him.

Soon Naomi padded downstairs in her quiet socks, rubbing her eyes. "Ryn, you're still here. Sorry for passing out on you. Hi, Dad." She kissed his cheek on her way to the stove. "It smells nice. How'd it turn out?" She fetched bowls.

"Perfect," Tom Bradford said.

Naomi spooned out borscht and glanced over her shoulder. "How was the Hill?"

"Rough." He hesitated. "Holland and Gordon are trying to ram through that security bill. Not happening. Trying to strangle it in the crib. If it escapes committee, I've got the votes— Lipset owes me after last November, and he puts me over."

"That's the bill on the news?" she asked, staring at her borscht.

Tom Bradford nodded, a silence opening between them that seemed a gulf. "I'm sorry. I rethought it after Banich. I just... I can't. It's too flawed, too deeply."

Ryn straightened when he mentioned Banich in connection with the mortal law. "What does the one have to do with the other?"

The senator explained something long and stupid and said the word "unconstitutional" the way old priests might have said "blasphemous." At one point he explained, "Private social-media companies would have to collect personal information on every user and provide the lists to law enforcement. Things as simple as your uncle's tinfoil-hat rants could put him on watchlists that violate a laundry list of rights."

Ryn stepped forward, bristling. "But this law. It makes finding Banich's associates... easier?"

"They bill it that way, but the bad eggs could just skirt the law. It's not about protecting people from lawbreakers, it's about controlling the rest of us."

Ryn could not care less about which mortals controlled which. "But it might help find them?" she pressed, heart blazing.

"It might put the website threatening her out of commission." Tom Bradford slid his bowl away. "It'd also chill speech all over the web, add about fourteen new ways for the government to jail people they don't particularly like."

Ryn didn't care. "You let these beasts exist, though they threaten Naomi? And for what? So fools might feel free to whisper in the dark to one another?"

"Rebels whispering in the dark started this republic."

Ryn's lip curled, caring nothing for republics. *Let them*

burn, to the last. Were one day of life a grain of sand, the sand of Ryn's immortality filled the length of every ocean and desert across all the Earth—no republic's days had yet numbered enough to overflow her cupped hands.

"Dad's right," Naomi whispered, sipping borscht from her spoon and shutting her eyes, as though to taste without distraction.

"He is *not*," Ryn snarled. Were Naomi's days sand, they would fill even less than her cupped hands—less than a teaspoon in her palm. Yet each grain was more precious to the deva than any contrivance of law.

"It's like with my bedroom." Naomi wove those skillful words: "That's what Dad sees that you don't, Ryn. This bill's just an ineffectual wall. It's theater. It's meant to make us feel safe, but instead it... becomes a cell."

"A cell for *others*," Ryn insisted. *And I care nothing for them.*

"Sorry." Naomi winked. "Not ready to sell out my fellow countrymen. We're all in this boat together."

Ryn growled.

"I sympathize." Tom Bradford scraped at his empty bowl. "I don't like it either. And Holland and Gordon are good at reminding me. Been hammering me in the press, saying not everyone can afford private security if their kid gets threatened."

"Did you tell them about your latest scheme to arm teenage girls?" Naomi teased.

"I *did*, and wouldn't you know it, that idea's not flying with the press."

"Have more borscht. You'll feel better."

"It'll make me fat and slow is what it'll do." He checked his watch. "I have some calls to make. Give me an hour, will you?" She nodded and he disappeared from the kitchen into a nearby office.

Naomi laid a bowl out for Ryn and sat opposite, blowing gently in a way that was interesting to watch. "My mom cooked this for Dad on their fourth date, except with tons of garlic. My dad *hates* garlic, but he was so scared of upsetting her that he choked down three bowls. The best part? Mom could tell he hated it, so she kept giving him bowl after bowl, trying to get him to be straight with her. His eyes watered so bad, he tried to pass it off as tears of joy. He threw up in her bathroom."

Ryn sniffed the borscht. "Strange."

"They had a strange courtship," Naomi agreed.

Courtship. "This food is part of a mating ritual?"

Naomi lifted an eyebrow. "For them. Maybe we don't talk about my parents mating?"

She nodded.

Leaning closer, Naomi grinned. "But if you don't like my borscht, you should shut up and pretend to love it anyway." Her eyes crinkled into a smile. "It's tradition."

Tasting the soup, she startled at heat and flavor wedded so rightly together; the beet and vegetables warmed her insides. Even the pork was fine, stewed into the broth's flavor. "Good." She wolfed down the rest.

Probably too fast, because Naomi watched with amusement. "I declare this Food Friday successful. Would you like to come to another?"

"Food Friday?"

"Old traditions are good, but so are new ones. My dad worries because Mark takes off Fridays. He likes it when you're here. So if you visit every Friday to keep me company, I'll make a different recipe—my treat, or you can help if you insist. We'll find out what you've been missing when it comes to cuisine."

One visit had been pleasing, but a promise of more was dangerous: too many opportunities to show this mortal too much. Despite currents of alarm, she couldn't refuse. Naomi had become like a sun that Ryn wanted to orbit. Feeling weak, and a fool, she whispered, "As you like."

~*~

Casper knew better than to conference Burns and Wilkins again, so he contacted them separately. Wilkins reported—disappointingly—that the guardian was only at Naomi Bradford's house on Fridays. Casper knew that wasn't true, so it meant the guardian was too stealthy to be noticed unless she meant to be.

Not good.

Wilkins' next job was to set up electronic surveillance near the Bradford home. Maybe it would help pinpoint the demon, but Casper doubted it.

Burns connected with him a few hours late, and when he came on screen his eyes were bloodshot and ringed in red. He was drinking a tall glass of water. "Are you hung over?" Casper asked.

Burns shook his head. "Negro woman maced me."

"Maybe you shouldn't call her that word."

"Not like I said—"

"*Or* that one."

"I can't keep track of what they like."

If I have a spare bullet when this is over... "What happened?"

"Found that hoodie chick's bitch of a caseworker. Got her name drinking with this burnt-out teacher. She gave me the lowdown on your little beastie. Ryn Miller. Stays at a group home off Oakland in commie town—sometimes—and she's fresh from the nuthouse. Anyway, tried to lift the caseworker's phone on the train; figured she'd have appointments. You believe that black bitch pepper-sprayed me?"

"Yes."

"I mean, she thought I was copping a feel, but still. She was a five—a six, *tops*—so it was practically a compliment."

"I'll let you know what our next move is." He cut off the video chat and drank a beer, digesting the information, finally typing it into an email for the benefactors:

> You won't like it. Wilkins never spotted the
>
> guardian except for when she wasn't hid-
>
> ing, so we can't identify her patterns. Burns
>
> couldn't figure out her routine either. She's
>
> a ghost.

Still, he included the guardian's name and address. The benefactors could use that, surely.

He clicked "send."

~*~

Ghorm's email dinged on the monitor to his left. With a pneumatic hiss, the chair spun and his hollow's greasy hands worked the mouse over its distended lap. Reading the email, he felt cold fear fill his vast center. "Mr. Saxby," he said in dulcet tones to his cabal-mate. "Oh, dear Mr. Saxby, did you realize—there is a tiny monster staying near Oakland Avenue?"

Mr. Saxby appeared at his side, the asura's middle-aged, balding, boringly average hollow dressed in a finely tailored suit, fingernails clipped to a level of impeccable symmetry. "Fascinating. Out of curiosity, do you remember who else fancies that neighborhood?"

"Dust," Ghorm ground out.

"Yes. Dust, with his long memory and loose lips." Mr. Saxby rubbed at a speck of dust on his sleeve. "Perhaps I should eat him."

"No," Ghorm said. "Dust is protected."

"By whom? A *monster*?" Mr. Saxby scoffed.

"No, not her; by someone who matters. A rival of our own paymaster, in fact. But I want to know what Dust is saying to our uninvited monster, and why precisely she is meddling in our work. I'll tell my peons to surveil Dust's haunts and we'll have a listen."

Mr. Saxby read the email carefully. "Ryn Miller, they call her. Why-oh-why does that name put the slightest shiver between my shoulder blades?"

"Might she cause you indigestion?"

A chortle, though Mr. Saxby's face didn't change. "What she did to Splat was special. She cut not the flesh, but the essence of him. That is something I'd like to study."

"And the gun you lent my peon—will it kill her?"

"That is no mere rifle," Mr. Saxby said. "That weapon has taken a hundred forms, suiting itself to the age. It's a... machine... and it came from my allies across the stars. The Hidden One said it would kill any god weaker than he." There was something malicious in his thin-lipped smile. "Though perhaps it would work against him too."

"You mustn't kill the one who pays us," Ghorm cautioned.

"Taking money from the Hidden One, who fights a cold war against another god—that was dangerous enough. But now he wants us warring with a monster. Our arrangement rather leaves us the pawns, and I prefer the space behind the board to being on it."

"Suggestions?" Ghorm asked.

Mr. Saxby removed his spectacles irritably and polished the lenses to banish nonexistent smudges. "I will need one of your toy soldiers. As well some tarp."

"Oh?"

"I'll have him war ready. We let them take their crack—my twisted lovely with tooth and claw, and your pet Bible-thumper with weapon from alien world. We eliminate Ryn Miller, then move on to Naomi Bradford. No two-front wars. And believe me," he smiled mirthlessly, "I would know."

Ghorm waved his chubby hand in the air. "Fine. Take one of my toys. I only have the three ready—still chipping away at the fourth. Which would you like?"

"Someone violent. Unhinged. I'm feeling... inspired."

~*~

Ryn had evaded Ms. Cross too long and agreed to meet her at the beginning of March. Outside, a heat spell had turned New Petersburg into a city of slush, and runoff trickled down the exterior brick walls of the office. They sat opposite one another, Ryn perched on the sofa's edge. Ms. Cross had populated a coffee table with stress balls and trinkets meant to distract patients.

Stacking cards in the style of the Eiffel Tower from Naomi's bedroom, Ryn understood from Ms. Cross's stare that she was upset.

"Good to see you at least read some history this month," Ms. Cross said. "A shame you weren't there to take the exams."

"I need no examination," Ryn said.

"I want you to get your GED."

"Meaningless."

"It means something to employers," she said sternly.

"You think without this thing I will starve?"

Ms. Cross firmed her mouth. "Listen to me very carefully.

We both know that at your age, there is precious little I can do to punish or reward you. But we also know a girl like you will—eventually—get into some kind of trouble. I know this city, I know how it works, I know police, prosecutors, and public defenders. When that day comes, I can be your greatest ally. Or: I can be your worst enemy. So what I want from you *matters*."

Ryn scowled, leaning two cards against one another. "What I do is important."

"Can you do it and study too?"

"Yes."

"Then study. And show up for your exams. And we'll take it from there."

Yet even now, Ryn vibrated with the need to fly across the city, to where Naomi had track practice at this hour. She loved watching her friend's pole stick, loved that instant as she soared over the bar when she seemed to float, body bending as supple branches in a windstorm. It was also a dangerous moment, where sabotage might snap the auburn-haired girl's life away.

"Ryn," Ms. Cross said. "Study. Take your exams."

Ryn relented and nodded. "As you will it." The words tasted bitter.

"Eiffel Tower." Ms. Cross nodded to the card tower. "Do you want to go there someday?"

"No."

"Why not?"

She shrugged.

"You don't like to try new things, do you?"

"I try new foods," Ryn said.

"With the girl. Naomi?"

"She shows me new things."

"Do you trust her?"

Ryn realized she did.

"What if she took you to Paris? Or I did?"

"I don't want to go to Paris."

"Why not?"

Because even if she weren't banished from their lands, the Fates lived in Europe. Because they would hunt Ryn, and because she couldn't protect Naomi there. The gods in America were fewer and younger. "I don't want Naomi to get hurt."

"She's the girl people are threatening?"

"Yes." Ryn fidgeted, irritable.

"You want to help her. That's interesting. What do you see in her?"

"Who cares?" she snapped.

"There's no need to be defensive. It's healthy to form emotional attachments to people. It means you're making progress. How would you characterize your relationship with Naomi?"

"We meet on Fridays." Other times Ryn just stalked her.

"Friends then."

"Yes."

"Nothing more?"

"No," Ryn said firmly.

"You seem very certain of that."

"Friends."

"Ryn. It's not uncommon for a woman who's seen abuse at the hands of men to form her most intimate relationships with other women."

"We are not... intimate."

"I'm just saying. For some women, it's a natural part of the healing process. For others, it's always been a part of them, and their abuse just leads them to discovering it."

"I'm not healing."

"Do you want to talk about the men who hurt you?"

"Why?"

"It might have—"

"It's done. They died; I lived."

"Sometimes the wounds go deep. They affect our ability to trust people. Were those the only people who ever hurt you?"

Ryn batted the tower she'd built, sending a cardstock cloud fluttering to the carpet. By the time they settled, she'd crossed to the window, her back to Ms. Cross as she stared at trickling runoff from the roof. "I've fought worse."

"You couldn't have beaten them, Ryn. There were too many. You shouldn't blame yourself."

"I was weak."

"You're not weak."

"I was weak in that moment. The moon was dark." She remembered the weariness, the girl screaming; how loud they'd made her scream. "It was empty, but for her voice and those monsters and the terrible things they did to her."

"You tried to save someone."

"She died." Her body hadn't yet cooled, though. "Her spirit was gone. It is... difficult to drag a spirit back through the gates. Your God doesn't like us poaching her works, but I do as I please. It's difficult; your souls are small but heavy as worlds. Pulling her back into ours nearly broke me."

"I've lost the thread of this metaphor." Ms. Cross had that doubtful look Naomi had worn after Ryn showed off her speed.

"I was weak. Made so by helping her, and also her brother. It was then, when my power was expended, that their knives came out."

Ms. Cross leaned forward. "They cut you?"

"Cut me. Shot me. Burned me. One of them urinated on me. They taunted me."

"Did they do other things?"

"What other things?"

"Did they rape you, Ryn?"

"No."

"All right."

"I said no."

"It's all right."

Ryn smashed her fist through the window frame, strong enough to shatter the glass pane. Tinkling fragments dropped down the building side. The sounds of traffic and whistling air filled the small office. Turning, she found Ms. Cross had stood and stepped back. "I said *no*," she hissed.

"You don't think I believe you?"

"I don't know what you think!" she roared. "I don't know what *any* of you think!"

Holding both hands up, Ms. Cross nodded slowly. "That must be frustrating."

Ryn bowed her head, containing her wrath in bunched-up fists. "I know you're afraid of me now."

"That's not true."

"It is. Your heart races. Fear comes off you like waves. I don't know faces, when you are happy or sad, joking or serious, lying or confessing, or what half your strange habits do.

But I *smell* your fear." She stared Ms. Cross down. "So now I know you lie. Why should I trust you?"

Ms. Cross expelled a breath and lowered her hands. "You're right. I did just lie to you. So from this point forward, I won't. Could we both sit?"

Not knowing what else to do, she lowered herself to the sofa.

Ms. Cross eased into her chair. "That's the most you've ever said at one time."

"I know."

"You expressed yourself."

Ryn said nothing.

"And that's progress," Ms. Cross urged.

"Progress broke your window."

"Progress is always a little destructive, a little painful. Building new things always breaks down the old things. Tell me more about how you can't understand faces. When did you realize that was a problem?"

"With Naomi. Because I can understand her face."

"Why is that?"

"Because..." She struggled for the words. They came haltingly. "She has... a larger soul."

"Pardon?"

"Her soul isn't just heavy as worlds, it's large too. It spills onto her face. It's in her scent and eyes and face; it cannot be ignored."

CHAPTER THIRTEEN
Muse

The March thaw had been a feint, all that water transformed into ice by a frigid cold front next afternoon. New Petersburg was a beautiful, crystal city, the guardrails, cars, and lampposts glistening. Stray snowflakes tumbled from the sky and melted on Naomi's cheeks where Ryn met her after school to walk her home. She wore too few layers and shivers racked her vulnerable human body.

Stripping her kanaf, Ryn folded her friend into it as they walked.

Naomi smiled back at her in a shy way, that spicy-strange scent on her skin again. "How are you never cold?"

"This isn't cold."

"Siberia. You were there, weren't you? The Russian you speak, the borscht, the cold—it had to be Siberia, right?"

Ryn mentally compared her many homes to maps from school and nodded. "For a time."

"I hear it's beautiful. Hundreds of miles untouched, unsettled."

"You could walk forever and never see or smell a person." *Once, nearly all places were like this.*

"Do you want to go back?" Naomi asked.

"There is no 'back' for me. My home is gone."

"What do you mean 'gone'?"

"Changed. Time makes us all homeless—eventually." She'd known this land before it had been paved. *And yet, time unmade my home so that it could build yours.* Ryn frowned, as this thought made her profoundly sad: a reminder of the distance between not just her and her friend, but between their two species.

Naomi put fists deep into the pockets of Ryn's hoodie, spinning to walk backward as she faced her. "I wish you could take me there."

"I could." *There are still places without the flavor of man.*

She laughed. "You're supposed to tell me, 'No, it's too dangerous!'"

"All places are. Except those next to me."

"God!" Naomi's eyes twinkled. "Your arrogance—why do I like it so much?"

"It isn't arrogance."

Naomi clapped her mouth shut, dipping her face low with eyes lifting, though the smile remained. "Then what is it?"

Something in that expression invited Ryn, propelled her forward not as mortals walked, but more fully what she was—her locomotion fluid, silent. "My strength. The truth of me." *You like my power because I show it; because you've been trained not to notice your own.*

And the way her scent had changed—it was delicious. The auburn-haired girl examined where her hands stretched the kanaf's pockets taut, her pulse skipping and body warm, all felt through the conduit of that mystical fabric. "Take me to Siberia someday and prove it." There was a challenge in her tone; the way she invited it while scrunching into the hoodie, backing away, and grinning all made Ryn want to... chase her.

What would I do once I caught her? She didn't even know.

But Ryn would have swept her friend off to Siberia and away from asura, deva, and mankind itself if she'd thought there was the slightest possibility the teenager wouldn't feel imprisoned. Naomi was wild in her own way.

That night, while Naomi slept fitfully and her father's soldier patrolled, Ryn hopped the train across the city to a Palisades museum just off the bay, sandwiched between the water and Commonwealth Plaza. She'd discovered it weeks ago while tracking Naomi during a day trip and had realized Dust haunted it on occasion.

She broke in through the skylight and descended on a single, bright gossamer cord from her kanaf. Dust roused awake in an exhibit of old instruments in a display case, the spirit occupying a recently donated violin of aged and sweet-smelling wood, the only sign of his presence a slight accumulation of his namesake on varnish that otherwise would have been pristine. When he moved, she could hear him in the way a hiss shot through the instrument's taut strings.

"Come to hang out, Erynis?"

"Where did you learn that name?" Ryn growled.

Dust hesitated. "Heard it around. Had no idea my baby monster was quite so... discussed. Shame on you, though, big famous beastie wakin' a humble spirit from his rest—disrespectful."

"I need to find Splat and his cabal. Now."

"I don't keep tabs, and nobody wise does either. They don't let on where they bed down their hollows."

"Then who. I want to know about his cabal."

"Hold on. There's no love lost between Splat and me, but why would I wanna upset so many hungry spirits?"

"If you know my name, you know I will not be denied."

"There's nothing to say, goddamn it. They ain't friends of mine."

Ryn approached, purring: "You know—or you know who does."

"Ah." There was an apprehensive hitch in his voice. "Suppose that's the question, ain't it?"

"You're stalling." She fanned her fingernails, let him see the glint of their sharpness.

"Don't rush me! Can't give you nothing if you gut me, so just—back up! Not gonna be kicked around by no one, least of all some short beastie with sharp teeth."

Ryn stopped at the case holding the violin, dragging one nail along the glass enclosure until she'd carved a neat circle. Removing it, she reached through, stroking the instrument's skin. "Tell me."

"You wouldn't dare. It's a Stradivarius, you bitch!"

"You like these man-schemed things." This museum was thick with them—instruments, baseball cards, pictures of the city in its infancy. "Yet I lived when the Earth was rock and mineral, and I have seen every wild and beautiful thing shattered, remade for mortal souls. Do you think I care for your violins?" She let her nails graze it, close enough to scrape off a few atoms and no nearer.

He hissed at the razor kiss. "You know how many masters

have touched this wood? Any clue what it's like to taste the passion of every fella who ever worked it?"

"You have ten seconds." Ryn tasted her fingertips—to her, just the flavor of old wood.

Dust waited nine seconds. "Muse. Muse knows." Then, his voice harder: "And here I thought we were getting chummy."

"I don't play games."

"Then you're gonna love Muse."

~*~

The email was priority flagged and held an audio file, curtailed to the interesting parts. Listening sent a shiver through Ghorm's hollow. He hit an icon on his screen to dial his second-in-command and on the sixth ring, Mr. Saxby picked up.

"I have you on speaker," Mr. Saxby intoned. "Afraid I'm elbow deep in your peon at the moment."

"The electronic surveillance picked up our monster."

"Ah! She's with Dust, then." Mr. Saxby shushed a pleading voice. "Fortuitous. Send the other mortals to kill Naomi Bradford while she's elsewhere. I'll nudge my latest masterpiece along shortly—just need to put in a handful of stitches and sign my work." There came a sob, cut off by the sound of Mr. Saxby tut-tutting.

"No. We have to send them after Muse. Dust—the blasted idiot—he told the monster about Muse."

"Muse? That adorable little empath we almost recruited? I remember how she went all wide-eyed when she realized what we were about; so charming! Why should it matter? We met her in the Palisades. She has no idea where the nest is."

"*It matters because she knows our names.*"

"And? It's not as though she's the only one."

"I heard the name of the monster. *Erynis.*"

Mr. Saxby sucked in a breath. "My, what a complication," he muttered. "I daresay, I'd love to pry her open to see how she ticks."

"Maybe. Or maybe she opens you. But she cannot be killed for long, and she won't rest until we're destroyed. The Fates named her the Implacable One. When the oldest, most vengeful deva call you *that*, it's a clue that maybe this monster holds a fucking grudge. She'll remember our names. She'll hunt us."

"What about Splat?"

"What about him?" Ghorm tapped a few keys.

"If Muse doesn't surrender our names, he will."

"Splat has been a convenience for us. If he's no longer convenient, I regard him as expendable. But let's wait until after we leverage him against Miss Bradford." Ghorm typed out a new message. "I'm sending our peons after Muse; the one named Wilkins has a mirror box to trap her with. Hopefully they bring her to us before Erynis finds her."

"And if not?"

"If Erynis learns our names, then Bradford is no longer our sole target. We'll have to kill Erynis, too, buy ourselves some time while she regenerates. There are rumors of magic in Europe that can alter an asura's name, change our scent—maybe the Fates would help us if we brought them tribute. There will be no appeasing her, no stopping her. What about you? Did you finish work on Burns?"

"Patience! He's nearly perfect. Stitching in one more heart and I'll clean up the hotel room."

Ghorm sighed. "By 'clean up' do you mean 'incinerate'?"

"Of course. He had three degenerate friends when I got here—plenty of extra parts to work with, but no amount of bleach is getting them off the walls."

~*~

Following Dust's instructions, Ryn took the train to Whitechurch and walked toward Graystone University, sniffing around the bars for asura. She caught the scent outside one called Pandora.

Inside, the tall ceilings made it less claustrophobic than Ryn had anticipated. One side room had a number of televisions anchored to the walls, patrons drinking and hollering at sports competitions—the rest featured a polished wooden bar, decorative lighting and shelves for brightly colored liquor bottles, and stairs leading to an upper floor where she detected the asura's scent.

The patrons seemed a blend of young and middle-aged, and Ryn picked up on the way men would chat more closely or kiss; the women, too, she realized were engaged in mating rituals with one another. Upstairs was a dance floor presently empty, duos and trios drinking at a second bar, and a billiard table in back. An older pair of women at the bar leaned into one another, whispering comfortably, so perfectly at ease it pinched Ryn somewhere deep.

"Look what the cat dragged in," purred a feminine voice behind her.

Ryn turned, facing a woman with an asura flesh-riding her. She wore a black suit with a thin tie of the same color, contrasted with her cream dress shirt; her spiked black hair matched exactly the tie and jacket. The caustic odor or her cigarette seared the insides of the deva's nostrils, and when she drew on it, Ryn saw the tattoos that gloved her wrist, hand, and the two innermost fingers. She strode past Ryn to the billiard table. She was tall and androgynous, casting an over-the-shoulder grin that showed some teeth.

"Muse," Ryn said.

"The one and only." She leaned on the billiard table and blew smoke from her nostrils like a dragon. "Play me?"

"I don't play games."

"I'd be happy to pop your cherry. Come on over, half-pint. I'll show you what you're missing."

Ryn scowled and approached the table, a foot shorter than Muse.

"Looking for trouble?" Muse held out a pool cue.

She snatched it. "Usually." Glancing the stick over, sensing its purpose, she added, "Not with you."

Muse gathered bright pool balls into a wooden triangle. Ryn examined a game played on one of the video screens nearby.

"You're here for information. And you're old. A new player in New Petersburg? Admission to the great bazaar of secrets and lies will cost you a name."

"Ryn."

"That's not your name. Or at least not your only name. But that's fine. I didn't specify."

"How did you know—"

"Empath." She tapped her temple twice and lined up her cue to strike the white ball. "Not good at faces?"

"No."

"Faces are my thing." The cigarette jounced on her lower lip when she spoke, a pinprick of fire smoldering in front of her face. "Can do downright beautiful things with bodies, too. I get a look at you, I look straight through. I see your heartsick glances at those two women holding each other; I see the rage bunch your shoulders when I come too close."

Muse paused to explain the rules of the game to Ryn—having apparently noticed her glances at the video screen—and then continued. "Can't see everything, of course." She cracked the cue ball into the racked balls and knocked a solid into a pocket. She proceeded to the other side of the table and brushed her finger across Ryn's waist as she glided past.

Ryn straightened. "Don't."

"So you're heartsick, but for someone in particular."

"Don't do that."

"Touch you? Or ferret out your secrets?" she teased.

"Either."

"Someone hates flesh riders."

What was there to like? "You push yourselves on them."

"Got that one wrong." Muse ashed her cigarette. "This girl's name is Mel. We're long friends. I take the weekend, she takes the weekdays. We split the memories down the middle."

"She... lets you?" Ryn had to shake off a wave of psychic claustrophobia.

"Hell of a deal. Smoke a pack a day, drink every night, fuck like a tigress—and Mel never gets tired, old, or sick. She's thirty-six, still gets carded. Then there's my empathy. Has its... uses." She winked, then leaned in deep for her third shot. Ryn noticed the curve it produced along her body and how well the suit was tailored to her. *Does she do that on purpose?* Muse snapped her cue and the ball missed its target by a hair. "Shit. Your turn."

Ryn chalked her cue. She went perfectly still, studying the table. "Tell me about Splat."

"Fuck. That why you're here? Not happening."

"Why?"

"Because he'd eat me, sweetheart. And I have to look out for Mel—what he'd do to a mortal woman is worse by a mile. All asura come from great moments. We're born from passion, obsession, sin. Splat burst into existence decades ago from a snuff-porn ring—spawned from the sadistic boner-rage of a hundred of the sickest humans to own a VCR. I steer clear."

"He won't bother you."

"It's not in you to stop him. He's fatter every year. All he does is eat and grow, and he's bigger now than some deva."

Frustrated, Ryn squeezed the cue tighter but still hadn't budged. "Tell me more."

She leaned on her own stick, closer. "What'll you give me?"

"Life."

"It's not in you to kill Mel—or me. You can't bluff an empath."

"Then what?" Ryn growled.

Muse took her time, eyeing the monster curiously from head to toe. "Old but inexperienced. Heartsick for someone else. And even though you flip out when I get too close, you're attracted."

Ryn bristled.

"It's like I said: can't bluff an empath." She pointed with the ember of her cigarette. "You're a monster. Can't pass for human, so you live in the wilds. Who the hell let you back into civilization? Whoever fucked it up, I should thank them—I've never met a monster before. You're my first. Bet it's lonely out there. Lonely and cold."

"I enjoy it."

"Not me. I need to touch. To be touched. Got to feel the beat of a heart beneath my ribs; got to feel someone else's race against me. Ever felt that?"

Ryn glanced away.

"Chin up, half-pint. Tell you what I want. I want to bed a monster. Want to show you the ten thousand things you've missed living outside the cities for—what, a hundred years? More? I want to see how much I can make a two-hundred-year-old virgin twist in the sheets."

Ryn bared her teeth. "No."

"Easy, put the chompers away. I'm a creature of delights—I only get pleasure from giving it. And your pleasure is guaranteed. There's not a rough bone in my body. Not unless you need it rough, and even then—I'd make you beg."

The outrage came alive, uncoiling inside her until she

knew the shine of her eyes glowed through blue-tinted lenses.
"No."

"Whatever you say. But I hope you're a billionaire or something, because I'm no saint. I don't risk my neck for free."

Ryn finally glanced from the pool table. "Then a wager."

She screwed out her cigarette in an ashtray. "Loving your
confidence. You've never shot pool in your life. But all right, if
this is your game: I win, I want you. Not for a night—too skittish, you'd need more time. A month. Never further than you
can handle, but on your honor, you'd give me a real shot at...
teaching you." Her gaze was too bold. "And I want you on the
full moon—want to see how it makes you move underneath
me."

"When I win, you tell me what I want to know."

"Deal."

They both crossed their hearts. The bet couldn't be re-
scinded.

Ryn glanced back at the table, examining it once more.

"You going to shoot?" Muse asked. "My beer buzz is fading." She waved her hand for another round and lit a fresh cigarette.

"Soon." By the time Muse's drinks came, Ryn had finished
studying the table, searching for whatever trick was meant to
make this game challenging—it dawned on her there wasn't
one. It was exactly as it appeared, and the fact irritated her.
*Everything in this realm is clumsy—this game can only be
enjoyed by the clumsy.* She'd won before she'd even shot and
all that remained was to show Muse that truth, so she raised
her cue and did so.

She fired the cue ball into a single stripe and knocked it
clean to the pocket, shifted to a new table side, and lowered
her cue to the precise spot where the white ball coasted to a
stop, shooting again. It bounced over two solids, pocketing another stripe. Rounding the table, she sank two stripes with a
shot, and finished by sinking three more in one go.

"There." She pointed at a corner pocket and cracked the
eight-ball home. Straightening, she laid her cue on the con-
quered table. "I win, yes?"

A thick column of ash fell off Muse's cigarette. "Fuck me."

"No. Now tell me about Splat and his cabal."

Muse nodded, her face pallid. "You going to kill them?"

"Yes."

"Can you?"

Ryn narrowed her eyes.

"All right. I'll tell you everything."

~*~

They sat in a shadowed booth, Muse burning down another cigarette and swallowing two shots of whisky before she explained.

"Two years back, my friend Drake tells me there's a flesh-riding cabal that's recruiting. Never been in one, and with the asura population in New Petersburg going up, I figure, 'Why not?' Could use the protection. They needed an empath. I met them over in the Palisades on top of a parking deck and found out why they needed one: to mark fresh targets; sniff out the vulnerable. It wasn't the kind of cabal I thought it was."

"Their names," Ryn said.

"According to Drake, Ghorm leads it. Born out of a cult—maybe it was nine hundred people drinking poisoned fruit punch, maybe it was something older. He's a deceiver. He can worm into a mortal's head and move all the furniture around."

"He controls them?"

"Tugs their strings. It's gradual, a kind of gravity that pulls people further and further into madness. He can do more directed stuff with effort, especially under a full moon. He doesn't control, he perverts. It's his specialty. Used to work with religion, but nowadays in this part of the world, politics is easier—it's like he can twist an idea until it's turned back on itself.

"Ghorm's number two is Mr. Saxby. Don't let the suit and funny name fool you. They say he was birthed from a Nazi experiment on twins. Strongest shifter I know. Bends the mortals he flesh-rides, molds them. He can add six hundred pounds of muscle to his hollow in under three seconds. Unnaturally strong, poisonous, and he can grow fangs, claws, stingers—biology's his arsenal. And his work on mortal bodies, what he does to their skin, to the symmetry of their form—it's unnatural. Between him and Ghorm, they can remake a person, body and mind."

"And Splat?"

"Strong and durable. Weaker than Saxby, but more sadistic by a mile. Addicted to hurting women and he hates them. Didn't even like me for flesh-riding one. I can't look at him, can't think of looking at him, without..." Her cigarette trembled in her hand and she stabbed it out, drinking another whisky from a row of glasses and wiping her mouth with the back of her hand. "I could see what he's done in his eyes. He's worked on women, on kids. The less said about that, the better."

"Is that all?"

"No. There's a fourth—a new one. Tooloo's the empath they got when I turned them down. I know her through Drake. Most empaths can't work with those guys—we can't stand suffering. We feel every piece of it. That's why we're all such fucking hedonists." She circled her thumb over the shot glass's lip. "Way more fun to watch pleasure than pain. But Tooloo's wired wrong. She's got a mind like a supercomputer; she can see all a person's inner workings, but she doesn't actually *feel* them. Feelings are just clockwork to her, and bodies are just sacks of blood, and... well, she's born of the digital age. People are just things to her on the other side of her eyes, the same way the internet is just a bunch of things on the other side of a screen."

"Where can I find them?"

"I'm not supposed to know, and if they knew I did, they'd eat me. But they think empaths are about reading minds. We're not. It's a kind of perception; it's about noticing things. So I could see the concrete powder on Saxby's penny loafers, I could smell the kerosene from a heater on Splat. They piped Ghorm in through a web connection, because he's basically immobile, and his voice had an echo, like from an empty space. They were in a housing project. My guess is Primrose—supposed to be a residential highrise on Park Ridge, but it's been delayed and half-built for years."

"Do they all stay there?"

"No, just Ghorm. But it's their nest, and they'll meet on the full moon. Best time for Ghorm to work his magic on a new hollow. Splat ruined his a few months ago and Drake says he's burning through the new ones too fast—he's sick, broken. Something's the matter with him and he can't keep them from rotting."

"He's wounded."

Muse snorted. "That's not possible. We exist or we don't. There's no 'wounding' an asura. We're spirits. We don't work like that."

"A sharp enough edge will cut anything. Even a soul."

"So someone cut Splat's soul?"

"You're the empath. Am I lying?" Ryn stood.

"Holy shit." The next shot glass shook in Muse's hand and she gulped it down. "You serious? You can cut an asura?"

"I can cut anything."

Muse breathed out a curse, but her fear gradually changed into something else. "You wouldn't cut me. I can tell. Have a drink with me. Or five. Bet you'd be a fantastic drunk."

"No."

"Who's the other woman?"

Ryn hesitated.

"Go on," Muse teased. "Ask me what you've wanted to all night."

Damn her. "There is no question to ask. She isn't... interested. Not like that."

"Let me tell you something a monster might not know. I've been in men and women, straights and gays, closeted and open, and everything in between. From where I've been sitting, you'd be surprised who wants what. Some people play their desires close as a hand of poker, and some won't even look at their own cards. Bring her by sometime and I'll have a closer look. Maybe she's more interested than you know. Maybe I'll see something you can't."

Ryn glared.

"Hey. Relax. I'd be respectful."

The glare continued.

"Well. Respectful-ish."

~*~

Muse proved persuasive enough to draw Ryn into a conversation—or, at least, to sit and listen to Muse's end of one.

The asura expounded elaborately on her experiences with humans and their drinking rituals—it involved a lot of waking up in distressed or mysterious circumstances. But whatever else Muse could do, she couldn't withstand a half-bottle of whisky, and she begged Ryn to help her to a cab.

"I will, but you won't... touch me."

"No, no, all the touching will be you—strictly carrying-me-related touches," Muse slurred from her half-cocked position in the booth seat. "Honest! I'm not sneaky. I attack head-on."

Ryn sighed, easing one of Muse's arms over her shoulders and assisting her out of the bar. "We are not friends," she growled.

"Not even slightly," she agreed, touching her mouth to hold back a wet belch.

The cold air of the street licked her skin and Muse groaned her approval.

An explosion transformed a line of twenty windows to Ryn's side into glittering shards of glass. She snapped her hand up and caught the bullet in her palm before it could tear the asura's body in half.

The force threw Ryn and she adjusted her stance. Concrete scraped underfoot. It kicked her four yards before she regained traction. Smoke poured out of her open palm, which was on fire, and she clutched in her right hand a dense, alien metal intended to murder gods.

Her gaze zeroed in on the distant smoking speck of the rifle's barrel.

"Stay." Ryn eased Muse into the crevice of a storefront, concealed from the sniper. He fired a second time, air pulsing from the bullet's passing—it would have broken through both sides of a bank vault, but instead the unearthly metal struck Ryn's palm and flattened.

The force only kicked her back half as far, but the shockwave ripped the doors from four cars and whisked them down the street. Car alarms went off up and down the avenue and the streetlights had shattered, casting them into darkness.

Muse clutched her bleeding ears and shouted, too loud, "Shit, what is that!"

"A dead man." Ryn vaulted to the wall, gripped brickwork, and ascended to the rooftops.

CHAPTER FOURTEEN
Achilles' Heel

Ryn flew across the city's uneven roofs. The distant muzzle flashed, a flicker of warning before its thunderous shot struck her outthrust palm. The force hurled her backward, feet planting into a building side; the mortar popped, bricks cracking in a dusty spiderweb of fractures. Ryn's calves tensed, and she pounced forth again with hands shedding burning powder like twin contrails behind her.

Another flash. She deflected the stinging metal with the back of her hand, the bullet sparking white from the collision and hurled into the heavens.

A third flash, and she batted it over the bay.

It never broke her stride.

He's less accurate than at the rink. Different shooter or is he nervous?

Then she sensed it. Risking a glance over her shoulder, she spotted another figure sneaking from a van on the street near Muse. He wore dark-rimmed glasses and carried a shotgun and something on his back.

A mirror box.

Ryn was caught between the sniper and another mortal intent on capturing Muse, equidistant between the two. Deciding, she bore down on the sniper. *Do it. Shoot me.*

The rifle clapped. Lightning erupted from the barrel's mouth, another wave of thunder and alloy tumbling through the air. She stretched the thread of time thin until the bullet was visible and caught the angry metal between both hands. She twisted her body from its path and arced the freight-train force off its tracks, casting it to the street where it bore down on the bespectacled man hunting Muse.

It struck him center mass. The bullet obliterated most of him, rending what remained into two great, uneven pieces sundered clean apart. The top parts slapped onto a car hood like wet laundry.

Ryn completed the spin she'd started to evade the bullet, flitting to another rooftop, and rocketed toward the sniper. She angled her approach from his side, forcing the barrel to waver and track to follow her, but the firearm's size made it hard to reorient.

She ate the distance. Her snarl was a long, vicious sound that grew in volume across her final leap. He fired one more time, point blank.

Ryn's claws glinted, cutting the bullet in half. Its two neat segments wobbled through the air above and below her shoulder and she traced her claws along the length of a Deep One artifact disguised as a rifle. Unnaturally cold metal casings, rune-inscribed plates, and hissing fluid filled the air—no sign of bolts, pinions, or springs, as it wasn't built from those things in its true form. The Kl'thunian weapon screamed its death rattle, its remains falling to the rooftop in a rain of viscid blood and tinkling metal shards.

Transitioning fluidly from claw to kick, Ryn cracked the mortal's jaw and tossed him into a brick smokestack. It cratered and he hung limp in the indentation.

Ryn traced her fingers across the tarpaper and sniffed where he'd lain. *Different mortal.* Then where was the one from the ice rink? This one was ugly. In fact, she wasn't sure he was human. He was... lumpy. His face didn't look right. His skull bulged out like he had a grapefruit under his scalp and his swollen shoulder was hunched, one arm a foot longer than the other. *Saxby's work. But to what ends?*

"I know you're conscious." She crouched, ready. "Where is the other shooter?"

His eyelids peeled open, but only one held the eyeball—the other was ringed in hooked teeth, a tiny mouth. Both his regular mouth and the second one in his eye socket smiled sickeningly together. "Look-it you, you're just a little girl. I could take you home in my pocket." He fell out of the crater and coughed out a molar. His neck was two vertebrae too long. "You're the reason they did this to me. You're the reason I haven't got half my working parts, you're the reason for the pain, for the fact I got Cody's brain stitched into mine and can't stop hearin' him *scream* about his missing face. I kill you... and maybe they let us die."

She fixed him with a stare. "Death is here now. Come closer. It sleeps in my hands."

He flicked his elongated arm her way, as though making a shooing gesture, but instead a spike of hardened bone squirted from a pucker in his wrist. Ryn batted the glistening spike aside, pouncing on him.

She struck his chest knees-first, claws out, intent on his throat.

His neck inflated to twice its size and blowfish spines puffed out. Flaps behind his ears had sucked in the air, so she clubbed the vents with her fists. He seemed to gag, the inflated skin protecting his windpipe sagging.

Flipping off his chest, she dropped and swept his legs.

There were no bones in his legs. They slapped wetly from under him, and though he collapsed in a thrashing pile, both legs wriggled on the tarpaper. Abruptly, his pant legs bulged and tentacles shredded through the fabric—dozens of them, bristling with claws or very human eyes with some teeth mixed in. The root of one tentacle patch held what seemed to be half a flesh-covered skull, no jaw but a tongue, screaming gibberish.

"See? *Don't you see?*" the creature said from the mouth in its head but not its eye. "It's crowded in here," he sobbed.

Barbed tentacles slapped the rooftop, dragging their mass closer to Ryn, so she kicked the bricks from the bottom of the chimney stack beside them. Brick powder clouded the air and the heavy stack leaned toward the fallen creature. She slipped behind it, giving it a shove that dropped a ton of rubble on the aberration's mewling flesh.

The air filled with choking, abrasive dust, and she heard him worming that slimy, near-boneless body from beneath the weight, crying and screaming and blubbering from four different mouths. She didn't even know where the fourth mouth was—didn't want to know, really. She could hear the beating of three hearts.

Something orange glowed in the fog of brick dust. Ryn thought of bombardier beetles and their chemical ignition system.

Fire roared through the air, but to her side. The blistering-hot film spewed a wet trail of flames, covering the tarpaper rooftop. *Children live here.* She had to take that weapon out, or the building would burn.

Ryn hefted a loose brick, flicked through the cloud, and launched a flying kick that planted both heels into the creature's torso. It knocked him stumbling out of the debris cloud, burning oil thrown into the air, spattering down in fat drops. It hissed against Ryn's cloak and clung to her forearm. She ignored it.

Out of the cloud now, she saw how his fire worked: his puffer throat filled with fluids from chambers in his guts and when he spat the flaming gel, it sparked on contact with oxygen.

She chucked the brick into his gaping mouth where it lodged firmly between his teeth. His puffer throat swelled, but couldn't contract. The fluids backed up, dribbling weakly from the corners of his mouth.

Ryn's claws flashed through his throat and she booted him off the building. He fell into an alleyway.

About halfway down, the glass-clean cut in his throat forced the chemicals from his guts to mix and let just enough oxygen seep in. The explosion started inside him, roaring out of his throat, mouth, and eye sockets, finally erupting like a wet bomb from his center. He landed in a dumpster and Ryn lost track of him as he detonated twice more in geysers of liquid fire.

Her cloak shivered, smothering the fire she carried on her shoulders and forearm. The rooftop still burned, and she launched a tether from her cloak to a water tower one building over. It smacked a wooden strut and she gave it a mighty pull. The strut bowed and snapped, the tower crashing down, overturning its contents on the adjacent flames. Water surged up to Ryn's hips and she had to anchor with three more tethers to keep from being carried over the building side with the deluge.

It made a waterfall into the alley where she'd dropped the creature, the torrent filling the dumpster and extinguishing the flames.

Ryn dropped down to finish him. He lay blackened with his throat split open and vertebrae exposed, but he'd half re-generated from the wounds already. He screamed and cried and cursed from his many mouths, but all of them a chorus of pleas for death.

Obliging, she ripped the first of his sinful hearts from the screaming corpus and wolfed it down. The meat slid into the center of her, a place not her stomach but nearer to her wrath. That dark furnace was buried deep, folded parallel to normal space so that it was tucked away from the world—necessary because its heat was like a star's. It was called *gehenna*, and the moment wet flesh touched that pocket of space within her, the organs burned to black ash. A scream vibrated through her, her inner fire so hot it ate his soul next, burning until that too was obliterated.

Digging for the other hearts, she sent speckles of blood to the alley wall, dissecting the monstrosity Saxby had stitched together. The second heart she slurped down in four snaps of her bright teeth, that one's soul stickier, the vagaries of their individual evil modifying the flavor. Coming to the final heart, she tightened her fist around it, stared down into the mangled face of her quarry and asked one more time: "Before I release you, you will tell me: where is the other shooter?"

"Kill me," rasped the bloody head. He was little more than severed spine, a cobweb of blood vessels, heart, and brain, but the unholy work done to his biology kept his soul rooted, and might for days yet. In a way, the eternal end of gehenna was a mercy, and the only one she knew. "Please... kill me."

"The ice-rink shooter," she insisted. When she spoke, glowing cinders from annihilated souls floated from her mouth.

"...Casper wouldn't come. Casper said it wasn't the mission. He went to finish it."

Tearing his heart out, she sprinted for the train at full speed and ate him as she went, ripping into hard muscle a bite at a time until his screaming soul joined his friends, first shrill, then silent forever.

Yet there was no satisfaction, no warm glow at her center knowing the world was cleaner for her efforts. There was a hard lump, and a rising, terrifying knowledge she might not be fast enough.

~*~

Casper had studied details of the Bradford security system emailed to him by the benefactors; studied Sgt. Mark Brody's dossier and patrol patterns using Wilkins' surveillance. Brody wasn't his idea of an easy fight, but at least he wasn't some kind of hell-spawned demon.

The backyard had three motion detectors. Casper scaled the outer wall and then walked carefully through an inch of snow, using a blind spot between their sensor ranges. Reaching the house, he stood flush to the wall and dusted the snow from his body as best he could, not wanting to leave a trail of slush in the house that could alert Brody.

Near his place on the wall, he found a disconnected hose. It was cold, but the water ran. Screwing it in, he set the sprinkler timer for fifteen minutes.

He worked a gap in the window just wide enough to insert a small magnetic strip meant to fool the alarm—the only trick was figuring out where to insert it, and he'd brought a compass to show him. It made him think of his daughter. *Julie used to do this to our windows at night. Sneaking out to see that asshole boyfriend.* Sneaking out ran in the family, he supposed. *Sure surprised her when I installed that backup sensor, though.* He smirked at the memory and jerked the window up. No alarm sounded. *So far, so good.*

He pulled off his boots before ducking into the darkened house. Would there be motion detectors inside? *No idea. They don't have a dog, so almost no reason not to.*

With the shrug of a man who realized he had no real options, Casper padded on socked feet across the floor and slid the taser from his hip. No alarms, no flashing lights. *Could be silent alarms.*

Ignoring the thousand what-ifs, he stationed himself in a shadowed nook, observing the hallway Brody would take if he left Bradford's office. Brody was sharp, almost restless in his patrols. *A good soldier.* He wasn't a bad man, but he'd fallen in with the devil. *Been there, done that.* Better not to kill him, though. Naomi Bradford was enough; no one would die tonight except the ones who had to.

The sprinklers hissed and he heard no alarm, so it must have triggered in the office. Brody pushed out his chair on the other side of the door and Casper tensed.

The office door slid open and Brody patrolled briskly through the home, his pistol readied in a two-handed grip.

Casper slipped from his nook behind him and planted the taser into the back of the soldier's neck. It emitted a series of sharp, staticky clicks and Brody crumpled to his knees. Casper followed him to the ground, device held flush until he'd snatched the pistol and tossed it over the sofa.

An elbow cracked into Casper's ribs, absorbed by his armored vest—but the soldier threw his weight back, twisted, and flipped Casper onto his back.

Brody was quick, wound up on top and landed a series of shots. One to the throat set off alarms in Casper's head.

His training kicked in. Tucking both arms close, shielding his neck and face, he weathered the attacks until he could club back with either fist. Their foreheads knocked together, and he had no idea who threw the head-butt. They rolled, exchanging positions, and then did it again in a struggle for chokes, arm bars, punching any time he had a fist free.

Brody's knife flicked out, but Casper locked down the arm, straining it almost to the point of breaking. The knife clattered to the floor.

With a snarl, Brody threw them into another roll that freed his arm, but Casper found his taser on the floor, wedged halfway under the sofa. Planting it into the soldier's ribs, the electric charge hit them both together. Every muscle snapped taut—it was like being shaken in a paint mixer. His finger tensing on the trigger, he tased them both until it slipped from his sweaty palm and a stray kick sent it skating away.

It had stunned Brody harder, so Casper threw himself behind the soldier and wrapped the crook of his elbow around the man's throat. He hoisted with all his strength, Brody elbowing his armored vest, kicking over a lamp, slapping his hands across the floor in a vain search for weapons and, at last, gagged and went deadweight.

It wouldn't last. Casper rolled the unconscious soldier to his belly, zip-tying him by wrists and ankles, then hogtying them together before he could recover from his daze.

Only need a minute, he knew. His pistol had—miraculously—stayed holstered at the small of his back, and he drew it now. *Easier to shoot the man, but glad I didn't.* Turning, he was just in time to witness a willowy girl exit her bedroom and cross the upstairs balcony, stretching sleepily without quite looking down. "Mark," she yawned, "I heard a noise. Is everything—"

She froze. Casper did too. He was at the bottom of the stairs in black face paint, wheezing through a sore nose that bubbled snot and blood, his gun dangling from one exhausted arm. Brody groaned, coming to beneath him. Naomi Bradford, the daughter of the Apocalypse, stood at the top of the stairs and registered all this.

"Oh God," she whispered.

"I'm sorry." He lifted the pistol, knowing what had to follow—resigned to it, but without the heart he'd once had for killing. *Just a fucking girl.* Disgusted, he opened fire.

She sprinted across the hall—his heavy arm hadn't been steady enough, and the slugs spanked into the wall behind her, one shattering the glass on a family portrait. "Shit." *Stupid to one-hand my gun—half-assed, sloppy. Don't care if you don't want to, Casper, this is the fucking mission.*

He pounded up the stairs. *It's fine—she's got nowhere to run.* Odd that she'd gone into her father's empty room and not hers. "I'm going to make this easy," he called, pistol now in a sturdier two-handed grip, leveled on her father's door. "I'm not like the other one. I'm not going to rape you." *Just the bullet,* he thought grimly. *I wonder if we'll both laugh about this after we're dead.*

He shook it off and approached the closed door to Tom Bradford's bedroom, where she was cornered.

"Are you still there?" she sobbed. It sounded so goddamn pitiful. *I wonder what I would do to a man who tried to kill my daughter.*

"I am," he said. "It doesn't have to be hard. I know how to make it easy. You won't feel it." *Like flipping a light switch.*

"You don't have to do this," she said through the door. "No one has to get hurt."

He shook his head. "Wish the world worked like that."

"Then you won't leave?"

He shut his eyes. "Afraid not."

Three shots ripped through Bradford's door and the first hit him square in the chest. It knocked him flat to his back. Five more shots penetrated the door, all over his head. He picked the slug off the cracked plate in his vest. *Of course he has a fucking gun in his room, you dipshit. He's a Republican.*

Casper fought to his feet, breathless like a hippo had sat on his chest, and kicked the door open. No Naomi Bradford—just an open window and spent pistol on the floor with its slide ejected back. He peered out the window. There was a narrow section of roof to one side, dusted in snow so that he could see footprints from where she'd jumped.

Casper hoisted himself into chilly air and leapt for the roof, almost skating off. He scaled to the apex and leveled his pistol at Naomi Bradford's retreating figure. "Don't move," he gasped. "Don't move."

He had her—nowhere to go, she stopped running. She lifted her hands in the air and collapsed to her knees, facing away. Head bowing as though in supplication, the wind whipped her gleaming auburn hair. Casper's mouth was tacky with drying spit as he approached, licking chapped lips. Snow crunched softly underfoot. "I wasn't lying." He swallowed. "You won't even feel it. I promise."

Her shoulders shook with another sob. "Did you kill Mark?"

"No. He'll live."

"So you just want me. Why?"

"It's complicated."

"For money? Are you being paid?"

"No."

Her hands trembled above her head and she panned her gaze, perhaps looking out at all those slumbering, snow-capped homes and quiet sidewalks where she'd grown up. Somewhere in the distance, sirens—but none would make it in time. He felt for her, felt the helpless knowledge that in four minutes cops would arrive and find her body.

And him. He wasn't leaving here a free man.

"Tell me why," she whispered.

"I said it's complicated." He stared down the barrel, a peace settling over him. The urgency was gone. *All that's left is the trigger, and I have minutes to do it. Just... squeeze it off. Do it while she's talking, when she won't expect it.*

"Uncomplicate it." She wiped at her face with one hand, the other still over her head. "I want to know why."

His finger closed over the trigger, tightening until he felt that tiny hitch of tension before it usually popped off. His heart had never been steadier. "The world ends if I don't."

She started to turn.

"Don't. Don't you fucking move." *Don't look at me.*

She froze. Their warm breath spilled into the air, misty and bright from the streetlights below. She turned again, so he jumped forward, putting the gun almost to her temple.

"I said don't!"

Yet she turned still, all from her knees, so that their eyes met and the muzzle was suspended in front of her nose. Some part of him knew he shouldn't stand within arm's reach of someone he meant to shoot—he ignored it. He knew from her eyes that the fight had gone from her.

More than that, when the wind caught her hair, streamers danced over her cheek and mouth. Her eyes were almost black, reflective, and they could have been Julie's. The way she looked at him was absent hate, anger, even fear. There was a roundness in her eyes, concern— *Shit. It's pity.*

"I said," and his voice caught, "turn the fuck around!" He ratcheted the hammer back.

"What if you're wrong?" she whispered.

"I'm not." He'd studied, he'd prayed, he knew. "I'm not wrong." But seeing her face made the words hollow. When he went over the evidence and the signs now, it looked different— like an old cellar exposed to daylight, the shadows gone and shapes all unfamiliar. The story, scriptures, it was all... bent wrong—or maybe bent right for the first time.

"I'd be dead if you believed that."

"I have faith. It brought me here."

"Conviction brought you here. Faith is the reason you haven't finished it. You're so sure you have to, but it's faith that's telling you: no, don't do the bad thing. Even if you're certain it'll make things better, trust God. Trust you don't have to do anything bad."

Something hot blinked out of his eyes, ran down his face. "You think the world works like that? What would you do? If the world were ending and you could stop it with a bullet? Because that's our world. It's falling apart, it's *always* falling apart, and it's held together by... willpower. By laws and the armed men who make them real. You think any of this shit—*any of it*—" He waved all around them. "—exists unless someone will pull the trigger? Everything, all around us, it's all here because hard men do mean jobs."

She kept her voice steady. "I think the point of dangerous things is to protect people who aren't."

"And when it's gone to hell? When God takes you to account at the end of days, what then?"

"Look up and say, 'You gave me hope and a bullet. I come before you with hope and an unfired bullet.' "

He snorted and tapped the scar on his armored vest where she'd shot him. "We both know it doesn't work like that."

Her smirk was nearly playful, surreal from a kneeling girl held at gunpoint. "In my defense, that was Dad's bullet, and you're way scarier than I am." Mentioning her own father seemed to bite her like a snake, though, and a sadness filled her. She no longer looked up at him.

"He's the reason—can't kill him without doing you first. He's the Antichrist."

"No, just a regular, old libertarian." Still frowning, she stared off into the distance—the sirens were two blocks away. "You're right about one thing, though. After Mom... if you kill me, I don't think he'll make it." She blinked up at him. "You're a dad too, aren't you?"

"Shut up."

"How old is she?"

"Shut up!"

"Can I ask you a question?"

"No." The gun felt heavy. He was so damn tired.

"You knew about that other one—Banich. The one who wanted to torture me. Rape me. Someone's convinced you to hurt me, but they keep telling all of you different stories. What if you've been lied to?"

He'd seen the rapist in the news. He'd met Wilkins and Burns firsthand. Shaking his head at fresh doubts, he wasn't sure why it had never occurred to him before. It was like she'd cast a spell; or lifted one. The rising fear that he was crazy swept over him. What was this new voice—his inner critic or his conscience? "What about the demon girl?"

Her brow furrowed. "Ryn?"

"She's not human."

"She's exactly what you should be. Dangerous—but good."

Casper's barrel wavered. The sirens were almost to the street. He had to do it now: there was no more time.

Naomi stood and he backed off a step, keeping the muzzle centered on her chest. Without flinching, she wrapped her hand around the top of the gun, stepped closer until it pushed against her, and looked over the gun as though it weren't there, meeting his eyes. "Tell me your name."

"Why?"

"We're familiar enough to talk about God and politics and to shoot at each other. You could at least tell me your name. It's etiquette."

"Casper Owens."

"Casper. It's cold up here. Let me have the gun and we'll go inside. We can make sure Mark is okay. Maybe sit for a while. You look tired. Like a man with a lot on his mind. Like maybe this isn't the time to decide whether to take my life."

"I have to. No time left." The sirens were close, flashing blue on the pale snow. But his finger wouldn't squeeze, not while she looked him in the eye, and when she tugged at the gun, he released it. "I have to kill you."

She put her hand on his shoulder. "Let's go inside."

~*~

Ryn tore across Commonwealth Plaza and sprinted the rooftops in Garden Heights, cutting through backyards and taking risks with being seen. She didn't care. The sight of flashing lights at Naomi's house made her heart lurch.

They were parked out front and Ryn froze atop a house across the street.

An ambulance sat in the driveway but didn't move. In the back of a police car was a middle-aged man who smelled of the ice-rink shooter. Her animal mind refused to piece it together, processing only what was before her: the shooter caged, blood in the air, the noise and bustle of authorities. Ryn dropped from the roof and approached the police car, fingers curling. She'd peel the car's chrome shell to get the meat inside.

"Ryn!"

Naomi's voice. It cut Ryn in half, doubled her over with relief. She caught her balance against a van in their drive. Gods and beasts and alien bullets could not bow her, but one look at Naomi stole all her strength.

Naomi ran straight into her and threw both arms around Ryn, forcing the monster back a step. The girl's entire body trembled and Ryn could feel terror radiating from her. "I'm glad you're here," Naomi gasped. "Have you heard what happened?"

Ryn's hands wrapped around Naomi's shoulders, the only thing she knew to do, and she inhaled the citrus of her friend's precious hair, a needed reminder: *She's still here. Still here, and I don't need to fight her God to take her back.* "You're unharmed?"

"He couldn't do it," she whispered. "Thank God, he couldn't do it."

Then he almost did.

Bitter, hard feelings contracted in the pit of Ryn's stomach, hit a flashpoint, and burned hot. She'd let the asura fester too long. *They will gather next on the full moon, when I will visit a reckoning on them all.*

~*~

Kessler spun a full circle to survey the scale of the disaster: all down the Whitechurch street was shattered glass, not a storefront, car window, or light left intact; the doors to four cars were torn off their hinges; the strobe of crime scene technicians' cameras highlighted gore plastered to a hood; a small media circus reported live, their shots framing a horde of angry college students hemmed in by police tape, all screaming about hate crimes. Down the street, a smoldering dumpster contained unidentified remains—some human, some just bizarre. The building above had flooded and its denizens were out on the street, an old man holding three cats in his arms wailing about his ruined apartment.

At the center of it all was a tall woman in a business suit with spiky, black hair. She chain-smoked and hit on a female uniform.

To Kessler it was a natural disaster. To her it was a Saturday night.

"So," Kessler said as O'Rourke tapped on his electronic tablet. "How much of this—exactly—is black binder?"

"Say what you will about this town, but it's not dull." O'Rourke pointed to a van on the street. "See the panel van? The one that looks like it's rented from Rapists 'R' Us? Front door was open when we arrived. The perp on the car hood over there—and a little more of him in that sewer grate and on top of that awning—came out of the panel van. Registered to a Trevor Wilkins. Bet our perp turns out to be Wilkins, soon as they find out where his teeth landed. He also matches a profile for one of the anti-Bradford lunatics posting online— username 'Gaia_Warrior.'"

Kessler blinked. "So this isn't just some nut shooting up a gay bar. It's Bradford related?"

"Or the hate crime's incidental. Let's talk to our witness."

They approached the dark-haired woman. O'Rourke nodded. "Melony Wiercinski."

"Call me Muse."

"Muse, then. How do you know Tom Bradford?"

"Who?" she asked. "The senator?"

"That puddle of human remains over there had a hard-on for Bradford and his kid. Now I don't know your business, but if the puddle was gunning for you—and I think he was—it means your path crosses with a senator's. Not to presume anything, but there's a typical reason for that."

"What, like I'm a campaign contributor? No thanks."

"Prostitution."

She arched an eyebrow. "You see the bar I'm at, right?"

"Maybe you're open-minded."

Her grin was all-knowing. "Insulting me and hoping it gets a rise—using that to make me blurt the truth. You have a thing for the classics, old man." She wagged a finger. "But you pronounced my last name right, which means you looked me up. What was it? My TED talk, right?"

O'Rourke shrugged.

"Wait, she's a professor?" Kessler asked.

"*Senior* professor. Biochemistry. God, I love how earnest you two are. It's adorable. I feel as though I ought to throw you a bone. But this is one of those crimes you don't want to look at too closely. Trust me."

"That what you did?" O'Rourke asked. "Got too close to something?"

"You could say that. Then again, I'm not the one lying in pieces, so maybe it wasn't my fuck-up."

"What do you mean?" O'Rourke pressed.

But she buttoned up.

Kessler tried another tack. "Ryn Miller."

That got Muse's attention, and O'Rourke's. But Kessler had only been guessing.

"What about Ryn?" Excitement danced in her eyes.

"She's woven into this every step of the way. And... sorry to say, if you don't give us a lead, she's our suspect. She's already attacked one of these anti-Bradford assholes. She's violent. And, I don't like it, but she's the obvious choice. Unless you give me another."

Muse nodded slowly. "Surprisingly honest for a cop." Tilting forward, she whispered: "I could give you suspects. More than one. There are layers to this, more than even Ryn knows."

"What kind of layers?" Kessler asked.

"That splatter of blood over there was street level. Some dupe. He's got puppet masters pulling his strings. But the puppet masters themselves have a paymaster."

"What sort of paymaster?"

"The highest of the high. Sort who might want a senator in his pocket—or to influence him any way he could. And everyone who isn't working for him is working for his rival. Except me, of course; I don't work for anyone." She smirked. "I've got tenure."

O'Rourke rubbed his bushy beard. "A conspiracy?"

"These two entities don't conspire—they despise one another. They're at war. We're all just caught between them, made into pieces on their board. It's hard to know whose piece you even are, but mark my words, if you don't even know the game's being played, that's how you know you're in it. And this whole thing? It ends in a place so high up we're all just ants eating dust."

"How do you know this?" Kessler asked. "What evidence do you have?"

Muse shrugged, stuck a fresh cigarette in her lips, and lit it. O'Rourke ground his teeth in the fashion of an ex-smoker who badly wanted one, and she blew the first cloud into him. "No evidence. But if you're friends of Ryn's, you're not my enemies. So I'll do a wicked thing and send you in the right direction. Look into Orpheum Industries, for one. And the Ostermeier Trust Fund scandal for another. Then have a little peek at Zmey-Towers Consolidated."

"And what are we looking for, exactly?" O'Rourke asked.

Muse ashed her cigarette on O'Rourke's shoes. "For history's real villains. For gods and kings."

CHAPTER FIFTEEN
Gazing Long into the Dark

Ryn scouted the Primrose construction site. The partly finished residence highrise was nine floors, nothing but skeletal girders on the top five, and surrounded with dirt mounds and rusted trailers. It had the faint odor of an asura and Ryn's claws ached to murder it, but she needed to wait for the full moon at the end of March.

The asura would gather then for the creation of a new hollow. If Ryn struck during the ritual she might slay them all. If she attacked just the one, the rest might scatter to places she couldn't yet follow. It might take centuries to hunt them down.

She suspected they had swept most of Ghorm's mortals off the board. The one called Casper Owens was in prison, repenting his crimes. For daring to hunt what was hers, Ryn ought to have gutted him—except the way Naomi spoke about him made her want to do it less. A little, anyway.

The droning humans who reported news showed pictures of Pandora, talking about body parts on the street and in the alleyway.

The Veil—a powerful deva enchantment that ceaselessly lapped at human memories of magic until it was sipped clean—did its work by fogging minds and burying whispers. By the time it came to light that the assault was committed by anti-Bradford fanatics, the media had moved on. Naomi remembered, though, and one day read a description of the second gunman's remains, of how he'd been ripped to pieces and half devoured. She'd cried.

That bothered Ryn.

Even with the brief relaxation of threats against her, Naomi wasn't at peace. The auburn-haired girl tossed in her sleep more than ever. She vocalized soft cries for help, pleas for phantoms in her dreams to stay back. Her voice floated through the roof. She would wake gasping, face wet with tears. Once, her scream pierced the rooftop and stabbed Ryn so deep that her nails—the only thing sharper than her palms were hard—cut the skin until her immortal blood dripped.

Thus, when Naomi announced an upcoming double date with Horatio and Wes a week later, Ryn agreed—anything, if it put her friend's mind on mortal things and not the night-mare creatures of her world.

After agreeing to the date, Ryn overheard Naomi on the phone with Horatio. She explained Wes had to avoid wearing scents, because Ryn had a sensitive nose. "She always wags her head at strong odors, especially cologne. So none of that, and none of that rank shower gel either. She hates it." Ryn should have been offended that they talked about her, but part of her kind of liked that Naomi had noticed.

The afternoons became a pleasure because they consulted every day after school. Ryn savored every minute in her friend's presence, in her bedroom, appreciating its warmth and general superiority to the roof. Naomi explained dating things, though she rambled and bumped around, the sleepless nights taking their toll.

Examining her ashen face and heavy eyes, Ryn interrupted one of her dating-related lectures. "If it is important to—as you say—'look nice'... perhaps you should rest."

Her smile was only half-lit. "That obvious? Maybe I need a prescription." She scrubbed at her face. "I'd hoped to sleep easier after talking to Casper. But when I heard about what happened to his friends in Whitechurch, how one was butch-ered— I don't understand how someone could do that to an-other human being. It's twisted."

Her words struck like a blow and Ryn's gaze flinched down. "But those men wanted to hurt you."

"Someone who kills like that, who mutilates, is still out there. Who knows what he wants? That's terrifying."

A cold space opened inside her, yawning wider, chilling her. "Is that why you can't sleep?"

Naomi considered it. "Not really? I don't even have night-mares about Casper getting into our house. I only ever dream about the parking garage. Like my brain is trying to tell me something." She shuddered.

Ryn nodded, soothed that the cause was Banich's grotesquerie and not her own murderous touch. She could almost digest that cold bubble now.

Naomi also insisted Ryn dress differently, for reasons unclear to the monster, so two days before the date they met at Center Square Mall.

"What is the matter with my clothing?" Ryn asked.

"I *love* your clothes. They're very... tomboy-mystique. But you need to dress special on a date."

"Why?"

"To feel awesome."

"I feel fine."

"Fine, by definition, is not awesome. Fine is a notch below awesome. Let's do better—I want to make jaws drop."

As usual, Naomi's enthusiasm was bulletproof.

"So, I know you like the pants look, but I was wondering if you would maybe try on a skirt?"

Ryn looked dubiously at the clothing rack. Her friend shuffled various skirts from the rack, skirts of every color and length, holding each to Ryn's waist. None interested her as much as the closeness and attention from Naomi. Truth told, in another era, she'd worn something like a skirt. But the men had worn them too. Since then, pants had been widely regarded as a technological advancement, one of the few Ryn personally enjoyed. There were times she believed pants to be humankind's most worthwhile achievement. That women didn't reap the full benefits was somehow typical.

"This would look good on you. It'll show some calf, you won't trip over it, but it's still kind of conservative."

"It's... frilly."

"Those aren't frills. They're pleats. *These* are frills." Naomi showed her and Ryn hissed.

"O-kay. No frills. But do you want to try this one on? For me?"

Ryn tried to say no, but to her horror found herself changing anyway. The "for me" had done it. *That wasn't fair.*

She toed out of the dressing room. Naomi beamed and clapped her hands together at chest level. "Perfect!"

Examining her bare calves, Ryn felt uncomfortable with the drafty sensation. When she turned to glance in the mirror, her spin flared the skirt just so.

"Wow, look at you," Naomi said. "I like seeing your calves; it shows off your grace."

It kind of *did* show off her grace. Her chin tilted up.

"You couldn't be more of a cat if you tried."

"Will you wear one?" Now she wanted to see Naomi be graceful in a skirt.

"No, I'm going in cargo pants and a hoodie." She was teasing again. She came up behind Ryn in the mirror, winked, and started tugging and pulling the skirt in places.

The touch sent a startling thrill through Ryn's body. She'd never been touched that way, not along her thighs and hips. She'd never imagined it would feel so nice and yearned for it to happen again, just once.

Naomi stilled, met her gaze in the mirror, hands dropping away. "The fit's perfect. Let's look at blouses next. And shoes."

Ryn wavered. Something bothered her. "I have no money."

"Don't worry about it."

"I should steal it, then?"

"No! No, no. I'll pay."

Normally Ryn didn't care, but there were more numbers on these particular clothes, and she'd gathered lately that the size and quantity of numbers was significant to people. "It's a lot, isn't it?"

"I'm the one begging you to dress differently. I'm being weird and pushy, so I don't mind paying. Besides, I'm a socialist. Just ask my dad."

"What is a 'socialist'?"

"Someone who flagrantly redistributes her father's money."

Ryn insisted on a blouse with sleeves, because she didn't like to show people the scar on her wrist where the men had pounded in a tent spike. The shoes, though, proved contentious. Naomi wanted Ryn to at least try on high heels, but Ryn regarded them as she might one of a Gorgon's vipers, and refused to stray too near. They appeared specifically designed to slow her down and would twist her feet into unnatural contortions.

"Just try them on," Naomi said, pursuing her through the shop, shoes in hand. "You're short."

Ryn retreated behind a display and kept it between her and the shoes, realizing they weren't what scared her. It was her friend's relentless desire to put them on her. She mirrored every step the taller girl took.

Naomi soon realized she would make no progress getting Ryn and the shoes into the same space without permission. "Please? They'll give you almost two inches."

She shook her head. If she'd wanted to be taller, she would be.

"They won't bite you."

But Ryn feared her friend would work her basilisk magic and the immortal deva would find herself in another dressing room staring down those shoes. Alone. She growled at them.

"You are the most difficult person in the universe. Fine." Naomi disappeared down an aisle and returned. "Try these on. They're flats. They match the outfit. You realize you're not even up to Wes's shoulders, right?"

"He can look down."

"He'll have a crick in his neck by the end of the night."

"His problem."

"You're terrible."

"I prefer being small."

"Why?"

"Lighter, faster. Less targetable body mass. Easier to hide."

"Weirdo."

They paused outside a store that sold human undergarments. Naomi rubbed her elbow with the opposite hand and gazed up at the cursive sign. Ryn paused too.

Naomi sucked in a breath. "What do you think?"

"About what?"

"I guess there's zero chance the boys would see us in them. I mean, set aside the fact I promised you it wouldn't get frisky, just the logistics. It's a double date. Not like it'll go there. So I guess we wouldn't need anything special."

Ryn canted her head to one side, confused by some of the garments and their functionality. "Where does the string go?"

"Um. Use your imagination."

She did so. One eyebrow lifted higher than the other.

"*Why?*"

"It erases the panty line in a tight dress. And some guys think they're sexy. Okay, most guys."

"They can wear it."

Naomi laughed. "I *like* dressing sexy. But Horatio isn't going to see my panties. That's what I meant—it doesn't matter. Betting Wes won't see yours either."

"I don't have any."

"Thongs?"

"Undergarments."

Naomi's face did the oddest thing. It reddened and her mouth and eyes opened wide. She gaped at Ryn, away, and at Ryn again. "You aren't wearing any?" she whispered, like it was a secret.

"No. It's uncomfortable."

"*Ever?*"

"Should I?"

"*Holy shit in a hat*, yes!" Naomi clapped her hands over her mouth. She whispered numbers, counting to five, head bobbing with each one. It was something she'd only done before with Denise. "Sorry. But yes, you should wear underwear, *especially* on dates with boys, who are easily confused and believe their presence or absence... signifies things." Naomi glanced at Ryn's chest, eliciting a prickly feeling all over. "There's no way you don't have on a sports bra."

"I wrap it in a long cloth." One produced by her kanaf.

"That sounds so convenient. Come on, we're doing this." She seized Ryn's arm.

"I— Naomi, I'm not—" Terror filled her.

"This is not like the heels. This is the thin line that separates us from the Hobbesian jungle. You will wear underwear on our date."

That sentence perked up heads in the shop, Naomi's face pinking in response. She tucked her head down while dragging the deva through aisles, finding a saleswoman who took them to a stall. She was tall, emaciated, with prominent cheekbones—much like the malnourished prisoners in the store's advertisements. *Do they make her wear the perfume?* It made Ryn's head throb.

The saleswoman led her into the stall alone and uncoiled a

tape measure. "Take your shirt off, sweetie, we'll get a better measurement that way."

Ryn backed out, growling.

"I'll... come back later." The saleswoman breezed away, causing Naomi to glance up from her phone and register that it hadn't gone well.

"I want nothing here," Ryn said firmly.

"You don't want a bra, or you don't want to take your shirt off in front of a stranger?" Naomi asked.

"Both."

Her expression softened. "Will you at least try it if I help instead?"

"I don't want it touching me."

"It's fabric. The only one who will touch you is me. And only if you let me. I— I know that's a big deal for you."

Everything in Ryn despised the idea of human artifice constricting her body's most intimate regions, and yet something in the auburn-haired girl undid her. It was that she seemed to understand her, and while Ryn had been many things—despised, worshiped, most of all feared—she'd never been understood.

"And listen, you know this is just for the date, right?" Naomi glanced sheepishly down at her own clasped hands dangling past her waist. "Forget what I said about Hobbesian jungles. I have these plans in my head. I just— I want that TV thing where we come downstairs dressed to the nines and the boys' faces light up. I've always wanted that."

But in her moment of uncertainty, biting her lip, she was already gorgeous; Ryn had known beauty before as a kind of symmetry in form, but the familiar and kind lines of Naomi's face tightened the monster's heart, made her lungs draw shallower breaths, and everything in her craved to touch her friend's cheek and promise her whatever she wanted. That was the power of her. Unable to look her in the eye, Ryn bowed her head. "As you like it."

"Thank you for this." Naomi cleared her throat. "Go into the changing room and take off what's wrapping your chest. I'll be right back."

Once inside the stall, Ryn unfurled the slip holding her bust, the cloth dissolving and untangling from beneath her shirt with ease. It rewove in her grip and she wound it nervously around one fist.

A knock sounded. "Just me," Naomi said.

Unlocking the door and letting her friend into the cramped space, she shied at the tape measure.

"We'll do it over your shirt and keep the weirdness to a minimum," she assured.

Ryn felt ticklish in the confines of the stall—it might be the absence of the slip over her breasts, feeling exposed even through the hoodie. She wanted more than usual to look away from Naomi.

"Take off your jacket and turn around."

Remove your armor and present your back. A more submissive thing could not be requested, and yet Ryn shed the jacket. She couldn't shed the lump pinching off her voice, though, nor conceal her loud heart. Hanging her coat, she rewound the loose slip of kanaf around her opposite hand.

"Is that what you wrap your chest with?" Her voice sounded close to Ryn's ear.

"Yes."

"It's pretty."

Ryn kept the black slip as soft and smooth as her magic could make it, and when Naomi reached to stroke it, she marveled.

"What is this? It feels like a cloud."

She wanted to yell, *See? My ways are fine.*

Sensing her chagrin, Naomi giggled. "Yes, you are wise and I'm a fool. But I like that you humor me. Put your hands up, you doink."

Lifting her arms intensified the exposure, Naomi's tickling breath at the nape of her vulnerable neck setting every fine hair straight as a razor. It should have evoked a warning growl, but instead, she shut her eyes and her breath stilled. The measuring tape smoothed around her ribs—she tensed.

"Relax," Naomi whispered, extending the word, saying it in some magical way that made Ryn's body obey. Just one word—one little word—and the monster exhaled, the coiled predator inside lounging like a cat. She felt as safe as she'd ever been, and so didn't understand why her heart galloped, why her blood pumped hot, why her knees threatened to buckle.

The tape measure tightened beneath her bust, unlooped, and constricted twice more at mid-bust and above. It felt good in a way that embarrassed Ryn, electrified her flesh, sharpened her senses to the point she felt Naomi's body heat and scent wrap her up, the fragrance having developed her favorite spicy-sweet edge.

"All right. I've got your size," Naomi said. "The good news is you won't need an underwire."

"Underwire?" Ryn crinkled her nose.

"You don't want to know. Arms down."

Ryn folded her arms around her middle.

"You can turn around. We're done."

No, she couldn't. It would mean looking at Naomi.

"Are you okay? Oh no. I pushed too far, didn't I?"

Ryn shook her head and turned, but there was nowhere to look that wasn't her friend, so she ended up looking into Naomi's eyes. A current seemed to pass between them, and Naomi's eyes dilated even as her face softened. She bit her lower lip, which seemed as full as it had ever been, and Ryn suppressed a wild desire to taste it.

"You did great." Naomi's voice broke and she glanced to one side, rubbing the back of her own hand with her thumb. The edges of her ears went pink. "I'll, uh, go get you some bras to try on."

She left the stall and Ryn stood in silence, listening to her own quick heart, and then to Naomi's. Her friend paused outside the closed door, relaxed against the wall a moment, breathed out, and wandered off.

Their hearts were both beating normally when Naomi finally returned with an armful of bras. Though she'd chosen every color, Ryn knew her preference immediately and pointed. "That one."

"Black. This is my surprised face." Naomi presented the bra. "And look: no frills, no lace. Do I know you or what?"

Ryn studied the satisfaction in her friend's smile as she picked through the rest of her selections, and realized something: several were too large. It dawned that they'd fit Naomi just fine. "What are those for?" she blurted, though she knew.

"For me. I *do* like lace," she teased.

For the first time, Ryn imagined the undergarment on her friend instead, and was so flustered she bolted for the exit, worming past the auburn-haired girl.

"Where are you going?" she laughed.

To hide. Her flight was wholly instinct.

Naomi fortunately let her go, shutting the door to try on her choices, but it did the deva's imagination no favors. "You should at least try yours on," she called.

Hearing her friend talk while presumably in a state of undress was frighteningly intimate.

It did do a small amount to alter her appreciation for the undergarment, and when Naomi purchased a red one, she couldn't look at her for the last hour of their excursion.

Together they left the mall, and their footsteps echoed through the parking deck. They passed beneath a broken light and a pungent fear odor wafted from Naomi's pores. Alerted, Ryn's senses scraped through the shadows for danger, but there was none. It was a reaction to the parking deck itself.

"Your tormenters aren't here," Ryn said.

"I know."

"Only us."

"I know." Naomi walked faster, outpacing her.

"Wait." Ryn stopped, forcing Naomi to do so.

"What? What's wrong?" Turning, Naomi glanced around the cavernous space, large eyes centering on the *plink, plink* of water drops into a distant puddle.

"Look into the shadows," Ryn whispered.

"I know! They're empty. Can we just go?"

"This matters. Look at them."

"I don't care. I want to go. This is— Seriously." Naomi shook and there was no color in her face. "Please."

Tucking their bags against a pillar, Ryn advanced—Naomi retreating step for step, until the deva closed the space in a startling instant, hand extended between them. "Take it."

"I don't want to do this."

"As you told me before... the only one who will touch you is me."

Her eyes tensed with indecision, bright with building tears, hands cupping around mouth and nose as she wrestled her fears, seeming again to bob her head in a silent count. At last, she took Ryn's hand, her fingers trembling like leaves in a high wind. "What now?" she asked.

Ryn pointed to the darkest corner. "Look there."

Setting her jaw, she followed Ryn's finger with her eyes. "Can we please go now?"

"Soon." Ryn led her friend into the shadows a halting step at a time.

Naomi's pulse hammered through their connected palms, fear-scent bleaching her palate and burning her eyes. On such bright-souled skin, the smell was obscene.

"You see?" Ryn asked once they stood in the pool of darkness. "It's empty."

"I see." Her voice wasn't quite as high or thin as before. "But how do you know before you're in it?"

"Because I'm from places where shadows aren't empty. I know the difference." Ryn guided her deeper, to the blackest part of the deck. "What do you see from here?"

"The garage." The reckless tempo of her heart had steadied.

"There is no shadow here darker than ours."

"I guess."

"I like it," she whispered.

Naomi licked her dry lips. "Why?" Shadows had a way of tugging voices lower, lower, until they were carried on small currents of air.

"Because nothing is cleaner than the heart of a shadow. It washes away their staring eyes and leaves nothing but me." *Us*, she realized. *Nothing but us.*

Naomi's heart relaxed to a normal rhythm. "You like that?"

"You asked once to see my home." She gestured. "Here it is."

"I'm afraid of the dark," she admitted, eyes shutting. "I never was until that night." Glancing sidelong at Ryn, her pulse spiked—an explosion of fear rolled through her and she jerked, trying to escape. Her mouth widened in a frozen scream.

Snapping a look over her shoulder for the threat, Ryn realized then—

I'm it.

Naomi squirmed her hand from the deva's grip, flailing out

of the corner and into the brightness of the deck lighting. Covering her mouth, she gaped into the pool of black, fixed on the gleam of Ryn's sunglasses.

"I won't hurt you," the monster whispered from her hideaway.

The words startled Naomi to her senses. With more control, she said, "I— I know, but please come out."

Stepping into the light, the monster bowed her head. A cold reality had dawned.

"I'm sorry, I didn't mean to freak out. It's just—"

"It's the thing you saw that night," she said.

A nod. "Not Banich, either." Naomi folded herself in her arms, as though a chill had crept over her. "No one would believe me if I told them."

"I would."

Nodding, she whispered, "Banich wasn't the only monster in the parking garage. There was something else. Something that came from Hell. Sometimes when I walk through my house at night, I know it's close. I can *feel* it out there, creeping between shadows. I sleep with my lights on because even though it can't be, I know it's there, and I— I don't know if I'm crazy."

Ryn tried to breathe, to inhale around the skewer through her center, more painful than knives, bullets, and tent spikes, more painful by far. Every beat of her own heart cut her.

Naomi rushed forward, throwing her arms around the monster, holding her tighter than Ryn had ever been held— and yet she couldn't feel it. She could only listen as her friend, her victim, whispered, "I'm so sorry. For a second, I saw you in the darkness and the way you blended into it, I thought you were *it*." Her laugh was too manic. "Thank God you're here. You're probably the only thing that makes it go away."

CHAPTER SIXTEEN
Those Who Fight Monsters

Her friend's nightmares had never hurt Ryn as completely as after she'd learned she caused them. Once being close to Naomi had been electric; what remained was a crippling hole in the deva's center, one that introduced her to a unique torture every time the girl whimpered in her sleep.

Ryn guarded her still.

On Friday, date night, Ryn brought her new clothing to the Bradford home.

"You didn't even wash anything?" Naomi gasped, incredulous the tags were still in place.

"No," she snapped. How was she supposed to know that? Her wings required no laundering—how was she supposed to know any of this?

"Not a problem. I'll throw them in the wash. Are you okay?"

No. Every glance and word was a reminder she was alien and unwelcome in the warm halo of her friend's bedroom lamp. "All is well."

"It's not." Naomi reached to touch her shoulder. "You don't have to—"

Ryn flinched from it—and hissed. She didn't mean to.

Startled, the auburn-haired girl froze, confusion knitting her brow.

What the deva wouldn't give to explain. *I have quills.* She stared into Naomi's eyes, willed her to understand. *They're on my inside. Every little brush massages them deeper.* She locked onto that image and tried her best: "Inside-out porcupine."

Maybe it somehow clicked, because Naomi eased back a step and said, "Go clean up. I'll try not to prick you again."

That she understood made this worse—she could reach into Ryn in ways no one else could, but whenever the monster reached back, she infected her friend's life with some new horror.

She retreated to the bathroom, where soon cold water needled her body and soaked her hair. She stood beneath the water, regaining her composure.

My world poisons her. From now on, I am only her guardian; never her friend. But she couldn't bring herself to vow it.

Water sleeked down her kanaf as she unwove it, retracting the countless fibers into six slits on her back, which closed and appeared only as thin scars. She donned a bathrobe, still naked without her wings, and padded to Naomi's room with arms around her middle.

"Your clothes are in the dryer. Let me braid your hair and I won't say a word about makeup. Promise." She started to cross her heart.

Ryn seized her hand before she could.

Naomi arched an eyebrow.

"Do not vow. Unless you mean it." She despised when mortals made vows so lightly. It reminded her that humans were capable of breaking them.

"Your hand is freezing." She ushered Ryn in, shutting the bedroom door.

"I showered."

"In cold water?"

Why wouldn't I?

"No one explained hot showers to you?"

No one had, and no one needed to. *Because when this task is done, and you are no longer around to ask, I will take them cold as the mountain stream and no one will care.* She eased onto Naomi's bed, wishing to make her face a placid mask and let time skitter ahead to their date.

But she couldn't, because Naomi slammed a chair down opposite her, sat to face her, and Naomi's face always made time stretch out. "I'm going to guess what's wrong," she said with steely determination. "I'll guess until I'm right, and I'll

loose. This would keep a lot of blood out of her hair.

"It shows off your face," Naomi said. "Which I like."

The dryer dinged, and Naomi fetched their clothes—she changed in the bathroom and Ryn felt wrong and excited at once, completely nude in her friend's bedroom. Unsure what to do with such feelings, she hurried into the outfit. The panties applied unwelcome tightness, the bra stiff and forcing her chest into a shape she wasn't accustomed to.

The blouse and skirt weren't so bad. It was hard to tell what humans liked, but she enjoyed the lines of her own body in the mirror and it was possible she was attractive. *I should be humiliated.* Compelled by the strange reflection staring back at her, she spun instead—just once. She could be humiliated later.

Naomi knocked before entering, wearing leather boots, tights, and a belted earth-tone dress with shorter sleeves that accentuated her long arms. "How do I look?" Her smile was more nervous than she had a right to be.

Releasing a held breath, Ryn murmured, "Beautiful."

Her friend's smile bloomed sincere and she slipped close to tug the edges of Ryn's blouse. "You're perfect."

"Girls!" shouted Naomi's father from downstairs. "There are two young gentleman callers who claim to be your dates. Should I have them shot?"

"No, Dad!"

"Are you sure? They look really handsome. Just a warning shot over their heads."

"I said no, Dad, now let them in and be nice. Give us five minutes."

Ryn heard the front door swing wide. "The girls will be down shortly. Have a seat. I want to get to know you boys. You both drink scotch, right?"

Naomi shut the door and bustled to her desk, kissing a photograph of her mother, then settling on another long look into the mirror, where her eyes met Ryn's. "I'm nervous."

"Why?"

"Other than school dances, this is my first date. Do you think we'll get food? I'm kind of hungry."

Being at the mercy of two juvenile males irritated Ryn deeply. "Next time, we plan. *They* dress up." Though if Naomi did too, she wouldn't complain.

Naomi summoned her courage and they left the bedroom, pausing in the hall to spy from the balcony.

Tom Bradford swiped through his tablet's screen while Horatio and Wes sat stiffly on the sofa opposite his chair. "And what do we have here? Horatio went from 'in a relationship' to 'single' just six months ago. Frowny face!"

"Sir, I promise this is not a rebound thing."

"Of course not, my daughter is much better than anyone else you could have dated. It concerns me you haven't un-friended this ex, though—"

"We have friends in common."

"And you're certain it's over with her?" Naomi's father tilted in, a maneuver that silenced Horatio's attempted reply. "You're certain *she* knows it's over?"

Struggling for a response, the boy merely shrugged.

Tom Bradford swiped a few more times. "You 'like' a lot of memes about marijuana legalization, Wes."

Wes's knee bounced so quickly it shook his voice when he talked. "It's not like—"

"I, too, support the legalized use of cannabis, though I don't condone it under my roof or as a parent. I'd rather not see young people's lives ruined for toking."

"Oh," Wes exhaled, relieved.

"But if you smoke it around Naomi, I might still ruin *your* life."

"Oh, no, never," Wes insisted. "I never smoke it in front of people who don't— I mean, I don't—"

"Of course you do. What else do you do?" Tom Bradford tilted his head to one side. "Too smart and cleaned-up for meth or heroin, but I'll bet anything you've tried at least one amphetamine. What was it—friend's ADHD medication?"

Wes's knee vibrated faster now, bullets of sweat working down his face. "I don't think—"

Horatio blew out a sigh. "His sister's meds, just once to study for a test, and he just sat in a corner writing sonnets to techno music all night."

"Still got an A on the test," Wes whispered in defeat. "On the bright side, I don't drink."

"That's because kids these days don't have the fortitude for

proper scotch," Tom Bradford observed. "They want everything in a nice, neat pill."

Horatio snorted, opened his mouth to retort—but stopped
himself just short of saying something.

"*Dad!*" Naomi hollered, going from lurking at the balcony
to hustling downstairs with Ryn in her wake. "You did *not*
make our dates friend you on social media."

Tom Bradford clapped his tablet shut, standing. "Gentle-
men. This is why you protect your data from the government.
Someone's always watching." He pointed at his eyes, then at
both boys. "Post lots of pictures from tonight. *Adieu.*" On his
way to the study he told the girls, "You both look nice. No babies, enjoy, and... Ryn... keep her safe."

Ryn nodded.

"He's unbelievable," Naomi said to the boys, even though
she'd spied on it happening and giggled at parts.

The boys stood, reflexively wiping their palms on their
thighs, eyes widening at the sight before them. Their hormones raged, but Ryn scented no aggression.

"You look fantastic," Horatio breathed.

No one else spoke until Horatio elbowed Wes, who jumped
and added, "Yeah! I mean, Ryn, you look... different. I mean
great! Not that you don't always look girl— er, great. Wow."
He tugged his collar, scanning for an escape route, and Ryn
was pleased at the way he twisted—it reminded her she was
still the predator. "From the top." He flexed his mouth, as
though to limber it up. "I like how you look."

Unsure what to say, she told the truth. "You smell harmless. I like that."

Horatio offered his hand to Naomi and they chatted on
their way out the door. When Wes offered his, Ryn stared at
it.

"Oh, I got you this." He removed from his pocket a thin,
black metal object sharpened on every edge.

"What is it?"

"A batarang."

That didn't clarify anything.

"You throw it. To disable bad guys." He made a tossing gesture and a sound from his lips, like air swishing. "I figured after the club... just figured you'd probably like a batarang."

It was thoughtful. Ryn hefted the weapon, testing its weight. "Sharp," she complimented, fingering its edge.

"It's totally not a toy. I bought it online and tried throwing it a few times. The less said about that the better." He rubbed a fresh scar on his chin.

Horatio's battered, four-door sedan had a recently placed Bradford campaign sticker on the bumper and he turned the radio down while driving.

"Where are we headed?" Naomi asked.

"Big surprise," Horatio said, sharing a cryptic grin with Wes.

"Holy smokes, your dad's intense," Wes said, changing the subject. "Was he serious about ruining my life?"

Naomi chuckled. "Joking. I think. He called the president's drug czar a 'scrofulous snorter of...' well, I won't finish that. You can ask him someday."

"C'mon, you can't leave us hanging," Horatio cheered.

"Rhymes with 'paint.' "

Everyone laughed but Ryn.

Swiping through his phone, Wes muttered, "Crap, still got memes posted about term limits. How far back on my wall you think he'll go?"

"How about you cut the cord?" Horatio said. "New date rule: no phones."

It was agreed and they turned them off.

"What's your read on Naomi's dad?" Wes asked, pulling Ryn unwillingly into the conversation.

Naomi half turned in her seat. "Why do we have to talk about *my* dad?"

"My mom manages a department store and never called the president of her own party a 'chucklehead' on live TV," Wes pointed out.

"Fair." Naomi relaxed back into her seat.

"You follow that stuff?" Wes asked Ryn.

She shook her head, staring out the window into the dark.

"Got to be *something* you care about," he pressed.

"I care about the things her father does." Ryn stared at the passing houses. "I hate flags, prisons, laws, schools, and self-important fools with badges or titles telling me 'go here,' 'do that,' 'don't think.' But that is the end of our similarity."

"Sounds close enough," Naomi grinned.

"No. He thinks humans are... bigger... than they are; that they can fend for themselves."

Wes seemed confused. "What do you believe?"

She'd never put words to it, but she believed most humans wanted laws—to feel safe from people with the wrong amount of money, the wrong color skin, the wrong religion or thoughts or words, and so they begged for them. They worshipped laws, because laws were how they puffed themselves up and pushed their foes into the mud. In one blink of Ryn's eye, though, the laws turned around like tigers and mauled the ones who made them. It was idiotic, and she felt bad for Naomi's father, because he had a principle; but there weren't many like him. Most of their kind loved flags. Most deserved to choke on them.

"What's going on in that head of yours?" Naomi asked.

Not knowing what to say, she mumbled, "I don't care what senators do, as long as they leave me alone."

They took highways beyond the city, where countryside whisked around them. An ache worked through Ryn, her limbs burning with the need to climb trees of hard bark, to sink into snowy litterfall and disappear into the wind that wove between trunks. She wanted to smell sap and lick it and hold the bitterness on her tongue, to drink the forest and be swallowed by it.

Naomi yawned and slackened into the car door, breath fogging the window, and the deva finally realized that the moment she dealt with all threats to Naomi's life, she would do exactly that: disappear into the wilds. That would end the nightmares, the quills—all of it.

"This is some drive," Naomi murmured. "How far are we going?"

"Like I said—it's a surprise." Horatio kept his eyes on the road.

Ryn had a mind to demand answers, but Wes recommended they stop for food.

Off the highway, they parked at a brightly lit restaurant next to an odorous gasoline station, climbing out of the car beneath a backdrop of tall trees. They flooded the deva with a need to slink into the shadows. Snow drifted in thick flakes, the smell of March's last storm in the air. "It will blow cold tonight," she said, and Naomi shivered without a heavy jacket.

Flakes stuck to the teenager's gleaming auburn hair, and Horatio hastened to wrap her in his coat the way Ryn wished to. "There are blankets in the trunk if you get cold," he said.

"Blankets?" Naomi's eyebrow rose.

"No spoilers." Wes unsuccessfully offered his coat to Ryn.

"Give her a minute," Naomi said, wisely assessing the way Ryn stared at the trees. "Think she needs a break—and she won't freeze, she's never shivered once while I've known her." She and the boys went into the restaurant.

Slipping off her flats, Ryn strode barefoot across the snowy lot, past the perimeter of lights, and deep into the slender black wood at the edge of the buzzing illumination. Once there, everything inside her uncoiled, a warm glow in her heart because Naomi had been reaching into her again, assessing her moods and needs in ways that were no longer uncomfortable.

She knows me. Not every dark corner, but enough. *Yet how she would scream if these glasses slipped even an inch.* That put an end to the warm glow.

Between the trees, she let the elder things stretch from her and touch the snowy boughs, the sky—everything in civilized lands tasted wrong, but in places without pavement, electricity, or shaded from artificial light, she could still feel the cold, unworked earth. Extending one hand east, she let the wind shiver through trees and unsettle flakes from her hair. Another hand west, and a second gust swept that direction.

Her laugh was a cold, high noise carrying far. The city's layer upon layer of brick and steel had not quite beaten this out of her. Savoring her comfort in the tiny patch of wild, she returned at last to the diner, refreshed.

Naomi had ordered for her. They ate, and the boys paid. It was all too familiar, the mortals treating her like someone to be looked after. The date tasted different, the wood having reminded her who and what she was.

Merging back onto the highway, Wes and Horatio kept the conversation afloat while Naomi slumped into her side window, dozing, a victim of restless nights and the rhythm of dark highways.

Her pulse quickened in her sleep. Realizing why, Ryn's hands balled into fists at her knees.

They turned onto narrower roads, lines masked by fresh snowfall. Naomi's head rolled fitfully to one side and she jerked awake with a shout. "No!"

She panted and everyone refused to look at her except Ryn.

Horatio rushed to fill the silence. "C'mon, my driving's not that bad."

"Where are we?" Naomi coaxed a stray lock of hair behind her ear, head bowed.

Ryn had no answer. The boys had driven them far from New Petersburg.

"Just wait—it's up the next rise," Horatio said.

They crested the hill and Naomi shot forward in her seat. "Is that what I think it is?"

"Yup." Horatio pulled into a gravel lane behind a line of cars working through the ticket booth.

"A drive-in?" Naomi asked. "They still have these? I've never been to a drive-in before."

"Real piece of history," Horatio said. "My family used to go all the time. They open earlier and earlier every year trying to spin a buck." He peered into the black-clouded sky. "Hope the snow holds back, or we won't make it through both features."

With only a few other cars out in the weather, they found a prime spot in the middle and Horatio left the engine running, the heater pumping warmth into the interior. He tuned the radio to a station broadcast from the theater. "Going to turn the engine on and off to save gas," Horatio said. "Hence the blankets."

He retrieved them and passed two back to Ryn and Wes. Then he unfurled a large one up front.

"Just so happens you only have three blankets, hm?" Naomi asked.

"I can go without if that's a problem," Horatio said.

"Just making sure you know that I see through your machinations," Naomi grinned. She scooted under the blanket and folded her feet beneath her.

The screen rose like a cliffside of white, and she furrowed her brow at images projected onto it—the noise and flashing pictures captivated the mortals. She'd never watched anything on their screens more than a few minutes, but it startled her how their mouths closed and their eyes subtly opened wide. The pictures were jouncy, garish, but something visceral in them held the mortals' attention, and she couldn't blame them: mortals couldn't control the speed of their perception, couldn't make an hour disappear or stretch a moment to infinity. These moving pictures did that for them: she'd seen how they erased hours by cutting suddenly between two scenes, or how they distilled a moment with music and held onto it; in a way, a hint at how the divine saw the world.

This film started with text insisting the events were based on a true story. Eerie piano music played and the picture swooped over a small, coastal town amidst trees and hills.

"Is this a scary movie?" Naomi asked anxiously.

"Yeah. Uh. Is that a problem?" Horatio asked.

"No. No, it's fine." But Ryn could tell it wasn't, and that feeling—guilt, Naomi had insisted—twisted in her belly, too real now to deny. *This is my fault.*

In the film, a family moved into a house against the pleas of a menacing, elderly man with a leathery face. As the story unfolded, ever-less-plausible horrors befell the family.

Naomi slid into the nook of Horatio's body. Whenever something popped out on the screen—first it was just a cat, then later an eviscerated doll—she jumped, almost into his lap. Her fingers dug into his arm, his other wrapped over her shoulders.

Ryn wished she could guard Naomi instead of sitting by Wes. *Guard her from what? Yourself?* The thing in her gut squeezed harder.

"That little girl is creepy." Wes shifted closer, then when she glared, further away. "Bet she's possessed."

"She isn't the ghost," Ryn said. "It hides in her mother."

"You seen this one?" Wes asked.

Ryn shrugged. "If I were an asura, I'd be in the mother."

"A what?"

"A spirit," Ryn said.

Wes rubbed his chin. "I feel you. The girl's got that psychologist, and they're trying to make the shrink look evil, because she hates the mom. Bet it turns out the shrink is the good guy."

"Would you two stop guessing the ending?" Horatio grumbled.

"What do you think's going to happen here?" Naomi asked, her voice small. She squirmed as the mother entered a corridor full of groping shadows.

"Ghost jumps out of the attic door," Wes said.

"No." Ryn shook her head. "It's inside her. So it appears from the mirror in the bathroom, down the hall, to the left."

The woman rounded a corner and a black thing flew from the bathroom mirror. Shrieks sounded from other cars, the camera shook, and Naomi whimpered.

"Ha. Ten points to Ryn," Wes said.

"Whoever talks next is walking home," said Horatio.

In the rearview mirror, Naomi's face drained of color, her shoulders tensed. That shadow—it had looked almost like Ryn when swaddled in her kanaf. One more turn of the screw and the deva's fists trembled. She wished she could open Naomi's mouth and eat her fear, drag it into her gehenna and burn it to nothing.

The scenes grew darker, emphasizing the menacing shapes inside the family's house at night, until Naomi's hands shook. Horatio seemed concerned, but Wes—oblivious—whispered about potential ghost weaknesses.

"One spirit can kill another by eating it," Ryn said, "because they're made of the same substance. For non-spirits, you must have Hell-fire or something sharp enough to cut a ghost. I only know one such thing."

"A plus-three vorpal sword?"

An odd piece of lore to know, for a mortal. "Two things," Ryn allowed. She kept her gaze on the movie screen and the rearview, where Naomi's eyes were bright with fear. The smell was worse than the parking deck and Ryn clenched her teeth.

Onscreen, the shadow creature pounced twice more, from a dark window and through water in a bathtub, where it drowned the family's patriarch. Each time it appeared, Naomi squirmed. Finally, the ghost sucked the little girl beneath a car in the garage.

Naomi threw her door open and bolted. Horatio sat momentarily stunned before following her.

Ryn stayed put. *What if she mistook me in the dark?* But

part of her wanted that—part of her wanted Naomi to scream
and to see the truth of her.

The teenager fled to the concession stand and restrooms
with Horatio's coat over her shoulders, disappearing between
the lights, where her long shadow vanished.

"She okay?" Wes asked.

Ryn unclenched her hands. Blood seeped from thin
wounds in her palms.

Naomi's scream cracked the night like a gunshot. Ryn
threw her door wide. Wind bit her as she hurdled a car hood,
forgetting her pretense of humanity, and slid to a halt at the
concession stand. Horatio held his jacket, calling into the
darkness: "Naomi! Come back!"

A blond boy of middle-school age with an impish face and
backward ball cap laughed hysterically. Horatio spun and
lifted him by his shirt, slamming him into the wall by the
women's restroom entrance. "You shithead. Why'd you do
that?"

"What did he do?" Ryn's desire to harm the boy laced every
word and for a moment, she didn't care that he was only a pup.

Horatio glanced at her, then lowered the boy an inch or
two. "He jumped out. Scared Naomi." He nodded toward a
mask matching the creature from the movie, discarded by the
wall.

"I'll get her. Deal with the pup." Kicking off her flats, Ryn
jogged into the snow. She tracked footprints into a lightly
wooded area beside the drive-in, where a copse of trees
opened to a picnic area. Naomi sat hugging her knees on the
picnic table in a ring of artificial yellow light from a single
lamppost. Beyond the light, black trees hemmed her in.

Ryn circled in the wood, looking in, a soundless presence
that pricked at her friend's intuition until she looked up.

"Hello?" Naomi wiped tears and shivered, sensing the
predator—sensing Ryn.

A blanket of snow muffled every sound but the panting of
hot breath from Naomi's fear-squeezed throat. She blinked
through glassy tears. Ryn stilled, her friend's gaze panning
across her, failing to catch. The pulse in her jugular quickened.

"Stop following me," she pleaded. "Stop sleeping under my
bed. Stop stalking through my house. Stop hunting me. Kill

me or don't, but show yourself."

Ryn stepped from the trees, into the light, and Naomi jolted back. Her mouth opened to let out a scream. The monster silenced her with one finger to her own lips. "Shh."

Recognition came next and Naomi sprang from the picnic table, rushing closer. It was the hardest part, because it made Ryn's hope flare briefly to life. *But there is only one way for me to end this.* Naomi had to face her demon—they both did.

"Thank God it's just you." Her arms flew around the deva's slight frame.

Ryn didn't embrace her back.

"I'm such an idiot." Naomi shivered against her. "So worn down, only ever half awake. I saw something jump at me, I just reacted—and I can't stop shaking because apparently I dropped Horatio's jacket."

"It's not the cold," Ryn whispered. "It's the monster."

"I— I'm sorry you heard that. I thought there was a monster out there, the one I keep dreaming about. I was sure it was there, I could feel it, and I think part of me still does. Am I crazy?"

"No."

"Was it the fear, you think?"

"No."

"Then what?"

"You're right." Ryn's voice was a ghost. Her chest tightened. The words were hard. Not hard to find, like usual—hard to *say*, as if each one was a mountain to be pushed over.

"What do you mean?"

Ryn stepped back. "There's a monster out here. Tonight."

Naomi's face changed and something flashed in her eyes. "Don't even joke."

It wasn't exactly anger. *Betrayal.* The lash of her friend's gaze burned and felt good at once, replacing some of the guilt with pain. Ryn far preferred pain. "Monsters are real. One has lived in your shadow for a while."

"No. You said you could tell. You said—"

"I missed one. It stood in the lightless parking deck with you. It moves through your home's dark passages. It stands here now looking at you."

"I don't understand."

"Yes you do."

Her soft face changed again, lips parting even as she accused with her eyes, a hurt so brilliant it burned through Ryn—all the pain her words wrought, she inflicted on them both and couldn't stop.

Shaking her head, Naomi glanced back toward the distant concession-stand lights. "Let's go back."

"Look at me."

Naomi shook her head. "No, let's—"

"Look at me!" Ryn growled.

The sound snapped Naomi to attention. She didn't turn right away, squeezing one hand in the other, her skin matching the color of snowflakes caught in her glossy hair. When at last she faced Ryn again, her large brown eyes had dilated with prey-fear.

"Watch now and understand what I am." Ryn took measured steps back, pausing after each. A stiff breeze tugged on Naomi's skirt, and she hugged her trembling body. The monster melted into shadow, wrapped herself in it like the wings of a bat. On the twenty-first step, Naomi's gaze unfocused, and on the twenty-second she lost the deva. Easing behind a tree, Ryn slid from trunk to trunk, using not just the darkness but the blind spots produced when Naomi's eyes searched for her—pausing when the gaze neared, flitting silently when it focused elsewhere. From inside the dark wood, she circled the clearing and her friend.

The predator in Ryn smelled her friend's rising panic, but Naomi couldn't quite see her, couldn't find the slippery movement. There was one human facial expression she could always read—a lurching fear at the realization one was being hunted. That expression crossed Naomi's face; she pivoted and fled.

Chase her! screamed Ryn's instincts. Her blood sweet and muscles warm, she snarled—*I shouldn't have done that.* But the sound rose as though plucked from her depths by dark magic. She burst from the trees, cutting off Naomi's retreat while she was still glancing wildly back over her shoulder.

Naomi thudded into the monster, stumbling back and collapsing into the snow. "This isn't funny," she stammered, crab-crawling away as Ryn advanced inch-for-inch, giving no quarter from the truth. "Why would you do this! Is— Is this some kind of test? Are you trying to prove anyone can do that?"

"Not anyone. I am shadow and wind."

"Stop it." Tears lanced down her cheeks. "You're not. You're my friend."

Ryn knelt and her only mercy was in not removing her glasses. "I am a killer and a predator. I hunted Walter Banich in the garage that night; I saw his ruined face. Do you remember how he lifted you with one hand? I could do that, and more—as I did to that man I tore apart in Whitechurch. Do you remember pulling out Banich's stitches? Did it feel good? Because I think I was laughing when I broke his ribs. His femur? It snapped like tinder. I enjoy breaking things—breaking humans. It makes my spirit sing. *And it is easy.*"

Naomi's breath quickened and her head shook.

"*I am* a monster. I am the one who lurks outside your bedroom at night, and I am the one haunting your nightmares." The gorgeous self-destruction flowing through Ryn's veins crescendoed as she tilted down to whisper, "And when I kill, it has nothing to do with war. It's what I am."

There. It is done. Now she sees me—all of me.

"Please," Naomi whispered, her body curled into a ball and her arms shielding her head. She hid her eyes, voice barely audible. "Please."

"Please what?" Ryn didn't like the pleading, and now the guilt returned—it didn't replace the searing pain of having betrayed her friend, simply added to it. "Please tell you I lied? Please go away? Please never speak to you again?" She needed to hear it, needed to remember it forever, to clutch it like a talisman in case she ever let a mortal make her feel this again.

Naomi's breath and body seemed frozen. "Please don't kill me."

"Kill you." The words echoed. Ryn wanted to laugh. Kill... Naomi? Was it a human joke? No. She knew the position the other girl lay in now. She'd seen ten thousand mortal women like that before, kicked, spat on, beaten, raped. Ryn flinched away, stumbling. Snow fell in the dark wood all around them and it made her dizzy. *"Please don't kill me."* The words stamped into the core of her and the deva had no answer.

She found herself wandering through the trees, Naomi sobbing in the distance. It was a while before she realized Horatio was shaking her. "What's wrong? What's the matter?" How was he so far away if he was shaking her?

Ryn pointed to the distant speck of lamplight in the woods. Horatio ran off.

She wiped melted snow from her cheeks, where it seemed to have gathered, its taste too salty.

She hid. She didn't know what else to do, how better to shrink into nothing, than that. Eventually, Horatio carried Naomi to the car, where he wrapped her in a blanket. He and Wes seemed to argue by the light of a phone's LED screen, and the car turned on.

Naomi had convinced them to leave Ryn behind. *Good. Good and wise.*

But the car hit black ice on its exit. The tires whirred uselessly, lost their grip, and the vehicle lurched into a slow spin that planted its back wheel in a ditch. Horatio and Wes got out and pushed in vain. Ryn approached, uncertain, but decided to send Naomi along.

"Get in the car," she told them.

Horatio glanced over his shoulder from the bumper. "Oh, thank God. You disappeared. Naomi won't say a word, but... look, we had our phones off, and it turns out something happened at home. It's bad. We need to get her home *now*, there's people after her tonight, and there's a blizzard coming in."

Ryn slammed her shoulder into the bumper with the boys at either side. It shot up onto the road.

"Got a good angle on it that time," Horatio said, dusting his hands proudly.

Ryn strode past them. "Get in." She slid into the driver's seat.

They scrambled in, Horatio asking if she could drive, but Ryn didn't answer. She adjusted the seat so she could reach the pedals and looked sideways at Naomi in the passenger seat. The human girl shifted into the door until she pressed the window glass. The deva lowered a console divider that had been lifted for the movie. Naomi glanced down at the divider, then at Ryn, as if to ask if she was serious. They both knew it was barely more than a gesture, and gestures from monsters meant nothing.

"Seriously. Can she drive?" Horatio asked.

Ryn stepped on the gas and pushed the vehicle over sheets of black ice. She manipulated the wheel, edged the rubber over clean asphalt, and the tires gripped. She smoothed them out of a fishtail and sped down the road.

"Apparently?" Wes said. "Yeah."

Ryn drove through blackness and flying snow. Other drivers nailed their horns when she shot by. Horatio begged her to slow down, swore elaborately in Spanish, and Ryn sped past two accidents.

Naomi never spoke, never moved.

They pulled up outside her house. Ryn glanced back at the boys. "Get Naomi."

She went directly to the front door, pounded twice, and Mark answered. He had his pistol drawn. "Where is the senator?" she demanded.

Naomi's father stood from the sofa. "Is it her?"

Ryn dodged past Mark. "She's here. Safe. What happened?"

"Police called us. Carol disappeared from the district office tonight. They..." His face was anguished. "They say someone pulled up in a van. Grabbed her. In front of her goddamn husband and kid. They saw it happen."

Wes and Horatio escorted Naomi inside, her father rushing to lift her off the ground in a crushing hug, and Ryn used the moment to slip into the night unnoticed.

They had taken Carol. Their plan would be to break her, possess her, then use her to get close to Naomi. They would probably hope to bypass Ryn, use Carol to sow doubt about her among the Bradfords, not that Ryn hadn't done that job for them already. But turning Carol into a hollow would draw them all to their nest—all in one place at the same time.

That was fine. It was a good night for endings.

CHAPTER SEVENTEEN
A Reckoning

The blizzard's cold came in through every uninsulated surface of the metal trailer, came into Carol through knees pressed too long into the floor, wrists rubbed raw by shackles, her head clouded by the sour smell of her own vomit. If she lay down, the icy floor would suck the heat from her shivering muscles.

A television lit the stark chamber, playing horror movies featuring tortured captives—the kind that made an audience fidget when the drill went into a shrieking actress.

But this was no movie. He'd stripped her to underwear and left a workbench littered with things: carpentry tools, a book of matches, a coil of barbed wire, oily rags, and a single beer bottle.

He wanted her to guess. That was the purpose of the movies: to make her wonder which things in the room were just there, and which he would use.

Frozen hinges on the trailer door wailed, a horrid sound that made the skin along her spine tighten. His flashlight blinded her, forced her to glance away, clanking door and shuffling footsteps her only sign they were sealed in together.

"Hello dear," sang a man's voice—his tone was playful like a drunk's; it had no inhibitions. "Guess whooo?"

Carol straightened under the gaze of a monster, an old habit. "Remember General Gambari? Ever watched him on the news? War criminal. Had whole villages... cleansed." And she'd been surprised when his eyes hadn't seemed special: neither empty nor cold, just wrinkled like a father's. "He came to the States once. I got him coffee."

"Oh. That must have been *nice*," crowed that singsong

voice. He kept the flashlight in her eyes, his silhouette examining the carpentry tools.

"I spat in his coffee. I'd say you're only the third-, fourth-scariest thing I've ever spat on."

"Ah, getting a little ahead of—"

Carol hawked and what was left of her spit flew above the flashlight. There came a satisfying smack, a short growl. Her courage liquefied at the sound.

His shadow knelt. "Did you know," he said with the clear enunciation of an instructor capturing the attention of children, "that a human can be addicted to anything? Isn't that fascinating? Why, I once met a man who liked to..." He yanked her manacled hands closer to the darkness masking his face. "...cut his fingernails."

Rather than biting, he play-chewed—loud lip-smacking noises dragging from Carol a squirm and a short shriek.

"He'd trim and trim and trim, down to bloody nubs. Then the roots. Do you know what the flesh looks like, that gooey stuff where fingernails nestle? He does. He'd hollow his fingernail holes into wet, red cavities, and poke poke poke—looking into his own body in horrified fascination, every electric current of pain as satisfying as an orgasm." Each of his words, a nursery rhyme to a child; and the shadows on his face weren't right—there were ridges in all the wrong places. "The right kind of addict will scrub his hands until they seep. Castrate a rapist and he'll rape with broken-off broom handles. Why do you suppose that is? What's he really want? Do you suppose for some people, they do these elaborate, bloody things for no other reason than... habit?"

Carol tried to speak. To say something flippant. To goad him. Nothing came.

"You know what I am." He shined the light beneath his chin and she flicked her gaze down. She didn't want to see.

He roared: "*Look at me*, worm!" All the singsong had turned upside down and animal.

"F-fuck you."

"It's almost like you *want* me to start with the barbed wire."

When she refused to look he bunched her hair into one fist, jerking her face upward. Through slitted eyes, she saw him: a

patchwork face of jigsaw stitches stretching down to an emaciated, shirtless torso and, below that, a scabbed patch of bris-
tly hair where a dick might have been. He'd cut it off, mailed
it to her office. Not someone else's—his own.

Carol couldn't possibly throw up again, her body heaving
nearly inside out with the effort. She gagged out, "Go to hell."

"We already did." He was back to the melodic instructor.
"Probably some time ago. No one noticed." He frowned, uneven patches of his stitched face rumpling like a poorly made
quilt. "We just kept trimming, scrubbing, fucking. Same thing,
every day, and we'll keep doing it again and again until we've
whittled the flesh off our bony fingers and walked until our
feet turn black from gangrene. The last man alive will die
humping the—"

He coughed. It cut off his words, thank God, but a second
cough speckled his blood on Carol's face. Crimson oozed off
his lower lip. His naked chest cracked like dry wood, producing a shudder, and something slick with black blood erupted
through him. It appeared as though a girlish hand had just
sprouted from his flesh—it flexed there, turned over, and drizzled. Then it sucked wetly back into him and he crumpled.

The flashlight bounced and rolled across the floor. It illu-
minated his heaped body, then a trailer door left open, and at
last a figure who'd been behind him—*oh God, what is that*. At
the briefest glance into its burning eyes, fear overrode her
senses and Carol passed out on the icy trailer floor.

~*~

Four kerosene space heaters blew warmly against Ghorm's
flabby mass, keeping him comfortable in the cavern of Primrose's third floor. Bare wood frames separated the chambers,
marking where someday contractors hoped to erect walls.
Taped-down cables spread in elaborate webs of Ghorm's design and black tarp sealed every window. The darkest corner
was for his monitors and the pneumatic chair holding him
aloft.

Most of the remaining space featured a sterile operating
theater and lab belonging to Mr. Saxby, as well a backroom
caging his menagerie of rats, monkeys, and dogs, all silent in

the face of an inevitable fate. Each animal's cage door was marked with a time, day, and serial number, and all cages marked with a time and day prior to this moment were empty.

Ghorm squinted at his email while tapping at a keyboard set atop the great crest of his distended girth. "News from on high," he intoned. The pneumatics of his chair hissed and he spun his corpulent hollow to face Mr. Saxby and Tooloo both. "The Hidden One sends word. He understands our... reticence... to deal with Erynis. However, he offers us sanctuary and generous payment if we finish off the Bradford girl."

"I'm unconvinced we require such 'sanctuary,' " Mr. Saxby said. He removed a gold-chained watch from his waist pocket, waiting for the second hand before snapping on thick green gloves and reaching into a cage to extract a wriggling white rat. He held the thrashing animal down, calmly injecting it from a syringe. The animal squealed and curled into a ball, unmoving. "How about instead of begging for the protection of deva, I simply deal with the monster."

"Absurd," Ghorm sniffed. "You saw Splat. He came back *broken*. His hollows ooze from the pores—can't stitch them up fast enough to keep it all together. His flesh-riding days are numbered. She could do that to us all!"

Tooloo was sunk into her beanbag chair and staring into a large-screen television as she mashed the buttons on a controller, her gaunt face lit by periodic flashes of light and gore. Muting her headset, she spoke without ever facing them: "I've analyzed her attack patterns based on her fights with Splat and Burns. Two things."

Sighing, Mr. Saxby inserted the twitching rat into a jar where it withered, hair sloughing off in fat clumps and skin blooming open like a flower—what remained beneath was a pulsing cluster of eggs feeding off its tissues. "What, pray tell, do you have for us?" He sounded bored; bored with his experiments, frustrated with the ramshackle lab and animal subjects he was reduced to using.

"One: you underestimate her. You've killed two deva, both born in the last six centuries. This one is from the Long Ago; she remembers the time before history shattered. The eldest deva in this hemisphere, the Hidden One, and Set the Pretender? They're using you because to move against her is...

dangerous."

"Oh please," Ghorm scoffed. "Deva? Frightened of a little monster? Who cares if she frightened a few Romans and Greeks."

"As well the Sumerians," Tooloo hissed, "depending on who you believe."

"Your second point?" Ghorm demanded.

"She can be defeated. There is a strategy."

Now even Mr. Saxby paused to listen.

"Her claws are death." Tooloo stared at her flickering screen. "Neutralize them, poison her, rely on brute force. You'll never be faster—but you'll out-heal her. It's all about those claws, though. They'll end you—end any of us." She unmuted her headset and went back to her constant stream of simulated violence, the opium that kept her mind relaxed enough to reason.

"We could just leave," Ghorm suggested. "There are more places she *can't* go than she can. And surely the Hidden One has bigger things to worry about than one measly mortal daughter of a senator."

"No!" Mr. Saxby snarled, the mask of pleasantry gone. "You think my research *cheap*? I'm no longer tinkering, Ghorm—what I'm planning will knit two worlds together! I am subsisting on rats and chimpanzees, but I need human skin and sinew and teeth, and..." He dashed a beaker into the corner, where it shattered. "...*proper equipment!*"

Ghorm sneered. "You think I don't yearn for finer things? I'm trapped in this dank cavern when I could be lounging poolside, or on safari."

"Spare me," Mr. Saxby moaned.

But Ghorm couldn't help reminiscing. "There is this lovely island, and they get the most exquisite prey shipped in—only the finest. Lithe, intelligent coeds; none of these hopeless indigents, no, they'll let you gun down a svelte little doctor or lawyer and their taxidermists do top-notch work. I had three trophies before I spent the last of my money. Had to sell them. I *miss* them; they were a matching set."

"Completely unreasonable waste of money," Mr. Saxby grumped. "I could organize a hunt in the Appalachians for a fifth of the cost, you extravagant fool."

Ghorm sniffed. "It's not a *real* safari unless it's hot enough to be served cold drinks and you're fanned by cabana boys."

"So at least it's settled," Mr. Saxby said. "We stay. For the money. If you're worried about the monster, we'll fetch some vicious dogs using what's left of the advance."

There were still a few dozen gold bars left, plus a little paper money. "You think hellhounds, then? Why not use one of your dogs?"

He snorted. "These are family pets—chosen for their docile attitudes. We'll start with something half mad. I'll rework the flesh, you program the... proper motivations. We'll store them in the basement and set them on our monster once it's time."

"And what, pray tell, do we feed them?" Ghorm demanded.

Mr. Saxby shrugged. "We've buried nine drifters and a federal investigator since we nested here." He positioned his camera, photographing the rat as it decomposed into more eggs, each wriggling with strange inner life. "The dogs will eliminate our drifter problem, and the drifters our dog-food problem."

"Truth," Tooloo said.

Ghorm tilted back, sucking his teeth. "Fine. Who cleans up their waste?"

"Splat," said Mr. Saxby and Tooloo at once. He was always given the messy jobs: disposing of bodies, washing under Ghorm's fat flaps.

"I accept," Ghorm said, magnanimously enough that Mr. Saxby rolled his eyes. "Tooloo, you have a knack for picking out vicious humans. Go see if your talent extends to dogs." Ghorm's chair hissed as he spun to face his monitor before she could protest.

Swearing, she turned off her console and opened the safe that secured their dwindling supply of gold one-kilo bars and cash. Swiping a stack of bills, she slipped through the steel fire door.

Ghorm sighed and glanced at the open door. "For the six-hundredth time, Tooloo, *shut the door*. You weren't birthed in a barn." Returning to his screens, he muttered, "That I know of." Tooloo didn't reply, nor did the door close, so Ghorm spun his chair. "I know you heard me, you unfeeling knob! Get back here and—"

But he didn't sense her. Only two asura inhabited the building: he and Mr. Saxby.

"Something's the matter," Ghorm whispered.

Mr. Saxby glanced from his jar of pulsating eggs, tilting his head to the side as one human ear sharpened to a dog-like point. "I hear something."

A *drip, drip, drip* plinked from the shadows beyond a yawning doorframe.

"And I smell blood," Mr. Saxby whispered. "A lot of it."

"Impossible." Ghorm's eyes searched the darkness. "She's stuck to the Bradford girl; she's *always* with her!"

Something oblong rolled awkwardly from the doorway, into the light—Tooloo's head. It emptied Ghorm of feeling, thought.

Mr. Saxby peeled off his gloves, unsnapping his collar. "Distract her while I change into something more comfortable."

"*How?*" Ghorm wailed.

A shrug from Mr. Saxby. "Die slowly, if you must."

Ghorm's frigid, syrupy blood pumped through an overworked heart the size of a cantaloupe, which at last convulsed and stopped from fear. Yet before his spirit could flee the dying body, a crack resounded from beneath his chair. "Oh dear." Something had undermined the floor, and gravity—ever Ghorm's harshest foe—seized hold, dropping him through the layer of crumbling concrete. He struck one level below, chair buckling beneath his mass.

There she was: perched upside down on the ceiling, the claws she'd used to cut away his floor gleaming in the dim. For eyes there were just two pinpricks of frosty blue light, a stare that was nothing but hate. When she dropped from the ceiling and bowed close, he saw how that light came from her irises. She had eyes of truest black, the rings of blue contracted thin—a sign she'd consumed psilocybin mushrooms, allowing her to spot him even if he fled his body.

"Wait," he pleaded, daring to catch her gaze. In so doing, Ghorm could stretch a moment into half a year. It was his gift, to hold his victims still while he whispered poison into their minds. Their stares fused. True, this moment would pass no faster or slower for Mr. Saxby, but Ghorm still had a chance.

He could hold her hostage to time and plead his case, whittle her down with bargains and assurances.

The words flowed from his mind, modulated low and sweet, honeyed promises that he would not only spare the girl, but protect her—he could provide names of those who meant her harm and enlist defenses for her that Erynis could only dream of. But wait! There was more: she was the victim of a conspiracy, after all, a pawn in a war among deva, and if Erynis vowed to spare his life, he'd spill secrets, bind his will to whatever the monster desired. He said all these words, said them elegantly, in the time it took to blink.

"What is my name?" Her voice was deadly and thin. She'd seized control, ignoring the way he teased the seconds longer, and spoke with words, not thoughts.

"Why, it is Erynis," he said, mild as milk.

"No." Her fingernails fanned, each glinting with unnatural light, sharper than a mother's scorn. "What am I *called*?"

He tried again to hold her gaze, but time marched onward, steady as the beads of cold sweat trickling down his plump throat. "They— They say many things about you that are plainly false, else you'd—"

"Say it," she hissed, hand rising, "and you live one second longer."

Such truth in her words—and so he said it to buy himself one second, with which he might whisper a saving plea or be aided by Mr. Saxby. "The Implacable One."

"About that, they do not lie."

For a certain type of immortal, one second stretched nearly to the corners of eternity. Ghorm stole from it what felt like a month of contemplation, and at its end, he tracked the arc of her nails as they traced the air, so quick their gleam formed a crescent of light edging ever nearer.

Perhaps he could have used his last moments to brood on how it had all gone wrong, or to hope, or to mourn his three perfect trophies lost to him decades ago. Instead, he could think of nothing but the strange beauty of that crescent of light coming to end him.

The instant before she touched him, he surrendered—he let go of the moment, she split him in two, and he heard the great gush of blood from his body splash across the room's four corners, washing over her ankles.

The claws didn't stop until they sliced to the center of him, to the essence, which they also split in two.

~*~

Ryn sucked the last of Ghorm from her fingertips, swallowing him into the burning hell that had already ended Splat and Tooloo. It might have pleased her any other time. Tonight, their terror only reminded her of Naomi lying afraid in the snow.

She leaped to the hole above, struggling through because her limbs buzzed with numbness, an effect of the mushrooms. Crouching, absorbed in the drug's curious tunnel vision, she ignored Saxby's mutating body and stared instead at crimson staining her hands. Was arterial spray always so mirror-bright or was this also from the mushrooms? She thought she could see her image in them, a reflection of her hair in the blood and the blood in her hair. Naomi's braid had loosened.

"Have I failed to hold your attention?" Saxby asked.

Ryn glanced up.

"Ah. Glad to see I have it now."

The room was faded white except for the asura's scaly black body—a great wyrm with coils thicker than ancient trees and a bull's horns pushing forward from his plated skull. His every breath was hot and billowed the fringes of her kanaf, all that mass coiled like a spring in the midst of a lab full of cages, workstations, and canisters of compressed gas.

When he spoke, his image vibrated and light zinged between his scales like electricity through a circuit board. "I've killed deva. I've tasted your kind's blood, and it is sweet."

Her head canted. "Then make me bleed." She wanted it. A disturbing, alien thought, so dreadful and backward she hardly noticed the blow from Saxby's tail.

A wall came from nowhere and cracked into her, shattering. A follow-up swipe from the tail's backlash beat her all the way through the dented cinder blocks and she blew through a second wall, smashing into the third amid spiderweb cracks.

Up lost its meaning. She tasted blood, could feel it seeping from fissures in her skull, and it felt good. All the pressure of her building rage vented from her broken scalp and soaked through her hair. She tossed the fraying braid over her shoulder, speckled blood on the wall, and centered her stare on Saxby.

"Again," she said.

His dark coils spilled like ribbons through the hole in the wall and he sneered with dagger teeth. In a flick of motion, his venomous tail opened three red gashes across her chest.

Yet the red-hot glow of pain didn't exorcise her demons.

Beneath the bleeding cuts, she felt the wyrm's searing venom thread into her veins, weakening her. Her body fought the poison, but it wasn't the thing slowing her down; it wasn't the thing dragging twisted desires from her soul—she'd ingested the psilocybin willingly, and whatever a deva consumed by her own will, whether alcohol or drug, affected her fully. She could see an asura, true, but now when the serpent licked her blood from his spiny tail and grinned, she could think only: *To her, that is what I am. Bloody-mouthed, grinning.*

He struck with the twin spears of his horns.

Ryn caught the glinting point of one horn and stopped it an inch from her throat.

The force bowed the cinder blocks she was pressed into and the crumbling wall swallowed her, spat her out the other side where she tumbled through wind and snow. Hitting the top of a cargo container, she skidded across slick steel and jumped to her feet.

On great and ragged wings Saxby descended, displaced air scouring whorls of snow from the broken ground where he alighted, just forward of the container. He rose, towering high.

Ryn spread her hands to either side, cool air tickling between her fingers, the ache of poison and fractures not enough to slake her thirst. She met the wyrm's unfeeling gaze, finding nothing in his soul but hatred and arrogance; nothing that wasn't also in hers. "More."

He sneezed globs of ooze that smacked both her hands, viscous so that when she clenched her fists they wouldn't reopen. She could wriggle individual fingers, but her deadly nails were each secured to the only thing they couldn't cut: her palms. *No more claws.*

Saxby pounced, snatched her in his hind feet, and on wings as wide as city buses, carried her up, up, to the top of Primrose, where he broke her spine against steel girders. Feeling winked from her limbs. She slid off the girders, dropping to a worker's platform, helpless.

Saxby brought his spiny tail overhead for the killing blow.

But she still had cards to play. Threads from her kanaf pierced the back of her neck, shooting through her vertebrae and fusing a connection. Sensation woke throughout her—agony like black lightning—and she caught the tail's downswing. Spines ripped through her forearm and broke off in the wound, the impact shattering her platform and dropping her through space.

She caught an I-beam in the crook of her elbow, dangling over the building's metal skeleton while the broken-off spines pumped her other arm full of venom—worse venom than before, blowing through her veins like wildfire.

It was melting her arm.

Before, the poison had slowed her. This one bubbled her flesh inward in bloody honeycomb clusters. Cinching a razor-thin thread from her kanaf just below the shoulder, she bit and pulled the line taut with her teeth, slicing off the offending limb. It thumped onto the platform below and she stitched the stump closed.

Saxby thudded onto a steel strut below, slurping her arm into the back of his throat, gulping it down. "Lovely how my poison brings out your flavor," he purred. "When I tasted your blood before, it helped me tailor this venom just for you. This sampling will evolve it even further, sharpen it so that my next sting will end you—from now until the End of Days, every little piece of you I take makes me better at killing you. I have your scent, monster, and now it is *I* who will follow *you* through the ages, killing your every incarnation."

Wind whistled against Ryn and undid her braid, the loose, whipping strands filling her with a sense of loss. Naomi's kind hands would never do that for her again.

"You hear me?" Saxby spat. "I am what you've always claimed to be—I am the thing that eats *you*."

She fastened her attention back on the dragon, its fury bunching all that killing power into a tight S-curve.

It reminded her why she'd come: not to feel sick, not to mourn the phantom of a thing that never could have been. *I came here only to kill.*

"—and when you wake from this death decades from now, I'll bring you the girl's bones."

Yes, Ryn decided. *Too much time among mortals—I've forgotten what I am for. My purpose is simple.* She tossed herself from the beam and flew past Saxby down the building side, sensing his mass behind her when he lifted his wings into a V and dived.

At the third floor where they kept the laboratory, she snapped a tether from her kanaf to the building side and bent her momentum through a tarped-over window, rolling to a stop amidst workstations. Saxby overshot, shaking the whole structure when he hit the earth.

Outside, Saxby threw a truck, roared, blew chemical fire into the sky. Inside, Ryn mixed his chemicals into an acrid concoction using the limited dexterity of her glued hand and her feet.

He pummeled through the wall, dusted gray from concrete powder, all jaws and burning strands of spit. Ryn stood atop his station and punted a smoking flask into his throat. She shoulder-rolled beneath him before he could chomp down and landed a blow to his tenders that forced him to aspirate the flask's acid.

With the serpent choking and thrashing, Ryn dodged between his legs, bounced to the wall, the ceiling, and alighted on his spine. But his venom weighed her down and he bucked hard, sending her to the floor; he shouldered a workstation over and pinned her by the waist.

His laughter echoed, interrupted by a wet cough that brought up sizzling mucus; he laughed again, louder, as he leaned his tonnage onto the workstation. A loud pop and jolt of pain signaled the dislocation of Ryn's hip. Reflexively, she snapped a tether from her kanaf around a distant stool, jerking it into her palm, swinging it in line as he made to swallow her. He snapped his teeth closed on the stool, and she twisted it, jamming his maw open.

But the metal bowed. The bolts strained. He had her.

Almost. Bracing the stool with her shoulder to keep him at

bay, her kanaf opened to let Wes's batarang fall into a gap between two knuckles. She took aim and flung it, curving the
whizzing steel around the room, to a stack of half-knocked-
over gas canisters where it clipped off the stems of two pressurized tubes. They jetted like two steel torpedoes and one
pounded Saxby in the ribs, setting off another hacking fit that
teetered him, taking his weight momentarily off her.

Wriggling from the debris, she lashed her kanaf onto her
right leg, using one sharp tug to sink the ball joint into its
socket. She bit off a scream, rolling to her feet.

Saxby wheeled, mouth opening wide—he blew fire and the
world turned molten.

Ryn whirled her kanaf entirely around herself except for
her remaining fist. Fire beat harmlessly off her cloak, and
when it had passed, she snapped the burning cloth down, extinguishing the flames. Still wreathed in fire, Saxby's scales
had a hellish glow and the room was flooded with barking
dogs, shrieking monkeys, and the scurrying of escaped animals. In the midst of the pandemonium, she extended her in-
vulnerable hand, which he'd bathed in that fiery expulsion—
the hardened glue had turned black and polished like volcanic
glass and, with a flick of her hand, it shattered and released
her claws.

"My turn," she said.

She dove into the maze of his coils and cut him—cut off his
tail, sent his lower jaw sailing, laughing as she took him apart
a piece at a time. He lurched away, steering for the entry hole
he'd made, but her nails clipped off a wing, so that when he
escaped through it he helicoptered to the ground like a maple
seed.

When he landed, he roared back at her while limping away.
Ryn returned a snarl and leapt after to finish what she'd begun.

But her killing blow never landed. With vision altered by
mushrooms, she witnessed his spirit spread from a concentrated point near his heart, burn through the blood and separate into almost every cell of him, until he erupted. Flesh and
spirit both split into ten million tiny pieces and Ryn dropped
through a cloud of snakes, centipedes, wasps, and scorpions,
each carrying a piece of her quarry's soul.

Swaddling herself in the protective fabric of her cloak, she hit the ground and rose, stepping on a single beetle, crunching it underfoot as all the rest of him slithered through grates, buzzed up into the sky, or skittered into distant crevices—too many to count, or to stop.

Crushing the beetle had winked out that piece of Saxby's spirit. Transporting his essence into so many pieces left them vulnerable to something as simple as her heel, but battling him in this form would be like fighting the tides.

Soon they were gone and it was just Ryn and the whistling wind, the darkness, and the descending snow. She'd killed three asura, badly mauled the fourth, but there was no "almost" to this task. Saxby had her taste—enough so that if he stung her again, it might end her present incarnation.

It wasn't finished. Naomi wasn't yet safe.

~*~

She returned to the burning lab, knowing the asura could use mortal currency to purchase leverage against Naomi. Slashing the safe open, she shoved money and one-kilogram gold bars into it, slowed by poison and her missing arm.

Sirens wailed in the distance, a sound distorted by the swimming in her head. She zipped the bag shut, stumbling from the lab. Blood drops fell like beads from her fingertips, pattering a trail on the floor. It would reduce to black dust once parted from her body a while, but she wasn't confident she could slip past the police in her state—not while weighed down by the bag.

Shuffling past Tooloo's headless corpse and up a stairwell, she felt the chamber shift and slumped into a wall.

Blackness covered her vision like a ribbon.

When she came to, voices were rising up the stairwell, beams from their lights cutting through the precious darkness that hid her. *I cannot black out again.*

Teeth gritting, she ascended the stairs to a floor open to the elements, surrounded by skeletal beams. Wind brushed her loose hair, cooling her sweat-soaked face. Blood now drizzled from her wounds, which wouldn't clot—perhaps, like a mortal, she'd bleed until she died. The kanaf stitches in her wounds tightened, forcing a grimace, but staunching her blood loss to a drip.

Below, more police cars arrived. They seemed small like toys, but there was no way past them. To shake off this poison, she had to sleep.

Collapsing against a vertical girder and slumping to her knees, she scanned the work area and spotted a stack of un-placed cinder blocks. Too weak now to walk, she was reduced to crawling, leaving behind her a slick of blood and some of her pride. Lying parallel to the stack of cinder blocks, she pulled her remaining fist back, punching a critical block at the base of the heap. It powdered and the stack teetered, heavy blocks dropping atop her. They thudded into her hard, small body, an avalanche that covered her and the duffel bag.

Lying still in her concrete cocoon, she slept.

CHAPTER EIGHTEEN
Hollow

For the third time since Ryn Miller had come out of the institution, Kessler stared at a New Petersburg crime scene reduced to chaos.

It took the fire department a half-hour to extinguish the third floor and the process frightened about a dozen soaked dogs, countless mice, and several monkeys out into the frigid night. Animal control were now attempting to round them up, having to bob and weave around firefighters and their hoses.

Kessler and O'Rourke sat on the hood of their unmarked car eating burritos in the flashing glow of emergency lights.

"Is this beef or mutton?" It tasted a little gamey.

O'Rourke shrugged. "Big mystery."

Examining the burrito's contents, Kessler frowned. "Where the hell you get these at this time of night?"

"Part of the mystery."

An explosion upstairs ripped an outer wall open and a pressurized gas canister whistled through the air, smashing through the front grille of a parked ambulance. O'Rourke took a large bite.

"If you told me," Kessler said, glancing from the empty ambulance to his food, "I wouldn't eat it, would I?"

O'Rourke nodded, chewing.

With a sigh, Kessler finished it off. Wadding up the foil wrapper, he asked, "Is this burrito some kind of metaphor for the city?"

"The burrito is a burrito." O'Rourke swallowed the last of his and glanced peevishly down at his bandaged thumb. "This city, on the other hand, is a pain in my ass. Monkey bit me before you got here."

Uniforms had interviewed Carol Metzler, the senator's legislative aide, who had woken a block from the scene, apparently carried to a stranger's car and left there. Kessler had also snagged an interview with a senile woman hooked to an oxygen tank, whose apartment overlooked the scene.

According to Metzler, someone dressed like the Grim Reaper had killed an anti-Bradford fanatic in front of her. As for the old woman? She was the reason animal control was already on scene, but she'd called them about the dragon.

"I sure hope they don't put it down," she'd said. "I think they're endangered."

After assuring her no one would put the dragon down, he'd excused himself. Now he was considering a second round of interviews, maybe getting a better description, like how many horns it had and if it looked like it was from around here.

Summoning the courage, he glanced at O'Rourke. "You... you think it could've been a dragon?"

"Firefighters are cleared out." O'Rourke pushed off the car hood, ignoring the question. "Let's have a look."

The bodies were upstairs. Kessler mistook the first for a beanbag stitched into clothing, but up close, he realized someone had neatly bisected a morbidly obese person. He nearly lost the burrito.

There was a headless one a floor above and a uniform found another without a heart in a trailer outside. They located the head in a room next door to the body, but no one ever found the heart.

The room with the head looked like a lab, maybe twenty surviving animals still locked in their cages, along with workstations and a massive computer set up with six monitors and a hole in the floor where someone might normally have sat—likely where beanbag-guy had been before someone dropped him down one level and did to him precisely what they'd done to Banich's gun a few months back.

"Huh." O'Rourke steered the monitors to the side and set the keyboard up on a desk. "Good thing it's stuck back in this corner, or the fire and water would've done all this in." He flipped the keyboard over, peeling off a sticky note. "And look at that. Passwords."

O'Rourke started to work at the computer, and when the

uniforms shifted to another part of the room, Kessler leaned in to whisper: "This was Ryn. Had to be."

The fat detective snorted. "If she did this, are you really going to arrest her?"

"You approve?"

"No. I mean... if a teenage girl did *this*," he motioned all around—to the shattered floor, howling animals, scorched room, and the severed head two detectives were delicately trying to roll into an evidence bag—"are you going to walk to her fucking door and read her rights?"

"Then what do you suggest?" he hissed. "This is a triple homicide and about seven figures of property damage."

"Keep your eyes on the prize. I believe that Wiercinski woman, the one who talked about this being a war between 'gods.' Or powerful men. Whatever. This place is a war zone, and I'm not interested in soldiers. I want the generals."

Kessler noticed how quickly and fluidly O'Rourke moved through the computer. "You think this helps?"

"Whoever that guy was," O'Rourke said, pointing down through the hole, "he was not overly worried about information security. Whatever he's up to? I think it's all here. The anti-Bradford site's in his browser, and I think he was an admin. These guys were the whole middle tier—maybe they got wiped out by Ryn or, more likely, a team of Army Ranger fucking ninjas paid by someone rich. I don't know, but from the safe back there, it's clear these guys going after Bradford were mercenaries too."

"So maybe there's a connection in the computer?" Kessler asked. "Emails? A way to figure out who was paying them?"

"Maybe. And Wiercinski gave me a hell of a lead. Zmey-Towers, she said—they lobbied in support of that security bill Bradford's fought all year in the Senate. And there's more, I can feel it. Just need to find all the pieces so I can make them fit." His attention was laser-focused on the monitor.

Shining his light on the safe, Kessler approached it and crouched. A small puddle of blood had gathered there and he leaned to get a closer look. It dissolved before his eyes into a patch of black dust. "The hell?" Swiveling the light, he spotted other drops dissolving a few feet away. He stood and followed the disappearing trail.

~*~

O'Rourke copied files onto a portable drive, running a hand through his thinning hair. Sweat plastered his stiff shirt to his chest and his brain zinged over what he'd found, disassembling the pieces he had so he could fit the new information.

Yes, this computer held secrets—a tingle of excitement and fear electrified his skin, one that meant he was brushing closer to those parts of New Petersburg most folks ignored. It was not in O'Rourke's character or job description, though, to ignore a thing just because it muddied the prevailing theories of reality. He wanted to see the grimy insides; to pry open the casing and see what made his city tick.

He'd researched the Senate security bill Melody Wiercinski had hinted was center stage, which, though thwarted, had come close to passing after a series of suspicious defections. Four senators who'd opposed it had abruptly flipped sides. Two had been subject to harassment: one's dead son had had his memorial page vandalized online; the other's niece had slit her wrists after strangers passed around images her ex-boyfriend had sent to a revenge-porn site. Whoever operated this computer had coordinated those attacks, plus blackmail leveled at the other two defectors.

It had the whiff of Soviet-era psychological warfare and manipulation. While O'Rourke couldn't yet connect this computer to Zmey-Towers, they were involved. The company had formed after the fall of the Soviet Empire a decade ago, a corporate haven for oil oligarchs and former KGB. A member of their board had been implicated—but never tried—for war crimes in Yugoslavia.

On paper, he knew Zmey-Towers had lobbied hard for the bill. Now he knew they'd done *more* than lobby; how much more was the question.

O'Rourke paused by a rack of spilled gas canisters, picking up a dinged sliver of metal with his handkerchief. "You've gotta be shitting me." It was a shuriken in the shape of a comic-book batarang—the kind idiot kids bought online. O'Rourke owned four. He deposited the batarang in an evidence bag.

~*~

Kessler tracked the disintegrating blood drops up a stairwell and into the blistery air on the unfinished fourth floor. It led to a streak across the floor where someone had crawled, disappearing beneath a heap of collapsed cinder blocks. Dragging a block from the stack, he aimed his flashlight into the crevices.

He spotted a limp, girl's hand.

"Ryn!" He tore the blocks away two at a time. "Can you hear me?"

He uncovered her face, flashing back to finding her strapped to that post in the desert. But no—she lifted her gaze, eyes no longer swollen to slits and no longer empty of color. Irises of flaming blue lit her eyes in a way that seized his heart, stole his reason. There was power in her eyes that made him believe all her strange tales of ghosts and demons.

"No hospital," she said.

But blood covered her chest—his stomach lurched when he saw she had no right arm below the shoulder. "You're going to die if I don't." He reached for his phone.

She seized his wrist with an iron grip. He struggled to pull away, not wanting his hand anywhere near those eyes. "No. Hospital."

It was her burning stare that convinced him. Relenting, he nodded, unable to think until she at last collapsed and stopped looking at him.

~*~

O'Rourke's phone rang when he was midway through the laptop's cache of incriminating file folders—the call a welcome distraction, as everything in the one labeled "Splat's Recordings" would haunt him till he died.

Clicking the folder shut, he answered before the second ring: "O'Rourke."

"Remember how you told me to keep you... informed... when I do something a little off the books?" Kessler asked.

"Yeah."

"I might be sneaking a certain teenager down a stairwell right now. She's hurt."

"You mean she was actually here? No way she was the one who—"

"Look, you going to arrest me for this or not? Just asking."

Glancing again at that folder—remembering the things someone had done to a young drifter with a corkscrew— O'Rourke made a snap decision. "Fine. Whatever she did, whoever helped her, she's still not the one I want." Whoever had hired these bastards was used to slithering through the shadows unseen. *But I see you now.*

"Thanks," Kessler huffed through the phone.

"Why are you panting? Thought she was tiny."

"There was also a bag of gold."

"The fuck?"

"Look, I dunno, she had a bag of gold, it's heavy. What do you want me to say?"

"Ask her about the batarang."

Now it was Kessler's turn to ask what the fuck.

"Just do it."

A moment passed and Kessler muttered, "It, uh, was a gift from her date. She said."

O'Rourke glanced at Splat's folder on the monitor again, shivered, and then looked to the room ravaged by some light-weight package of savagery and—probably—a dozen Army Ranger ninja sidekicks who'd helped her. He hoped. "Use the back stairwell. Leave through the fence's rear exit. I'll meet you in the alley behind in the car."

He hung up and popped the portable drive into his pocket, knowing evidence like this tended to disappear—swallowed down a weird memory hole, like everything else he regarded as black-binder weird, or else destroyed by someone on the take. He told a uniform to bag the computer as evidence, but kept the drive to himself.

Sucking on his bandaged thumb, he swore for the hundredth time that one day he'd stop being surprised by this goddamn city.

~*~

Ryn slept only during the new moon or to heal, but it was always dreamless—her awareness would have sharpened for danger, except Kessler placed her somewhere warm that smelled of him, and her slumber was disturbed only when he bandaged her. His hands startled her and she woke with a snarl, but his scent and clinical ministrations quieted her. Once bandaged, she sank into a fortification of covers.

When dawn's light touched her eyelids she roused and stretched, Kessler's coffee mug shattering as it hit the floor. He'd wandered into the bedroom where she stayed and was now transfixed on her regrown arm.

"You didn't put me in jail," Ryn whispered, unsure why. He was police now and it was what his tribe did—police were for jailing lawbreakers, as surely as she was for killing monsters.

"Your arm." He still gaped. "I thought—"

"Are you not honorable?" She'd thought Kessler unlike other mortals—capable of being one thing, unchanging, of having no duplicity; closer to her kind than his own. "Why am I not jailed?"

Shaking himself from the sight, he took his time figuring out her question. "It's complicated. But I had a dad once, and he died half a world away fighting for these people—people he didn't know, who I didn't either. I never understood until I met you. When I got you out of that hell, I felt a piece of what he must have. That... connection you can have to kids who aren't yours, family that's found, not made." His eyes tightened and he unclipped his badge from an inside pocket, examining it. "You're big on honor. I get that. But I brought you here, you're my responsibility, and I'm not sending you to jail." He set the badge face-down on his bureau and turned his back on it, walking out. "Get some rest."

Family. The idea felt claustrophobic; like she belonged, yes, but also belonged *to* someone, and its first taste wasn't good. Tossing her blankets off, she flicked the kanaf from her back, cloaking herself and scaling from the window with Saxby's gold in tow.

A few months and the Veil would swallow Kessler's memories of her regrown arm; a few more and it might eat this absurd idea about "family" too.

I was wrong about him. He's like the rest. Like Naomi.

They didn't understand what it was to be constant as the stars—to be forever just one thing.

~*~

With Saxby loose, all Ryn could do was hide his gold in an abandoned smokestack and guard Naomi during those nighttime hours when the beast would most want to take her. She was loath to approach her former friend's home, its roof unwelcome and the scents producing the most rending sensation in her heart, urging memories forward that hurt for being so blissful.

But immortals held mastery over the passage of time and what they beheld. Ryn banished all perception of Naomi's heartbeat, voice, and aroma, attuned to danger while inoculating herself from memories too happy and bitter. She made the girl into a living ghost—into a gaping hole in the world.

And what a hole it was. As Ryn lay awake on the roof, she knew that to surrender her control for even a moment, she'd be allowed to inhale Naomi's scent and listen to her strong pulse and the oddly soothing rhythm of her breathing.

Any time she wanted to, she remembered Naomi in the snow, lying still and clutching herself, sobbing. That memory haunted Ryn most of all, making her want to flee into those unpopulated forests where she could live decades without bothering to have any thought beyond: *hunt, eat, drink, rest, run,* a part of the earth without being distinct from it; no different from the stones she slept upon or the animals she devoured.

Some days, when Ryn felt certain Saxby's presence was far away, she went to school simply to spend time alone—a large school, she'd finally realized, was as good as alone, if she could endure its smells.

After hours of staring at dead words, a strange thing happened, and some of them came alive. One piece in particular she read over and over, as though there was something special in it. It was about a bird coming down the walk, its restless eyes and feathers somehow brought to life with ink stains, until at last:

> Like one in danger, Cautious,
> I offered him a Crumb,
> And he unrolled his feathers,
> And rowed him softer Home –

Something in the lines came off the yellowed page and pinched, the syllables stamped into her brain, and she found herself watching birds and wondered if she ever again could simply watch them, live like them, without remembering those branded words.

The time in school also brought higher marks, but thankfully no new attention. Other than a colorful sticker and different letters, it was the same.

The cold weather broke, the days lengthened, and the moon swung around without so much as a whiff from Saxby. When the new moon arrived, Ryn stumbled through a day at Parker-Freemont half aware, even as Harper Pruett and his pack once again mocked that blue-haired girl. They'd Named her, so often and well that the entire school called her those things.

The Naming and the mocking must have broken her, because on this particular day Ryn had to catch a knife the blue-haired girl tried to bury between Harper's ribs from behind. Tearing the blade away, she tossed the girl back into some lockers.

Harper spun to face Ryn, his sneer transforming and face going ashen when he saw the knife in her hand. "Help!" he belted out, shrinking away while gesticulating wildly at her. "That fucking psycho's armed. Shoot her! Someone shoot the bitch!"

The blue-haired girl slunk into the crowd with the same frightened eyes as that bird in the poem, disappearing even as the resource officer in her uniform strode from among the gawking students, leveling her electric weapon. "Drop the knife!"

Ryn blinked through the haze, weary. "It wasn't—"

The officer fired and Ryn was barely cognizant enough to catch the barbed prongs in her palm, the tingle rousing her. The snarl she loosed sent everyone, officer included, clearing the floor around her. She presented the knife to the officer, then drove it forcefully into the wall's cinder blocks, to the hilt. "Take it," she spat. "If you can."

She stalked from the school, its bullies and cowards and clumsy administrators, intent on never returning. No one stopped her.

Detouring through the parking lot, she cut Harper Pruett's car in half.

That night, Naomi and her friends attended a religious gathering called a "lock-in." None of her father's soldiers would attend, so Ryn did her best to shuck off gravity and follow the girls to an old part of Garden Heights with a stone Episcopal church, its iron fences hemming in a lawn of spring grass. Neither asura nor deva were permitted in temples of the new religions, which afforded some protection from Saxby—though Ryn couldn't enter without herself being damaged, so she folded into a ball on the laundromat roof across the street, breathing in warmth from nearby steam vents.

Heat made her muscles spongy, her brain fogged, and the weight of other sleepless new moons pushed down on her until she slept; hopefully she'd rouse if there was trouble.

She woke in the dead of night, alert.

Rolling to her feet, the sight of Naomi startled. Though Ryn lived most nights on her roof, she never really looked at her—but there she was, sprinting joyfully across the fenced-in lawn. That smile broke something in Ryn's chest—broke whatever thing let her pull deep, clean breaths. At a full run, she was perfect in the way her hair flowed, body sharpened, all her grace on display. Ryn wanted to run with her like it was the only thing she'd ever desired.

Naomi didn't seem troubled, or to be running *from* anything, and soon disappeared into the church. Unable to put it to rest until she'd sniffed around, though, Ryn dropped to asphalt, jogged to the fence, and vaulted over. She knelt in the grass to savor its tickle against her palms, grass Naomi had enjoyed moments ago.

"Hey! What the hell are *you* doing here!" hollered Denise.

Ryn's stomach tightened and she stood as Denise approached from around the corner, flashlight in hand.

"Some nerve showing up here." As Denise closed in, her expression remained inscrutable as ever.

Blinking through the haze, Ryn shifted back a step. "I'll leave."

"Fucking stalker." The words were barbed, and she jabbed two fingers into the monster's shoulder, more fearless than she had a right to be. "You hurt my friend—did I not explicitly warn you? And following her is screwed up. Hope you don't plan on ambushing her out here."

"*No,*" Ryn swore. "Don't tell her I'm here."

"Don't tell me what to do. I'm twenty seconds from screaming some things that shouldn't be uttered in the shadow of one's church." She set fists to hips, examining Ryn with an intensity that suggested she was deciding what exactly to do with her. "Not here and not tonight, but you're going to fix her."

"What?" Ryn asked, retreating another step.

"Fix her. You broke my friend. I thought it was her dad's aide getting kidnapped at first, but she hasn't talked about you since that night. What'd you do to her? If you *hurt* her, I swear to Christ I'll—"

"I showed her the truth," Ryn growled. "What I am."

"Bullshit. You did something to her." Denise strode forward, almost nose-to-nose as though searching for the truth in the deva's blue-tinted lenses. "You kiss her?"

Ryn stiffened. "No!"

"Too bad."

Now Ryn was confused. It was the norm around Denise.

"I stayed over at her house a few times." Backing off, Denise assessed the deva again. "She seemed to want me there with her; she was scared."

Ryn tensed, remembering a few nights with Denise in the bedroom below. She had no idea what Naomi had been like those nights.

"She jerks awake from the nightmares. Sits up with this wild look. But she screams *your* name."

How her palms ached—she'd balled her fists, cutting them again.

"Of course, some nights she's not jerking awake; she's gasping, rolling around, moaning." Denise smirked. "Not 'in pain' moaning, either. The other kind."

"I don't understand."

Denise's eyes rolled upward and she shook her head, patting Ryn's shoulder in a humiliating way—but she knew things, clever and sideways things, and if the deva wanted to hear, she knew to ignore the gesture. "Sometimes when she dreams, it's like she's running from you; other times, more like she's fucking you."

Ryn sputtered, a torrent of started words that never finished.

"Since that night, my friend's only ever half smiling. She broke up with Horatio—said it was because he's going to Alaska this summer and she hates long distance, but *Horatio* says she wouldn't even kiss him. Not interested. And that is a boy who's not used to disinterest, trust me. So I don't know, maybe she is and maybe she isn't, but for a while, all that attention she poured into you made me wonder. I can't tell what screws with her head the most: that you scare her, that you turn her on, or that you disappeared."

Remembering Naomi's scent, how it changed when Ryn got too close, she shut her eyes and shook her head. "No." She couldn't let herself believe it; it made the loss too large if there'd ever been hope.

"You'll fix her, but you don't get to make up with her tonight. You're in pain, and you deserve it, so you have to wait. But in June, we're all going to camp together. A week of outdoor adventure, right up your alley. You're coming as my guest, and you'll approach Naomi—timid as a pussycat—and grovel until she forgives you."

Ryn's fine hairs went bristle-brushy, her words low and dreadful: "You have no concept of what I am."

For only a moment, Denise wilted in uncertainty. But she found her footing and turned her back on the monster, headed for the tall church doors. Over her shoulder she called, "See you in June."

"You won't."

"You must be confused," Denise smirked. "Because I *always* get my way."

The heavy wood doors swung shut, a dull sound that vibrated in Ryn's chest, shutting her out from Naomi's world.

~*~

The city thawed in April, warm spring winds teasing Ryn's hair; she walked the parks, starving for things green, and touched every blooming tree. Her school expelled her for the fight, though security footage showed her thwarting a stabbing, which plucked her out of legal trouble.

She didn't stay out of legal trouble. She'd been avoiding Roosevelt Place, but Ms. Cross's fury at her expulsion led Ryn to return to the group home early one night. Coming in through the window, she caught Albert Birch masturbating beside Susan, asleep in her bed.

In retrospect, she shouldn't have thrown him *through* the wall.

But she didn't feel bad in the least about what she did to his nose. It deserved to be as crooked as the man.

It was her first night in a detention center. She spent it worried sick about Naomi, planning to break out if they kept her more than a day. Kessler had posted bail by morning, and he and Ms. Cross both set to work—their case was helped along by the testimony of Susan and two of the Rabble, who described Albert Birch's lewd behavior around boys and girls alike. He was implicated in the suicide of Susan's old roommate.

There was also the fact that it wasn't generally regarded as possible for Ryn to have thrown a grown man through drywall, insulation, a wooden beam, and out the other side.

The hearing came at month's end, the judge saying plenty of angry things to Albert Birch before dismissing the case against Ryn. The Rabble and Susan were divided, sent to different homes. Susan got one with all girls.

Kessler and Ms. Cross both insisted Ryn find a school and live with Kessler, but she was legally allowed to drop out and live on her own, so she did. When they asked about supporting herself, she fetched one of Saxby's gold bars, thumping it onto the table in Kessler's apartment next to the butter dish.

Ms. Cross folded her arms over her chest, eyes narrowed. "I want to know where you got that."

"You really don't," Kessler said.

He exchanged the bar for a large sum of money, though Ms. Cross warned they wouldn't exchange another for her unless she continued therapy. That rankled, but if someone had to sway her life, Ryn preferred it to be Ms. Cross. She was at least formidable.

Her new home was near Dock Street in a 150-year-old structure called the Fairchild Building. Her top-floor room was a long, narrow chamber with towering ceilings, the space voluminous enough to echo. It had once housed a clothing factory and tall windows let in all the wonderful nighttime cold. Bathroom aside, it was a single, unpartitioned room with a balconied platform at one end overlooking the rest.

It was infested with bed bugs, sporadic gunshots sounded from the neighborhood, holes opened the windows to whistling air, and the pipes leaked rust-red water. Ryn chose it over everyone's objections, even the building owner's, and it kept her busy: tossing out furniture, installing a steel door, replacing pipes and windows. At her presence, the bed bugs and other pests fled except for a single, gray rat.

Since the rat was dust-colored, shy, and unobnoxious, she named it Susan II. It deserved the room, having lived there before Ryn, and it didn't complain when she fed it crumbs or slivers of radish, often wedging itself into a cardboard toilet-paper roll beneath the radiator. Ryn imagined it kept the rat warm in the way its old colony had before its exile.

While Ryn guessed Susan II missed its old home, she wondered if it could be lonely. Were cardboard and radiator good enough for a rat? They probably were. Envying Susan II, sometimes Ryn lay next to the radiator too and tried to feel as warm as she had when Naomi embraced her.

Ms. Cross hated her space because she had to sit on the floor. Ticking off demands on her first visit, she made Ryn buy chairs, carpet, and a bed and kitchen table. "A bed is psychologically necessary, even if you never sleep," the human explained. "It's not just about sleep—it's your private space; refuge, comfort, all those things. The kitchen table's the opposite: it's your public forum. You need a sanctum and a gathering place for loved ones. You understand?"

"Yes." Ryn waited to see if she was better at lying yet.

"No," Ms. Cross sighed. "You don't. But buy them before my next visit anyway. I know you can afford them." Patrolling the space with hands on hips, her brow furrowed. "What do you do in here all night and day?"

"Watch the sun move." At night, she guarded Naomi.

"You need a hobby. A television. Books, maybe."

Humans were like this. Their short lives compelled them to fill every second or they despaired.

She nonetheless obeyed Ms. Cross's dictums, filling her room's corners with stacks of books she found attractive in look, feel, or smell, positioning the kitchen table at an edge, always keeping floor space as wide open as possible. She bought a laptop but never used it—it kept Ms. Cross's criticisms at bay, which was its only purpose. The bed had curtains, Ryn having taken to heart the words about privacy, and it was the only thing about her furnished room she liked.

In May, Ryn moved from pipes and windows to the wall, smoothing its patches with stucco and replacing panels. The room felt more whole, and she appreciated the great, hollow, intact chamber.

"You're going to wallpaper, right?" Ms. Cross asked during their mid-May checkup.

"No," she said.

"Why not?"

Why would she?

"The blankness doesn't bother you? It's so sterile." When Ryn didn't answer, Ms. Cross sighed. "You were making progress. Now, it's like you've stopped trying. You don't express yourself. Is it because of the fight with your friend?"

"She was a mistake."

"Because she's not interested in you?"

"*Because*," Ryn growled.

Ms. Cross paused in her circuit around the room.

Ryn's hackles rose, sensing something was coming.

"You're afraid you'll hurt her?" Ms. Cross asked at last.

Trying to stare her down, Ryn wound up glaring at Ms. Cross's back. "I fear nothing."

"Avoidance implies fear, Ryn. What do you fear?"

Anger rising, Ryn spun and strode for the door.

Without raising her voice, Ms. Cross spoke, somehow aware Ryn could hear her at any volume from any point in the apartment. "Have you apologized?"

Turning back, Ryn bared her fangs. "Why?" *Why do they insist I stoop and scrape like a mortal?*

"Do you want to know what I think?"

"No."

"Too bad." Ms. Cross took a seat facing her, smiling now. "Naomi is the first thing you've loved and you hurt her. Badly. You did it by being true to your nature, but you're guilty—and you're afraid of guilt. You're afraid she won't forgive you, that she'll reject you, but most of all, you're afraid she can *change* you."

Ryn sneered at the blasphemous charges. "I am no more mutable than the constellations."

"Stars don't feel. You never did either; not until this. You're not in the unfeeling heavens anymore, poor girl." It was hard to be sure, but Ms. Cross's eyes seemed softer. "You're trapped down here with us. That's what you don't see. Naomi? She's already changed you."

The accusation rocked her. "Get out."

Ms. Cross lifted an eyebrow, but she stood and made her way out the door. Whispering from the other side—Ryn could still hear—she said, "You love her, you idiot."

Ryn activated her computer for the first time. A day later, she still couldn't send messages on the damned thing, so she tracked Denise and strode up behind her when she was alone after school. "I will go camping with you. But," she warned, "only because I wish to. And I will not grovel." She gave her hardest stare and stalked away, burning from even that much.

Denise made it no better by shouting after her, "Okay, pussycat."

The hot days of late May and early June burned off the calendar one by one, and she lay on Naomi's hot rooftop never listening or scenting, just waiting for that fearful trip. It felt like the end of an era. She, a goddess, had to go before a mortal and beg forgiveness.

Yet it spiked her pulse, sweetened her blood, because though she couldn't imagine what would happen, she knew Naomi would be there.

CHAPTER NINETEEN
Summer Storms

Denise's father brought them to Cold Spring Highlands, a half-day's drive from New Petersburg in the heart of Appalachia. It was a campground nested in steep hillsides of dense pine and deciduous trees, interspersed with buildings, a basketball court, soccer field, and pool. Structures stood on any surface flat enough to build on.

Ryn fought the buttons in the car until she found the one that made windows disappear, then jammed her head out and sucked in a breath of the minty-sweet pine.

They parked and Denise carried a box of her father's cookies, so Ryn took her bags, having only brought a duffel for herself—filled mostly with a loaned bedroll. They registered, waiting around in front of an outdoor stage facing log seats.

Campers clustered into their assigned groups all around, Ryn silently hoping hers stayed small.

When she turned, Naomi stood ten feet away and Ryn heard the thump of her bag on the ground without remembering letting go. Having transformed the girl into a living ghost, she'd had no way to hear Naomi's approach, and now ten short feet separated her from the thing she craved and feared more than any other. *Everyone can hear my heart.* She was certain of it.

Releasing the barrier that had locked out her friend, Naomi was suddenly all she could smell: the fragrance of rain and sunlight crushed her senses. The auburn-haired girl wore jean shorts and a too-long T-shirt accentuating her height and casual athleticism, and Ryn wanted to touch the shirt's hem just to ensure she was real.

"Elli, let's find the counselor," Denise said, but it didn't matter because she and Elli weren't actually there anyway. It was just her and Naomi, gazes locked.

Naomi's was fragile and she took tentative steps closer, arms folded around her middle.

Now they both stared at their own feet.

"Guess we should talk," Naomi said.

"Yes."

Except neither did.

A pressure built in Ryn's chest and she wheeled, searching for escape. *I don't want to do this.* She'd never done anything like it, so her mouth opened and moved without producing sound. Trying a second time, she made words happen: "I... I am sorry." It was done. Her chin tucked against her chest and she felt as though Naomi could smite her with a word.

Naomi's hesitation stretched the moment painfully. "I didn't tell anyone," she whispered. "About what you did to Walter Banich. Or those others."

"...that is not what I'm sorry for."

"How can you not be? You were ruthless. My father told me Banich still can't walk. It might be years."

"I'm adept at breaking things."

Her brow furrowed. "Then what *are* you sorry for?"

"For hurting you. Terrifying you." More words rose to the threshold of her mouth and she swallowed them, afraid of the tremor in the ones she'd already spoken.

Naomi bit her lip and shifted a step nearer to whisper softer still. "That night I thought you were going to kill me."

"I know."

"Did it ever cross your mind?"

Ryn shook her head briskly. "Never."

"You seemed so angry. Your voice... changed. Everything about you changed."

Sealing her eyes, Ryn could only nod. She hadn't even known that, but didn't doubt it. "I wasn't angry at you."

"Who?"

She shrugged, inspecting her shoes.

"Yourself?"

Another shrug.

"Why?"

"Because it was my fault. The nightmares were about me." The pressure in her chest burst, the words all gushing out at once. "I don't like your fear, Naomi, I don't like it at all, it doesn't taste right. I only want you to be safe, to sleep, to not scream at night. But how can I hurt what haunts you when it's *me*?"

Naomi stepped closer, both hands making push-down motions. "Shh, shh, I get it." Setting her finger to the deva's jaw, she raised it like she was raising all of Ryn with it. "You're not a nightmare."

"I am."

She smiled, eyes gleaming strangely bright as she tilted her head to the side. "You are, aren't you? But I'm not afraid of you now; I'm never afraid when I look right at you."

"Maybe you don't see deep enough." Ryn's throat was dreadfully tight.

"I don't always understand you. But I'll look at anything you show me, and I'll try."

Ryn shook her head in disbelief. "You still... wish to see me?"

"Naturally," she said with a wink. "But you have to apologize."

"Yes." *Anything.*

"Say you're sorry for running away. For scaring me and disappearing without any explanation. And then never do it again—it's not how friends act."

Friends. "I'm sorry for leaving you in the snow." It felt good to say, like a vise on her insides had released. It was a singing relief she'd never had before—relief from pain she'd lived with so long it had started to feel normal. It made her lighter; made her stone mouth smile.

"Don't do it again," Naomi repeated, touching Ryn's face once more, and the deva wondered if she was allowed to touch back. The auburn-haired girl's scent had turned dark and lovely.

"Hey!" Denise shouted.

Naomi straightened and jumped to face her.

"Guys, meet our counselor." Denise guided over a college-aged brunette in jeans, a T-shirt, and multi-pocketed vest with dark sunglasses, ponytail hanging out the back of her ball cap.

"Ladies, I'm Counselor Jane. Welcome to Adventure Camp. Let's see." She checked a clipboard. "Ryn, Denise, Elli, and Naomi are here. We have two more girls and we'll meet the rest of our family group at the cabin."

"Family group?" Naomi asked.

"The boys are the other half of our family group," Denise said.

"Yes, there *is* a cabin of young men who join us for most activities." Jane scanned them all. "They have their own counselor and quarters, the interior of which you won't be touring, particularly after hours. Everyone copy that?"

"Yes," they all agreed, though Ryn noticed the way Denise crossed two fingers behind her back.

Their group included a pair of sisters, Phoebe and Cara. They hiked a winding forest path that opened to a firepit flanked by two cabins, one belonging to the girls. "Cabin's built for twenty, but this week we only have seven, myself included," Jane said. "Plenty of space to sprawl."

"How many boys?" Elli asked.

"Closer to ten."

Elli pumped her fist. "Ka-ching."

The cabin had concrete floors and bunk beds, the restrooms in a separate building through two hundred yards of hilly forest. A breeze passed through screen windows and Ryn could hear scurrying rodents in wet branches outside. Everything would come alive by night, and she ached to hear rain pattering through the leaves.

She set up near the door, but Jane summoned her to the midst of the pack in one corner, ordering her to "be social."

The boys arrived at the firepit, another noisy Rabble except ten strong. Most were younger, disappointing Elli, but an older one caught her eye immediately. "They call him Patrick," she whispered, returning from her reconnaissance. "He's got to be a senior."

Indeed, Patrick was tall, graceful, and strong, with dusty-blond locks and a broad jaw raspy with stubble. He wore ragged shorts, a T-shirt and a hemp necklace.

Elli, Naomi, and Denise all glanced out the window at him and spoke at once: "Look at his *shoulders*." "Wow, he's tall." "I hate his stupid necklace."

They all looked at Denise. "What? I *do*. Kind of want to light it on fire."

"Check out his tan," Elli cooed. "I heard him say he's from the West Coast. I'll bet he surfs." She glanced back at Denise. "Since you hate his necklace, you can't have him."

"Don't look at me." Denise shook her head. "After the Nine Lives, I'm taking Mom's advice and only dating well-trained males. Less work, emotionally simple, good cooks. That boy looks... needlessly complicated."

"Yeah," Elli sighed happily. "What do you think, Naomi? Since Horatio's done, we could flip for him. You want to let Patrick fill the hole in your heart?" Under her breath she added, "If not, he can fill the hole in mine."

"It's your heart you're talking about him filling, right?" Denise grinned.

"I'm talking about whatever he wants to talk about. Unless Naomi wants him—she's got free Saturday nights, and I'd have to put my Craig-related plans on hiatus." She considered the male again. "Long, *long*-term hiatus."

"Leave Naomi out of your web of sin, dork," Denise said. "Let her heart mend however it likes." She cast a look Ryn's way the others didn't catch.

Ryn felt a prick of something in how they fawned over Patrick. He was tall, certainly, but his face was dumb. And Denise was right: so was his necklace.

Outside, they joined the boys and played an introductory game with a ball. Whoever caught it had to share something—the first circuit, a name; the second, a single word describing themselves. Ryn lost track of every new name.

Denise caught the ball and said her word: "Loyal." She underhanded it to Elli.

"Fun-loving." Elli glanced with meaning at another boy and sent the ball to Naomi.

Naomi looked right at Ryn, her smile sending electric currents through the deva. "Joyful."

Then Patrick caught it, and his gaze also held meaning, directed at Naomi. It rankled. "Single." Cara—she was only thirteen—blushed in his direction. Patrick underhanded it toward a boy beside Ryn.

But she snatched it from the air and held the tall male's

gaze, narrowing her eyes behind her blue-tinted sunglasses.

"Ryn?" Jane asked. "What's one word that describes you?"

She kept her stare level on Patrick. "Territorial."

They broke for dinner, crowding outside a dining hall as scant drops of rain fell from the darkening clouds. A storm rolled steadily over them, Ryn dragging it closer so she could taste the rain. Before it started in earnest, though, everyone around her did something terrifying.

They sang.

Counselors led the songs. It was a human game. Naomi sang avidly, of course; it was brilliant to watch her find a melody and laugh at the childish rhymes. It soured when Patrick glommed onto her enthusiasm and joined her.

Denise elbowed Ryn. "I'm with you. I never sing for my supper."

"Come on," Elli whispered. "It's camp. Go ahead and be stupid, no one cares. It's fun!"

"You can have my fun," Denise scoffed. "I'm about topped off watching this actually happen."

Ryn despised the very idea of singing, or talking in crowds, or crowds generally. This activity rolled it all together in one. Worse, Patrick and Naomi whispered about having so much fun.

Camp fare disappointed her, as it came from cans. There was fresh game within a hundred yards, but somehow she doubted they'd let her kill anything. While Naomi made quick friends with Phoebe and Cara, Ryn gave terse answers and avoided talking.

Rain caught them on their way to the cabins. A crack of far-off thunder broke the air and scattered the campers. They sprinted; Ryn strolled. She tilted her head back, drinking fat drops that rolled from the leaves.

Naomi cut through the abandoned soccer field and stopped midway across. She held out her arms; she accepted it, the only other person who understood she could get no wetter, and so instead smiled. The downpour lit her in a white halo of scattered droplets, framing her sleek hair in soft light, painting her shirt to the skin of her torso.

Ryn didn't realize she'd been approaching until Naomi whirled, scattering water from her fingertips. She laughed, flashing her teeth and those bright, bright eyes, framed by dark lashes that held pearls of water. "You look different in the rain," she said.

Ryn had no answer for that.

Naomi beamed at her. "You look... content." She eased nearer. "Like you and the rain belong together."

A smile teased its way to Ryn's lips, still unused to the way Naomi saw to the core of her.

Denise and Elli returned through the downpour. "You coming?" Denise called.

"Come on," Naomi challenged. "You've got all week to be dry."

They found the soccer ball and at first Naomi and Denise played one-on-one, darting with practiced ease, two rivals who'd done this together enough to have each other's measure. When Naomi fired the ball sideways to Ryn, she popped it into the air with her knee and head-butted it over Denise, further downfield.

"She's on my team!" Denise called.

"Nope! Everyone against Ryn!" Naomi said.

They played through the storm and mud, shouting and shrieking, every motion kicking sparks of water through the air. Ryn wove through the trio, letting them snap the ball from her a few times. It was relaxed until the boys joined, transforming into girls versus boys, and against them Ryn was less magnanimous. She still passed the ball more than she took shots, disliking the attention of scoring, but she loved to slip into the pack and steal the ball effortlessly, to rocket it unexpectedly to Elli's feet even if Elli lost it every single time.

Jane waited an hour to break them up and they retreated to their bunks, Naomi throwing an arm around Ryn, hollering, "MVP! If we had you at Madison, we'd go all state."

Ryn glowed with delight.

In the cabin, the girls hung wet clothes and towels on crisscrossing wash lines between bunks. Ryn dripped water and Naomi dragged her into a corner where hanging towels cordoned them from everyone else. "You forgot towels, didn't you," she teased.

She needed no towels—if she could get free, she'd flick her kanaf once and be bone dry again.

"Here." Naomi ruffled a towel through Ryn's hair before she could protest.

The friction felt good and the deva leaned into the contact, her friend releasing the towel so that it draped like a hood.

Naomi snorted. "More kitten than tiger when you're wet, I'm afraid." She reached for the monster's sunglasses, but Ryn darted back.

Smiling apologetically, Naomi fetched her own towel and did something in the quiet corner that put Ryn's spine flush to the bedpost: she peeled off her own shirt. It exposed dew along her abdomen, water beading at her chin and running teasingly across the ridge of her collar bone. Then she skinned off her pants and tossed them with a wet slap to the concrete floor.

She never looked at Ryn and dried off mechanically, though her ears were pink and her scent changed again—it felt almost like she was pretending not to see Ryn, planting one foot on the bunk beside the deva. Her coltish leg went on and on, higher than Ryn had seen before, all the way to rain-soaked underwear, and the sight sent a delicious, terrifying curl of warmth through her belly. Tearing her gaze away while Naomi changed into dry panties, she folded herself protectively under the towel, heart galloping in her ribcage.

Naomi scrounged in her bag, tossing a shirt to Ryn. "Here. I brought too many clothes and you probably forgot PJs too, knowing you. And..." She finally glanced back. "I know you don't wear certain *things* regularly, but that'll be long enough to cover you."

The old shirt had a cartoon tiger on it, though not a dangerous-looking one. Ryn would have preferred her kanaf, but felt trapped. She started to undress, slow and uncertain.

Denise peeped through their blanket partition. "Oh, there you two are."

Naomi smiled, her back to them both as she shrugged out of her bra. "Just getting Ryn situated."

"I see." From Denise's tone, Ryn wondered what she saw.

Naomi rolled her eyes, snaking into a nightshirt and pajama bottoms, slipping out of their partitioned compartment. Ryn changed into the tiger shirt, hanging her wet kanaf close to where she slept since the shirt's length stopped slightly above her knees and left her feeling exposed. She scampered immediately into her bedroll.

Nearby, the other girls chatted long into the night. Ryn avoided the conversation, but Naomi was in its midst, sitting up Indian-style on her bunk. Lying on her side, covered in a shirt imprinted with her friend's scent, the deva savored the sight of Naomi speaking. She liked watching her do anything, but liked it even more when the other girl's gaze slipped back to her, which it did every so often.

Naomi slept a few feet away and that was best of all.

~*~

The rain let up by morning and Ryn rose first, twisting the kanaf around her body. Naomi shivered in her bedroll from the morning chill, the deva fixated on her friend's parted lips, where foggy breath spilled out.

Her fragile, sleeping form returned the curious heat to Ryn's belly, made her want to crawl into the bedroll and hold the auburn-haired girl close. She was in the midst of those thoughts when she sensed eyes on her and swiveled to face Denise, who grinned up at her.

Ryn narrowed her eyes.

Denise made kissing motions with her mouth that only made the deva's eyes narrow more.

They hiked to breakfast through wet mist that settled around the knees, blanketing the forest's ferns in a way that put Ryn at ease—at least until the singing. Worse, when Patrick joined Naomi, they goofily slung their arms around each other. It was the same arm that had been around *her* after soccer and she wished for once in her life she could make song. Scenting Patrick for asura in case he needed to be decapitated, it unfortunately turned out he was just a boy.

Ryn wanted to catch her friend's eye during breakfast, except she was engrossed in conversation with Cara. After breakfast came something called trust falls, where Ryn panicked at the realization she had to drop backward into someone's braced hands. She sought Naomi to save her, but Patrick had again intercepted Ryn's favorite human.

Fortunately, Denise fast proved her second favorite by

partnering with her and convincing the counselors Ryn "totally just did like four" while they weren't looking.

It still rankled to see Naomi fidget and smile shyly when Patrick's big paws caught her shoulders. She even laughed at something he said! Not only couldn't the monster sing, but she wasn't funny either.

It wasn't until Denise snorted that she realized she'd been growling at them. "You are so unsubtle," her second favorite whispered.

Then came other group activities: helping each other cross a wire line suspended eighteen inches above the ground, or climbing a wall together, or carrying a beach ball up a hill on a blanket. It was meant to be done as a team, an idiotic concept: Ryn could have done it all much easier alone. Or perhaps with just Naomi.

And Patrick told them all what to do. Worst of all, *they listened.* When he ordered Ryn to let him boost her up the wall since she was lightest, she stared him down and then scaled the wall on her own.

At lunch, Naomi sat with Patrick so Ryn cut out early, using her afternoon free time to brush up on archery. She loosed shaft after shaft into distant hay bales, ignoring their awful instructor. Every satisfying thump of arrow to target unspooled her violent urges, perhaps since the target's size and shape wasn't a total mismatch for Patrick's face.

"Who are you imagining in that bullseye?" Denise leaned against a nearby post. "Patrick?"

Her concentration wavered and her arrow planted an inch too wide. Out of anger, she thumped three more into the red dot, one-two-three, so fast the instructor said an oath in front of campers. *How does Denise always know my thoughts?* "Are you an empath?" she demanded.

"Uh. No?"

Ryn sighed. "I'm confused."

"For what it's worth, I know why Patrick flirts with her. I'm fuzzier on why she's flirting back."

Lowering her bow in resignation, Ryn sank to the bench seats behind the firing line. If Denise was confused, Ryn had no hope of understanding.

"I do have a theory." Denise shifted to face her, hands in

pockets and weight rocked back against the post. "It was weird that she'd date Horatio right after you two met. She's normally slow to let guys take her out. At first, I thought she wanted that first kiss, but the double date actually makes scoring a kiss slightly more challenging. Fast-forward to now, and the moment you two make up, boom: she's hanging off Patrick."

Ryn stared ahead at the target bristling with her arrows. "I don't understand *at all*."

Denise shrugged. "It's just really damn convenient that every time she's around you long enough to get her panties tickled, she tries her damnedest to fall in love with the closest guy."

"So I'm insufficient." Ryn frowned, unwilling to admit surrender. "Denise. I must make jokes. Teach it to me now."

Her second-favorite human sighed. "Think what I'm saying is that you're very sufficient. Overly sufficient, even. This time it's not your fault. For once? It's the princess who's screwing it up."

For dinner they served a congealed meat tube inside bread. That was Ryn's limit, so she crept out and found a raspberry bush in the forest to pick over. By the time darkness spread over the campground, the solitude had fortified her and she returned to the firepit, looking in on the popping coals—how often had she done this? Except this time she strode from the brush and her presence among the mortals was unremarkable.

She froze. The humans were huddled close, and Naomi clung to Patrick as they whispered scary stories.

Noticing her, Denise stood and approached, uncertain. "They're a couple," she whispered, more gently than she'd ever said a thing to the deva.

Nodding, Ryn stumbled back into the dark, only returning to the cabin after everyone else had. She slumped into her bedroll fully clothed.

"You need a nightshirt?" Naomi whispered from her bunk across the aisle.

Ryn rolled over, her back to her friend.

The next day, rain chased them off the ropes courses and trapped them in the cabin, where the others chatted and played cards. After lunch, some of the boys started a tackle game on the field with an oblong ball, and Ryn thought it would be a relief to do something away from Naomi. She asked to join and they fought over who would take her until one with a twangy accent rolled his eyes at the bickering and invited her to his side.

Her toes curled when she spotted Patrick on the other team.

Intuiting the rules from a few plays, she waited for the ball to snap and darted across the field, separating from the others in a burst of speed. The thrower who had invited her to his team fired from back in the rain, ball spiraling wide of her trajectory. She sensed Patrick coming up on her, caught the scent of his exertion—it tasted aggressive and wrong somehow.

Pivoting in the mud, she cut hard and the ball thudded into her outstretched hand. Its spin squeaked in her wet grip and cheers shot abruptly from the sideline—the girls were watching. *Naomi is watching.*

Patrick dove at her from behind. Ryn flicked low and nailed his middle with her shoulder. As he folded into her and went rolling over top, she used her strength to fling him higher so that he sailed end-over-end. When he hit earth, he skidded, flipped, skidded again, and splashed into an enormous mud puddle.

She had no idea what was wrong with Patrick, but her gut told her something was. *Untrustworthy.* Glancing up at Naomi, though, she saw the auburn-haired teen's mouth was an angry, straight line. Ryn tossed her wet hair over one shoulder, meeting her friend's glare.

The thrower who'd invited her to play jogged over, helping Patrick up. Patrick groaned, stumbling.

"Let's... let's play two-hand touch," the thrower said, with nervous looks at Ryn.

"I'm done." She stalked away, headed for the field's other side, away from them all.

Denise caught up to her, though. "Jesus. Ryn! Hold on."

She halted, wheeling on the girl. Her throat clicked out a growl. "Why?"

"Because... because I'm worried you're about to murder someone."

"I'm not."

"You didn't have to smile like that when you hit him."

"I smiled because I enjoyed myself."

At dinner Naomi wouldn't even look her way, a frosty anger in the teenager's demeanor. But Ryn was angry too. Her friend had coupled with a boy with a wrong scent. What if he was a monster? *Perhaps I should eat him to be sure.*

"That wasn't cool," Naomi hissed on their walk back from dinner. "You were trying to hurt Patrick."

"If I were trying, he'd be hurt," Ryn growled.

"What's your problem?"

"I don't trust him."

"Why?" she demanded.

"Because." Ryn's lip twitched. "There's something wrong with him."

"I'd like more to go on than your gut feeling. It seems like you just don't like me spending time with him."

"Why would I care who you spend time with?" she snapped.

"Because I... because he..." For once, Naomi was speechless.

Ryn bolted into the woods to escape the rising bitterness, the disillusioned sense that Naomi was playing some stupid, dangerous game. She lurked along the fringes of the forest, staring into the clearing and those licking, orange flames—relegated again to her proper place at the light's periphery, looking in.

Patrick's skin glowed in that light and he seemed to drink it, as well the affections of the campers and Naomi, who all smiled at him.

I'll bet he doesn't even taste good, she fumed.

That night, Naomi slid from her bunk while everyone else slept. She padded across concrete, easing out the door. It didn't fit her usual nighttime patterns, so Ryn sneaked after, ascending into the trees and trailing her along the winding paths.

Naomi's flashlight joined Patrick's, and the two embraced. He stooped for a kiss and Ryn's stomach tightened, but Naomi danced to the side, smiling instead. She dragged him off the path and into the shadowy wood.

Ryn glided after, from trunk to trunk. Thunder rumbled in

the distance.

They perched together a few hundred yards into the forest, on a jutting rock overlooking the steep drop-off of a ravine. Patrick had laid a blanket down and they nestled side by side, staring into the night while rain rattled the leaves. Their pulses were at ease, and Patrick's scent seemed fine now. *No. It was wrong. He's wrong.*

They spoke in hushed tones. Patrick had lived with his father; his mother had been killed in crossfire at the hospital where she worked when two gangs had opened fire on each other. "The bullet came through her office window."

"Oh my God," Naomi whispered.

His hands clenched, unclenched. The aggression was back—now that Ryn knew why, it didn't stink so bad. *No! It's bad enough; it's not right for her.*

"It was fast," he said. "At least there was that. Went through her neck. She sort of coughed, fell over. She shook really hard and she was gone before I could get a doctor."

"You saw it?"

He shrugged. "Yeah." Glancing off into the ravine, his fists squeezed and released again.

"My mom didn't die in the car," Naomi murmured at last. "She was hit by a drunk driver, but she made it to the hospital alive. She lived about a day." She sucked in a breath. "People hear about car crashes, picturing it like it's sudden, clean. Broken metal and smashed glass, then you're just gone. It wasn't like that. It was... ugly. She was my mom, and she was so, so beautiful. But at the hospital, I could... I could barely recognize her. There were tubes everywhere." Her voice was barely there. "She didn't have any legs. It made her seem small. I remember not being able to find a good place to touch her—nowhere that still felt like her." She wiped at her eyes. "I wish she'd been awake. I wanted so bad for her to hear me one more time."

Ryn realized it went deeper than songs and jokes. She could never relate to Naomi like another mortal could. The deva had no mother but the dark sky. Death was not her enemy; she had nothing it wanted, nothing it could touch except, perhaps, Naomi.

The teenagers leaned into one another, and though their

sizes were different, their bodies seemed almost made to rest together as they stared off—and then their fingers laced, their hearts sped, and they looked into one another's eyes.

This is how it's meant to be, Ryn realized. *I'm not a part of their world.* It was all in front of them, precisely as Denise had once described at the Nine Lives: a first kiss; making love for the first time in six more months; married in a church where Ryn couldn't enter, and then to live short lives, rear children, and die. Precisely the life Naomi had always dreamt of.

Sorrow filled her and she wanted to see them kiss; wanted a clean end, as hard as she'd wanted it in the snowy forest next to the drive-in. Her nails sank into the bark.

Their lips neared.

Her heart flared—with anger, yes, but also hope made defiant. *No!*

Lightning broke the sky and lit the forest in neon brightness. It seared the imprint of trees into her vision, thunder rumbling through the old trunk and into her bones.

Naomi jerked away before Patrick's mouth touched hers, and they both stood under the sudden deluge from Ryn's sky.

In that instant, the kiss, the lovemaking, the wedding, children, and even death itself—all were swept momentarily away.

"I— I should go," Naomi said.

"You don't have to." Patrick offered her his hand. "We're not getting any dryer."

She shook her head. "Let's talk again tomorrow." Together they ran for the trail, shadowed by a monster from the treetops.

They were stopped at the firepit by Jane and the male counselor, whose name might have begun with a T.

"You two have a fun stroll?" Jane asked.

"Nice of you to escort her to the restroom," T-counselor said.

Ryn dropped to the wet ground and stayed in the forest.

"It's not like that," Naomi said. "We just talked. Nothing happened, relax."

"You can't wander around in the dark. It's dangerous." Jane glanced around. "Where's that little angry kid?"

"Ryn's not in the bunk?" Naomi asked.

Not good.

"Of course not." Jane folded her arms. "That kid's never where she's supposed to be. You didn't see her out there?"

"No." The word was angry enough that everyone took notice of Naomi. "She's only seen when she wants to be. But I'll bet she's been with us all along."

"What?" Patrick spun to look around. "Seriously? Who, that short one with the attitude?"

Naomi turned to the forest and folded her arms. "Get over here," she called sternly.

Ryn froze, confident no one had spotted her.

"Ryn! Get your ninja butt out here! Now!"

The deva slid from wet brush; Naomi fixed on her and everyone else startled back at her presence. Rain pounded her as she approached.

"You have a lot of nerve." Naomi's voice was coldly furious.

"Wait, was she following us?" Patrick asked.

Ryn glared at him, but Naomi ignored her boyfriend. In spite of how bad this was, Ryn liked it when she ignored him.

"All right," Jane said. "Everyone's alive. Todd, get Patrick to his bunk." Todd the counselor did so, and that left the three of them in the rain. Planting hands to hips, Jane took note of Naomi's aggressive posture. "Whatever this is, settle it. I mean in the next five minutes, ladies. Then get to your bunks, sleep, and tomorrow we'll raft the crap out of that river. Naomi? If you had sex, go talk to the nurse."

"I didn't have sex!" Naomi shouted. "We never even kissed."

"She didn't," Ryn confirmed.

"You're not helping your case." Lightning flashed again and lit the outrage in Naomi's eyes.

Shaking her head, Jane went into the cabin.

Naomi wheeled on the deva. "How could you! After scaring me to tears, after filling my nightmares for weeks, how could you do that to me again?"

"I didn't frighten you!" The accusation hit Ryn hard, because she never wanted to do that again to her friend.

"It doesn't matter. You invaded my privacy. It's creepy and wrong."

Ryn bristled. "I was guarding you."

"From what? My boyfriend?"

"I don't like him. I don't trust him." Ryn straightened, saying the truest, most damning thing of all: *"His smell is wrong."*

"So? You don't get to sniff all my boyfriends and grade them pass-fail! You're not responsible for guarding me. The people my dad hired do enough of that!"

Now the deva smirked. "They're not a tenth of what I am. You think they kept the monsters from your room every night? No." *I did that.*

But Ryn had not concealed those last words cleverly enough. They must have been in her eyes, because Naomi froze and a look of horror filled her face. "Wait. What do you mean you kept monsters from my room?" She took a step back. "You were there, weren't you? Outside my house at night."

Tired of the lies, Ryn nodded. "Every night. Except once, the night they sent Casper Owens. That night I... failed you."

"You failed me," Naomi said, eyes gleaming too bright, "when you *stalked* me every night for months. When you came in through my bedroom window, it wasn't the first time you were on my roof. You'd done that before; you do that almost every night. Sit on my roof. 'Guard' me." Now her eyes were sad. "Oh my God." She blinked and looked away. "God, you're insane. You're actually insane."

"I'm not."

"You're a deluded, insane stalker."

"I'm not."

"Then leave me alone!" she shouted. "Leave *us* alone! He's my boyfriend."

"He's not right!"

"He's right for me!"

"No!" she hollered, the loudest she'd ever dared to be in front of Naomi—energy shot through her, heels to shoulders, her face buzzing.

But Naomi stood her ground, eyes narrowing as though she saw something she'd missed. "How do you know?"

Ryn covered her mouth with one hand. Had yelling displayed her canines? She whispered, "He is fake. He hides his aggression and smells wrong and is *not right*. Not... right for you." She clenched her eyes shut. "You want this thing. With...

with a first kiss, and six months before mating, and a wedding in a church where I cannot go, and fine. Do that. If you don't want to be with one like me, be with Horatio. Just... don't be with Patrick." It made her feel lower than a worm to grovel, but she peered up into her friend's eyes and whispered: "*Please.*"

Rain drummed on them and Naomi's face was still with shock. "What did you say?"

Her pulse quickened.

"You said... if I don't want to be with *you*."

It had been said too fast and she'd therefore said too much. But she just nodded. "I did."

"Ryn. Oh Ryn." Everything in her friend's face was gone now except pity, and pity had such a bitter taste. "I'm so sorry, but I'm not—"

"Don't." Ryn shook her head.

"I want to be your friend, but I want you *as* a friend. Not as a competitor who wants to wreck my relationships so she can get a date with a straight girl."

"You want to hold hands with boys in front of me? Fine. Laugh at their jokes, because they're funny and I'm not? *Do it.* But not *that* boy."

"But you understand, right?" she asked. "That I'm straight? That *we* can never work?"

Ryn shrugged.

"Tell me you understand."

"I do not."

Her friend's anger flared. "You need a chart or something? It's a Venn diagram of 'women' and 'people I date' that's two circles, never touching."

"Let me tell you what *I* understand," Ryn said. "I won't call you any words—straight, gay—I don't care for them." She edged forward. "I know this." She tapped her nose. "I smell how your body changes when I'm close. It changes even now. I didn't recognize why, because your smell is different—special. But you have desires, and they're stronger when I come close."

"Ryn, I don't— And how would you— You can't *smell desire*, that's crazy."

"I can. Don't lie to me and don't tell me what I can't do."

She was close enough now to touch her friend, and the girl had gone rigid like prey. "I can smell the sun in your hair, the rain on your skin. And when I step very close, like this, and when we stare at each other like we are now, your scent changes. I like that change." Now she was near enough their breath spilled together. "It changes now."

Naomi exhaled sharply, lips parting. She shook her head, but so minutely it barely registered. Then she shook it harder, stepping forcefully back. "I'm not gay. Okay? I like boys. I'm going to fall for a guy, I'm going to marry him in the same church as my mom and dad. Denise is going to be my maid of honor and you—you were going to be a bridesmaid. That's how it *goes*." Her eyes glassed with tears.

Ryn frowned and suddenly didn't want to push her, didn't want to so much as nudge her friend for fear she'd crack in half. "I cannot do that with you. But you should do as you wish."

"Leave me alone," Naomi whispered.

"Very well."

"Not just tonight. Leave me *alone*, Ryn. Leave me alone forever. Stay the hell out of my life! Stay away from Patrick. Just... stop ruining my plans, stop ruining everything." Her voice trembled, and though the words stabbed Ryn's heart, they must not have penetrated nearly as deep as they had through Naomi, because she wilted before running for the cabin. The door slammed shut behind her.

Standing in cold rain until her skin went as numb as her insides, Ryn wandered indoors to lie wet on her bunk. It didn't matter. When she turned her head, she saw Naomi with her back presented, shoulders quaking. She cried until she slept.

CHAPTER TWENTY

The River

Dark dreams held Naomi underwater until first light. The soggy chill reminded her she was at camp, the memory of her fight with Ryn tightening the knot in her stomach. She rolled over and Ryn's bunk was empty. For a brief, terrifying moment, she wondered if the raven-haired girl had actually left her alone—forever—as she'd demanded.

No. Her bag is still there.

So what if she had? *After what she said, maybe that would be best.* Ignoring the jittery panic, she packed her bathroom things, put on sandals for the long trail to the showers, and hoped to trek it alone. She needed a broody walk.

Except Denise waited for her in the cold, gray wet, leaning on the cabin's outer wall with bathroom gear in hand.

Without a word, Naomi strode up the trail. Without a word, Denise followed.

Halfway there, Denise asked, "So what's this Patrick thing about?"

"I'm not in the mood."

"I heard your blow-up last night. Everyone did."

Naomi winced. "What parts?"

"Not all of it. Just the loud parts. And where Ryn yelled that he's not good enough for you. She's right, by the way. Patrick's... shady. He's got some deep-seated anger below the surface."

"I know."

"You know he's sketchy and you're still dating the guy?"

"Yes." Naomi stopped, facing her oldest friend. "You don't think I know? I can tell he buries his anger; squeezes it off when I bring up his mom. He's broken, just a little bit. So is Ryn. So are *you*. We're all a little damaged, so don't talk to me about fake. That's none of Ryn's business."

"Okay, okay." Denise started walking again.

She had to jog to catch up, arriving at Denise's hip before she realized she'd spent her anger giving chase and didn't know what else to add. *She did that on purpose,* Naomi realized.

Denise had on her clever smile, which Naomi hated. "I just didn't think you were doing the boyfriend thing yet. Not so soon after, you know..."

"Horatio?"

Denise snorted. "No. After that striptease you did for Ryn the other night."

She guffawed. "Striptease?" Her voice came out sharper than she liked.

"First bad thing you've ever done, and with a girl no less. I was proud."

"I was changing clothes. You change in front of me all the time. It wasn't like that."

"It was so like that, and you know it was. And you know you *liked* it like that. So no, I don't understand this Patrick thing. It's like you're trying to win back your straight cred. You know you can tell me, right?"

"Tell you what?"

Denise stopped, so she had to as well. Her friend looked Naomi straight in the eyes. "Tell me you're gay."

The words caught in her throat. "Denise." She shook her head. "I'm not gay." She'd built the list of reasons already, but knew if she went through all eleven, Denise would try to shoot them down one by one. "Didn't we both go through that Tom Hiddleston phase together?"

"Not saying you wouldn't fuck Tom Hiddleston. I'm simply saying you'd prefer to fuck his sister."

"Denise!"

"Do you have, like, a physical list of reasons you're not gay, because it'll be faster if you just give me the piece of paper."

Her ears burned. "Of course not."

She raised her hands. "Tell me Ryn doesn't turn you on."

"She *doesn't.*"

Denise cracked a smile. "Liar."

It wasn't a lie—there were aspects of Ryn she found thrilling, but she just needed to find those aspects in a *boy*. "Ryn and I are through."

"Ryn's the kind of girl who—if you tell her to leave you alone forever—she's going to. So I hope you're sure about that."

"I am!"

"...she said, with not a hint of fear in her voice."

"It's *not* fear, it's anger. Stop telling me how I feel. You don't know."

"How much you want to bet?"

Naomi spun and strode back toward the cabin.

That forced Denise to stop. "Hey. Where you going?"

"What, you don't know? Guess you're not omniscient, Denise. I'm going back!"

"Why?"

"Because it's away from you."

Her friend quieted, which was highly unusual to say the least. Guilt gnawed on Naomi's stomach. What if she'd actually upset her? Pausing, Naomi glanced over her shoulder to check.

Denise stood there with a huge smirk.

She knew I'd look back. Her whole face burned.

Denise winked.

~*~

Ryn kept out of sight until they loaded into two vans for their rafting trip. She avoided the one with Naomi in it. During the long drive to the river, it sank in: her time with Naomi had finally ended. Only dealing with Saxby remained.

They arrived at a boat launch and boarded yellow, rubber vessels suitable for whitewater, the plan being to raft downstream, camp overnight, and raft again the next day to a rock-climbing locale.

Naomi joined Patrick in the forward raft; he guided her into the boat, even though it wasn't a challenging step for someone with her superb balance. Ryn boarded the second raft with Denise and their group pushed into the brisk current.

Rain had fattened the river until it hissed and spat and beat on their vessel.

Jane plunged her oar into the stream, angling them with a white-knuckled grip. "I know this river. You do what I say and no one goes for a swim. Trust me and listen to me, because you don't want to fish our tents and food out of the drink. Copy?"

Everyone else cheered. Ryn stared ahead at Naomi's bobbing raft, sensing she was near to never seeing the auburn-haired girl again.

The rapids tossed them around, but Jane kept their raft true. Ahead, Naomi's jarred over rocks, washed down sluices between stacked tablets of stone. Their boat trailed, rarely losing sight of the other. Campers shouted and squealed their delight, and even Ryn savored the spray of cold water against her body, its flavor alive on her tongue.

When the river later flattened into a stretch of glossy, unbroken ribbon, Denise scooted closer, whispering, "It's not so bad, you know. It's not you she's really mad at."

"She wants me to leave her alone."

"So you're going to run off again?" Denise asked. "Just like that?"

"I'll protect her until she's safe." Staring grimly ahead, she added, "It won't be long now."

"That's how it is?"

"That is how it was always going to be. And it's what she demanded."

Denise leaned closer. "Let me tell you a horrible secret. I'm planning to kill her."

She twisted on the mortal, eyes wide.

"Oh yeah. It's because she won't come clean about how she feels. So unless she convinces me I'm wrong, I've got diabolical plans to end her life. In a slow, agonizing manner involving a crate of hungry weasels. So with that in mind, I don't think she'll be safe for a while, and you'd better keep a close eye on her."

A smile tickled the corners of Ryn's mouth. "Denise?"

"Yeah?"

"I don't desire to kill you."

"Aw. I love you too, weirdo."

Ahead the river narrowed, funneled into churning white-water that roared louder as they approached, misting over the edge of their boat. Jane shouted orders, tensely focused as they whisked down a steep slope, sank abruptly off waterfalls, and cracked their raft off dense stones with whip-snap force. She'd call for them to paddle or crowd different parts of the boat to manage the impacts.

"These are class-five rapids," Jane announced. "Ahead's the Devil's Drop, so I want you razor sharp. This is dangerous. People have died at the bottom of that waterfall. So do *not* fall out. We're going to try zagging across the river to miss it, but the best route down's like threading a needle. If we have to flip, crowd right and we'll at least flip away from the water-fall."

Todd steered their craft from the left bank, across the river, and Ryn tensed—Naomi leaned out to paddle on the side with the falls.

Their boat turned, swept close to the lip of Devil's Drop, but Todd stabbed his paddle into the water and cut their vessel to the side. It slid onto a sloped rock and bobbed wildly on its way past the waterfall. They'd done it.

"Look out!" Patrick pointed to the right side of the boat. Everyone glanced that way, the passengers in Ryn's own boat focused on Jane's commands.

In that moment, Patrick grabbed the strap on the back of Naomi's life jacket. She'd already leaned partway out, facing the river instead of her boyfriend. He heaved her over. She tumbled into the water, disappeared without words or commotion. Gone.

The deva tore off her life vest, straps busting with a loud rip, and dove into the river in the same clean motion. Kicking beneath the rapids into the dark, cold underworld, she heard only the roar of the moving water. Her glasses washed off her face; she ignored it.

Beneath the surface, away from air and light and in the sanctum of crushing water, she surrendered any pretense of humanity. Body flexing along her powerful spine, she kicked both feet together, careening through the water in a frantic search. She couldn't hear Naomi's telltale heartbeat over the thundering of the river, so she dove wildly and wound between the stones, following her into the deep.

~*~

Naomi's world flipped end over end. Water pushed into her nose and ears, grabbed hold of her whole body, wrestled her into the dark. It was strong—stronger than anything that had ever held her; she belonged to it, and it was trying to kill her.

The current sucked her down and squeezed her head. The river pushed its thumbs into her eardrums until she wanted to scream in pain. It ignored the buoyancy of her life vest and held her there, pinned her to a cold, dark blue space and somehow the river bit her ankle—her whole foot was wedged in the lip of a heavy tablet of underwater rock.

I'm going to die here.

It pounded at her chest, as if beating at the doors to her lungs, demanding the last sliver of precious oxygen locked beneath her ribcage. She jerked on her pinned foot with all her might, and when that failed, fought to undo the waterlogged laces. No good. She'd double-knotted them, a habit from running, and her fingers were numb and trembling.

A wild thought to cut off her foot shot through her brain. *No knife,* she realized.

Her lungs burned. She focused on calm. On surviving, on having faced worse things than rocks and rivers. She fought the wet strands of her laces again, and when the knot finally released, hope sprang to life—but even untied, her foot wouldn't budge. The river had her, and it wasn't going to let her go.

Hope died.

She bit her own mouth, hard, to fight the reflex to inhale. She clung to her last breath, but the oxygen burned down lower and lower, a sputtering candle flame on the last of its wick.

Her vision darkened. Bright spots popped off behind her eyelids. An ache blossomed like a hand grenade in her skull, her mind shuddering off and then on, as if she'd drowsed, and adrenaline kick-started her brain in time to watch the trail of silver bubbles escape her mouth and rise through the murk.

Now her chest felt concave, and the urgent need to inhale grew.

The escaping bubbles distorted around a shadow. A thing descended toward her—a thing from her nightmares. It rode on draperies of fine darkness and its pale face was the only thing on it with form. *Death. Death is real, and it's here now.* It had eyes that were at once beautiful and terrifying, something Naomi had only felt staring into lightning storms.

Yet Death had an oddly serene, oddly familiar face. *Not Death. Ryn.*

She'd followed Naomi down into the frigid, lightless void and ignited it with the strangeness in her eyes. Not that it would help, with Naomi's foot wedged in the crevice.

No time. She tugged her knee again, but there was no give. *No time.*

Naomi's eyes shut and her mouth opened. Reflex kicked through her willpower and she inhaled, her whole body expanding to fill the painful vacuum in her chest with water.

Instead, precious air surged into her throat and sweet oxygen flooded her lungs. Naomi's eyes shot open. Ryn's hand clutched the back of her head. Naomi felt her lips on hers, fused. She drank the air greedily from Ryn's mouth.

The raven-haired girl floated a few inches away and again Naomi saw her eyes. The irises burned bluer than stained glass backlit by the sun. They produced their own light, eerily illuminating the water. But where a human's eyes would have been white, hers were matte black. Nothing on Earth should have eyes like that. And it confused Naomi, because she hardly recognized Ryn—it was a small part of her face, but utterly changed the meaning of every other line, and so it was the first time Naomi had *really* seen her.

She tried to push her away, but not from fear. Ryn had just fed her the air in her lungs. They might both drown if her friend didn't surface now.

Ryn's hand stroked the side of her face. Soundless, the girl's mien was placid, unconcerned. It was her calm that stopped Naomi's struggling. She drifted lower, to the pinned ankle, and stretched one hand back, striking the stone tablet with four stiffened fingers. A crack of thunder. A tremor hummed all the way up Naomi's leg to her hip. The world split, it must have, judging by the sound ringing in her ears. Then, the strange girl rolled away an engine block–sized stone with one arm.

Again, the oxygen in Naomi's lungs was spent. Again, her vision darkened. Ryn took her chin in hand, leaned in, and briefly their eyes met. Had the water paralyzed her, or had something else made her timid? Their lips touched a second time. Naomi's eyes widened as air once again filled her. She only stole half a breath, likely all her friend had to give—every last whisper passed from Ryn to her.

And yet Ryn didn't die or pass out, didn't slow. With unflagging strength, she tugged Naomi close and powered through the vicious current, carrying her, dragging her inexorably to the surface world. A ceiling of glassy water jumped closer with each of the girl's kicks. They broke through.

She collapsed onto a rock slab, Ryn beside her. Coughing, sucking in gulp after gulp of air, she hacked out mucus that dangled from her lip in a slimy strand and inhaled again. Blackness at the edges of her vision receded. The oxygen starvation left needle-prick burns in her face, ears, and lips. "God. Ryn. What are you?"

Ryn settled onto the other side of the slab. Her shoulders rose and fell, no more winded than if she'd been jogging, instead of battling the river without a drop of air in her lungs. Her head bowed. She wrapped her arms around her knees and made no response.

All the pieces settled into place: the men she had hospitalized or killed; the way she'd faded into shadow; her vicious speed, unearthly grace, and strength enough to overturn great stones. *Her eyes. Oh my God, her eyes.* They burned in her mind, a fire that wouldn't go out, and she couldn't tell if her limbs shook from the near drowning or from the creature who'd saved her.

Creature. Because Ryn wasn't a person. She was something else.

CHAPTER TWENTY-ONE
Eye to Eye

Naomi sank to her knees atop the stone slab and lowered her terrified gaze. When the edge of her vision caught Ryn, a jolt ran through her, as though her entire wet body were an exposed nerve, and she snapped her eyes back down. A hundred thoughts collided, locked up, and she didn't know what to do: run, hide? Some errant part of her thought to bow.

Yet when she at last dared to look, Ryn faced away with arms folded around her shins and forehead to her knees. She didn't seem dangerous that way; she seemed small, alone.

They must have stayed that way twenty minutes. It was Jane lurching from the brush, stumbling upon them, that woke Naomi from her mental paralysis. The counselor appeared to count them over and over, confirming both were there. "The *hell* was that?" she asked Ryn. "Your life vest!" She stabbed a finger at the river, as if accusing the monster and river of conspiring. "What. The. *Hell!*"

Shifting, Ryn only presented her back to Jane. It deepened the counselor's rage.

"Stop it." The words sprang from Naomi unbidden, and she said the next words as much for herself as Jane: "She saved my life."

"What?"

"I almost drowned. She dove in after me, and I'd be dead if she hadn't. Don't yell at her. We're both freaked out enough."

"All right." Jane seemed to be collecting herself. "All right, but you fell in; she dove. Let's not do that again."

Fell. Had she? Frowning in thought, she tried to remember how it had happened. It hadn't felt like a fall. But the only person next to her had been Patrick.

Denise hit the slab a moment later, rocketing directly into Naomi so hard she almost knocked them both into the river. She tightened her long arms around her friend, whispering "Thank God" over and over. Elli appeared from the brush as well, but instead of hugging, she stood back and sobbed uncontrollably.

When the hugging and crying had started to work itself out, Jane said, "Come on. The others are downstream, worried sick. They'll want to know you're all right." When she reached for Ryn, the creature scooted away.

Ryn's eyes were shut, head still bowed. *She's hiding her face.* Remembering those unnatural eyes that marked her as a predator, she realized Ryn had lost her glasses. She sat next to the girl, swallowing, body buzzing harder the closer she got. "You don't want to show your eyes?"

Ryn nodded.

"Wear a blindfold." Her mouth was weirdly dry. "We'll tell them the light hurts your eyes without your glasses. We'll guide you."

"You would do that?"

Heart in her throat, she nodded.

Ryn produced a dark strip of cloth seemingly from nowhere, putting it on.

When Naomi stood, she offered her hand by reflex before her brain could remind her: *Don't touch. Danger.*

At the contact of the raven-haired girl's palm, she shivered reflexively as another jolt leapt up her elbow. The strange energy that entered her seemed to pour hot oil into her heart, making it pound faster. Shooting back a step, she severed the connection. *What was that?* It summoned a vivid mental image of Ryn's mouth pressed to hers underwater, one that left her lips tingling. A terrible thought worked through her: *That's why I can't forget her. Why she sticks to my senses for hours after she's gone; why she haunts my dreams, both good and bad; and why my skin remembers her when she comes closer. It's some kind of... spell.*

That dreadful thought seized hold. She was helpless before

the power of this spell, but it put all these past months' confusion into sharp relief. Denise had been right—she'd poured her attention into Horatio and Patrick, trying to find in them the things Ryn had unleashed with her clever magic.

Staring at the slight, dangerous creature before her, Naomi tried to hate her.

She couldn't. That was how deep the magic had rooted.

Denise stepped in to guide Ryn by the elbow. Naomi trailed, but for the entire walk her head swam with sensations. The air was delicious, and every current of wind exploded her senses. Colors had brightened, refined, and she could distinguish minute shades that changed the foliage from a swaddle of green to something infinitely more nuanced and beautiful. Her brain absorbed details until she felt dizzy.

At first she wondered if it might have been caused by nearly drowning in the river—but no, this was more than sensory overload. The air tasted alive. She could distinguish smells she'd never known before—that Elli was on her period, that Jane carried enough of Todd's scent that she could tell they were an item.

Her thoughts warred: though Ryn had saved her, she'd also done *this* to her; changed her senses, how she felt, and against that spell she was defenseless. If Ryn could do all that, what else was she capable of?

Downstream, the rafts were dragged to an embankment and Todd had corralled everyone around untouched lunches. Relief overtook all their faces at the sight of them—everyone except Patrick, who sat on a cooler with guys on either side of him. He registered only surprise, and maybe guilt.

Naomi could feel from ten feet away Ryn's skin tightening, hear the low-frequency growl purr from her throat and gradually swell into the range audible to humans. Slipping close, she set her hand to Ryn's damp shoulder, sensing that coiled-spring body beneath her fingertips. "Please don't," she whispered. *If he threw me into the river on purpose, she might hurt him. Or worse.* She didn't want this creature to murder Patrick on her behalf.

Ryn wore her intensity like a cloak. Simply in touching her, Naomi became somehow aware of her friend's body, of its shape beneath wet cloth—from powerful heartbeat to the soft contours of her skin, an intimate knowledge that burned her ears. Jerking her fingers away, she was scalded by the swell of desire it produced.

Hovering there, the raven-haired girl danced on the balls of her feet with the energy of a lightning bolt with nowhere to go. She stormed across the beach with Denise at her heels, the blindfold not seeming to hinder her one bit.

It took a while to explain what had happened to everyone's satisfaction: to describe Ryn's rescue while editing out the supernatural parts—and also how their mouths had touched. She echoed assurances that she was all right again and again, more frustrated each time, because all she really wanted was to puzzle out this otherworldly girl who had bespelled her.

Jane finally ended the explanations by asking if Naomi wanted to leave. "We can hike the radio up to the road."

"No," she said automatically. Though terrified of what Ryn was doing to her, she couldn't risk letting her disappear again—maybe this time forever. *Maybe I'd get my regular feelings back.* But did she even want to? Some dark part of her liked being in its thrall.

"You're sure?" Perhaps Jane sensed her uncertainty.

Looking to the distant log where Ryn sat alone, she nodded. "I want to keep going."

The crowd clung to Naomi, trying to drag her into more detail about her brush with death, but anyone who spoke to Ryn ran into a stone wall of silence and eventually gave up. Patrick stayed on his cooler, nodding wanly when a boy muttered, "God, that was lucky."

But when she next looked to the log, Ryn was gone. Edging from the crowd and making excuses all the way to the trees, Naomi slipped into the forest. *No, she's not gone.* She could feel Ryn, taste her in the air, and she peeled through brush until she found the girl gliding between trunks—angling for Patrick's position. *No blindfold.* The sight stilled her, because she'd come upon a predator in the woods, and her heart crushed against her ribcage. She managed to ask, "Wh-what are you doing?"

Ryn crouched on a splintered stump, head bowed to hide her searing gaze. "What I'm best at," she whispered, and Naomi was seeing her for the first time—seeing the animal in her stance, her voice. "Hunting."

"Please don't hurt him," she whispered. Bowing in turn, hoping supplication would win her over, she said, "I don't want you to kill because of me. And... I want to know why he did it."

She loosed a low, clicking growl. "I hunt other monsters. This is my way."

"Please. Is it because you think he'll hurt me?" She risked a glance.

Ryn nodded, thankfully keeping her gaze low.

Taking a breath, she tried to bargain with the monster who was her friend: "If I rescind my... request... that you leave me alone... if I ask you to watch over me instead, will you agree not to hurt him?"

"Do you know what promises are to me?"

"I'm beginning to understand." She lowered her head again, aware she was bargaining with something far different from the shy creature she'd befriended. "The truth is, I don't want you to go," she confessed.

"Why?" When Ryn lifted her gaze, the sight forced Naomi back into the crux of two slender maples. "You know what I am."

"A demon. Or an angel. Or something stranger. I don't know, but I don't want you to disappear again, and I don't want you to hunt Patrick." She at last looked up, eyes pleading.

With a solemn slowness, Ryn crossed one finger over her heart, as she had several times before; except now Naomi felt the gesture's gravity. "I vow to protect you until you're safe from him. And I will not harm him—unless he first tries to harm you. Then he is mine."

It would have to be enough, because Jane was calling the campers back to their rafts. With a quick aside, Naomi convinced the counselor to swap her onto Ryn's, mostly to avoid Patrick.

She paddled one seat ahead of Ryn and, in spite of the blindfold, could feel how the monster's attention fixed on her. It marched a prickly sensation up the ridge of her spine, the fine hairs on her neck abuzz. Her heart came alive at the crisp spray of water against her face. Sophisticated river smells danced through her forebrain, and Naomi marveled at the subtle difference between sweetly oxygenated surface water and the moldering fragrance of the nutrient-rich depths.

Ryn's attention had a texture to it, the sensation reminding her of the dressing room, where nearness had caused Ryn's teasing breath to tickle her hot skin; or how it had felt to dance with her for hours, reveling in their two bodies' intimate knowledge of each other without ever touching; or how safe she'd felt falling asleep on her bed while Ryn perched stalwart above her.

That last memory lingered, and Naomi had never been sure if the dream of soft fingers brushing her hair while she dozed had been real or imagined—because oh, she'd had so many dreams. Some unintelligible with terror, dark shadows in Ryn's shape prowling through parking garages or the corners of her house. Some not just frightening, but thrilling, the shadows wrestling her into dark, sweet-smelling places, tangling around her like bedsheets, tightening—but not too tight—capturing her and holding her exquisitely still. How often had she dreamt that and thrashed in anticipation of forming shadows whose soft breath brushed her body? How often had she woken in a state of half panic, half arousal?

Naomi had to shake off the redolent memories, as they'd joined with her sensitized skin and the rocking of the raft, leaving her acutely aware of how near Ryn was behind her. It changed something in the air—her own scent, she realized. The monster was right about her scent, and her cheeks burned with shame. She couldn't look up from the paddle or water for the remainder of the trip. *From the beginning,* Naomi thought. Ryn had worked this dark magic on her from the very beginning.

By the time they arrived at their campsite and had dinner, all Naomi wanted to do was get the monster alone and pry out why—why her, to what ends, and would it ever end? At least, she hoped that was all she wanted.

The sky darkened over their grassy embankment above the shore, where everyone erected two-person tents—boys on one side, girls the other, and a shared firepit between. Ryn took a tent away from the group, placing it among the network of roots and beneath the crowning of an oak's mossy branches. In spite of the blindfold, she found a gap in the roots and felt out locations for spikes with her fingers, sureness in every motion.

Naomi approached, hands clasped behind her. "Can I help?" She knelt, finding Ryn's blindfold hid those impossible eyes and she could get near; even reach for the hammer.

Ryn jerked away. "I can do it."

"It's our tent," she decided then and there, pulse racing. "I'll help."

"...our tent?"

"I was with Denise, but she can bunk with Elli. So I'll be with you."

Ryn fidgeted with the hammer until Naomi plucked it from her hand.

She started to tap the spikes in place. "I don't bite."

"What if I do?" the monster asked.

That pulled from Naomi something between a shiver and wiggle, between fear and... want. She cleared her throat. "I'll have to take my chances," she said properly. More quietly, she added, "I mostly need to talk. About... what you're doing to me. I'd like it if you'd stop." *God, it sounds like I'm asking a favor.* "Please."

"Stop what?" Ryn threaded poles into the nylon of the tent; it rose, taking shape.

"Whatever this magic is." She sighed. "I admit, it feels... kind of good. But it's scaring me. Like I'm losing control. And it's not who I am."

Ryn's eyebrows pinched together in bafflement.

"I understand you're maybe not doing it on purpose. If you are, I'm flattered, sort of." Naomi felt weak dancing around it, so she squared her shoulders and started over. "I'm not stupid. I see and smell and taste all kinds of things since you... put your mouth on mine. I know what I'm feeling isn't normal."

Now her friend nodded. "Yes. That. I'm sorry. When we touched, when you shared my breath, some of my power went into you. My power is chaotic. The effects fade."

"Good." But her heart dropped a little. "All of it, though, right? Including the stuff from before we touched?"

"Before?"

She nodded. "Yes. Like how you made me feel when we

danced. Or in the dressing room, or..."

"We shared no breath."

"You don't have to lie. I won't be mad, I promise. I just want to go back to normal."

Ryn crossed her heart. "I vow that I'm speaking truth. I didn't make you do any of that; I can feel when my power goes into a mortal, from any distance, and the river was the first time it touched you."

"Then how did—"

A shy smile appeared on Ryn's face, showing the tip of a sharp canine. "What did you feel?"

"That's— That's none of your business!"

"As you wish." Ryn's smile vanished.

Naomi glanced sharply down to tap in the final spike with fumbling, nervous hands.

Unzipping the tent, Ryn took her sleeping bag under an arm. "If you feel wrong things around me, perhaps you should sleep elsewhere. I didn't make you feel them; I can't stop you from feeling them again." She slunk into the dark tent.

Naomi stared into the shadows between those flaps, eyes not adjusted enough but still sensing her friend in the inky shadows, as she had in so many dreams and nightmares. *Something otherworldly is in there. Only a fool would go in.* "You don't actually bite, do you?"

Her voice slid from the shadows: "I won't harm you."

That wasn't a no. She had a vague memory of a long-ago conversation they'd had waiting for a train. "Didn't you once say you'd never bite someone you liked?"

"I've never liked someone like I do you."

The words shouldn't have made her want to go into the tent—but they did. Naomi inched into the lion's den and settled her bag, acutely aware she was near enough a monster to feel her movements stir the air. The creature was still, save for her breathing, and when it whispered against Naomi's forearm her skin tightened and she shuddered. "This is going to sound stupid, but just... can you talk? So I know where you are."

A click and Ryn had turned on a flashlight, aiming it upward so that she stayed shadowed, but outlined.

"Oh. That's a better idea." She laughed nervously and

noted the tent seemed more suited for one-and-a-half people than two. Her bedroll mashed into Ryn's once unfurled.

Everything felt close together and the nylon gave the illusion of privacy. The tent felt like its own tiny universe, but indistinct conversations floated from the campsite and with the flashlight on, their shadows might be visible to anyone with a mind to look. It was a reminder they weren't quite alone, though it wasn't enough to curb Naomi's reckless pulse.

Ryn's attention was fixed on her in spite of the blindfold. She slid her flashlight into a nylon sleeve hanging above their bedrolls so that it worked somewhat like a lamp, beam facing upward so they could huddle beneath. Naomi settled into her bedroll, facing the girl, and dusty-pale moths beat their wings against the flashlight's lens. Ignoring the black blindfold, she stared a while at Ryn's soft mouth and the way her glossy raven's-feather hair rested on her soft cheek, or how her ear cutely peeped from beneath the mane. Those features reminded her: *I still know this girl. Whatever else she is, I know her, and she's my friend.*

When she'd stared long enough, built her confidence, she whispered: "Are you really a monster?"

A nod. "I am."

Naomi swallowed. "You kill for pleasure?"

"I kill because I'm a killer. I do take pleasure in it."

"I don't understand. That's not an answer. That's tautology."

"Yes. Humans are born and they change; the wind blows and they are moved. I'm none of these things. I am... uncaused."

She managed to joke: "Still arrogant, I see." Bracing herself, she went on. "What do you kill? Who?"

"Monsters."

"You *are* one, and you hunt them? I guess I should ask: what do you mean by 'monster'?"

"The things civilization abhors. Men who steal life and sanctity: rapers, murderers, torturers."

"Why are *you* a monster? Do you... suck blood? Turn into a wolf?"

Ryn's brow furrowed. "I've never turned into a wolf." She said it in a way that suggested maybe she could, but hadn't gotten around to it. "And I don't suck the blood."

"You— You consume it, though, for sustenance?"

"I told you I hunt. A hunter eats what she kills."

"Would you want to consume mine?"

Ryn propped herself up on an elbow. "*No.*" She shook her head. "Why would you—"

"It's what vampires do. They want to drink the girl's blood."

"Vampires." She frowned, leaning closer. "I don't know that word, but if something drank your blood, I would get it back for you."

Oh. I guess that's... thoughtful. "So that means you probably can't be killed with crosses, silver, or a stake through the heart?"

"Why do you want to know how to kill me?"

"Those are always the two questions, right? 'What do you want' and 'How do the villagers beat you at the end?' "

"They don't. I cannot be killed and I have no end."

"Oh." She blinked. "Like, at all?"

"If my body were destroyed, I would be reborn. I'm too old to die for long."

The thing across from her was undying; immortal. Naomi looked upon something that rewrote the world from beginning to end, that tore apart all her textbooks and reordered the pages with addenda inked in arcane runes. Her jaw worked until she could get the question out: "How old are you?"

"My years cannot be numbered."

"Can you ballpark it for me?"

Rather than summon a number, Ryn thought a while. "It's difficult. The new religions split the old world apart, and time passed differently in the Long Ago. When time sundered, some worlds fell away and others merged. I lived through eras that were erased from time. Others who lived in the Long Ago remember it differently than I do, because they were part of different worlds. Your history books before a certain point are gibberish to me. There is order to history now, which didn't exist when I first inhabited the Earth. So the years I've lived cannot be counted."

"But... older than twenty."

"Older than twenty."

I am in so much trouble. "Are you a demon?"

"Our kind have many names. We use 'deva' most often."

"There are more like you? Other monsters?"

She shook her head. "Few monsters remain. When the old world fell away, the deva who were too chaotic to pass as mortals were deemed monsters and banished from all the cities and nations of the realm. Deva who could pass for mortal became gods and blended in; most older monsters left Earth or fell asleep."

"That's it?" Naomi asked, shaking her head. "Your eyes glow and that makes you a monster? And otherwise you'd be a *god*?"

"I'm a monster and my eyes glow because my power is chaotic. I can only live in these lands because your people invited me. My banishment subjects me to your laws. If not for that curse, yes, I'd be a goddess."

A picture had started to form, of not so much a monster, but a wild creature standing in the light for the first time. "If you added up all the centuries you've lived, it would be more centuries than I've had years. But if you added together all the conversations you ever had with human beings before coming here, and put them in a book, how big would that book be?"

"You could read it in a day."

"Oh." This creature was older than time, had power enough to never die, and yet she'd had to teach her the difference between pleats and frills. When she'd fed Ryn hot chocolate, it actually had been her very first taste. *I took a deity on a double date and—oh—I tried to make her wear heels.*

"Why are you looking at me like that?" Ryn asked.

"Nothing." She'd been wondering if Ryn had ever kissed someone. "I don't know whether to be in awe of you or..." *Attracted.*

Some moments weighed more than a mountain. Often, they were the quietest ones. Staring now into the face of a divinity, much of Naomi's world mattered less. Her life's plan? How loving a girl could alter how everyone saw her? Those things were dust. They were nothing when scaled against this thing, who had moved through all the pages of history and now offered her friendship. *And more,* Naomi knew.

"You never put a spell on me?" she asked cautiously.

"Never."

"I can trust my feelings?"

"They're your own." The deva fidgeted and, in that moment, didn't remotely look the part of an immortal or blood-hungry monster. She was an anxious teenager who, like Naomi, had never been kissed.

It was as though all those ages in total isolation had frozen the raven-haired creature in a kind of adolescence, the sweet insecurity of the goddess reining her down to earth where Naomi could touch her—wanted to touch her, and treat her with care. *You think you're a monster, but maybe you just haven't been made to feel human yet. Can gods stay cold when they live among us?* Shimmying closer until their breath mingled, she stroked the smooth ribbon over her friend's eyes.

Ryn tensed, prepared to dart away.

"Shh. Let me."

"You'll be afraid," she whispered.

"Then let me be. Let me see all of you and not just the pieces you feel safe showing me. I'll try to understand."

"I don't want to be your nightmare again."

"They weren't all nightmares," she said, tugging the cloth free.

Ryn opened her eyes.

They were eyes on fire—a fire that consumed fire. The black scleras had gravitational pull and if Naomi had to identify the kind of fear she felt, it would be the fear of falling; a sense those scleras were the new "down" and if she was careless, she'd tumble into them. Heart thundering in her ears, her urge was to flee for the safety of the firepit.

The deva closed her eyes. "You see now?"

A thrill swam through her on being released, but the memory of that cold light lingered, afterimages appearing when she blinked. "Not enough."

"You've seen more than enough."

Determined, she set her gaze on Ryn. "I want to see it all. Your eyes and your teeth."

"You'll run. It's instinct, burned into your species from the time I first hunted your kind."

Swallowing, Naomi inched closer, almost to the point of

touching. "Then hold me still."

The monster frowned.

"I know you won't hurt me. Hold me still and let me see." A mad request—but she had to withstand it, to get beyond the instinct to the other side, because it was the only way she could know Ryn. "If it's too much, I'll tell you."

"You promise?"

Showing more certainty than she felt, Naomi nodded. "I do."

Tentatively, Ryn wrapped one hand around her bicep, the other awkwardly at her mid-back, Naomi's body electrified by the sensation of her friend pressed close. "Are you prepared?" asked the monster.

"Do it. Just hold on tight."

Again those eyes lit her with bright, singing fear. Her breath caught and a plea died in her throat. True to Ryn's word, she tried to fight from her grip, to flee. She writhed, and the monster rolled abruptly atop her, pinned her—those eyes boring down into her.

The pinning changed everything. Her panic joined with a sensitive stiffening of her fine hairs. She found Ryn's gaze somehow predatory and alluring at once, realizing the flames subtly brightened and faded as though Ryn's breathing were a bellows. Her terror and attraction weren't in tension, they didn't seesaw—they both rose together, the desire to run and to touch raging through her at once, until she didn't want to be released for fear she'd get away.

"I smell your fear."

"What else do you smell?"

They both knew. The fire and shadow in her eyes and the flashing ivory of her canines painted a portrait of something equally divine and savage.

"You really are both," Naomi managed to say. "Goddess and monster." She lifted her face nearer to the one holding her still.

Ryn jerked her head back. "What are you—"

"Come closer. It's okay."

She didn't at first. "Mortals don't do this. They flee. If I let go of you, so would you."

Heart in a vise, Naomi lifted one hand and carefully—oh so

carefully—stroked Ryn's cheek. "Then don't let go."

She drew Ryn closer, unsure if the magnetism was drawing the deva in or trying to push them apart, but when their mouths were close she felt the electric space between—and in the end, that last finger-width of distance only disappeared when Naomi leaned up to erase it.

Her first kiss.

Sort of.

It was hard to know what it felt like, because outside the riot of her pulse, the shaking in her hands, that was her only thought: *My first kiss, sort of, not counting the river.* That might have been all there was if it hadn't lingered, the sweet press of her friend's mouth quieting the noise in her head. When the deva pushed down into her, a happy growl whirring from her throat, the tension released from Naomi's body and she melted until it was hard to think of anything *but* the sensation.

It was Ryn who pulled away, panting, and true to form the radiant brightening and dimming of her eyes kept time with her lungs.

Not letting her get away, Naomi's fists clutched the girl's shirt at both shoulders, dragging her into a second, less chaste kiss: somewhere in the heat of it, they rolled to their sides, knees entangling and Ryn's trembling fingers raking through her hair.

Naomi only broke for air when she'd let out a needful sound that might have carried to another tent, surprised enough at her own voice that she blushed.

And for a few precious moments after the kiss, she could stare into those eyes without anything holding her down. She came in close, brushing against Ryn's cool nose, warm lips, and confessed: "There is a chance... a small one... that I may be slightly less straight than I thought."

"I still don't care for your words," and she closed her eyes before they could chase Naomi away.

They lounged that way a while, breathing and grasping, and when they kissed one more time, Naomi ran her tongue against those sharp canines to prove it was as strange as it all felt. And it was.

Not slaked, but tired from their day and perhaps too afraid

of what it all meant, they both went still and listened to the chirping of frogs and indistinct chatter from the campsite. Naomi savored the pads of her friend's fingertips stroking her face.

When Ryn yawned, it displayed her pointed canines like a cat's, but the contentedness of the yawn dissipated and the deva was aghast. "What did I just do?"

"That's a yawn." *And it's adorable.*

"It felt like my spirit stretching out of my throat."

"You've never yawned before?"

She shook her head.

Naomi grinned. "Looks like when we, um... 'share breath,' it does more than crank my senses to eleven. Maybe it's a two-way street. Is my sleepiness rubbing off on you?"

She stifled the next yawn. "It feels like the new moon. Strange." Her face nuzzled into Naomi's shoulder, voice muffled: "It feels right, though."

Stroking her hair, she had to admit it did. "You don't sleep?"

"Not like you. Not with dreams. What if I dream?"

"I'll be nearby." She relaxed into her pillow, appreciating Ryn's warmth and the fact she didn't push for words to define what they shared. Were they still friends? More? Naomi had no clue, but there was a rightness to this moment.

For a stretch, they were silent and she drifted, asking a question that floated through her foggy mind. "What's your coolest superpower?"

Ryn murmured something that tickled her ear with breath. It sounded like, "...out here, away from concrete... the weather obeys my heart..."

"Clear skies from now on, you think?"

"Probably not."

Folded into each other, they drifted off, and in their dreams Naomi sprinted through a strange vertical forest of sharp stone and birdsong. It smelled of clean rock, wind, and wet roots. Ryn sprinted beside her. In the wilds of their dreamscape, though, the monster's unearthly eyes were at home.

~*~

The dream bent distances, distorting Ryn's knowledge of every stone in the Fortress of Needles, but it was still wonderful—made so by Naomi, who kept up, and together they tasted the same clean air.

Ryn stopped to scent. Something was wrong.

Naomi bolted past her, laughing. The dream defied logic by simply placing the auburn-haired teenager beside Ryn again when she asked, "What's wrong?"

"You're in danger."

"It's a dream, weirdo. I think it's safe."

"It's not."

Ryn caught the knife and her eyes snapped open in the tent. Naomi startled awake beside her.

The razor tip of Patrick's steel pocket knife trembled an inch from Naomi's throat, held back from her pulsing carotid by Ryn's hand.

The blond male threw all his weight into the knife, but Ryn dragged the point until it hovered above her instead. Glancing angrily at Naomi, she growled, "I only promised to spare him until he attacked."

There was fear in Naomi's eyes, and Ryn couldn't tell who for. "Please don't kill him."

That left her some latitude.

"What the hell," Patrick snarled, but when he caught a look at Ryn's eyes, his face drained of color.

Snapping the steel blade off his knife, she flicked to her feet and planted her shoulder into his middle, tossing him flailing through a hole he'd slit in their tent. He fought for balance even as she strode after.

"You think you can stop me?" he shouted.

"Yes." Ryn tossed him to the dirt, straddled his chest, and bludgeoned his face. Soon, other campers were unzipping tents and spilling out. Ryn took her time to disguise how fast she could be, which left her with an audience.

"Ryn!" Jane screamed. "Ryn, *stop it*, what are you doing!"

"Fixing his face." It had started to look about right. "Almost done." She gave it two more shots, releasing him so he flopped limp with drool and blood pooling from his shattered mouth.

With her gaze down to hide her eyes, she sensed how Jane

darted forward. Naomi called out, "Patrick tried to kill me. But Ryn, stop it—you're going too far." The quaver in her voice stopped Ryn and Jane alike, the crowd paralyzed at what was unfolding.

"He's not done yet." Ryn seized Patrick's arm, pushing him facedown and dragging the wrist into the air behind him. "Confession—" She twisted the bones into an alarming contortion. "—it's good for your soul."

"Ryn!" Naomi shouted.

"You work for Saxby." Ryn leaned down to hiss it in his ear. "No, don't look at them. They can't help you anymore. You're mine, little snake." She applied torque until he whimpered. "Tell me where your master is."

"What are you talking about?" Naomi asked. "Are you crazy? Ryn, you're hurting him."

"Shut up," Patrick snarled. He lanced Naomi with a baleful glare. "Stop pretending. Stop pretending you care! Let your pet demon loose—you know it's what you really want!"

Naomi stared, mouth falling open at the change in Patrick's voice, at the mask of hatred covering his face.

"You're exactly like your father," he spat. "Pretend to care. Preen for the cameras. But I know your kind for what you are. Fucking vermin. You eat this country from the inside."

Naomi was porcelain, unmoving.

"It started with your mother, didn't it? Is she the one who thinks gangsters should go free? Who thinks we should just sprinkle more guns on top of the problem? When you anarchists bribe your way to victory, you fucking *mug* for the cameras and call them 'gun rights' and 'rights of the accused,' and never mind the *bodies* you never had to bury!"

"You're one of them," Naomi whispered. "Those people. That website. You're one of them."

He laughed, a deranged cackle that shook him. "You got my message?" he asked in a broken voice. "I wanted to see your face. Watch it go still when you die." He looked up at her. "I want to see your dad's eyes when he hears how it happened. I want it to change him forever, the way he changed me!"

"He's been twisted by another." Ryn dropped him to the ground, setting her heel to his spine to pin him. She no longer wanted to kill him. He'd been bent this way by Ghorm before she'd ended the asura.

"Fuck you!" Red spittle flew from his gums. "You're all anarchists! Move back to that broken slab of concrete you call a country and leave us alone!"

"Why are the pretty ones always crazy?" Elli whispered.

Patrick lurched toward Elli, and Ryn shoved him facedown again with her foot. Jane apparently had had enough, binding his wrists with clothesline. "Everyone form up. Todd, get on the radio. We need the police."

Something disturbed the air above them and Ryn placed her palm square to Naomi's chest, throwing her effortlessly across the campsite, collapsing her into a tent.

Saxby's terrible claws dropped from the heavens and thundered into Ryn, knocking her senseless.

CHAPTER TWENTY-TWO
Who Owns the Skies

Saxby clutched Ryn in his draconic claws and pumped his wings. They sailed higher and Naomi shrank into a toy person, swallowed by the ocean of trees that spun below. A steel-fibered kanaf protected Ryn from the hundreds of stingers lining his grip, each one trying to drill an envenomed barb into her skin.

Ryn thrashed.

"Tut tut, little monster," rumbled the wyrm above her, a grin peeling across his scaly lips. "Any moment, I'll nick that smooth flesh and you'll be gone. I daresay my latest venom would follow you into your next life."

She inhaled, expanding her chest to strain his claws, flexing her shoulders with all her strength—then exhaled sharply. In that instant, using the smallest gap, she snaked one arm loose. With a *snap*, her claws cracked through him and she dropped through the air alongside the spinning remnants of his toes. She sharpened into a needle-point dive.

Wheeling, he screeched and bent his wings tight to his flanks, both of them plummeting for the same rapidly approaching, stony patch of earth. The wind sang through her ears as the stones swelled larger.

They struck the ground a split second apart, she on hands and feet like a cat. She rolled, and his claws cratered the spot she'd left behind. They were beside the riverbank and he was the size of a house now. Before he'd settled, she twirled and chopped off his barbed tail, the stump spurting blood.

"You smell like her," he snarled. "I didn't take you for a collector of pets. I wonder how long she'll live when I swallow her alive." He leapt for the air, wings flaring.

"No," Ryn roared. *"These skies are not yours!"* She reached out to the forest on both sides of her, eyes shut and spirit touching the air, feeling it tremble in anticipation—it was wind too long untapped by gods, too long abandoned to natural forces and allowed to twirl and rage inside a glass bottle. Ryn uncorked the bottle, lifted both hands, and poured it on Saxby.

The trees swayed and groaned, and then bowed. In the maddening whirl, Saxby's wings folded in an awkward direction and he sank to the other side of the river with a dull thud.

Already, he'd regrown his severed tail. Glaring across the river, his reflection was distorted when the water rippled into streaky waves from the gales. "No matter. To save your girl, you still have to get past me. Ghorm twisted that mortal boy so tight he's a killing spring. The boy told me he wanted to kill your pet with a machete. I told him: splendid. He's doing it now. This very moment."

Fury tinged her vision red.

"How many seconds does she have left?"

He was goading her, trying to get her to behave rashly. She didn't care. *I'll murder him as rashly as I please.* But no sooner had she started forward than he blew oily fire across the river and lit its surface aflame.

He laughed at her. "Tick tock, monster. Tick tock."

~*~

Naomi struggled out of the nylon canopy Ryn had tossed her into, standing and orienting herself, but seeing Ryn nowhere. She'd been thrown clear, everyone else spread across the ground, confused. A strange wind seemed to have blown through.

Wait. Where's Patrick?

By starlight, she saw his figure advancing with a duffel bag in hand, shucking off the last of the clothesline bindings. He tossed the bag off a length of metal that glinted in the moonlight. "You're vermin, Naomi," he called out with an unhinged lilt. "An invasive species. Brought here by your mother. Your kind infest the halls of our institutions and chew them up from the inside."

Mind swimming, she crept back a step to see if he noticed her—he did, and veered her way. Pivoting, she fled, feet carrying her swiftly even as she heard him barreling after. *He's faster than me.* She knew from playing games with him all week. He was laughing and gaining. *He knows it too.*

She sprinted into the edge of the wood, spun to face him—his black size swelled and he swung. But she'd danced between trees and the machete sunk into an elm. He struggled to pry it free.

"Listen to me," she insisted. "I'm your friend. You opened up to me, told me things. I know that was real."

"Of course it was real," he snapped. "I wanted you to know why I'm killing you." He wrenched the blade free, stalking forward as she retreated pace for pace.

The weather changed. Winds shifted and the cold prickled her skin.

"I've always wondered." He crept after her. "They wouldn't execute my mother's murderers. 'Cruel and unusual!' Courts all belong to vermin now. Do you think your father will ask them to give me the death penalty? I can't tell what'd be sweeter: him groveling for the judge to give it to me; or watching him give another fucking speech about my rights while you're cold in the grave."

~*~

Ryn brought the wind together, collapsed it from four horizons, and crushed it into the space around her. Storm clouds piled atop one another, circling overhead. She stroked the storm across treetops like a hand over velvet.

"Howl for me, monster, but know that's all you'll do!" Saxby laughed in the glow of a fire he'd lit across the river. "I know your beginning and your end! I've tasted your power."

"And now I'll make you drink it," she promised. "To the dregs." A fist of air struck the burning river and cut a gash down to the rocks below. The banks swelled, great waves rising on either side of the gash. Ryn crossed the barren divide made by her storm, glinting claws splayed at her sides.

Saxby reeled, kicking up dirt as he positioned like a cat to pounce, launching into the air where he tried to fly clear of her approach. His wings beat, he climbed a spiral path—and she sunk her fist low, winding the maelstrom around behind him. She caught him by his own wings, and with bullet force cast him to the earth. Trees exploded, sheared by his mass, and he left a hundred-foot furrow of raised ground and splintered stumps.

Pivoting, ignoring the dragon, she flew through the forest for Naomi—for the only important thing. Around her, the storm dropped the temperature of the woods to match her cold heart, her breath fogging as though it were a December midnight. Rain that streaked from the sky turned to snow and moisture in the forest froze to slick patches; tree trunks brittled with clinging frost.

Saxby crashed through the forest, toppled icy trees, and came at her on all fours. He intercepted her at a clearing, spitting a barrage of spines from his throat. Ryn sank behind a fallen trunk, quills thudding into the log's other side, thick as a porcupine's hide.

More quills sprouted from the ridge of his spine and his pointed elbows, each dripping venom. They furred his claws, bristled along the softness of his underbelly. "I'll bet he's got her blood on him by now." He spat a volley, heaved another from his tail, reared to fire a thicket of them from underneath his coils. But Ryn danced between them; she flicked between trees, always seeming to find another thing to duck behind as he launched his next barrage.

He's stalling me. She cut to his flank and tried to outrun him, but he gave chase and his body lengthened, growing yet more serpentine, winding through the forest in her wake with only trees, ridges, and stones to cover her from his glistening barbs.

~*~

Snow fell heavy through the air and settled into branches, whose cooling sap made them crackle when they swayed. It was snowing in June, during the time of raspberries and fireflies, and Naomi had never been so cold. The temperature stung her nostrils and lit her breath silver.

She couldn't run or he'd chase her down. Nor could she

stand still, because then he'd cut her in half. Instead she stepped cautiously backward, and Patrick advanced at exactly the same rate. He was savoring it, the slow pace of her murder.

"Listen." She raised her hands. "I'm not your enemy. They've twisted you all around."

"What would you know?"

"You aren't the only one who lost someone. I understand what it does to you."

"Mine was murdered. With a gun your father thinks should be legal, by criminals he wants on our streets."

"Mine was killed by a drunk driver. She—"

"It's *not* the same!"

"Your mother wouldn't want this."

"She always told me to follow my heart." His machete was painted in frost. "Guess what my heart's saying?"

She swallowed and tried not to imagine the bite of cold metal into her body. "Think of her face, Patrick. Think of her eyes before she went away, and tell me that doesn't make a difference. Tell me she's looking on you fondly right now, and I'll let you do it."

"You can't stop me either way." He swatted the machete through branches in his path, never slowing.

She backed into thick brush and the frigid branches snagged her. "Is there anything left in you except hate?" she asked, searching the shadows of his face.

"I thought about shooting you," he said, and it was clear he no longer even heard her. "Wanted to use the same kind of gun that killed my mom. More poetic that way. But I get nauseous at the idea of touching one." He lifted the machete. "At least this way, I get to make a mess."

Naomi tensed, wondering if she could tackle him—a near-hopeless prospect, but it had come to that.

It was Denise who came from behind him, shouting, "Eat it!" Her voice drew Patrick around just in time to catch a frozen branch to his face. His jaw snapped up, blood spraying from his mouth. The machete whirled into snowy litterfall.

The blow spun him almost a hundred eighty degrees, and Denise launched onto his back from behind. She pulled his hemp necklace taut, choking him with it. "You're mine, shit-bag!"

Gagging, he slammed an elbow into Denise.

A white nova of fury lit in Naomi's core and she burst forward, aiming her best kick between his legs. It thumped home with satisfying force. Somewhere in the chaos, Denise got the crook of her elbow around his throat.

Out of the trees came a screaming Elli, who sprayed Patrick in the face with something. He shrieked.

Together, they dropped him to the snow and kicked him until they were out of breath while Denise choked him out. She held on until he started to shake and, gasping, tore off his jacket, belt, and shoelaces, hogtying him. They were all Girl Scouts, but Denise knew the best knots for some reason.

"What— What was that you sprayed him with?" Denise gasped, rubbing her eyes as Elli stood back with a spritz bottle still leveled on an unconscious Patrick. "You can't bring mace to camp, you maniac."

She checked the label. "It's Binaca. Peppermint." Glancing down at Patrick, she added, "I think I contributed."

Denise folded her arms skeptically, but then looked around the forest with concern. "What the hell is going on? Someone broke summer."

Naomi stood, gaze drawn to the sky. "Oh my God." *Goddess?*

A ring of clouds the size of a mountain spun in the sky, a roiling black halo lit with flashes of lightning.

~*~

Ryn sprinted between two rows of trees glazed in crystalline encasements from roots to highest boughs. The forest groaned at the sudden drop in temperature, trunks threatening to burst from the pressure of expanding water within.

Sliding to a stop on one knee, Ryn stretched her hands to the ring of storm clouds overhead. The dragon was a scaly ribbon twisting through the trees, angling for her with jaws opened wide to disgorge more poisoned barbs. She stretched her power to the nimbus crown in the sky and drew down lightning.

Ragged bolts rained from the heavens, white-hot tongues of celestial fire dancing among the trees. Clean and pure as her wrath, she enveloped every tree Saxby neared. The power transformed the water inside to steam, a violent expansion that exploded trunk after trunk like bombs. Wood shrapnel peppered his hide, the impact clobbering him and spoiling his forward momentum. The dragon crashed headfirst into the snow, his slithering mass buckled like a train that had derailed. Fresh powder filled the air as he rolled to a stop.

Her claws flexed and she took them to Saxby's body; she carved him with method and malice—not to incapacitate, no, he'd only heal. There was no punishment there. She peeled him. She flayed until his body opened into bloody gills anywhere she could reach; she scraped off half his face in one swipe.

Her own eyes were flash-imprinted, ears half deaf from landing thunder at her own feet; but Saxby was rendered senseless, except of course for his sense of touch. He lived now in darkness, alone except for her cruel hands, and she worked him until he keened.

"Sing!" she snarled. "Sing for me."

And he did. There was nothing asura hated more than pain. It was enough to force a miscalculation—the last one he'd ever make. With a cry for release, Saxby split his essence again. His flesh rippled, spirit pushing through every drop of his erupting blood. The flesh foamed like the sea, burst, and transformed into insects, scorpions, and serpents. To her immortal eye, it happened slowly—and she leapt through the wriggling epicenter.

With her kanaf as armor to shield herself from stings, she snapped a single snake from the swarm, tucking it close.

Landing on the other side of the buzzing cloud, she reached again to the clouds above and pulled the sky down upon both their heads. The snowy earth lit with not just a few bolts—she brought them all down.

As she'd promised, she made him drink her power. To the dregs.

~*~

Naomi gasped as the sky opened up. She'd never seen lightning so bright, so vicious. It came from every part of the dark ring of clouds, a flurry of bolts that bent inward to the same central patch of ground. They struck a distant place she couldn't quite see. Shielding her eyes, she watched as thunder shook the stones and trees, trembling through her.

I kissed the thing that's doing this. Nameless feelings gripped her, too varied to comprehend, though her hands trembled, her heart pounded, and she wanted to hide from Ryn's eyes at the same time she wanted to... kiss her again. But carefully.

"That— That isn't— I don't..." Denise stared at the same sky, along with Elli. "What's happening?" She swallowed. "Is it the end of the world?"

"I don't know," Naomi confessed. No one could speak louder than a whisper. "We have to get back. Come on."

They bent to drag Patrick, who was groaning and probably concussed from Denise's branch.

Still, the lightning struck. It had not yet stopped pouring from the clouds, battering a single piece of ground as though artillery from Heaven. *She said the weather obeys her feelings,* Naomi remembered. *That's... a lot of feelings.*

~*~

Again and again, Ryn spent her anger in blinding neon strokes from the sky. She beat him like an anvil until her head rang, until her eardrums bled, until all she saw was blue and all she tasted was ozone.

When she stopped, she unfurled the kanaf from around her shoulders and stood alone on a singed patch of earth. When enough of her vision returned to make out shapes, she could tell nothing stood within fifty feet of her in any direction. It was only charred stumps, black ground, and boiling pits of vapor where once there had been water. A stink filled her nostrils: that of the ten million dead life-forms Saxby's essence had split into.

She extracted the snake, the very last piece of him, and could smell his essence inside the struggling serpent. "Stay your hand," Saxby begged, voice disconnected from any physical form. "I'll tell you who paid us."

"I've no time for lies."

"No lies. This is the work of other deva! The Pretender and his foe, the Hidden One, and the Hidden One cannot be found without my help. I know a way. He's paying for my experiments; he wants to use them for his plans. I could—"

Ryn tossed the serpent into the air and sliced it in half. She cut Saxby's essence with it. His stink was snuffed from the air forever. Dead and gone, in a flash of her nails.

She ran for Naomi, making quick work of the trek in spite of her near-sightless eyes, relying on scent and intuition to navigate the forest.

~*~

Jane and Todd had dragged their rafts beneath an overhang in a rock wall and herded everyone, blankets around their shoulders, into the rubberized crafts to keep stray lightning strikes from reaching them through tree roots. Both counselors jogged out to help the girls with Patrick, since it had exhausted them to drag him that far.

"Where's Ryn?" Jane shouted.

Naomi wheeled and stared into the forest, which was thick with swirling snowflakes. Something was coming through the gaps in the trees, a shadow pressed against the snow. "Take care of Patrick. I'll get her." Naomi ran toward the darker patch in the flurry.

It was Ryn. The deva hugged herself tight in her hoodie and kept her head bowed. Blood trickled down her cheeks from her ears and she leaned into a tree. Naomi could still see wisps of smoke rising off her shoulders and smell the stink of electric discharge on her clothing.

"Ryn! Oh God, Ryn, are you okay?"

Ryn stared at her mouth, and Naomi realized she was reading lips. But her eyes unnerved Naomi and stole all her words, making her want to retreat to safety with the other campers. Ryn nodded and collapsed against the tree, fell to her butt and curled her knees close, hugging them.

Naomi shivered and sank next to her friend, bopping her shoulder into the other girl's. The deva leaned back into her, and the heat coming off her felt amazing.

When Naomi spoke, Ryn watched her mouth again. "Could you t-t-turn the snow off?"

"Sorry," Ryn shouted too loudly. Then, more softly: "I

was... upset. Afraid. For your life."

Naomi stroked her friend's hair, the uncertainty in that voice softening her heart. "Will a hug fix the weather?"

Ryn glanced shyly to the forest floor. "It might."

Naomi wrapped an arm around her, squeezing.

Ryn's attention fell to something by her foot. It was a lone plant poking from the snow and coated in a film of glassy ice. She snapped it off by the stem and blew gently, her breath transforming the ice into water. A gorgeous, sunset-colored lily lay beneath, and now its leaves were dewy with melted ice.

With gentle hands, Ryn lifted the flower and put it in Naomi's hair.

The gesture fired her cheeks. "Thank you."

All around them, wintry gusts had died and the air warmed. There was no more lightning and the stars began to shine down from a smooth, clean sky.

CHAPTER TWENTY-THREE
The Pretender

Ryn had finally destroyed the asura threat against her friend, and so had no reason to haunt Naomi's rooftop at night. She did out of habit, liking the scrape of shingles and how it was close to the mortal but not too close. On occasion, when the auburn-haired teenager opened her window, she'd whisper into the balmy summer night: "Are you out there?"

Her voice paralyzed Ryn. That night in the tent had felt so right, but anxiety rose in her when she imagined the ways it could go awry. Perhaps Naomi knew her just the right amount to like her; if she learned more, this tenuous thing they had might evaporate.

So she stayed silent—listening, looking in, never slinking too close to the warm light of her friend's bedroom window where, deep down, she knew she'd never belong.

And her job wasn't wholly done either. Saxby had pleaded for his life, but he'd named names; now she had two deva to find. She didn't want war, but she couldn't kill just *one* god. Their web of alliances meant that touching one brought three more from the shadows, ready to make something of it. They'd once made a hobby of trying to cage her, some seeing her as the last wild thing to be hunted or tamed. Evidence of these battles still dotted this world: sunken nations and scars carved too deep into the Earth to heal.

She'd thought the deva too wise to cross her again, but if they so much as brushed Naomi with the hems of their robes as they passed, Ryn would commit deicide until the realm was emptied of their magic.

But now I have something they can take from me, she reminded herself, and that frightened her.

The generic-voiced people on the television reported Patrick had been questioned by police before they jailed him, and Ryn wanted to know if he'd told them anything about deva. She started her hunt at O'Rourke's apartment, since that one always smelled like secrets.

There were sensors in his windows and a pressure plate under his carpet, all triggered to an alarm. *He's clever.* She scuttled along shelves and furniture, exploring his workshop table, spartan kitchen, a refrigerator full of takeout, and shelves upon shelves of books.

One row of books all had black binders smelling faintly of goatskin. Sniffing, she drew one from the shelf. It creaked when she opened it, the words written in a code that might have been based on pictograms. *Strange tongues bound in the leather of sacrificial animals. Clever indeed.*

She heard his enormous heart long before he leveled the handgun on her. "Ryn Miller." He lowered the weapon.

She shut his notebook and slid it back into place. "The leather does what?"

He was dressed in a sleeveless shirt and boxer shorts that did nothing to hide the roll of belly fat protruding. Squinting at the shelf, he unloaded his handgun. "My reports had a habit of going missing. Maybe it gets lost, or the ink's too smudged to read, or a water main breaks in the records room..."

"The Veil." It erased memories and any other evidence of gods, monsters, spirits, and outsiders. It was always at work, a magic that had imbued their world since history had broken in half.

"Whatever you call it, it's damn annoying for a guy who hates to forget. The leather seems to hold it at bay." He motioned to the whole series of notebooks. "That's everything I ever learned."

"How did you know to use goatskin?" she asked.

"No idea. It's probably in one of those notebooks, how I figured it out. I forget what's inside if I don't reread them." He shrugged. "That's why I keep an index. Sometimes you need to know a thing, and you need it now."

She stroked a fingertip across the bindings. A god would

have burned this shelf the moment he found it, to protect the deva. Ryn couldn't care less. "Meticulous."

"You know things, don't you?"

She shrugged to avoid speaking a lie.

"I questioned Patrick Dailey. Boy said he was 'herald' for some kinda monster. A dragon. Occurs to me I can't really arrest a dragon, but he *was* emailing that enormous hacker whose corpse we found at Primrose."

He knows more than I do. "What else did he say?"

O'Rourke snorted. "Someone bought the kid a machete, paid for him to go to that camp. Kid claims he never met the guy in person."

"They knew I'd smell them on Patrick if they interacted in person."

"There was a go-between who gave him some cash. Got a sketch out of it, and the face matches some secretary who works for a corporation called Zmey-Towers. Those guys lobbied hard against Senator Bradford's security bill." O'Rourke eased into an overstuffed chair. "So I think Zmey-Towers is at the head of it all. Paying the hackers and the people who manipulated the Dailey kid. But I got nothing to go on. Unless you want to throw me a bone."

Saxby had told her the Hidden One was involved. Once, they'd called him Glycon. He'd been fond of mortal cults and it seemed little had changed. "They worship a master," she said. "His ceremonies occur on the full moon. Find who in their leadership this 'secretary' works for and follow her on that night. If you do, you'll locate their whole coterie."

"Who's this 'master'?"

"Someone you won't find." That was her job now. "But jail his followers and you'll stymie his plans."

"Can't arrest people for having kooky meetings."

"If they're Glycon's, they'll do more than meet." She turned from him, headed for the window. "Glycon kept the old ways. There will be sacrifices."

O'Rourke took a moment to respond, perhaps digesting what she'd said. "You're sure I can't find this Glycon guy?"

"He and the Pretender are beyond you."

"The Pretender?"

"I don't know that one. He's too young. Glycon will be hard

enough to find—he carries no scent and his appearance changes through the ages."

"The ages? Holy shit." O'Rourke glanced at his bookshelf. "Guessing you don't want me to start an entry on you."

"That would be a mistake."

"Look, from what I heard, those two... beings... Glycon and the Pretender guy, they're at war. I know Glycon wants the Bradford bill to succeed. So what if the Pretender guy's fighting against him?"

She snorted. "Then he's useless. I've turned back Glycon's pawns at every turn."

"Unless," O'Rourke said, "that was the Pretender's play. What if *he* put you in motion? What if *you're* his pawn?"

Ryn bristled. "*I* chose to defend Naomi Bradford. *I* chose to hunt Splat."

"Splat?"

"Walter Banich."

"And no one nudged you in his direction?" O'Rourke asked.

A dark mood passed over Ryn and a growl clicked from her throat. "Dust."

"Sorry, is that a person too? Okay. Well, whoever this 'Dust' is, assume he works for the Pretender. You want to find him? Go through Dust."

"Oh," Ryn said, flexing her claws, "I will."

~*~

Ryn shattered the museum skylight, dropping to the floor amidst tinkling glass and tattling alarms. Her dark eyes—dilated by psilocybin mushrooms—honed on Dust's presence in a display of crisp baseball cards, each sleeved in a slab of bulletproof glass and screwed onto a plate for display.

She ripped the card from its plate, claws fracturing the clear casing in spiderweb patterns. Slamming it facedown into the display, the impact punched her claws millimeters closer to precious cardstock. "*Where is the Pretender!*"

Dust had gone silent, still.

She squeezed. Her claws neared the tender card where his essence rested. If they pierced him, he would die. If he moved, he might scrape against her nails, which could also prove fatal. "Where is he," she hissed.

"I— I dunno who you're talkin' about!" He was awake now.

The glass cracked again as her nails burrowed closer to him. "A shame," she taunted.

"I ain't telling you a blessed thing till you swear to let me live."

She scanned the display case she'd pried him from. At bottom it read, "Donated by: Orpheum Industries." She growled at the asura in her palm. "So the Pretender owns that company. And you deceived me, an elder monster... for baseball cards? Violins and old junk?" She might have laughed at his stupidity if it were remotely a laughing matter.

"Not any old junk," he grumped. "The best old junk. Delicious old junk. You oughta try incentives sometime, beastie. Catch more flies with sugar than murder."

"I don't catch flies," she ground out. "I swat them." She ripped the front of the sleeve off and stroked her nails across naked paper.

"Okay! Okay! Wasn't even that bad, Jee-zus, you got *problems*, you know that?" She kept her nails close, but gave him space to breath. "He goes by Set—Set the Pretender. He mighta talked to me, asked if I could... redirect your attention a little. I naturally told 'im, 'Set. Buddy, c'mon, you know I wouldn't mess with someone like Erynis, I respect her too—' "

"Get on with it."

"Long story short, he begs me to point you toward Splat and his obsession with the Bradford girl. But hey, he said you'd probably want to get involved anyway, so it was basically win-win-win. The Pretender gets Splat outta the picture, you get to eat Splat, I get the 1961 Clemente card—what's not to love? Peace, beastie, we got no quarrel. Not with me and not with this innocent card, which, by the way, never did nothin' but give people hope. Kill me if you gotta, but this slip of paper? Let it be."

"How did he know I would be at the group home?" That was where Dust had first contacted her.

"He's got eyes everywhere. He told me where to be."

"And what about me getting out of Sacred Oaks and onto the street?" The timing was too convenient to be coincidence.

"Don't you get it? The Ostermeier Trust Fund—the private money that used to pipe into those facilities—he sank it through some kind of Ponzi scheme. Sent the whole system belly-up to free you."

Ryn scowled and tossed Dust's paper house carelessly across the floor. "What is his game, Dust?" She flashed her nails. "Tell me, or I shred the room."

"Peace, peace! Same game it's always been—Set and Glycon, going round and round each other, snappin' like dogs. But they can't touch each other, not really, or the Fates would step in. They've all crossed their hearts and vowed to play by certain rules. So it's all done by proxy."

"I am no proxy!"

"Yeah, I'm picking up on that, okay?"

"Why do you call him 'Set'? Set has passed on; he sleeps."

"Yeah, you been gone a while, must not have heard. That's why they call him Set *the Pretender*. He's only a few centuries old, tells everyone to call him Set, but the Fates know he's *not* Set. But rules are rules—gods can't name other gods. So they call him Set, and added the epithet to keep him in line."

"Then you tell me, Dust." Ryn approached, knelt, and stroked the card lying on the floor. "Tell me quickly, before the police arrive, or I'll end you. Tell me where this upstart calls home."

~*~

Ryn sensed no human life in the echoing, empty Docks warehouse. It wasn't supposed to be abandoned—it was a property of Orpheum Industries with gates, cameras, and forbidding barbed wire crisscrossing its perimeter. She descended to its rooftop and cut a hole in the skylight that was clean enough not to trigger sensors. Descending silently, she peered through the barren interior.

Scrape marks on concrete showed where they'd moved all the equipment in a hurry. The air was thick with bleach odor, the entire lofty space emptied and scrubbed of its original smells to take her off the trail of anyone who'd worked here. All that remained was a table with a single, thrumming black laptop and projectors aimed at the four walls around her. A lonely alley cat with a missing eye slept on the laptop's keyboard, snoring softly. The cat hadn't been put there; it appeared to have wandered into the room and found somewhere warm to rest.

As she approached, the laptop activated and the cat let out a discontented meow. It hopped from the computer, thudding to the floor and padding off to find a dark corner.

Projectors on all sides displayed forty-foot images that mimicked the laptop's display. She was surrounded by Set the Pretender. He was a dark-skinned man with chiseled features, black eyes, and extensive tattooing on his hands and bald scalp that disappeared into a white kurta. He knelt, bowing his head to her. "Erynis. A pleasure."

"If it is, come meet me," she beckoned.

"I cannot help thinking that would be a... poor decision." His mouth did something that might have been mockery.

She bore her teeth at him.

"You have many names, though none pleasant. Erynis— the implacable one. Adrasteia—the one from whom there's no escape. Nemesis? Yes, that has a certain foreboding ring, doesn't it? Let's not forget Lailah—pretty. At least to the tongue. Not so pretty for those who crossed you."

"My deeds speak for me, not that tangle of names that clutch at history. Tell me. What are your deeds?" She approached the computer.

"Numerous, dark, and manipulative." He shrugged. "Haven't you heard the reports? The Fates don't think much of me; nor does Glycon."

"I've never heard of you."

"Ah." He nodded. "I get that a lot too. Whatever my press, I'm the one who intends to survive you."

" 'Intends.' "

"I'll confess, it's not up to me." He stood, spreading his palms. "I'll start with an oath." He crossed his heart. "I swear to never harm your mortal, Naomi Bradford."

"As you swore not to harm Glycon?"

"I swear it for Naomi more deeply than I did for Glycon— I'll follow the spirit for you, not just the letter."

"I don't believe you."

"You won't at first." He sighed. "You've little reason to. If you haven't figured it out, I'm the reason for all this. Glycon had originally targeted the family of Senator Wulf. I took Wulf out of play through... various means. I knew when Glycon couldn't get to Wulf, he'd target Bradford and his daughter instead. I nudged him that direction, knowing it put your friend in danger."

Ryn's hackles rose. "For that, you'll die."

"I knew you'd defend her."

Glaring at him, she shook her head. "You don't know anything about me."

"Not true," he chuckled. "I know everything about you. And, while you're old and deadly, you're not terrifically complicated. For instance, I also know that no matter how mad you are at me, you'll go after Glycon for what he did."

"I'm coming for you both."

"Splendid." Another strange smile. "I cannot feed you information about Glycon directly without violating my own oaths. But I do wish you luck—at least, in regards to hunting my rival. As for me? Now I'll slink away and hide; avoid you and your mortal as best I can. Glycon, as you know, lacks my characteristic humility. You hurt him. He'll come for you; he'll come for Naomi. If you love your mortal, you'll deal with Glycon first."

She balled her fists, prepared to cleave this young god into a dozen pieces for daring to put Naomi in danger and manipulate Ryn for gain, all in one bold stroke.

"I'd love to talk more." He shook his head sadly. "But I'm afraid I've got to blow up the warehouse now."

"Why?"

"Tradition?"

"I'm unfamiliar with this tradition," she said.

"I'm keen on making new ones." He removed a smartphone from his pocket, punching a button. A large number "10" superimposed on the screens. It ticked to "9." It took until "8" for Ryn to realize what was happening.

Sprinting past the computer, she tore it in half on the way. She slid along the floor, snapped the hissing cat into her arms, and broke a side door from its hinges. She'd vaulted the outer fence when the explosion hit her back. It sent shrapnel into the sky for hundreds of feet.

Ryn rolled to a stop as fire and debris fell on all sides. She shielded the cat, and once the last piece of smoking sheet metal rang against the asphalt, she peeled the traumatized animal from her shoulder and tossed it aside.

"Two gods to kill," she whispered. A dangerous task, especially with her heart invested in a fragile human being. But she saw no other path, especially since Set had spoken the truth about Glycon—he wasn't humble, and he wouldn't let Ryn's encroachment on his territory go unpunished. They were on a collision course, one engineered by Set.

She kicked over a flaming stack of cinder blocks and waded through the rubble. *Let him come,* she decided. *I will darken his whole world.*

~*~

A tiny gremlin crouched alone in Glycon's pocket world, cold snow underfoot and dark trees towering on all sides of them.

The altar at the clearing's center was cut from an ancient stump, its roots burrowed like great claws into the ice. The emaciated creature was all knobby joints, combing down its bristled fur to make itself more presentable before him. It bowed, bat ears drooping in a show of submission. "...that is all I knows, Lord Glycon. I swears it."

"Spare me your groveling." How he despised gremlins. But he'd run into... issues... with his cult, and so was forced to rely on outside contractors. *Far outside,* he mused. "Were you able to recover any part of Mr. Saxby?"

"No part recoverables, not a one. We searches the forest high and low, my brothers and I. All we finds was the lab, the pieces police stored. Those is here." It waved to the two suitcases in the snow.

"Very well. Your payment." He passed the gremlin a manila envelope.

With deft fingers, it checked the papers. Six authentic certificates for the adoption of six young children. "They is healthy? Had their shots, teeth real good?"

He scowled. "I'm no roadside vendor. It's in order. Healthy specimens all. Now begone!"

The gremlin stooped and scraped on its way out of the portal. Glycon sealed his pocket world with a dismissive wave of the hand, knelt, and opened the briefcases one at a time. He lifted free a glass jar that contained the decomposed remains of a rodent, bristles of white fur still visible amidst the rot. In the center, though, pulsed several still-living eggs; and beneath the pink, Glycon detected faint signs life.

He smiled. "It's a start."

~*~

Mark stayed in the car but insisted on driving Naomi to her friend's apartment, since it was around the corner from a place dubbed "Murder Alley" for the fact so many corpses showed up there. David Kessler had given her the address after her dad started asking for it—apparently he wanted to send thank-you flowers. Upon hearing Ryn lived by Murder Alley, he'd asked instead about sending a thank-you gun.

Ryn's building was grayed with age, accented with fresh graffiti layered over the old. The elevator seemed a little deathtrappy, so she took stairs that smelled faintly of urine, climbing to the top floor.

Ryn had the only top-floor apartment, the stairwell exiting to a short corridor. The imposing door was made from steel and bolts, and after she knocked, it opened just a crack. Ryn peered through, wearing new glasses that were the same model as the pair Denise had bought her.

"I thought—"

The door shut with a clank.

"Okay." Naomi blinked at the door. "I understand communication isn't your forte, but you shouldn't just—"

A rattle of the security chain and Ryn swung the door wide, stepping aside to motion her in. "You're welcome here." Peering past her, she added, "But *just* you."

"I'll keep your clubhouse totally on the down-low, promise." She flashed the Scout's-honor sign. The space was open-aired and almost featureless, though all Naomi could initially think was, *She is way too short to have her own place. Especially somewhere so... tall.* It had bare wood floors with a drab area rug, and a dais on the farthest edge was furnished with a four-poster bed. Every wall was smooth, white, and un-painted. With its vaulted ceiling, she couldn't decide if it re-minded her more of a gymnasium or a barren cathedral.

"Why are you here?" Ryn shut the door with another clank and she fidgeted.

"Missed you." She toed at the floor. "I thought since we kissed, I might, um, see you once in a while. Not that I neces-sarily deserve that, after yelling at you and accusing you of putting a spell on me." She cleared her throat. "I was kind of a jerk, wasn't I?"

Ryn shrugged.

Something was the matter, and Naomi squinted, trying to figure it out.

The attention made Ryn transparently uncomfortable and she twisted one hand around her opposite wrist.

Why's she so freaked out? Naomi straightened at the real-ization: here was a deific creature who had never so much as had a friend before her, and now they had kissed. "Do I make you nervous?"

"No," she lied.

Naomi approached, gently touching her friend's cheek. The raven-haired girl startled, but didn't back away. "Don't be. I still like you."

"There's more." Ryn leaned slightly into her hand. "There are dangers. Beings who are going to hunt me; who I have to hunt. They may try to harm you. Everything is so fragile. Eas-ily broken, easily lost."

"They've already tried to hurt me," she said evenly. "You've saved me more than once, and every day's a gift I wouldn't have had without you. So there's no reason for guilt."

Ryn nodded but didn't look up.

"And they'd be coming for me even if we weren't together, wouldn't they?"

"Probably."

"So there's nothing to do except your best." Before she could disagree, Naomi drew her into a hug. At first, the mon-ster's whole body stiffened, but the longer she held on, the more Ryn relaxed into her. "Come to my house this weekend."

"Why?"

"Dad's orders."

"But why?"

"Big mystery. You'll have to show up if you want to know."

Ryn shifted, having locked her hands behind Naomi's back. "It sounds like an ambush."

Naomi inhaled, the deva's hair possessing a woody smell like oakmoss, but with something of a sweeter note. "What if I'm part of the ambush?"

The slight creature shivered in her arms. "I might like that."

"Then come." She hesitated and kissed Ryn's cheek, wanting to taste her mouth again but not yet as courageous as she'd been in the tent. The light of day had reminded her how much of her life was invested in being Naomi Bradford, future hetero wife and mother-of-two; there were so many unknowns. What if everyone talked? What if she fell for some amazing guy and ended up just leading Ryn on? The combined weight of those fears applied just enough inertia to keep the kiss affectionate but chaste. "So you know," she said slowly, "I'm still figuring stuff out."

"Do you want to do what we did in the tent again?" Ryn asked, blunt as ever.

She hesitated. "Like I said, I'm figuring it out."

Ryn bit her lip. "Did you like it?"

Naomi nodded, the heat in her face confirming the truth.

Neither could quite look the other in the eye, but Ryn released her. "Then I'll wait."

~*~

Ryn heard by way of Ms. Cross that both Kessler and O'Rourke were being praised for having followed the Glycon cultist. They'd stopped the worshipers from feeding someone to a giant snake and this was apparently good for their careers, especially since a lot of the men feeding people to the snake were rich or powerful—owners of companies and nonprofits, involved in the film industry or federal government.

She asked, but no one told her what they'd done with the snake.

In July, Ms. Cross and Kessler both visited at once and Ryn instinctively locked down at the sight of them together. They sat near one another and sometimes held hands; it didn't seem fair how they'd joined forces. It was cheating.

Ms. Cross cleared her throat. "You're going to finish school."

Next came Kessler: "What Victoria means to say is, rather, we think it's important. Not just for the degree, but because it'll integrate you better. We're here to encourage you to do the right thing, not make ultimatums."

"Though we also insist," Ms. Cross said.

"Gently," Kessler added. When Ms. Cross glanced at him and did something with her eyes, he cleared his throat. "But firmly."

"The school won't have me." Ryn folded her arms. "There's no point in talking about this." *There. Done.*

"We've researched private schools." Kessler slid a glossy pamphlet across the table. "Your grades are actually good. Given your, uh, 'inheritance,' money's not an object. This school is selective, but it's our favorite."

Ryn tore the pamphlet in half. "No."

"That's Madison Academy," Ms. Cross said.

Quickly matching the two halves together, Ryn recognized the gates on the front. "Naomi goes here."

"The thought had occurred to us," Ms. Cross said, pleased.

"School. With Naomi?" The idea wasn't wholly bad.

"It's prestigious," Kessler said. "Kids with your background aren't well-represented there, but I can get a letter of explanation that'll better reflect the reasons for your expulsion. With a letter of recommendation from Victoria and me, that gets us most of the way there. The fact that you've apparently pleased a sitting U.S. senator will round out your recommendations nicely."

Ryn nodded.

"You'll keep your grades up, of course." Ms. Cross said it like the thing was decided. Perhaps it was.

"And there's one more thing," Kessler said. "Madison requires a parental guardian. So you'll live with me."

Ryn shook her head. "I live here. I like it here. I own it for one year; that's the law."

"All right," he said. "Crash here now and then, when you need to. But take the spare room at my new place. It's closer

to Madison, since I'm in the Central Precinct now with
O'Rourke. It's closer to Naomi, too. I'll work up the foster-par-
ent paperwork. That is, if you trust me enough. I know that's
hard for you. I get it."

Ryn felt cornered.

"We care about you," Ms. Cross said.

"Why?" she asked.

"Because we do," Kessler said.

"But *why*?"

Ms. Cross took a breath and let it out. "Because we love
you, you silly girl. Both of us. Tremendously. We want you to
succeed; we want you to flourish."

"I tried to tell you before," said Kessler. "I had to go halfway around the world to find it, but you're part of my family
now, Ryn."

She stood, but they did too. She wanted to back away but
couldn't, not because her path was cut off, but because another part of her didn't want to. Instead, she took a hesitant
step forward and Kessler hugged her. She set her head into his
chest and, like always, he smelled like the safest person in the
world. She realized she was hugging him back and squeezed.

He let out a sound that meant he couldn't breathe. She
loosened her grip.

Ms. Cross hugged them both too and she wondered if *that*
was family. If it was, it still tasted funny in her mouth. But
maybe not completely, entirely bad.

~*~

Kessler and Ms. Cross drove Ryn to Naomi's house on the
appointed night, and Ryn had to dress nice—which meant
wearing the clothes Naomi had picked out for their double
date. It felt odd to arrive by car instead of rooftop, and when
she entered, Senator Bradford met her in suit and tie.

"The guest of honor," he announced. "I hope you don't
mind my secretly engineering this dinner through well-placed
calls to your loved ones. It's in your honor of course."

"Why?" Ryn asked.

"New family rule. Anyone who saves my daughter's life
more than once gets a dinner. Thank you, Ms. Miller."

"I am called Ryn."

"If we're being particular, call me 'the Senator.' I like to hear it."

"Do *not* call him that," Naomi said from the top of the stairs. She was gorgeous, her hair an auburn halo, dressed precisely as she'd been on the night of their double date. Except now it was Ryn who stood speechless at the foot of the stairs, listening to the flutter of her own heart. Naomi wore a secretive smile, knowing precisely what she had done. The clever mortal had finally gotten the thing she'd so wanted, but instead of a boy it was Ryn who gawped at her elegant descent of the staircase.

Dinner was served at the table, a spread Naomi and Denise had prepared, though Elli was supposed to have helped—they accused her of leaving it all to them, having spent all her time texting Horatio, who she was now dating with Naomi's permission. There was salad, some kind of mixed fruit, and steamed legs from a large crab.

"To open it, you do this," Naomi said, picking up a nutcracker.

Ryn figured it out first. She grabbed it at both ends, snapped it in half and rent it apart, plucking the meat from inside. "Like this?"

Naomi stared at the shell debris all over her plate. "Sure."

It was great fun, actually—the challenge of ripping the meat's armor off before eating it. Ryn enjoyed the entire process and Senator Bradford and Kessler both made jokes at her expense. It didn't stop Ryn from finishing perhaps one too many crab legs, because there was no hunger at all left in her belly. She disliked the satisfaction that came from too much food—it robbed her of her edge, slowed her down. But sitting at the warm table, part of her liked it. *Just this once,* she decided.

Senator Bradford tapped a goblet with his fork. "To round the evening out, I just got off the phone with the admissions committee at Madison Academy. I understand Ryn will receive an acceptance letter any day now. Also, I think Naomi has something for you."

"*We* have something for you," Naomi said. "We all chipped in." She held out a small box with a red ribbon around it.

Ryn took the box and pulled off the top, revealing a shiny, black cellular phone. She handled its weight and inhaled the plastic scent. "I don't understand."

"It's definitely not to eat," Denise said helpfully.

"It's to keep in touch," Naomi said. "This way I don't have to physically *go* to your house, or wait for you to show up here. Turn it on. I'll show you how it works. We've paid the first few months."

Ryn wasn't sure she wanted a phone. But she liked how close Naomi sat while they went over how it worked, and she maybe didn't catch on as fast as she could have.

Kessler and Ms. Cross excused themselves after dinner, since Ryn insisted she could take the train home. Elli and Denise left next, and when the hour grew late, Naomi yawned and stretched. "To bed with me. Denise and I are doing Scout things tomorrow. You're invited if you don't mind babysitting itty-bitties."

Ryn didn't like small children. They were clumsy. But because Naomi would be there, she nodded. "All right." After a stiff hug that seemed too quick, they said goodbye. Ryn left through the front door. On the porch, she smelled the summertime garden and savored the electric glow of their mothy porch lights.

Her phone buzzed and she clicked the button to receive a text.

Naomi

I'm not asleep.

Ryn wondered what that meant.
Another buzz from Naomi:

Dad went straight to
bed. Has to be in office tomorrow.

Ryn puzzled over the messages. Would Naomi send her a text updating her every thought? Based on the third buzz, she guessed so.

That means sneak in.

Oh. Ryn skittered up the tree behind their tall stone wall, across the rooftop, down to the windowsill, and pushed through the curtains covering the open window.

"You can be so dense sometimes." Naomi sat on the corner of her bed, legs crossed, so pretty it hurt Ryn to look directly at her.

"Did you want to talk?" Ryn asked.

"No," Naomi whispered. "I want you to sit. Here." She patted the bed and Ryn swallowed.

She did what Naomi asked, and the girl slid behind her. She noticed there were hair bands on her wrists.

"Can I touch your hair?"

"Yes." A shiver scrunched Ryn's shoulders together.

It was the same bliss as months ago, when Naomi had braided her hair the first time. Ryn shut her eyes and every touch soothed her.

"I'm sorry for that night when I yelled at you," Naomi said after a while.

"It's all right." It really was. Everything everywhere was all right.

"I was mixed up. I still am."

Ryn opened her eyes and could tell Naomi stared across the room at the plastic structures she'd built with her mother. She looked in particular at the unfinished, jagged model that was supposed to have been the Eiffel Tower.

Naomi glanced away. "I think kids are always trying to save their parents. Trying to learn from their mistakes and do it differently; do it right. Or just, you know, avoid the same tragedies. My mom never got the happily-ever-after, she never got the Eiffel Tower. I thought I'd get married in her church, and then go with my husband someday, and maybe that'd make it... cosmically right?

"And it scares me. Not just the church part, but because I never really talked to my mom about how she'd feel if I were gay. It never came up. I'll never know what she thought—but

I guess I have to believe she'd love me no matter what."

Naomi had stopped braiding, and Ryn reached back to touch her hand. Their eyes met through the mirror. "You smell like half of her. If she is even half of you, then you shouldn't worry."

"Thanks."

"I'm sorry too."

Naomi laughed. "What for?"

"Scaring you."

"You're not that scary; not underneath."

That worried Ryn. She looked at Naomi through the mirror. "I *am*, though."

At that, Naomi averted her gaze and went back to braiding. She did it for a while, and Ryn couldn't tell what she was thinking. Only that she was. Was she remembering all the people Ryn had killed? Humans always seemed especially bothered by that.

"Remember that deal we had last time I braided your hair?" Naomi asked.

"If you could still hug me after I told you what I was, you got to braid it and put a flower in." It was a sweet memory now.

"Want to play again?" She didn't look up from the work of her fingers.

"What is the bargain?" Ryn asked, heart beating harder.

"You let me put the flower back in your hair and I'll let you take me out on a date. No boys this time." She glanced up into their reflection again. "Just us."

Ryn smiled, turning on the bed and pushing Naomi back, enjoying the way she relaxed into the mattress beneath her. "I'd like that."

Naomi reached for her glasses, sliding them off, and Ryn's gaze chased her back to the headboard.

"One condition." Ryn prowled after her.

"What's that?" she asked, breathless.

"I dress how I like."

"Be careful." Naomi's eyes crinkled with mirth. "Some humans make assumptions about girls who don't wear underwear."

"Then you can wear it."

"Maybe I won't," Naomi challenged, and for some reason her tenor excited the monster.

Seizing the auburn-haired girl's ankle, Ryn dragged her close, Naomi's breath hitching as she was pinned under glowing eyes. They kissed again, and from her friend's sigh and arching body, it was as good for her as it was for the deva. "You should wear a dress," Ryn purred.

"So you do like them."

She nodded. "On you."

"You realize, of course, that I'm hopelessly bossy—if we do this, if we really do it, you're going to get dragged into things— things like dresses and family dinners and who knows what else. You hate change, but with me, it's going to happen."

The stars couldn't change and neither could Ryn. She was finding, though, that Naomi could unearth parts of her that she'd never known existed. "We'll see," she said, and before they could argue, she kissed Naomi again.

EPILOGUE

John Laek's buddies dropped him at the curb, blitzed and swaying on the short walk to his apartment building. His neck burned from a fresh tattoo and the whisky bottle sloshed. They'd grabbed it off an amputee vet in the Draintrap.

He rummaged for his keys, making three attempts at putting it in the lock before he got into the building. On the short elevator ride he checked his texts: two from Gregor congratulating him on the dropped charges for that dustup back at the Nine Lives; one from Senna looking to score, but he was sick of screwing her.

He was horny, though. Drunk and horny and he'd been jacking it in his cell for months, waiting on Gregor to pay off that Nine Lives bouncer who was threatening to testify. *Next time,* Gregor had warned him, *Try not to fuck with a senator's kid.*

Crashing in his apartment, he pulled up a few names, looking for that honor-roll chick he'd had almost a year ago. He found her picture, having entered her name as "A-Plus Mouth."

"Come over," he typed. "Want an oral exam." He giggled at his joke.

"Leave me alone," she replied.

"Nah. Get over here." He waited, blood going icy hot.

"You've got the wrong number."

He looked at the message a while, face souring. Laek shook his head and pulled up the footage from last September when she'd been high on his couch and a little more willing, sending it along. "Really? This ain't you? Shame."

A long, long pause, and he grinned while he waited. Finally: "You kept that?"

"Babe, it's on the internet."

A barrage of misspelled, raving texts followed: curses, threats that she'd call the cops, informing him her dad was one. He liked that one best. The last message read, "You know I'm underage, right? That's child porn. You'll go to jail, you pedophile."

He laughed. "I didn't post it. My face ain't even in it. Who says I did that shit to you?"

Another pause. "What do you want?"

He took his time typing: "Too late, bitch. Hope this doesn't go viral and ruin your life. If you want to beg, you know where I am." Laek wasn't sure he even wanted her anymore. Her mouth had been more of an A-minus, come to think, but he was interested to see if she'd show up with tears in her eyes.

It wasn't long before his door buzzed. Standing, he fumbled for his handgun—he gave it fifty/fifty she'd sent her pissed-off dad or older brother to knock his head off. When he opened the door, though, the hall was empty.

"The fuck?" He took off the security chain, stepped out, and had a longer look around: just the same old cracks in the plaster and an empty beer bottle on the hall's far window.

Back inside his apartment, he turned on some porn and picked up the phone, typing, "You out there, Miss College Scholarship?"

He went to make a sandwich and heard a ding, and was halfway back to the living room when he realized it hadn't sounded like his phone's usual tone—and besides, his phone was dark in his pocket.

Laek realized his fine hairs were on end. Through his drunken haze he felt a tickle of fear, and realized someone else was here. The question slithered through his brain: *Did I lock the door?*

Rushing back, he checked, and the security chain was firmly in place. "Stop freaking out, John," he told himself. But he heard it again: the soft ding indicating a text, but not from his phone.

It had come from the bedroom.

He cocked the hammer on his gun and trod to the bedroom with care, hugging the wall and focusing on being stone-cold sober. Hopefully the noise of his porn covered the occasional scuff from his sneakers.

His door was partly open, which wasn't unusual, and he prodded it further, using the hall light to look across his darkened bedroom. But it was empty. He realized one of Gregor's guys must have crashed at his place while he'd been in a jail cell—and left their fucking phone. "Christ." He dragged a sweaty palm down his face. "Going to kill Gregor."

He stormed inside, tossing pillows and blankets aside, going through drawers to find the errant phone.

Another ding, from under his bed. "Seriously?" But a split second later, his own phone chirped. He saw it was a video file and briefly wondered if that pretty high-schooler had sent something interesting.

The short video played. It showed two sneakers from a weird angle on the floor.

His shoes. The video had been shot from under his bed.

The number wasn't the high-schooler—he recognized it as Pavlo's, who he hadn't seen since the Nine Lives.

He whipped out his gun. "Who are you, you—"

The growl came softly from under his bed. It surged from the gap between the mattress and floor, made from wet ink and hatred. Its eyes stole every reasoning part of Laek's mind, familiar eyes that had haunted his nightmares too many cold nights. Razor fingers wrapped around his gun hand and he watched from beside himself as the whole arm came off. He heard the meaty rip, and was staring at the space where he'd used to have a limb.

It was only a moment later that the pain hit and he screamed.

~*~

Ryn didn't stop, not through the screams and not through the begging. She could have told herself this was because mortal prisons had failed to punish him, or for what he'd have done if she'd let the monster live. But the truth was simpler: she was made to eat monsters, and John Laek's heart was as good as any other. She plucked it free and devoured him, sending him off to the fires of gehenna, where the world would be free of him and he would be free of himself.

She picked up his phone when she'd finished, using what remained of his finger to access it. These were useful devices—she'd messaged him using the phone of Pavlo, the handsy one he'd been partnered with at the Nine Lives, whom she'd already eaten. There was a girl messaging Laek, afraid of images he had of her, but the phone also had contact information for the last monster who'd been with them at the Nine Lives.

Ryn's own phone dinged. It was Naomi yet again: "You're just full of questions about phones tonight. Glad you're taking to this. Sure you don't want to come over and talk date logistics?"

Her thumbs smeared blood on the screen as she replied, "No." The other good part of a phone was that Naomi had a harder time seeing through lies. "Going for a run. Talk again soon."

She stepped over the pieces of John Laek she hadn't eaten and left through the window.

Ryn will return

Sometimes Casey and M.A. Ray play together in the same sandbox—they are two writers who try to be friends even though they're very jealous of one another. M.A. Ray writes fantasy, though a different sort, set in the world of Rothganar, which has Casey's fingerprints all over it. Since they've developed their skills and worlds in such close concert, there's a good chance that if you like Casey's work, you'll also like M.A. Ray's. Below is a sample of Ray's take on a tiny, murderous creature falling in shojou-manga sparkle-vision love with someone of the same gender. Enjoy.

An excerpt from *The High King's Will*
© 2015 M.A. Ray

Eagle Eye lay broken and reeling on the floor of the cavern. The dark hulk of the great red Worm loomed over him, tail backlit by the gold that shimmered in heaps on the floor. Huge wings hung limp, casting strange shadows. The last dead twitches passed through Eleazar.

Eagle's head ached. His vision swam, and distantly he heard the Crown Prince call out, "Hey-la-hey!" Brother Fox struggled over the thick tail with a blob of golden mage-light hovering just above his head. He called out again: "Eagle, brave Eagle, you've done it!"

He didn't feel brave. He hurt so badly. The cruel black horns on Eleazar's head, the knife teeth, and the massive eye, which had only a few minutes ago fallen upon him with hungry menace, sent a trembling to his soul.

Brother Fox blocked his view, partially, and he was glad of that. Light wreathed the Prince, making a glowing spirit of a flesh-and-blood youth, and Eagle understood why his stomach clenched when Brother Fox smiled. Gold threads gleamed in his dark hair, and his face sent Eagle's heart staggering. Impossibly beautiful.

The perfect mouth moved, but Eagle couldn't hear. Black-ness teased at the edges of his awareness. When the Prince bent over him, shadows swallowed amber eyes, like the bruises that so often marred the face. Eagle had preserved Brother Fox's life, but he wondered if he had done the Prince a service.

Then—nothing.

Eagle had done for the Worm with a single, lucky arrow, but the Worm had nearly done for Eagle, too. More properly, Eagle had nearly done for Eagle. He'd dashed himself to pieces on the rocks. Broken bones, cracked skull. Two days he'd been deeply unconscious, in the care of the healers, but this morn-ing, when he woke, the High King had tacked *Vistridir* onto his name. Wormsbane. Father had hustled him home straightaway, after Brother Fox had given him a scale from the Worm's own hide. "You ought to have it," the Prince had said. "You earned it. And after all, I did promise you one."

He'd felt Rothganar's biggest fraud when the High King called him Wormsbane. All his dreams of great deeds had fallen to ashes before the terror he'd felt in the Worm's cave, and a numbness had come over his heart since, which he dis-tantly feared would never go away. Even all the loveliness of the flowers and the sweet songs of the frogs had lost their power to move Voalt Vistridir. Nothing seemed quite real after Eleazar, and Eagle himself the least real of all.

The royal gardens showed spectacular on a summer's night, especially a night like this, scented and breezy and clear. All the mage-lanterns shone in the cottage behind Eagle, who sat on a stool just outside the front door, gazing into his own shadow. In his hands he held the Worm's ruby scale, the size of his palm. He rubbed at it unconsciously with a small, callused thumb, over and over.

He was alone. Father had gone on a hunt that afternoon, to stock the High King's larder. He always took Eagle along, and today was no exception, but Eagle had asked to turn back. His leg, the site of the worst break, pained him. Normally there would have been no excuses accepted, but Father al-lowed it today, on the condition that he stayed inside.

He'd meant to obey, but the cottage stifled. Here he sat, with the achy leg stretched out in front of him, turning the scale over and over. Remembering, though he would sooner not: images cloaked in darkness, lit by flashes of red mage-light and gold, by a blast of flame bright as day. His memory tainted the sweet-smelling night with Worm stench. The world was half unremarkable dream, half nightmare, and Eagle wandered in it, lost, feeling only enough to realize, from a distance, that he hurt. So lost that when a figure stumbled around the yellow rose hedge, it surprised him. Ordinarily he would have heard someone coming, particularly someone so very drunk.

Brother Fox. The Crown Prince's bruised face dripped tears and blood, and he shuffled toward the cottage, cradling a swollen arm that surely must be broken. Not drunk. Beaten. Father would have sent Eagle away to do some chore right off, but he stared, rooted to the spot, so much that the Prince nearly tripped over him. He popped up, overturning the stool, and remembered to bow. "Your Highness," he rushed out, slipping the scale into his pocket.

"Please don't," Brother Fox rasped. He swayed on his feet. "Is your father here?"

"No, Your Highness." Eagle bit his lip. Father would have sent him away, but Father wasn't here, and one of Brother Fox's eyes was so badly swollen he couldn't open it, though tears still leaked from between the lids, a slow trickle. He couldn't think how the Prince had managed to get through the gardens to the cottage. Had he used the tunnel? In any case, sending him back up to the Palace would be a cruelty not even Eagle's numb heart could stand. "Come in."

The door slammed behind Brother Fox. Eagle knelt by Father's trunk, which he shouldn't have gone into, but he felt this warranted the intrusion. His fingers brushed one of the shiny wood boxes Father brought down sometimes after he'd answered a summons, but he didn't feel the least temptation to open it—not now, anyway. He found the little glass jar of all-heal.

"Where's Falcon Eye?" Brother Fox pleaded.

"I'm sorry, Your Highness. He went out this afternoon. Hunting. He hasn't come home yet." Probably wouldn't until late tomorrow morning.

"I thought he always took you with him."

Eagle said simply, "Not today." The agony in the Prince's voice made him rush. He went into the washroom and fetched a bowl of hot water, and a pile of clean rags. Brother Fox stood in the spot he'd occupied when Eagle left him, rocking slightly and staring into the distance, hunched with pain and—if Eagle read him right—shame. "Your Highness?"

"What?"

"I can help you, if you want. My father taught me. But it'd probably be better if you sat down."

The Prince nodded vaguely.

Eagle arranged the supplies on the window seat. "Your Highness. Please—"

"Bey." Fox.

Eagle shook his head and carefully guided the Prince a few steps, to the window seat. Brother Fox didn't sit, and he was the taller by more than a head. Eagle couldn't work on this mess reaching up. He screwed up his courage, laid his hands on the royal shoulders, and pushed. "Sit down, Your Highness," he said.

"Call me Fox." The Prince sat down hard. He probably jarred every injury at once. A pained little sound pressed between his teeth. Eagle clenched his hands, angry. So he could feel, after all; not entirely numb.

"If you're—if you're familiar enough to help me after—this—you're familiar enough to call me Fox."

"All right. Fox." He pushed the long glory of hair behind Brother Fox's shoulders. It whispered over the backs of his fingers. "Father calls me Eagle," he offered. The most serious injury, the arm, he'd treat first, no matter how badly he wanted to fix the Prince's face. He remembered it swimming over him in the cave, all the lovelier against his horror.

"How old are you, Eagle?"

"Fourscore years and two. Hold still now." Carefully, he examined Fox's arm.

"*Ah!*"

"This is broken." He could feel it just there.

"I know," Fox wrenched, sweat standing out on his forehead.

"Wait here." Eagle went and fetched the leather strap from Father's chest. "To bite on," he said, giving it over.

"I know. Talk to me," the Prince said suddenly. "What's it like being Wormsbane?" And he put the strap in his mouth.

"Oh, well..." Eagle didn't know how to answer that for himself, let alone Fox. He rubbed the nape of his neck. "I'm not really sure yet," he decided. "It's only today, you know? I was talking to Vercingetorix, and he said—"

"Vercingetorix?" Fox interrupted. He had the strap in his hand now. "The unicorn?"

"Bite down." That was none of anyone's business, though why anyone should be surprised Eagle didn't know. He wasn't anything special. The Prince obeyed, and he snapped the bone into place before he could lose his nerve. Fox's scream through the strap rattled his eardrums. He reached for the jar of all-heal. When he opened it, the scent drifted up to prickle green, herbal magic into his nose.

"You—can still talk—to Vercingetorix?" Fox panted.

Eagle's face heated. What a thing to ask about, while he stroked all-heal over the living silk of the Prince's skin.

"It's nothing to be embarrassed over."

"Well, it's just..." He wet a cloth in warm water and began to clean blood from the Prince's face.

Eagle had always been apart, and when the others around his age had started stealing kisses and touching each other, he'd been outside of that, too. He'd been outside of everything for so long, kids younger than he was were starting it. "Nobody notices me," he blurted. And if they did, it was only to call him odd or stuck-up, or witch-boy because he talked to fairy creatures. "Only Father."

Under the cloth, Fox's split mouth curved into a smile Eagle could feel. "You're sort of small."

That was true. He was small and slight, even for his age. "And quiet," he admitted.

"I see you," Fox said, with a husky note in his voice and a gleam in his amber eye. The open one.

Eagle's stomach jumped. "Mm-hmm." It was all he trusted himself to say.

"I do. I see you around, working with Falcon Eye." Fox dragged in a breath and added, "He loves you."

"He does." If there was anything real left in Eagle's world, it was Father.

"Why are you so serious? I never see you smile. But your father loves you and teaches you. You get to talk to unicorns. If anybody has a reason to smile, you do."

Eagle raised Fox's chin to clean his neck. It felt intimate, trading secrets. If he leaned in six inches, he could steal a kiss, and what would happen then? He longed to find out, but—no. He contented himself with sponging blood from golden skin, leaving it damp and gleaming. "Guess I just don't need to. Why do you smile all the time, when your father does this to you?"

Fox's larynx bobbed under the cloth. "I've never thought about it."

Not for one moment did Eagle believe that. He paused in his cleaning and looked Fox in the eye.

"I suppose... I need to, because if I don't, I'll cry."

He nodded slowly. He wanted to throttle the High King, even knowing he'd die for it. "It's wrong, you know. What he does to you."

"If I were a better—"

"Shut up." Oh God. He'd just told the Crown Prince to shut up. "It's not about you. He'd do it if you were perfect, because it's all and only about him. You think I never make my father angry?" He was always making Father angry and having things taken away from him, or being given extra chores. But this. This was fists and no holding back. "Difference is, I don't look like this after he punishes me."

Fox didn't answer. He looked ready to cry again.

"Why don't you just leave?"

"Where would I go?" Fox said, so small and sad that Eagle wanted to take him away this very minute, into the wood and the wild, and keep him safe.

"Where wouldn't you go?" Eagle stepped back, holding the cloth, reaching for words. Where wouldn't *he* go? "Anywhere," he said. "Everywhere!" He threw his arms wide, and his face broke into a smile for the first time in days. "You could have adventures, all kinds. See the world! Save beautiful princesses, and find buried treasure, and slay dragons and—and—"

Oh, the look on Fox's bruised face. That gleam in his eye, hotter now, hot as the lava sprites when they got too close. *You are something extraordinary,* the look said, and he couldn't understand it.

"Why are you looking at me like that?" he asked.

"Because," Fox said, "I just figured out why you don't smile. You don't want to be here any more than I do."

The Prince really *did* see him. He had *let* someone see him—the insane, secret part of him that wanted to run and never look back. "I want to see where the round-eared sailors come from," he said, feeling stupid, and went quickly back to patching up Fox.

He had his fingers under Fox's eye when the Prince asked, "Which ones?"

"All of them."

"What if I went?" Fox's voice: hushed now, murmuring. "If I went away and had adventures, would you come with me?"

In a heartbeat. "Sure I would." No doubt Fox would forget by morning, but Eagle would never forget. He wished it could be a true thing.

He pulled up the Prince's stained shirt to spread all-heal on his ribs. The bruises there took longer to fade than they should have. "You should go," he said quietly. "Before he kills you." He glanced up from where he knelt and found Fox's eyes on him, both of them now, those hot amber eyes. He couldn't look away if he tried.

"You're probably right," Fox said. His look held Eagle's for a long moment, unreadable.

Eagle slid his hands out of Fox's shirt.

The Prince leaned forward, near and nearer, until Eagle could feel air stir against his mouth. Fox lifted his chin with soft fingertips, whispering, "Eagle... I want to—thank you." The moment shattered. Fox withdrew his hand and rose. "Good-bye," he said at the door, and whipped out in a flurry of hair, leaving Eagle sitting on his heels with forgotten manners and fierce longing.

"I would've let you," he said, to the empty space the Prince had left behind. He would've let Fox do a lot of things, if Fox had wanted to bother. Sometimes the haylofts in Shirith overflowed with naked flesh. Eagle was never in any of them. It was a lonely feeling to have nobody want you, and it would have been nice to know what it felt like when somebody did.

With a sigh, he stood and went about cleaning. He stuffed the rags into the incinerator, rinsed the bowl, and scrubbed blood from the carpet where Fox had stood. He tried to turn his mind away from what had just happened, but in the cedar-paneled shower, surrounded by steam and scent, he propped his forearm on the wall and stroked his prick with a soapy fist. Whether it had meant what he thought it did or something else entirely, the memory of Fox's fiery gaze brought a moan out of him. Fingers of hot water coursed down his back. He came on his hand with a ragged little sound like a sob, and afterward leaned there trembling in the billows of hot vapor.

It felt like disrespect. Fox had spoken to him. Listened to him. Seen right into him. Whatever was there, the Prince had found it pleasing. And he was so used to the eyes skidding right over him, the mouths that called him spooky and strange where they thought he couldn't hear. He'd welcomed their thinking he was odd, and hardened his heart. Or thought he had. One look from Fox had been enough to crack him open to the soft meat inside. He was as weak and stupid as the rest of them.

He shut off the water and dried himself with a towel so old it was ivory rather than white. What he wanted, he realized, was for somebody to want to touch him, and most of all, Crown Prince Bearach of Shirith, who had seen Eagle's real, wild self, and liked it.

Eagle put on his nightshirt. He climbed into the sleeping cupboard and slept hard on top of the blankets with all the lights blazing and the windows and bed-door open.

When he woke, there was an emerald fairy perched on his nose. It took forever to get the glitter off.

~*~

If you liked this excerpt and want to find out what happened next, you can find *The High King's Will* on Amazon. In addition, M.A. Ray invites you to visit http://menyoral.com for free stories, a map of Rothganar, and a blog that doesn't get updated as often as it should.

ABOUT THE AUTHOR

Casey Matthews is a tall hobbit from a farm in the Rust Belt, preferring the intimacy of small gatherings and the fortifying effects of being surrounded by tall trees and familiar old rocks to sit on while thinking. Casey lives near Washington, D.C. now, where they could use more thinking rocks.

If you liked this book, the best way to help Casey do more is to leave an earnest review and tell your friends. Find more stories at www.caseymatthews.org, or look Casey up on social media.

ACKNOWLEDGEMENTS

Thank you, those who were my first readers, the people who cheered for Ryn when she was still hard to make out in the roughhewn words: Katie, Emily, Will, Amanda, all the folks at the Scriptorium and the Dragon's Rocketship crowd. A fandom of a dozen is all any author really needs, but I did need you.

And let's also thank the finishers, the ones who applied spit and polish to a filthy manuscript: my cover artist, Natasha Snow, who made me look as pretty as I feel; Rachel Bostwick, a friend and formatting guru; Emily again, for reading snippets at 2 a.m. and convincing me not to burn them to ash; and John Hart, for hours of work perfecting the language.

There were the background people, too, the influencers and the emotional support: parents, family, friends. This book only stands because of a foundation you provide.

The poem in Chapter XVIII is from Emily Dickinson's "A Bird came down the Walk."